Author's Note

Certain words are purposefully capitalized to show the importance of these words politically, powerfully, respectfully or emotionally to the people in the story. For instance, a very powerful or especially dangerous Darkness will have its name capitalized, while a weaker Darkness will have its name in lower case. Similarly, objects or people of great power will also be capitalized.

Some words are also occasionally phrased a bit differently, like normally singular words being written in the plural. This is done to reflect the unique predilections of the cultures represented in the story.

Dedication

To all those who helped make this book a reality and to all of those who dare to dream.

Chapter One

The sun was high over the Great Trade Road as it wound its way through the Barshom Forest along the edges of the kingdom of Klynsheim. All in all, it seemed a pleasant enough day, with the trees stained red and orange by the light, and the clean scents of the forest drifting through the air. Bird song and the chittering of squirrels arguing over the right to certain trees created a soothing cacophony, adding to the pleasing atmosphere. The Road itself did nothing to take away from the forest's charm, almost blending with the woodland due to the gentle green overgrowth that cushioned the step and lent a tang of mint to the air when crushed.

This far north of the heart of Klynsheim, The Road was more cart path than the grand thoroughfares of more southerly routes, which created a certain charm to the otherwise utilitarian affair. Still, path or avenue, the Great Trade Road had a sense of grandeur about it due to the carved protective Ward posts that flanked it on either side, pulsing a reassuring soft yellow light as they stood sentinel. The five foot tall posts of stout oak stood every twenty feet guiding and reminding travelers of the dangers inherent to the forest, while giving a friendly sense of home.

In essence, every bit of The Road was carefully designed, regimented and maintained. Precision was the key to security.

Along every mile of the tract lay Way Points, camp areas as tightly Warded as the trail, the Ward runes holding back The Darkness which could haunt the woods of even the most settled lands, but often felt free to run amok along the frontier. Just as important as a barrier to The Darkness, The Road served as an important link between the Klynsheim villages that seemed more numerous every year in the North Country.

The man responsible for maintaining Wards along The Road and, by extension, the protections of the surrounding villages along his assigned route, walked at a methodical pace, his long legs encased in knee high leather boots, laced tight over thick leather pants in a uniform dusty brown. His overcoat, open over his shirt in the heat of the day, was his best piece, being reinforced at the shoulders and lower sleeves with the additional protection of dulled brass strips.

This Warder Mage, as his kind were titled, was deeply tanned and a bit disheveled, his light brown hair in need of a trim and his face past reputable stubble. Dark brown eyes were set in a thin, angular face frozen in an expression of resignation and fatigue.

The resignation that the man was feeling was due to the fact that he found his occupation, well, boring. Yes, maintaining the protections that were key to Klynsheim's defenses sounded like an exciting and dangerous job. It was dangerous; the man was pretty certain that his predecessor had been eaten by something or other while stepping off The Road to take a piss. The problem with maintaining Ward Posts was that the chore was about as exciting as watching a painter. Not the artist kind of painter, but the men who whitewash walls.

When it came down to it that was exactly what a Warder Mage was; not an artist but a maintenance worker. True, he was the conduit that drew in energy and channeled it into the Wards, sparking them into life. However, in a lot of ways what he did was no different from priming a well pump.

The man spent his days walking the Ward line of the Great Trade Road, checking carvings, wood quality and looking for Darkness sign. The job was important, just not fun.

It was also a meticulously slow job, seeing as every Ward Post had to be carefully checked. The Mage's path tended to be a winding one as he worked his way from post to post on either side of The Road. His progress was slowed even more by the fact that he walked with a significant limp, a reminder that no matter how pleasant The Road seemed, The Darkness always waited to take advantage of the unwary.

He had to stop often and stretch tight muscles, a hazard of the trade, his thin frame betraying little spare flesh whenever he did so. The Mage was strong enough; he just had the build a man could only get on a diet of sparse food, stress, and harsh living conditions.

The Mage occasionally checked his weapons, another tedious, but necessary, procedure. He kept a quarter staff leaned against his shoulder and a fighting knife within easy reach at his waist, not standard issue for Warders but essential on The Road. It would have been nice if someone had told him about their necessity when he'd received his commission. If nothing else, he would have been a bit better prepared for a life that was nothing like the one he had expected when he'd graduated from The Academy nearly a decade ago.

He had been dressed in proper robes then, a new carving knife in his hand and the belief that the world held endless possibilities, even in a career as established as his own. The thought caused the Mage to quirk a rare smile. The Academy had never taught him the value of a good stretch or the cold comfort of a fighting knife. His instructors had never seen fit to teach him the need to keep his eyes continually roaming from post to surrounding terrain, and back to the posts, looking for problems both on and off The Road.

No, The Academy had never prepared him for an existence that could fit into a bandoleer of pouches across his chest and a large pack on his back. What The Academy had taught him was a radical adherence to duty above all else. The Wards were to be maintained as the sole priority. Everything else in life could be experienced once that duty was fulfilled. Years on and the Mage was still wondering when he was ever going to find time to experience anything else that life might offer.

There were so many villages along The Road now. So many settlers lured by the promise of free land for the taking by anyone who could hold it, despite the occasional Obari objection, the wild illusionists who claimed the North Lands as their own. The settlers were a mixed bag. Some were smart and cautious. Others were too used to the safer Wardings of the heartlands and could not quite grasp the need for constant vigilance. Some of the smart ones lived and prospered. All of the careless ones died. Either way there were always more settlers willing to take their places, which meant more Wards to be carved and maintained.

The Mage was rounding a bend in The Road when he came across an unwelcome sight. A caravan of settlers was blocking the way, seemingly camped for a time. Children were playing games, laughing and squealing as they chased one another, ducking in and around the wagons. Mothers were prepping meals as their men looked over wagon loads and checked the health of their oxen. Occasionally a parent could be heard scolding the children when one of them got too close to the oxen, but none seeming as concerned when the kids edged near the Ward Line.

While the wagons were uniformly plain, serviceable affairs with high sides, large wheels, and tarps stretched taut over hoop frames to provide protection from sun and rain, the people were not. Brightly colors dominated the scene, the women's clothing every shade of the rainbow, their long dresses swishing with every movement, bonnets tied tightly to their heads. The men seemed a bit more 'subdued', dressed mostly in shirts of startling blue and black trousers tucked into thick leather boots. Heavy beards covered most of the men's faces and wide brim hats of various - and often clashing colors - seemed to be a sensible requirement.

Farmer folk from the deep Southern Lands of Klynsheim by the look of them, still dressed as their ancestors had been when they lived in the Deeping Dells. The folk were from lands far from The Darkness, no threats having walked those fields in generations, which was the only explanation that the Mage could come up for why these people were being so careless.

He grimaced; the caravan was blocking his progress along the Ward line and he kept to a very strict schedule. These people were going to set him off his pace. The Mage grimaced again at the thought, wondering when he had become so set in his ways that a delay upset him. He was equally upset because he was going to have to talk to these people, not something that he particularly enjoyed. While he had never been outgoing before being assigned to The Road, he had become more withdrawn over the years. Socializing cost time that the Mage did not have and most importantly opened him up to the kinds of conversations that he would rather avoid.

Not that he was going to avoid such a conversation at the moment. Someone was apparently paying enough attention to their surroundings to call out when he came into sight. A group of men hurried out from the wagons to intercept him before he got too close. The men were barrel chested, eyes glaring suspiciously over bristling beards.

The Warder Mage stopped just short of the men, ignoring their suspicious looks and glanced to the left and right along the Ward Line, knowing that with all this racket The Darkness would be watching.

He opened his mouth to identify himself but was interrupted by the man he had already dubbed 'Stupid One', who stood on the right and confirmed his naming.

"You one of them Obari, we been hearing tell about? There's nothing here for a savage like you. We're decent God fearing folk and want nothing to do with your sinful ways," the man said loudly, clenching his jaw and raising a threatening fist.

The Warder Mage was momentarily surprised. He'd never heard such a ridiculous accusation. Yes, he could understand being mistaken for an Obari – his dress was patterned after theirs. But Obari worshipped God the same as Klynsheimers did, albeit with a less formalized religious structure.

The Mage could have answered the challenge but did not feel like wasting his breath. Instead he shifted his quarterstaff so that he could open his coat wider, revealing his knives. He quirked an eyebrow and gestured with a finger towards the blades.

"The son of a bitch wants to fight," Stupid Too swore loudly, attracting attention as more people gathered. The man standing to the left of center seemed to be a carbon copy of Stupid One.

The Mage split his attention between the Southlanders and the Ward Line. There was definitely something slinking in the bushes along the left of the Line, which was to be expected. Most Darkness threats came from the wild country north of the Line.

"No he isn't," the man in the center said, whom the Mage dubbed 'Not Quite As Stupid', gesturing for the other men to calm down. "That's a Warder blade next to the big knife."

The Mage coughed, needing to clear his throat to strengthen his voice, though the words still came out soft and hoarse. He didn't spend a lot of time talking between villages.

"I'm a Warder of The Trade Road," the man acknowledged, inclining his head slightly. "You folks are in a bit of trouble, lest I miss my guess."

"Dressed funny for a Warder," grumbled Stupid Too, not like being corrected.

The Mage ignored the comment. He knew that he was dressed outlandishly for a Warder Mage, having forgone more traditional robes of wool or cotton for leathers. But the leathers, like the weapons that he had learned to carry, were more appropriate for the rough life of travelling The Road. His robes had fallen apart during his first year on Patrol.

The Mage looked at the center man waiting for an answer. He was not going to give these foolish people more of his time or energy than was required. Maybe he was being an ass, but he was tired. There was always too much to do on The Road and these people just added to the burden.

The Warder Mage wished that Troopers were present so that he could foist off the problem on the Military. But since he was the only representative present of either the Warder Academy or Military, the two powers responsible for maintaining the security of The Trade Road, it fell to him to deal with the issue.

"One of the wagons broke an axel. Had to stop here to fix it," Not Quite As Stupid explained, shooting an irritated look at Stupid Too. "Should only take another hour or so to fix."

"I assume you folks were briefed on Road Protocols," The Warder said, shifting slightly away to get a better look at the Ward Posts nearest them as he tracked movement in the underbrush. You either learned to multi-task or you didn't survive for very long on the frontier.

None of the three men seemed to notice the movement even though The Darkness were becoming more confident as it judged the settlers as easy prey.

"We went through the briefings," Stupid One snapped.

"Fair enough," the Warder Mage acknowledged, hating the part of his job where he had to explain the difference between attending the briefings and actually paying attention. "Care to explain why you're violating the Protocols then?"

"We haven't been doing anything wrong!" shouted Stupid One, clearly believing that bluster could get him out of any situation. The man was puffing up his chest and trying to look as threatening as possible.

Yep, the Mage really hated these kinds of conversations. Never ended well for anyone involved, particularly himself.

"The Protocols clearly prohibit any caravan of over ten wagons. Camping or stopping outside of way points is strictly prohibited. Noise discipline is to be maintained at every stop along the Trade Route. Those rules are not suggestions; we are not in the heartlands, protected by hundreds of miles of Wardings.

"We are in the North Lands and you have brought The Darkness," he hissed angrily, trying to convey a sense of urgency.

The three men grew angrier themselves with each word; they had to know that they had done wrong but seemed unwilling to accept the consequences. Another group of settlers who didn't understand the difference between settled lands and frontiers. More deaths along the Trade Road.

Then his words penetrated that anger. He saw the moment when the men realized what he had just said. They began to glance fearfully in the wrong directions.

"Spike striders, north of the Line. They'll try to spook your draft animals and scare people into leaving the Ward Line if they can. Draft animals are the biggest danger. Spooked animals can cause damage to the Ward Posts under the right circumstances. You folks need to get the wagons that are clear of the blockage moving to the nearest way point. Abandon the ones that're stuck behind and get to an area of greater safety," the Mage advised sternly.

He caught a hint of a tail out of the corner of his eye, red and white, tufted and spiked. Striders were about the size of a large, very compact dog and pack oriented. Head to toe along their bodies were thick spikes of varying lengths, from a few inches long around a long snouted triangular head, to several feet along the spine and sides. These spikes rattled with every step and were designed to make it easier for the animals to drag down prey, impaling flesh and rolling to rip free ribbons of meat simply for the pain it caused.

"No way!" bellowed Stupid Too. "Everything we have is in those wagons! We aren't leaving them! You're a Mage. It's your job to protect us and our supplies."

"Shut your mouth," hissed the Mage, his voice low, but full of concern as he began moving down the Line, checking the Ward Posts as the spike striders began to shake the spikes on their tails, creating a rattling noise that jarred the teeth. "Noise discipline exists for a reason. Who knows what else you're going to bring down upon us.

"Spike striders are bad enough. They're like vultures on the wing. Other creatures notice them circling an area and they'll come looking for a meal."

The Darkness were not normally organized in any recognizable fashion. Different types of Darkness competed for resources. Only when The Darkness Rose, meaning unified under a guiding intelligence, was there any true cooperation between the beasts.

"That's your problem to deal with," argued Stupid Too.

The Mage stopped his inspection and turned to face him, frustration and contempt fleeting across his face. He move forward a step, his entire frame vibrating with tension.

"Listen clearly to what I'm about to say. I'm a Warder Mage. I walk the Line and Service the Ward posts. I'm not a guard and I'm not a Trooper. Heed my advice and get your people moving. Your stuff will still be here when it's safe enough to come back for them."

The Mage turned to go back to his inspection, but Stupid Too wanted to keep arguing. The Mage could sense it. As much as he disliked Stupid Too, Stupid Too didn't like him either. The man's face twisted with rage as he spat the words at the Mage.

"Not likely, you coward. Leave our stuff? Why? So bandits can make off with everything? We aren't going anywhere until that wagon is fixed and we all leave tog- oomph!"

Not Quite As Stupid must have heard enough and realized just how much danger the caravan was in. He twisted to the side and punched Stupid Too hard as he could in the stomach, silencing the man. In the sudden silence the rattling of the spike striders became audible.

The oxen were on edge now, eyes rolling in fear and stomping impatiently, wanting to run. The animals began to low plaintively pulling on traces and fighting the wagons' brakes. Most of the settlers, still oblivious to the danger, began to either curse or try to calm the animals. A few of the smarter ones were craning their necks, looking for the source of danger, eyes wide and fearful.

The Mage just shook his head, hurrying to check each Ward Post as fast as he could to make certain that the Line would hold. The idea of bandits was ridiculous; where would the bandits hide where The Darkness wouldn't find them? Troopers patrolled The Road often enough that no bandit camps could exist on The Road itself. At least not for long anyways.

"Get back to your wagons and spread the warning," Not Quite As Stupid snapped to the Stupid One, pushing the man in the right direction, moving away himself and urging the people who had gathered to see the Mage to hurry back to their wagons.

The men did not get very far before a young girl ran up to Not Quite As Stupid.

"Pa! Pa!" the girl yelled, out of breath and her eyes wide.

The Mage had to wonder if anyone in this caravan had any sense.

"Benny Se! Get back to your mother. It isn't safe here."

"But Pa, Ebry got caught carving his name on a Ward post!" the girl blurted out.

No one could be that recklessly stupid.... Not Quites As Stupid shot a look in Stupid Too's direction. No need to guess the name of Ebry's father.

"Which Ward Post?" the Mage snapped, moving quickly.

Benny Se's eyes went wide as she pointed behind her, less than helpful.

"Get everyone moving," the Mage said again, utter command in his voice and shaking his head as he tried to run in the direction that the girl was pointing. The best that he could manage was a fast hobble. "The Line might fail!"

The striders seemed to agree as they began to charge the Line.

The caravan erupted into chaos when the striders first hit the line. People stumbled backward, absolute shock on their faces as striders erupted from the underbrush to collide with the Wards which flared brighter with power, threat, and menace, throwing The Darkness back. The striders recovered quickly, tensing their red and white bodies and rattling their spikes, surprisingly small mouths gaping wide to reveal jagged teeth coated with thick ropes of saliva as the creatures drooled with glee.

People fell over one another as they tried to flee while still keeping their eyes on the striders. It was difficult to determine who was more panicked, the draft animals or the would-be settlers. Screaming started as men tried to reign in the animals and women and children raced to get out of the way. Not Quite as Stupid began shouting orders and this time the Warder Mage did not protest. He just wanted these people clear of the Line so he could address the damage and prevent a break in the Wards.

He had to shove his way past panicking knots of people to get clear of the wagons that took up far too much space. The Road was narrow along this stretch and left very little room for the large wagons that the settlers were using. Another infraction; the Way Fort commanders should have halted this caravan long before it got this far.

Some people shoved back, fear becoming anger. This was why he didn't like being around people. Too many chances for matters to get out of control as fear of The Darkness destroyed all reason.

The Mage avoided as much of the shoving as he could but was forced to lay into two men who seemed septa bent on beating him for some ridiculous reason. The quarter staff snapped out in a series of quick blows that were far from elegant but made up for the lack of finesse with efficiency. The men fell back, clutching arms and stomachs.

The Ward Posts were flaring brighter as all the defensive runes came to life in cascades of energy to drive back The Darkness. The striders flung themselves with seeming abandon at the Wards, being thrown back in crackles of light that so far only repelled and did not inflict much damage to the beasts. The Wards worked on an escalating scale of threat. It did not pay to have Wards that immediately sought to kill The Darkness. Such Wards would be seen as a direct challenge to The Darkness and attract things far deadlier than spike striders.

The Mage moved slower now, needing to watch the Wards, identify weak points, and find the damaged post. Some of the draft animals were beyond reason, oxen tearing free of their yokes and trampling settlers or smashing them aside in mad dashes up and down The Road and through the Ward Lines. Striders rattled louder, feeding the panic that brought them prey.

Two oxen fell tumbling, as they crossed the Line, the striders leaping forward and impaling themselves on the animals, sending great gouts of blood fountaining into the air. The Darkness went into death rolls, the motion continually impaling and tearing spikes free, rending flesh with every moment in a gluttonous orgy of pain.

A man and woman were knocked aside by a panicked animal, stumbling just clear enough of the Wards for the striders to get a hold and drag the couple screaming away from the protections. The striders did not even bother with death rolls. The Darkness simply blinded the settlers with swipes of their paws and began playing, herding the terrified people with sharp jabs and yips in one direction and then another. Each time the striders drew a bit more blood and a few more screams as the man and woman stumbled in desperation, their fear mounting with their inability to see The Darkness.

"Oh God, oh God, help me!" screamed the woman, blood pouring from the ruins of her eyes, as she blindly reached out, stumbling and falling. Her dress was shredded as she crawled and the spike striders drove her on. Even if terror and pain did not eliminate the need to worry about modesty, her breasts were unrecognizable ribbons of flesh barely clinging to her chest, lending any such concerns morbidly unnecessary.

The man screamed incessantly, his voice a ragged wretch. The striders were knocking him around, slamming in from every direction, flailing more flesh from his bones with every pass, yipping in delight.

No one made a move to help the man or woman because that was what the striders wanted. Crossing the Line at this point was death.

The Warder Mage wanted to feel pity; he didn't, but he wanted to. He didn't even feel horror at what was happening to those people. He could not afford to feel anything right now. He had to find the damaged post.

People were starting to find their way clear. Desperation and survival instinct were kicking in enough that the wagons that could be moved were now lumbering away from the attack, the draft animals needing no encouragement.

Others, instead of running for safety, were trying to get possessions out of the stranded wagons to take with them. These people were adding to the chaos and panic that was making it that much harder for Not Quite As Stupid and a handful of other men to get the remaining draft animals clear.

The striders reveled in the chaos, continually striking at the Ward Line to drive people to even greater heights of panic. People pushed and shoved one another, overburdened with possessions. One, then two, than five stumbled too far and were dragged down in a riot of blood choked screams and rattling satisfaction.

The damaged Ward Post revealed itself just two up from the Mage's current position. Instead of a cascade of properly functioning Wards, the post's defenses sputtered at best, indicating that more than one of the Wards was damaged. Man and striders discovered the weakness at the same time. As much fun as The Darkness had been having with their victims, the greedy beasts wanted everyone. The striders launched themselves at the weak point with renewed frenzy.

Wards flared, but did not inflict the right amount of damage, half-heartedly pushing The Darkness back and dimming with each successive attack. The Mage dropped to his knees, examining where the name 'Ebry' was crudely, but deeply gouged into the wood across almost a dozen rune Wards. The idiot boy had put a lot of effort into the vandalism. Obviously no one had been keeping an eye on him or bothered to teach him Ward Law. How anyone could think defacing Wards was a good idea was beyond the Mage.

There was no quick fix for the post. The damaged wards had to be filed away and re-carved. A lot of precision needed to be used to link the Wardings. Fine cutting that took time and skill. The Mage could easily accomplish the repair about half an hour after the striders broke through the Ward Line and began killing up and down the Trade Road. He needed time; a temporary fix to hold the Line while he worked.

He could try using his quarter staff as a temporary post but it did not have the right amount of mass to take the punishment of repeated assaults. The strain of the Wards feedback as they powered up and repulsed would crack the thin pole all too soon. It came down to a matter of equal and opposite reaction. As much force as the Ward post pushed forward also pushed back on the post itself.

The Mage needed something with greater mass; the best he could hope for was to buy some time.

He hobbled over to the nearest wagon and began carving one Ward over and over. The simplest Ward he knew and the first one he had ever learned. 'The Way is Shut' was also his favorite because of its simplicity. An open square with bars slashing across it. Designed to repulse and nothing more. Not strong by itself, but six in a row should buy him some time. The Wards flared to life, one after another, their initial emeraldine light flaring to the bright yellow-white of a fire seen from the distance during the night. Now, how to get the wagon over to the Ward Line?

Not Quite as Stupid was the answer. The settler was not panicking and had watched the Mage work as the last of the animals were cut loose. He grabbed four of his men and moved to the wagon, trying to push it where the Mage indicated. The wagon was heavy and it was slow going. A woman ran over and jumped into the wagon, beginning to unload it as fast as she could to lighten the weight.

The Ward Post was not going to hold long enough. The Mage really hated days like this because they were preventable and so unnecessary. He wished that there were Troopers present so he would not have to do what he was about to try.

The Warder Mage had been honest. He was not a Trooper or a guard but he did know how to fight – had learned through brutal necessity. Necessity born not from a fear of The Darkness but from a fear of his own People.

He dropped his pack, buttoned his coat and raised its reinforced hood. From the collar he pulled up a leather mask that covered everything up to his eyes. Not perfect, but it would have to do. He then stepped into the Ward Line next to the failing post, quarter staff raised and ready to block.

The striders didn't hesitate. They simply killed the man and woman that they had been playing with and surged towards the Mage. He was still enough in the line to prevent the striders from rushing him from multiple sides, but that was all the advantage that he had in this situation - especially since he had to minimize The Darkness's contact with the portion of the Ward Line covered by the damaged post.

Time. He only had to hold until Not Quite As Stupid got the wagon into position. The staff lashed out and a strider cringed back, the wood connecting solidly with a sensitive snout. Now if only the rest of this was going to be as easy. He prayed that the settlers hurried.

Not Quite As Stupid's name was actually Parsons. He was one of the leaders of the caravan, having been one of the driving forces behind relocation to the frontier. The lure of free land had been too intoxicating to resist to the hard scramble farmers of the village who had less and less land to farm each year. Parsons had begun to regret the decision as he'd watched the Orbons get mangled and stumble around blindly, pleading for help as The Darkness played with them.

There had been nothing that he could have done to save those people, but Parsons could certainly move a septaed wagon.

He rallied his brothers who had been helping push the wagon slowly towards the Line.

"This is heavy," his older brother Korin said, huffing as he ran up and began pushing.

"Problem is that you're heavy," grumbled Ikthin, the youngest of Parsons' brothers, as he slammed a shoulder into the wagon on the opposite side. "What the septa is in this thing?"

"Shut up and push!" snapped Parsons, hoping for once that his brothers would listen to him.

"Leave it to my brothers to be idiots," said Sharni, their sister, from inside the wagon. Shari shared the same hair and tall build, but lacking the sheer bulk and beards of her brothers. "Empty the wagon before you try to push it."

Sharni was emptying the wagon as quickly as she could, throwing pieces of someone's life out the rear with wild abandon.

"Sharni, septa it, get to the way point!" Parson's hissed between ragged breaths. The septa wagon was so heavy.

"Save your breath. I'm not leaving you idiots behind," said Sharni, her voice muffled by the wagon cover.

"Sharni, it's not -!"

"Kor'nta!" Klyde, one of the twins shouted, interrupting Parsons.

"What?" Parsons demanded, suddenly suspicious. "You better be pushing, Klyde!"

Klyde had made an art of appearing to work while allowing his brothers to do the bulk of the labor on the old farm.

"The Mage," Sharni said in terrified awe, standing at the front of the wagon now and pointing. "He's stepped into the Line. He's fighting The Darkness!"

Parsons' head jerked up and he froze, looking to the Wards. The Mage stood there, the Wards flashing around him in acidic fury as he stabbed and thrust at the striders, driving them back from the damaged post. The man was insane. Gloriously, magnificently insane.

But Warders didn't fight. Warders...well...Warded. How could this man think he stood a chance? Why was he risking his life for them? The Warders back home never would have taken such a risk.

"Stop grieshtataing around and push," snapped Orn, Klyde's twin and the last of the siblings.

The brothers pushed with renewed effort, creeping closer to the Line.

"No!" Sharni screamed, jumping from the wagon, grapping a small pile of pots that she had just thrown out and charging the Line.

"Sharni, what the septa-?" Korin yelled, stopping pushing in shock.

"The Warder's down!" Klyde yelled, swearing violently and pushing even harder, his face turning beet red with exertion.

Their sister was at the Ward Line throwing the pots at The Darkness, trying to drive it off of the Mage, who had ripped his fighting knife free and was repeatedly stabbing a Spike strider that was trying to get the man into a death roll.

"We're almost there!" Parsons grunted, pushing harder. "Push, septa it! Korin, move your grieshtatan ass!"

He had to hope that they got the wagon into position before the Warder was overwhelmed.

The quarter staff slashed to the left and right, smashing into The Darkness, keeping the deadly spikes from full on contact. The Mage could not keep the spikes from scoring gouges in the leather of the coat and pants, but he could keep the spikes from gaining purchase and dragging him from the Line.

The quarter staff was becoming increasingly scarred as the slammed it into strider hide and spikes, each blow a little less strong. The Mage himself was tiring quickly, his breath coming in ragged bellows. He was incredibly desperate as he prayed for the settlers to get the wagon into position. He was not a fighter. He shouldn't be doing this...

The inevitable happened. He overextended a strike and a strider got purchase on his coat, dragging him clear of the Line. He would like to believe that he cursed his fate or bellowed defiance. He didn't; he simply screamed, flailing desperately in every direction, rune light almost seeming to play along his arms in a final act of defiance as he yanked his fighting knife free. He stabbed with brutal determination at a strider that was tearing away at this coat.

The animal snarled, thrashing wildly in an attempt to hook him with its spikes. The knife plunged deep again and again, driving the animal into an even greater frenzy, which was all that kept the other striders from attacking him.

The wagon slammed into position. The Mage could feel it when the Wards on the wooden sides strengthened the Line. Given his current predicament, the Mage did not feel much satisfaction. Blind panic, but not satisfaction.

A soup pot rattled the nearest Darkness, causing it to draw back and Not Quite as Stupid suddenly needed a new name. Insanely Courageous might be a better fit because the man reached across the Ward Line and dragged the Mage back to safety, as the other settlers with him threw a variety of heavy pots and pans at The Darkness in an attempt to drive them even further back and cover the men's retreat.

Not Quite As Stupid took three ragged cuts across his forearms and began to bleed profusely but refused to let go of the Mage. The Mage kicked feebly at the strider trying to regain purchase, silently pleading for Not Quite As Stupid to get them clear. He held his knife ready, though it did him little good.

Both men eventually fell to The Road surface, gasping for air with deep shuddering breaths, having been rescued by the contents of some settler's kitchen. One or both of them was sobbing in relief; it was hard to tell.

He just wanted to lay there but he couldn't. Instead he reached for his pack, dragged out several bandages and tossed them to his rescuer. The woman grabbed a canteen of water and ran to Not Quite As Stupid and began cleaning the cuts before bandaging them to stop the bleeding. She looked close enough in appearance to be the man's sister. Not Quite As Stupid turned his eyes to meet the Mage's and gave him a quiet nod of thanks. The Mage returned the gesture.

He fought the urge to keep still. He had a Ward post to repair and the looming threat of further violence. As a Warder Mage, he had been in similar situations before. He knew how the settlers' gratitude would quickly sour into recriminations. The recriminations would turn to anger and sorrow would stoke that anger into a rage. As the sole representative of the branches of the King's government charged with protecting the people he would become the target for that rage. Hopefully, he had enough time to repair the post before that happened.

He took a file from his pack, grimacing in pain, and went to work, grinding away at the damaged Wards. The striders didn't give up their attacks. If anything The Darkness increased their frenzy, trying to distract the Mage from his repairs. He ignored The Darkness just as he ignored the small group of settlers that stood by him determinedly clutching a variety of makeshift weapons. He knew his duty and fell into the routine. It was better this way. He could ignore the fact that he had almost died.

Half an hour later the Mage re-established the Ward structures and the post stood sentinel once again. The striders gave up and wandered away, looking for easier prey. The few settlers still in the area began to clean up the mess, pushing the wagon out of the Ward Line. Not So Dumb supervised since there was not much he could do with his wounded arms. Thankfully the shock had not worn off yet; the settlers had not given into the anger.

He wanted to sleep, his eyes burning with frustration. He wanted to sleep but couldn't. He knew that he was hurt, but still needed to get clear of the settlers before tending to the wounds. He needed to move before the adrenaline wore off and the pain made it impossible to fend off the settlers' inevitable blows.

Luckily, after eight years he was prepared. There was a bolt hole, a small Warding just off of The Road and hidden in the trees a hundred or so yards away on the Southern side of The Road, away from the threat of the striders. The Mage maintained a network of these bolt holes every mile or so along the more heavily traveled sections of The Road. He'd had to use them more often than he liked to remember.

Thankfully, none of the settlers seemed to notice when the Mage packed up and began limping away, making for his small sanctuary.

"Parsons, where'd the Mage go?" Sharni asked, as she walked up to where he was directing the cleanup.

God did Parsons' arms ache. Each cut seemed to throb with an inner fire that made the stitches his sister had managed to give him seem to stretch and creak in his mind. Sharni had wanted to see to the Mage's wounds as well but had agreed to wait until the Mage finished his work. No one wanted that post to fail.

Parsons was just glad that the caravan had at least heeded the regulations about keeping basic medical supplies in each wagon. They'd all grieshtataed up enough that Parsons would not have been surprised to find himself still in blood soaked bandages bleeding out. Luckily he wasn't and those supplies were helping a lot of people. After Sharni had sewn him up she had been called away to set the broken leg of a man who'd been trampled by one of the oxen. There were dozens of wounded in similar shape.

"What?" Parsons asked, trying to concentrate past his own discomfort. He still couldn't believe that he had crossed the Ward Line to drag the Mage back to safety.

"I asked you where the Mage went to," Sharni reminded her brother, scowling. She always scowled at her brothers and they usually deserved the expression, though this time the scowling was also masking a bit of the fear that still hammered away in her chest.

"What do you mean, 'where is the Mage'?" Parsons asked, confused by the question. The man should be over by the Ward Post.

"I mean exactly what I said," Sharni snapped. "I need to tend to his wounds, same as I tended to yours. Only I can't find him."

"Man's over by the Ward Post," Parsons said, raising a hand to point in that direction and then wincing as his wounds raised an objection.

"If he was over by the Ward Post I wouldn't be asking you where he is, now would I?" Sharni demanded in exasperation, her hands on her hips.

"Klyde!" Parsons called.

"What?" Klyde called back from where he was pretending to be picking up scattered supplies.

"You see the Mage?"

The Mage could hear the shouts already starting. Idiots should have learned their lesson with the attack. But anger never made for clear minds. Sounded like he'd gotten to his bolt hole just in time.

Pulling off his coat proved to be a harder chore than he thought. There were tears all along the back matching gashes in his skin. The leather was stuck to the wounds, having helped to stop the bleeding, but now that he needed to treat the wounds the coat was a problem.

There was no way around it; the coat had to come off and the Mage eventually won the struggle. He had no idea how long it took to get the coat off; he'd passed out at least once and his eyes were swimming with black dots by the time he finished.

The Mage cleaned the wounds and bandaged them the best that he could, having had too much practice in the past. The coat would have to be mended when he was feeling a bit better. His pants weren't in much better shape. Thankfully he only had minor punctures along his legs. Bruises covered half of his body and hurt almost worse than the back wounds.

The shouting was becoming more heated. The Mage sighed in frustration as he chewed a bit of fever few and willow bark to help with the pain that was beginning to rack his body in growing waves. He grabbed his canteen and drank deeply, knowing that he needed the liquid despite his stomach's sudden protests.

The settlers would be at least a day or more before moving on, needing time to repair and clean up. It was a good thing that the Mage was in no shape to travel. Hopefully, by the time he could muster the energy to take up the Patrol again, the settlers would either be gone or at least their anger dimmed.

He tried to find a comfortable way to lie down on his stomach. The punctures in his legs protested but not as much as his other wounds would have if he tried to lay on his back. Bruises along his stomach and ribs wanted to force his body into a fetal position but the back wounds pulled dangerously. He prayed that sleep would take him so that he could find a bit of relief from both the pain and the heart wrenching terror of having been dragged down by the spike strider. Eventually he passed out, his body shuddering slightly.

Fever took the Mage at some point. He wasn't certain how much time had passed. He managed to cut a strip of leather from his coat with shaking hands and use it as a gag to keep himself from crying out too loudly if either the pain or fever got too bad. He couldn't afford to attract any attention. He trusted the Wards around the bolt hole to keep him safe from The Darkness. The Wards wouldn't protect him from angry settlers.

Days seemed to blend into each other. He ate, he drank, and he slept. When he emerged from the bolt hole, weak and exhausted, it was because he was out of water. He needed to get to the well at the way point.

The settlers were long gone, though signs of the disaster were still evident. His mind pushed him to move to the way point but his feet took him to the Ward posts. He inspected the Wardings with sunken eyes and hands that shook with palsy. He could move and he could walk after a fashion. No more excuses to keep him from the Patrol. The water would have to wait a little while longer.

Chapter 2

The incident at the damaged Ward post was several months in the Mage's past. Incident. He had to refer to the near death experience as an 'incident' to keep the thoughts and fears from overwhelming him. His clothing was patched and his wounds faded enough.

He was camped in a small meadow outside the Ward Line, near a pond that was one of his favorite sites. A well-hidden fire warmed his canteens, purifying the water inside. No food was in evidence, his meal eaten safely away from where he planned to sleep so as not to attract predators. The meal had been the highpoint of his day, which was depressing since he wasn't certain if the chewy gray strips had been bread or meat.

A few years ago the man might not have ventured so far from the protections of his Wards, but he could no longer find it in himself to be surrounded by the things that consumed every moment of his life. As a child the man had marveled at their different forms, eager to learn how to shape new runes. As an adult his world had devolved to endlessly walking The Road, no matter the weather, the season, or what his own personal wishes or health might be. None of the endless mantras about duty that the man had been forced to learn during his school days was the least bit of comfort.

He also had to face his fears so that he could continue his Patrol. He had nearly died in the Incident and he had to process that; staying on The Road, staring at the Posts was not helping. He needed time to think clear of the Wards and all that they represented.

Perhaps this need was why the Mage did not react to the shadows slipping free from the tree line opposite The Road. The shadows slunk low to the ground, circling wide of his camp and then paused, watching, waiting for the man's attention to wander a bit more.

Currently the Mage's attention was focused on a cup of warm water, a cake of scentless soap, a razor, and a hand shard mirror as he prepared to shave, one of the few small pleasures afforded him by a very lonely existence. He had waited four days for this moment, struggling through particularly rough country before he could relax his guard enough to shave and have a quick wash down. The man struggled to remember when he had more than a quick wash down. If it were not for a simple ruin called 'sweeten the air' the man probably would have scared The Darkness away with the power of his smell.

The shadows tensed eagerly as the Mage's attention seemed to drift even further away. The shadows stalked the camp now, waiting for just the right moment.

The Mage sighed, wishing that he could relax, but knowing that he couldn't because nowhere in the North Country was particularly safe. While he had so far avoided being eaten while defecating he had to admit to an extreme learning curve the first few years of his patrol. That was when he had realized there were brutal differences between book learning and theory and blood curdling reality. A Bael Wight was unnerving in a book. An enraged Bael Wight hammering at failing Wards while you tried to desperately repair them was soul ripping, pants soiling terrifying.

But the man had learned. He had had no other choice, having been given the patrol and then left to look after himself. Fifteen Darkness wrought scars among others, a missing finger, a slight limp, and haunted eyes were a constant reminder of every lesson learned. He tried, yet again, to convince himself that the Incident was just another lesson. Sometimes he thought he heard the rattling of spikes when there were no sounds.

The shadows stilled, watching the Mage's hand put down the razor and briefly closed on the haft of his fighting knife before letting it go. He took a deep and mostly calming breath, reached for the cake of soap, stopped for a moment and sighed again as he was momentarily overwhelmed by his situation. He wanted to go home. He wanted to sleep in a bed for more than a night before moving on. He wanted to be surrounded by people who did not cling to him with a desperation, praising him one moment and then cursing him the next when The Darkness pressed close and they doubted his craftsmanship or begrudged him the supplies he was due in exchange for his service to the Wards. He'd almost had to beg to get his coat repaired and a new pair of pants when the obligations due to his position should have guaranteed easy acceptance of the request.

Eight years the man had held this patrol. Eight years of being ignored by Academy Command other than terse replies to his annual reports and a refusal to send him help even though his patrol was seventeen times the size he had been led to believe when he received his commission. Sometimes he just wanted to scream, shout, and curse, but he did not, knowing that none of that would help.

The failed treatise he had written on the importance and various uses of basic Wards in combination was a painful reminder of just where he ranked with The Academy. The man had hoped that the treatise would not only help other Warder Mages in similar situations to his own but gain him enough attention to get him recalled back to The Academy. He would have enjoyed teaching a class or just getting away from The Road for a while. Instead the man had received a scathing rejection critiquing not only his grammar but 'foolish attempts to write children's books'.

He shook his head trying to shake the thoughts away; he was not normally this introspective, avoiding such thoughts as much as possible. Focusing on the job made everything easier and kept him alive. Introspection just led to frustration.

Introspection also allowed the shadows to move into their final positions, teeth gleaming in anticipation.

The shadows were not the only thing taking advantage of the Mage's inattention. The pond nearby, having moments ago been crystal clear, began to fill with a fetid mud that slowly bubbled to the surface. The bubbles roiled through the water before grasping at the air and bursting mournfully. A shuddering mass of weeds blinked open eyes that glowed with malice broke free from the water's surface and lurched towards the bank with a slurping shudder of anticipation and a slight giggle.

"I've warned you before that you have to be meticulous in your preparation. Laziness always leads to failure," the man said, not bothering to look up from the mirror.

The monster paused its movement, rearing back and looking as offended as mound of water weed could possibly manage. The man continued speaking, this time with a small smile on his face that spoke of affection and reminded him, as it always did, why he always looked forward to this area of The Road.

"Kelpin are creatures of the salt marshes, not freshwater ponds hundreds of miles away from the sea. Not to mention that Kelpin are made up of the materials that surround them. That

pond is full of duckweed. You've draped yourself in seaweed –
which I have no idea how you would keep it fresh long enough to
bring it here – not to mention the fact that Kelpin don't have eyes.
Glowing or otherwise," the man said, continuing to point out
inconsistencies.

The fake eyes blinked and the man heard a muttered curse.
Suddenly the seaweed blew apart in a spectacular display of light
and magic, leaving a woman of ethereal beauty hovering in the air,
her blond hair wavering in an otherworldly breeze as her dress
sparkled with star shine. The woman's appearance spoke of
ageless wisdom and timeless beauty that made the heart ache to
just be near it and the soul tremble when that terrible gaze was
turned upon all who witnessed it.

"You are aware that your wig is made out of skepin weed,
not flax? Skepin weed oozes an itchy sap when it gets wet," the
man inquired politely, neither heart nor soul suffering any ill
effects.

"What? Oh, nta!" the woman said, her voice squeaking
slightly as she frantically removed the wig, shattering the illusion of
wisdom and terrible power in the process.

Gone was the otherworldly figure and instead stood a
diminutive woman scratching at her shoulder length ebony hair.
Wisdom was replaced with a bit of panic and the ethereal beauty
was replaced with mortal prettiness, mischievous eyes, and the
trim, athletic build of the Obari. The man smiled. He much
preferred the woman's natural appearance.

The Obari were in many ways the opposites of the
Klynsheim, two peoples who differed not so much because of
genetics but philosophically. Where the Klynsheim relied on fixed

defenses, mixing Wards, walls, military might and unified leadership in the form of King and Academy, the Obari relied more on stealth and movement. The Obari were tricksters and illusionists, fiercely independent, acknowledging no king and no permanent home. As the old saying went, the Klynsheim confronted The Darkness and the Obari avoided it.

While some people could argue that both peoples continued survival stood as a testament to the success of their differing strategies, there was no denying that the Obari were in crisis. Facing pressures from Klynsheim expansion into traditional Obari ranges and a weakening of their magics' effectiveness their numbers had dwindled significantly under these dual pressures.

There were differing opinions as to why the Obari were losing their powers. Many leading academics at The Academy argued that the Obari magic had become diluted, shared among too many people. Unlike the Klynsheim, whose Warders made up only a small percentage of the overall population, all Obari were gifted.

The Mage had a different opinion. He believed that the Obari had become lazy; too dependent on using the same traditional methods over and over again. The Darkness was nothing if not adaptive; by relying on the same techniques, the Obari had become predictable, their illusions easily pierced under the right circumstances, leaving them vulnerable. Not that anyone wanted his opinion on the matter.

The Mage did have to admit that his own people suffered from too much traditionalism as well. That being said, the rune Wards were not subtle creations meant to distract and deceive as their only defense. The Wards were meant take a punishment, meeting The Darkness head on and repulse it. Yes, Wards failed, but not without putting up one septa of a fight first. Illusions held the strength of tissue paper, which was why the man was glad to see that his Obari friend had taken his advice and blended real props with her illusions, lending the impressions more reality and more resiliency.

"I put a lot of work into that illusion, Galeb Eielson," complained the woman, pouting. Her voice was strong and sweet, inviting conversation. "You could have at least played along for a little bit."

"Playing along doesn't help you refine your craft, Kieri" Galeb pointed out. He wished he could find more of the playfulness within himself that used to dominate his conversations with the Obari woman. All too often these days he found himself sounding stuffy as he lectured her. "Besides, you giggled."

"I did not!" Kieri huffed. "I was merely imitating the Kelpin's well- known hunting call.

"Kelpin don't have vocal chords. The only sound Kelpin make is the occasional 'slurp'," Galeb insisted.

"You were a lot more fun before you lost that finger," Kieri muttered, before realizing something. "Wait a minute. How do you know what sounds a Kelpin can or cannot make? As you pointed out there aren't any Kelpin within hundreds of miles of here. Where would you have possibly met one?"

"I wasn't born up in the North Country," Galeb said, tilting his head, to regard his friend.

Kieri was silent for a moment, regarding Galeb in surprise. He never spoke about his childhood.

"You grew up along the coast?" Kieri asked softly, wanting to know a bit more, hopeful that her friend was finally opening up after all these years.

"Well, no, as a matter of fact, I didn't," Galeb said, smiling.

Kieri glared at him. She should have known that the moment was too good to be true.

Galeb never spoke about his childhood to Kieri. Not because of anything bad that had happened to him. It was just that he hadn't had much of one. Books, Wards, and studying. Pretty boring; Galeb did not want to appear any more boring than he already was to Kieri.

"You're an ass, Galeb," Kieri said with a snort.

Galeb smiled at the jibe. His interactions with Kieri were the high point of his patrol and she could still lighten his mood even when insulting him. He yearned for these times when the Obari woman poked at his stern demeanor.

"Don't get snippy with me just because I called you out for being lazy," Galeb said, lathering up his face and beginning to shave swiftly, but carefully.

He really wanted the shave and a chance to look presentable now that he had company.

"You being an ass has nothing to do with accusations of laziness. Not that there was anything remotely lazy about that illusion!" fumed Kieri, clenching her fists and stamping her foot. "Do you know how much time and effort I put into setting this up?"

Kieri liked their exchanges as much as Galeb. Even so she had gone to a lot of effort to set up this trick. The least Galeb could do was to show his appreciation for how much time and effort she had put into trying to scare him.   A kiss, maybe. Yes, Kieri would definitely enjoy a kiss.

"Okay, maybe not lazy. How about sloppy?" Galeb asked, trying to keep his expression neutral and not cut himself because hands suddenly decided to tremble a bit. As fit and trim as Kieri was, certain things jiggled distractingly whenever she stomped her foot.

"How, so?" Kieri demanded, her eyes narrowing into slits. No, Galeb was not giving her the compliments that she so richly deserved. If anything he seemed to be withdrawing into himself a bit. She hated when he did that.

"Well, there's the dress for one thing," Galeb said.

"What's wrong with the dress? Besides the fact that it is a gown. A spectacular gown, I might add," Kieri stated running her hands over the fabric.

"Yes, you look very pretty in it," Galeb admitted, not noticing the blush on Kieri's face at the complement in the twilight.

Galeb rather liked the effect of the star studded gown, having seen Kieri wear it on several different occasions. He had even created a Ward combination that he had dubbed 'Star's Kiss The Water', in honor of that gown. Of course that particular Warding was a bit less pretty in that it sucked the heat out of a Darkness's body, freezing it from the inside out.

"The problem is not with the gown," Galeb continued gently, "You weren't moving with the illusion. I could see your real dress underneath. Your cousins weren't helping either; their shadow illusions contrast too darkly against the ambient light."

Kieri threw an irritated look in the direction of her cousins, looked down, quirked an eyebrow, and let the illusion of the gown lapse as she leapt the short distance from the raft to the shore and walked over to Galeb. Underneath she wore a knee length dress over thick leggings and boots of the same mottled browns and greens. A long narrow sword that curved ever so slightly was belted at her waist along with an impressive array of knives.

Galeb's own clothing mimicked Obari style, since the Obari had helped him learn to survive some of the more unexpected problems of continually living outdoors. Though Galeb had to admit that Kieri's clothing was in better condition.   His shirt was mended more times than he cared to admit and was tucked into thick leather pants that still needed replacing. He'd been lucky to get the coat mended.

Kieri was the bright point in his existence and sometimes he felt that he should avoid Kieri because he could not bear the thought of arriving back on this stretch of his patrol and not find her waiting for him with her latest illusion.

Fear of losing Kieri to The Darkness was why when Kieri teased him, joked, and tried to make him smile, Galeb responded with practical advice. He had to admit that his advice drove her mad, which made Galeb happy in a strange way. He loved seeing the passion in Kieri that he could no longer find so easily in himself. He worried sometimes that he was growing bitter.

Kieri, for her part, did not disappoint him, as her eyes filled with heat and her face lit up with a sultry smile.

"So, Galeb, are you saying that you were trying to see under my dress?" She asked, liking the direction the conversation seemed to be suddenly heading in. Kieri had been trying to head their conversations in this direction for three years.

Kieri Sonovonol and Galeb were old friends, having met years earlier. Galeb had been a supremely confident and inexperienced eighteen year old Itinerant Warder Mage and Kieri had been a precocious twelve year old determined to trick the Klynsheimer.

Kieri had taken one look at Galeb and instantly became fixated on testing her illusion skills on the foreigner, mostly because he was one of the few men she had ever met up to that point whom she was not, in some way, related to. Galeb had taken pity on a girl whose family seemed to be ignoring her and complemented her on an illusion of a butterfly in flight.

Eight years on and both had matured greatly in the time since their first meeting though Kieri had yet to give up on her goal to trick Galeb with one of her illusions. She claimed that it was a matter of pride; it was one septa of an excuse to keep seeking out Galeb's company. Neither one could say exactly when they had begun to look at each other as more than friends, though it was in the last few years.

"I thought you said it was a gown," Galeb reminded Kieri.

"I wasn't talking about the gown," Kieri said huskily, fingering the hem of her dress and lifting it slightly.

Galeb blushed to the roots of his hair and looked away, trying to find safer ground especially since he knew that Kieri was not alone. She would have family members nearby. The Obari lived in small extended family units, never more than twenty Obari in a particular range at one time, though in certain areas those ranges overlapped. Usually safe zones, the closest things to permanent encampments that the Obari considered maintaining. Places to rest and recover.

Ebko, Kieri's father, in particular was not very fond of Galeb and would beat the living nta out of Galeb if he were to see Kieri's dress lifting anywhere in the Mage's vicinity.

Kieri grinned wickedly. She may have failed to ever fool Galeb with one of her illusions but ever since she turned seventeen she had set herself an additional challenge. She tried to make him blush or stammer at least once during their conversations.

When the game started, Kieri just wanted to best the Klynsheimer in one thing. Call it the need for a small victory, but Kieri relished making Galeb uncomfortable. Not only was she able to break his composure but she was able to make him smile. Oh, she enjoyed knowing why he blushed, but that smile was precious to her.

Of course the teasing had changed in recent years as well. None of her early attempts to embarrass him had been suggestive in any way. It was only in the last couple of years that she had turned her efforts towards more adult pursuits. If her cousins were not watching she would have jumped Galeb right then and there and reminded him of just how passionate they could be together.

"Don't you like my dress?" Kieri asked, sauntering a bit closer, pulling the hem a bit wider. Oh, she was enjoying this.

"It is perfectly serviceable," Galeb choked out. He was an idiot. 'Serviceable' wasn't what he had meant to say. But who could think when they had a hemline to watch.

"Any other compliments?" Kieri asked sourly, as she dropped the hem of her dress, not having received anywhere near the reply she had wanted yet again. "Or would you rather criticize my illusion?

"Your cousins besides getting the shadow color wrong, were moving the lanterns used to create the halo effect too much," Galeb mumbled as he emptied the cup of now soapy water and repacked the supplies, having somehow avoided cutting himself. He was disappointed that the conversation had found itself back on to familiar ground, but he could tell Kieri was mad and didn't want to make things worse between them. So he went along, answering the question.

The shadows, which had been holding to their illusion just in case Galeb was guessing, stiffened.

"You try to crawl through grass while holding a lantern," came the offended reply from one of the cousins.

"I didn't even want to do the 'enchantress' illusion," protested the other shadow. "I wanted 'Warrior Princess'. That one would at least make it easier for Kieri to kick the crap out of you when you make stupid comments like calling her dress 'serviceable'. Smooth. Real smooth, Klynsheimer."

Galeb couldn't dispute Kieri's cousins' comments. This was the way that their conversations had seemed to be going the last few years. Kieri kept pushing at him and he retreated, unsure of how to give her what she seemed to want while still keeping his attention on the dangers around them.

"Of course they were," Kieri muttered in disgust, recognizing that he was withdrawing into himself again. "You seriously want to talk about my cousins right now?"

Kieri ran her hands down the front and sides of her dress as she asked the question.

"Well, you did ask about the illusion," Galeb pointed out, almost choking with the amount of restraint that it was taking to control himself. He was actually shaking a bit.

No, Galeb did not want to talk about Kieri's cousins. He very much wanted to return to the topic of her dress, but he would not. He had his patrol and nearly a year between now and when he would see Kieri next, Galeb reminded himself.

Galeb fixated on the old arguments that he had been having with himself since Kieri turned eighteen and he suddenly noticed that there was a septa of a lot of difference between the woman she was and the girl that she had been.

"You are a very frustrating man, Galeb Eielson. How is it that you see through every one of my illusions when no one else seems to be able to and you can't even compliment a woman?" Kieri asked in exasperation, finally acknowledging defeat. If she pushed anymore Galeb would only become more withdrawn.

"I use my eyes, Kieri. I pay attention. I listen. I do everything that you, yourself, have taught me to do," Galeb answered honestly, as he settled his pack closer and picked up his quarterstaff, searching the dark around him for threats, falling into the comfort of old habits. This he knew how to deal with, though he was silently calling himself an idiot again.

Kieri's cousins, having shuttered the lamps, sent illusions of fireflies sparkling through the night air, distracting the eyes as they shifted their positions, taking up their own guard as Kieri and Galeb finished their business. Kieri was never alone, always surrounded by loved ones. Galeb was almost always alone. Yet another reason not to return to the topic of the dress.

Kieri shook her head and then stood patiently waiting for the request that she knew was coming. As part of their long standing game, Kieri had to help Galeb with one of his experiments if he saw through her illusion. Of late these experiments entailed Kieri standing still and slowly raising an illusion around her while Galeb studied the magics as they swirled and solidified.

Kieri had no idea what Galeb gained from the study. As a Warder Mage – Itinerant Warder Mage, as Kieri had to often remind herself since Galeb felt the distinction was important – Galeb did not work with illusions. Not that the man had need. His Wards were the most powerful that Kieri or her relatives had ever encountered, elegantly simple in their construction, belying the Wards great strength.

Kieri and her cousins had once tricked an Ulanimani, a Darkness roughly shaped like a bull with a hide of solid rock, into charging one of Galeb's Ward posts. Wards in quick succession had flashed a myriad of colors, first stopping the Ulanimani's charge so swiftly that The Darkness actually flipped over to land on its head before another Ward pulsed forth and sent the stunned creature cartwheeling through the air away from the Ward line.

Ulanimanis weighed over a quarter of a ton. Kieri and her cousins had been stunned, almost falling from the tree they had been hiding in from the shock of the encounter. The Ulanimani had looked dazed and stumbled off into the distance.

The Wards were a reflection of Galeb. Simple and effective, with no effort wasted. Even her father begrudgingly admitted admiration for Galeb's skill, which were a cause for speculation and consternation among the Obari.

As an Itinerant Galeb stood among the lowest ranked of the Warder Mages. Among the Obari, given his strengths and time of service, Galeb would be among the most esteemed. This was a contradiction that the Obari did not understand.

Obari may have been culturally different than their Klynsheim cousins but they were not ignorant of Klynsheim customs. Knowing the workings of The Academy and Military was essential to continuing Obari survival in the face of Klynsheim migrations into the area. Even by Klynsheimer standards Galeb should have ranked at least Journeyman Warder Mage status, if not Master status by this point in his career. Treating a talent and dedicated Mage like Galeb so disrespectfully was beyond Kieri's families' comprehension. Though that low ranking did give Ebko more justification for disliking his daughter's friendship with Galeb.

When Galeb nodded that he was ready, Kieri slowly raised an illusion, a simple one that heightened her pale features in a manner which Galeb found quite alluring. Kieri knew that Galeb liked the effect, which was why she chose that particular illusion time and again and noticed that Galeb never once complained about the repetition.

Galeb smiled briefly in anticipation. He never tired of watching the intricacy of Obari illusions. He was fascinated with the way in which the magic adhered to Kieri's body. Who was he kidding? He was also fascinated by Kieri's body. How was it that he seemed to be able to counter the worst that The Darkness seemed to offer but he could not show simple appreciation for a beautiful woman? He turned his mind to less maddening thoughts and concentrated on the illusion in front of him.

Doctrine tied Ward magic to inanimate objects like stone, metal, and wood. Strong substances that could stand the test of time and assaults. The idea of tying Wards to the body was considered ludicrous considering standard practices would have the Wards carved, chiseled, or burned into their holding medium. Besides the obvious pain involved, no one wanted to have a Ward on their skin since the feedback from a fully active Ward would probably severely burn a person at the very least. The detonation of a failed Ward would be lethal.

The illusions of the Obari did not pose such risks and could somehow be molded close to the skin. The illusions were masterful creations even if they failed to fool Galeb once he had learned to look at them properly. The mistake most creatures made when confronting the illusions was seeing the whole and not the pieces. Obari illusions weren't single pieces of magic, but hundreds of interwoven strands that twisted around one another, creating a strong weave that was greater than the sum of its parts and breathtaking in its intricacy. Galeb strongly suspected that the Obari managed to visually create what the more intricate Wards of The Academy sought and failed to imitate. Whatever the truth, once Galeb learned to look at the pieces and not the whole, he found that he could pierce the illusions.

Galeb was always amazed at the seemingly effortless nature of Obari magic. Creating comparable styled Wards would take days of preparation and months of work.

Well, using traditional Klynsheimer methodology would mean months of work. Years of studying Obari magics had given Galeb ideas. Ideas had become experimentation and experimentation had given rise to many failures, but some stunning successes. Galeb now knew how to craft Wards with lightning speed. Not powerful Wards, not permanent or long lasting Wards, but Wards that were filled with potential.

These Wards, which Galeb dubbed 'light Wards' were based on Obari principles. Obari illusions worked by manipulating light and shadow to build impressions, like a master artist with his paints. Once he had figured out how the Obari gathered the light for the illusions – well, once he figured out that the Obari were gathering light – he was still not certain the Obari even knew how they did this – Galeb was well on his way to making his own innovations.

Since Galeb wasn't Obari, he used the Ward posts for inspiration because he was most familiar with their workings. A Ward called 'Gather the Light', which was what caused the Ward posts to glow so travelers could never lose sight of The Road, gathered the necessary raw energy, drawing from whatever light source was available, which was usually the sun. A second Ward, 'Pool the Water' condensed the light into a manageable ball to secure the light in one place, and 'Leavens the Bread' gave the light an almost doughy consistency that ensured the gathered light released the energy slowly and not all at once.

The Warder Mages who had established the initial defenses for the Great Trade Road had used a single Ward to achieve the same lighting effect on the Ward Posts. 'Rises the Sun' was an elegant defense in the heartland's style of decorative Warding. Not only was the amount of time needed to service the Ward prohibitive given his patrol, but Galeb did not like relying on a single Ward. Galeb saw redundancy as the key to strong defenses. He could also fit three separate simpler Warding combinations in the amount of space 'Rises the Sun' took up on the posts. The chances of three Ward arrays failing due to damage or overloading at the same time was much less than the chances of one Ward failing.

Galeb had based his light Wards on the three Ward combination, guiltily using the Ward posts themselves to power his experimentation. It had not taken Galeb much of a leap of logic to see that that the doughy globs of light that lit the Ward posts could be shaped. Using his hands had not been an option since he was not fond of burns, so he had originally tried using 'The Way is Shut', his favorite rune Ward. Using that particular Warding meant that he had to constantly hammer each portion of the light ball, like a smith working metal. Eventually the more subtle 'Turning the Tide', a Ward meant to redirect Darkness away from the Ward line, proved to be more helpful. 'Turning the Tide' was more of a feather stroke to "The Way is Shut's" brute force.

Well, that was a bit of exaggeration. Even realizing that 'Turning the Tide' was the Ward to use had not meant that Galeb did not have to spend quite a lot of time practicing and adding other Ward combinations to get it right.

There had also been the matter of what to anchor the Ward combinations to so that he could utilize his light Wards away from the Ward posts. Despite considering a variety of mediums, from his coat to his quarter staff, Galeb had eventually realized that he had to place the Wards dangerously close to his hands no matter what he did. Accepting that fact had taken more courage than he had in him considering that Wards exploded spectacularly if too much energy was pulled through them. Or more stupidity. Sometimes it was hard to tell the difference.

Yes, he had 'Sweeten the Air' etched into his clothing. But it was a maintenance Ward at best, one of the few non-Darkness related Wards ever mastered. Galeb suspected that there used to be many other non-Darkness related Wards in the ancient past, but the need to defend against The Darkness had limited teaching and most non-defensive Wards had probably been forgotten.

But back to the point. If 'Sweeten the Air' was damaged than the worst Galeb had to fear was a brief instant of mild heat and then his clothes would probably start to smell rather quickly. The kinds of Wards that Galeb had contemplated if damaged would release a lot of heat and probably char his hands if not completely severe them at the wrist. Not that the fear stopped Galeb for more than a week. The idea of his light Wards had been too tempting to ignore since the excitement he had felt had chased away the boredom.

Galeb had sought a way to not only weave the Wards he would need out of out of light like the Obari, but permanently anchor the Wards a few feet around his hands giving him a modicum of safety. Trees had been unwilling participants in the experiments, quite a few finding rings girded into their bark by the failures. He felt a little bad about that, quite enjoying the trees since the vegetation broke up the monotony of The Road. But not bad enough to want to experiment on himself.

In the end, he had managed to create an array of Wards around both wrists, hovering a good two feet away. Galeb had shaped the initial Wards from the light globes, building off of the material to gather further light and built from there. Wards to gather light, Wards to condense the light and shape it. Other Wards to hold these Wards in place, which turned out to be a combination of 'The Way is Shut', to repulse the Wards away from his skin and 'A Lady's Smile Beckons', which attracted the Wards to his skin. Balancing the opposing forces had been the most difficult task, probably made more difficult because Galeb always sought ways to incorporate his favorite Ward into any construction.

The Wards were individually very weak, but designed, as always to work in concert to create a greater effect.

The only continually nagging problem that Galeb had was an unanswered question about the way the Wards moved. The Ward array continually rotated around their anchor point in a sinuous dance. Galeb had tried once, and only once to fix the Wards in place and still the dance. The tree he had been working with had not been girded. Its entire midsection had been ripped in half. Galeb had decided that he liked the rotation after that experience.

There had been one departure from the Obari and Ward post inspired craftings. Both the Obari illusions and the Ward posts were meant to be seen. Galeb had not thought that having glittering Wards around his wrists would be easy to explain to his fellow Klynsheimers and would definitely be a temptation to The Darkness. He wanted to delay revealing his abilities as long as possible. Especially considering how hostile The Academy seemed to be towards innovations. Galeb didn't need to give his superiors any more excuses to react negatively towards him.

So instead of keeping the Wards visible, Galeb bent the light, twisting it upon itself so that the Wards would be invisible. Galeb had honestly wondered why the Obari had never attempted this technique. He was still trying to figure out a way to broach the subject with Kieri.

One last Warding in the array had been added as an additional measure to keep the Wards hidden but also so that

Galeb did not have the threat of live Wards around his body at all times. Galeb still sweated a bit when the Wards were active.

'Sleeps the Baby', was a Ward used to create passive defenses similar to the type that Klynsheimer scouts used when going on spying missions against The Darkness. Temporary Ward posts, much smaller than The Road Wards could be laid out in a circle around the scouts. 'Sleeps the Baby' kept the Wards inactive until Darkness directly threatened the scouts' position, helping to keep the scouts undetected. 'A Parent's Sleepless Night' was the counter to 'Sleeps the Baby' and nullified the other Ward bringing the Ward circle into full power when The Darkness got too close. Both Wards were worked into his array, though in Galeb's design, 'A Parent's Sleepless Night' could not be automatically triggered.

Kieri had been the inspiration and the teacher, helping him to realize that the Wards could be shaped from light and had to be woven together, like the separate strands of the Obari illusions. Not a few strands either. Galeb could now weave thousands of Ward strands together, twisting around one another in an eye watering tangle of complexity with each individual strand reinforcing the whole and becoming nearly self-sustaining. The process was slow but the results were worth the effort. He called it Deep Ward Weaving.

Galeb should really write a treatise on the process but did not want to irritate his superiors with more 'children's books'. He knew that he was being petty, but could not give a septa.

These Wardings were the only reason that he had survived the Incident. He had tried not using them when holding the Ward Line, but when the Spike striders had dragged him down he had lashed out in desperation. Fear of how the settlers would react had held him back; he had been stupid and wounded because of it. Even now, when he should share with Kieri what he could do, he was holding back out of fear of rejection.

Kieri had no idea what Galeb had discovered; he seldom talked about his Wardings anymore, assuming that she would be bored by such talk. He was right of course, but she did not tell him that. Instead Kieri built her illusions piece by piece for him. Illusions that Kieri could build in seconds she stretched out into minutes, creating an intense kind of intimacy between the two. In a way these moments were all about seduction for Kieri because Galeb's eyes always seemed to light with hunger as he watched.

If Kieri had talked to Galeb about his experiments with the weavings she would have known that he had hit upon the idea of templates to speed the work. The pouches on his bandoleer contained dozens of specially treated leather patterns, meticulously shaped so that all he had to do was summon the light and pass it through the template to create strands of Wards that were more powerful than the light Wards but not as powerful as what Galeb could create when he took the time to Deep Ward Weave.

For most things the templates were a good compromise. Stronger than traditional Klynsheimer Wards, but not as time consuming as deep weaves. There was too much ground to cover in his patrol to allow him to Deep Weave as much as he wanted to but all of his Ward Posts had the template created Wards upon them.

There were limitations of course like the damage to the Ward post during the Incident. The idiot boy had damaged the Wards in a way that required a precision repair. He couldn't burn Wards into the wood with as much precision as he could carve.

Even so, he used the templates whenever he could. One in twenty of the posts even held Deep Ward weavings. He was trying to increase that number with each trip but no matter what he tried he could not manipulate the strands as swiftly as Kieri, which he supposed was only fair. Kieri could not shape and power a Ward to save her life.

Kieri's life was a thought that dominated Galeb's thoughts for the better part of a year after he began mastering the light Wards. The Darkness was unrelentingly in its savagery; He knew that it was only a matter of time before Kieri was hurt...or worse. The Incident had only hardened his determination to protect her.

He did not like to dwell on such thoughts but Darkness attacks had become more frequent in the past several months. In places where Galeb would find Darkness sign once every few years he was always finding fresh tracks that spurred him further along The Road to ensure that there had been no breaches. And Kieri was right; he had not been the same since he lost the finger to the Darkness.

Maybe it was the exhaustion clouding his perceptions or the fact that his reflexes were also admittedly slowing; he did not seem to be as fast or strong as he once was. Galeb guessed that age was finally catching up to him. He grimaced. An old man at twenty six when Kieri seemed to be bursting with youthful enthusiasm and fresh faced beauty.

Galeb shook his head.   As Kieri raised the illusion around her he pulled out a stone from his pack. The stone acted as an anchor for the countless Ward Weaves that he'd crafted in every spare moment that he had had over the last twelve months, which was why his own Wards were limited to the area around his wrists.

Galeb would finish his own defenses once he knew Kieri was protected.

As tightly packed as the Weaves were around the small stone, the air seemed distorted around it and Galeb was careful to keep the stone away from curious eyes at all times. The Ward Weaves, thick ropes of Wards unwinding in a seemingly endless stream as they unanchored from the stone, slowly swirled around Kieri, and found their place exactly where he intended them to be. A delicate web was forming around Kieri visible only to his eyes, as he bent their light to keep them hidden. Galeb wished that he did not have to hide the Wards' light; he had crafted each Ward to compliment the beauty he saw every time he looked at Kieri. The vibrant colors that silhouetted her frame in a protective dance spoke more of his feelings for the Obari woman than he could ever voice.

But no one but Galeb could see the Deep Weavings; like so many aspects of his life, he was alone in this ability. Kieri would not see the depth of the passion he felt, would not know that he had septaed near killed himself with exhaustion in the months since the Incident to make certain she would always be safe from the monsters he defended against.

Keeping the Wards four feet from Kieri's body was critical should the Wards fail. Figuring out a safe distance had been tricky since the Deep Wardings were exponentially more powerful than the Wards around his own wrists. The Wards were all directed outward should they break, taking any energy bursts away from Kieri's body in theory. Well, more than in theory, Galeb hoped. He was proud of that particular directional Ward, which was of his own devising. He called it 'Watches the Way' in partial honor of his favorite Warding and used it to help direct his shaping of the light Wards. Still, if the Wards failed and there was blowback towards Kieri's body, the four feet would make the difference between injury and death. He'd also used an experimental design to disperse the opposing forces.

Instead of the usual equal and opposite reaction, the force acting towards Kieri would be partially deflected to either side. Not that it was guaranteed to work perfectly – there was a reason why he wasn't using this technique on the Ward posts themselves. Even so Kieri wouldn't be able to stand up to any Darkness of significant mass. Her Wards would protect her but she would be blown backwards.

"What's that tingle?" Kieri asked, starting to drop the illusion as she felt the Wards flowing around her. She may have been unable to create Wards but she could feel active magic.

"No excuses. You owe me a full illusion and this one is particularly breathtaking," Galeb said, hoping to distract her. Why couldn't he think to say things like that to her when he wasn't too preoccupied to take advantage of the situation?

He wanted Kieri Warded and he did not think that she would approve of what he was trying to do. Obari were a proud people and took offense to the suggestion that they needed more than their own magics no matter how true that suggestion might be.

"What do you think I'm doing?" Kieri snapped, reinforcing the illusion until her skin glowed with moonlight and shadow, such a contrast to Galeb's deeply tanned skin. A beaming smile at the compliment took some of the sting out of her words and had her reshaping the illusion to better highlight the parts of her body she would not mind Galeb focusing more attention on.

Not that it seemed to be working and there was definitely a tingle; not a threatening tingle, but a feeling none the less. Kieri was certain of this fact. Her cousins better not be trying to play a prank on her – or Galeb. Only Kieri got to play tricks on Galeb. She had ensured that her family members understood this rule explicitly.

As soon as she finished with the illusion and Galeb had his minutes to examine it, Kieri was going to find out what was going on. But not until she was finished. Kieri did not get to see Galeb as much as she wanted and enjoyed the way he watched her now, the pride and awe that he felt for her clear upon his face. Maybe her illusion was working after all. She unconsciously played with the hem of her dress again, lifting it slightly in invitation.

Galeb watched Kieri intently as the last of the Wards wove around her body, completely missing the movement of the dress. Sweat was on his brow from the strain of anchoring so many Wards at once. He would have liked to illuminate the Wards to double check his work but had to trust that everything was as it should be.

Kieri slowly let the illusion drop, noticing that the tingling had stopped around the same time. She frowned, but put the thoughts aside when she noticed how Galeb suddenly seemed to deflate in front of her.

"Satisfied?" she asked him, moving forward, her sudden concern ending her attempts to entice him.

"Yes, thank you," Galeb said, stretching a bit as he tried to shake off a little of the fatigue, and turning slightly away from Kieri so that she would not see the brief tremor in his hands.

"Well there goes any hope of a bit more fun. Galeb, go to sleep. My cousins and I will watch over you tonight," Kieri said softly, worried that her friend was not well. No, she knew he was not well; she just hoped that he was no worse than usual.

Galeb nodded, lying back, cradling the quarterstaff, without a single protest, which was not like him. "Thanks, Kieri."

She smiled in pleasure at how much he trusted her. The smile faded to be replaced again by worry. Kieri did not like worry. She like Galeb's smiles and she dearly wanted them back.

Galeb quickly fell into a light sleep. Kieri looked at him and sighed, noticing that Galeb did not even relax as consciousness left him; not a bad habit, but she had hoped that he would relax more around her. She walked away a few yards, staring out into the night.

Her cousin Elboab, affectionately nicknamed 'Bob' for his fondness in making illusions of bobwhites, which made no sense since Bob had never actually seen a living bobwhite outside of the drawing of a book, walked over to her. Bob insisted that his fondness for creating the birds was a reflection of man's struggle to gain what he could not have beyond all reason and logic.

Bob was like most Obari males, slightly shorter than Galeb, lightly muscled, with forgettable features. Forgettable features worked well with illusions, not distracting from the overall effect. Bob was dressed similarly to Kieri, except he wore a thick tunic instead of a dress.

Bob insisted that he was most unlike other Obari males. Usually with his chest puffed out and a smug look on his face. The smug look never lasted long; usually a woman was smacking the expression off of his face.

Bob glanced back at Galeb with an unusual look of concern on his face as he leaned on the spear that he favored as a primary weapon. The haft was decorated with what he insisted were bobwhite feathers but looked suspiciously like crow.

"You worry too much about him when he's here," Bob said. "You worry too much when he's not in our range. The first I don't understand because he never leaves your sight when he's around here. Strange, really, when you consider that I'm much better looking. As for the other, you can't worry about what's not in your range. Though if you lift that dress up any higher your father is going to make certain that Galeb is never in your range again. At least not with his balls intact."

"Bob, we're cousins. I'm not going to be watching you anywhere near the way I watch Galeb, unless it's to see you being driven away from the bathing pool because that never ceases to be entertaining," Kieri said blandly before sighing. "Where Galeb's concerned, it's not that simple.

"Galeb leaves our territory and I no longer have to worry about him? We're long past those days, Bob. We have been for a long time now. And there is nothing wrong with the height of my hem line," Kieri said primly, "Which you should not even be looking at, you pervert."

"I'm not the pervert here. You'd be dancing naked around Galeb if Kawen and I weren't here to remind you that there is Darkness waiting to bite your ass, clothed or not. Stop changing the subject. It might be better for you if you let him leave your mind when he's away," Bob said. "Kind of like the way I forget the way the women scream at me at the pool. Or at the very least change the way you think about events."

"What do you mean by changing the way I think?"

"Well, when the women are chasing me, threatening bodily harm, you see unreasonably enraged women. I, however, see women driven mad with lust for me."

"It's not lust, Bob. I'm pretty sure it's intent to maim."

"Eh," Bob said, shrugging.

A few moments of silence stretched out.

"He's my friend," Kieri eventually said stubbornly, not liking the thought of forgetting about Galeb.

"He's a good man," Bob acknowledged, as if conceding that there was value in Galeb, while at the same time not acknowledging that he was simply Kieri's friend. "That you want to see you naked. Never going to happen while I'm around, mind you. Man would be too embarrassed in the comparison."

Kieri huffed at her cousin, pulling her hemline down a bit. At least Bob was more understanding than Ebko. Kieri's father thought she spent too much time focused on Galeb and not enough time worrying about her own people. Personally she thought that everyone should worry more about Bob being down by the women's washing area. Kieri had caught him just last week dressed in the illusion of a wash cloth.

60

"Friend or not, good man or not, he has to live his own life," Bob reminded her with a shrug.

"Am I not part of that life?" Kieri asked.

Bob wasn't certain if Kieri was asking his opinion on the matter, herself, or the sleeping Warder Mage.

"I did notice that whenever he's near our territory the Warder grants you opportunities to play tricks on him," Bob acknowledged with a smirk. "One would almost think that he didn't have more important things to do in his life. Or people to do for that matter."

Kieri's concern for Galeb almost caused her to ignore Bob's playful comment.

"Galeb isn't 'doing' other people, Bob," Kieri said, scowling.

"How would you know? You see him once a year. Man probably has women in every village," Bob said with a grin. "I know I would."

The idea of Galeb becoming interested in another woman was one of Kieri's greatest fears.

"He is *mine*!"

Bob arched an eyebrow at that bit of possessiveness.

Kieri sniffed.

"I am the only woman in his life. And I will cut you if you dare to say otherwise."

"You aren't going to cut me," Bob said dismissively. He had it on very good authority – his own – that Kieri considered him her favorite cousin.

"No? Well then the next time your mother decides to go to the bathing pool instead of Marel or Krina, I'm just going to let her grab your 'wash cloth'."

"Gack! That's sick!"

"Then you should stop saying stupid things and definitely stop pretending to be a wash cloth," Kieri said sternly.

"Shouldn't you be worrying about your Warder Mage?" Bob said, scowling. "Or wondering what trouble he's getting into when you aren't around to moon over him?"

"I don't 'moon', Bob" Kieri said, firmly, even though she knew she was lying poorly. "Though I'll admit that I'm very curious about the part of his life that I don't get to see. Why's he gone for so long between visits? Why does he come back more tired every time we see him?"

Bob pondered the question before answering as was his habit when asked a serious question. He felt it made him appear nobler. Women liked noble; or he supposed that women like noble. It was hard to tell some times. Usually because they were too busy shouting at him. You would think that women would have quieter ways to show their appreciation for him.

"He has the burden of his duty. Klynsheim take their duties very seriously. I sometimes wonder if they know how to have fun," Bob finally said by way of explanation. "They certainly have a hard time noticing the heights of hemlines."

"That doesn't explain the fatigue, Bob," Kieri insisted. "And will you please stop fixating on my hemline!"

Bob was quiet for some time before he responded. Bob wanted to make a joke, deflect, but knew that he couldn't – Kieri was his favorite cousin; she didn't rat him out to his mother when she caught him staking out the bathing pool. She kicked his ass, but didn't rat him out.

"Galeb's not fatigued. He's worn away." Bob said, not failing to seen the look of pain that flashed across his cousin's face, "But you know this."

Bob also knew about how Galeb had recently fought to hold the Ward Line west of the territory.   He did not and would not tell Kieri.

"But why, Bob? Galeb is ranked an Itinerant. How much territory is assigned to an Itinerant? Two, three weeks of travel time? How can that patrol be doing this to him? And don't you dare say that he is weak! We both know that's not true."

No, Bob admitted to himself, Galeb was not weak. He had heard of how the Klynsheimer faced The Darkness armed only with his knife and held The Road when Bob himself would have only wanted to run away. In a manly fashion of course.

Then there was the time Kieri had convinced him to bait an Ulanimani to test Galeb. Kawen had nta himself when the creature had collided with the Wards.

"Nothing makes sense about this. Not even the timing of his patrol matches up with what it should be. Galeb's gone ten months between visits to where The Road passes by our range. Last year he was a full year between visits. It was so long that I thought he was dead," Kieri said, her voice straining at that admission. "I don't understand...."

Bob looked at his cousin sympathetically. She was scowling at the memory. He remembered her melancholy all too well. Ebko had been quite angry. Bob still wasn't certain if Ebko had known why he had been angry any more than Kieri had known why she was so melancholy at the thought of losing Galeb. Bob found the Klynsheimer and his cousin exhausting at times. They complicated simple matters and sucked the fun out of life.

Galeb was a good man. A strong man. Kieri was a good woman. A strong woman who would gladly share a man's burdens. Bob was getting to the point where he felt the need to grab the both of them and shake them to make them see reality of their situation before it was too late. Of course, he kept getting distracted by the bathing pool.... Maybe he should be encouraging Kieri to lift her hemline more. But that was a disturbing thought. Bob did not want to accidently see what was under his cousin's dress and Kieri could sometimes get carried away where Galeb was concerned.

No, he just wanted Kieri and Galeb to face the facts of their relationship. For God's sake the woman was guarding the man's sleep! Anyone with half a brain knew what that signified.

But if his cousin didn't want to face what was going on Bob was going to push a bit. It might be fun and Bob was bored. He was also curious. Kieri was right. Galeb's long absences and fatigue did not make sense either because of Galeb's rank or his proven abilities. The Road Wards were proof enough of that power. Though no Obari liked to admit doing so, the family had sheltered behind Galeb's Wards a time a two when The Darkness became particularly malignant. Yes, Bob needed to find out what was going on with Galeb. This had nothing to do with his mother's increasingly pointed questions about Bob's own social life.

"Follow him," Bob suggested, liking the idea immediately. He like any idea that took him out of the reach of his mother. Kieri never ratted him out, but that didn't mean that Bob hadn't been caught by others. A man gets caught masquerading as a wash cloth near the women's bathing pool once and suddenly there are a thousand questions about his intentions. Sometimes he envied the simplicity of a bobwhite's existence. No one ever screamed at a bobwhite when the bird happened to wander past a bunch of naked women.

"What?" Kieri asked, surprised by the suggestion.

"Follow him. See where he goes. See what he does. Find out what troubles him so." *Give me the excuse to escape my mother for a bit. Come on, Woman! Take the bait! Oh! I might even get a chance to see other women naked.* Bob perked up at that thought.

"Ebko wouldn't allow it," Kieri said, shaking her head, though the idea appealed to her for more reasons than just Galeb. It had been quite a while since she had been outside the family range.

The problem was that while Obari were fiercely independent, resisting a centralized authority did not mean that the Obari did not have a hierarchy. Obari family units obeyed the words of their matriarchs and patriarchs.

"Demand a test of skill. Ebko can't deny you the chance to challenge your abilities," Bob explained reasonably. Internally he was all but shouting 'take the bait! Take the bait!' Besides, Bob had a sneaking suspicion that Ebko's dislike had more to do with encouraging his daughter rather than discouraging her affections.

"How's traveling with Galeb a challenge to my skills?" Kieri asked, a wistful note to her voice. "Though they're skills of his I would like to test."

Kieri licked her lips when she said the last words.

"I said follow Galeb, not travel with him. I definitely didn't suggest any of...that. Probably wouldn't be any good at such things anyway. No, follow him undetected. Avoid his notice for once. Not even Ebko can deny Galeb's abilities. Avoiding Galeb's notice would take extreme skill."

And get me away from here long enough for my brothers to screw up and take my mother's attention off of me, Bob thought to himself, trying not to seem too eager.

Kieri thought about the idea and smiled.

"Who's going to judge my challenge?" she asked.

"Kawen and I'll accompany you, Cousin. We'll judge," Bob said with a smile that was equal parts triumph and relief.

"You'll guard my back?" Kieri asked, still smiling.

"Haven't we always?"

"Yes, yes you have. Thank you, Bob."

No, thank you, cousin. I hope there is time to visit the bathing pools before we leave. A tree didn't work. Maybe next time I'll try an animal. A fish or maybe a bobwhite?

Bob wandered off distracted by his thoughts but not enough that he didn't keep vigilant for threats. He was not stupid, just very hopeful, which was why the woman's bathing pool had been relocated twice.

Chapter 3

Galeb woke as refreshed as he ever did with no sign of the Obari. He was not surprised, though he felt a little bit of disappointment. It would have been nice to see her before he left the area and get another peak at where her current hemline stopped. But Galeb knew that Obari did not stay out in the open for long and always sought the safety of illusion.

He hefted his pack after a hasty breakfast of pemmican and water to fill his stomach and give him the energy he needed for the slightly chilly morning. Galeb's body wanted more, but would have to make do. Thankfully the region containing the Great Trade Road was prone to rains and not snows. Though it got cold, Galeb never had to worry about trying to slog through snow drifts. Still the chill was enough to remind him of the many aches that he had acquired over the years.

That day and the next was spent walking The Road, checking Wards, repairing areas that had become worn by time, and adding to the overall defenses. Galeb tried to always leave another layering of Wards on each trip. Occasionally Galeb came across sign of where The Darkness had tried to challenge them.

He was careful at those moments, never leaving the protection of the Wards. He examined the sign and recorded as much information as he could about what kind of Darkness was in the area. He would file a report with the nearest Way Fort and spread the word among the villages.

Even behind the Ward barrier, he activated the arrays around his wrists and kept two Wards in mind, ready to spring when he saw sign of an Ilmuth, an ambush predator with a venomous bite. 'The Way is Shut' and 'The lost Drunkard'; repel and confusion Wards were his bread and butter and less likely to trigger aggressive responses in the less purposefully harmful types of Darkness.

Kieri was bored, her elation at Ebko acquiescing to her request quickly dimming. She never realized how painfully repetitious Galeb's job was, though she should have had some idea since she had watched him spend hours repairing a pair of Ward posts on The Road one summer without his shirt on. Come to think of it, repairing the Ward posts was another thing that did not make sense.

Kieri understood that Galeb had to be the one to carve the Wards onto the wooden posts. What she did not understand was why Galeb had to be the one to physically install the posts themselves. She knew enough about the Klynsheim homelands to know that there were regular work crews who should have been tasked with that job. That got Kieri thinking about what other jobs Galeb had to do on his patrol that were not the normal responsibilities of a Warder.

Eventually Kieri's thoughts returned to how mind numbing Galeb's routine seemed to be. She wished the day were warmer so he could take off his shirt.

Kieri and her cousins had been following Galeb for several hours at this point and Bob was signaling for her to hang back and let the distance between her and the Klynsheimer increase. When Kieri gave her cousin a puzzled look, Bob leaned toward her ear and whispered an explanation.

"The purpose of this test is to be undetected, Kieri," Bob explained, whispering across the short distance that separated them. "Not to follow the man like a lost, drooling, puppy."

"I know what the purpose of the test is, Bob," Kieri hissed. "And I know what undetected means, unlike you. Yesterday was what, the third time you got caught at the women's bathing pool?"

"Stop changing the subject. This isn't about my admittedly magnificent skills. This is about you and the Warder who has to know that you're following him," Bob answered defensively. It wasn't his fault the women wanted to show their appreciation for him. He just wished that they'd stop using their fists when they did so.

"If Galeb knows that we're here, it's because someone keeps making illusions of bobwhites," Kieri grumbled.

"My illusions are – stop changing the subject. If Eielson doesn't know we're here, Cousin, then explain something to me. Does Galeb talk much to anyone besides you?" asked Bob, ignoring the comment about the bobwhites. Bobwhites were awesome.

"He – well...no, now that you mention it Galeb doesn't talk much to other people," Kieri agreed, looking slightly perplexed by the realization and feeling a little defensive on the Klynsheimer's behalf. "He talks plenty around us."

"I thought he was a mute the first three times I met him," Bob pointed out sarcastically.

Kieri felt a sudden urge to punch her cousin, which would have definitely revealed her presence to Galeb. She was wrapped in an illusion of rock and moss as she hugged a tree a hundred yards away from where Galeb stood writing in his log. Seeing moss rear up and hit the ground where Bob crouched would have been a dead giveaway. It also might be worth it.

"What's your point, Bob," Kieri asked, annoyed.

"Every time Galeb stops and examines Dark sign he offers the world a running commentary of his findings. I don't think that the Warder is talking to himself or the trees," Bob explained. "He's offering you warnings about what may be in the area."

"Nta!" Kieri hissed, feeling a little panicked. "I've been careful. He can't know we're here."

If she failed the test, Bob would insist on going home. Right now he was still smarting from the beating Esie had given him. The poor woman had found a chipmunk leering at her and figured out that Bob was spying on her at the pool. The memory of Esie's outrage might buy Kieri some time, but a failure was a failure and Bob would lead the group back home a lot sooner than Kieri wanted. Of course, if Kieri had stopped to consider the matter she would have realized that Bob had no intention of going back home anytime soon. At least not while Esie was on the war path.

Not that Bob couldn't outrun Esie. The woman was so top heavy it was a miracle she didn't topple over with ever step. At that thought Kieri realized that she really needed to stop hanging around Bob.

"I am starting to think that Galeb always knows when you're around," Bob said. "He has studied your particular magics for years what with that silly bet you two insist on. That's assuming he is actually studying your crafting and not just openly leering at your body. Hard to tell with that one... Either way, he may sense your crafting."

"What do you mean, 'sense my crafting'? Do you mean like taste or smell? Are you saying that I smell, Bob?" Kieri demanded angrily.

"What I am saying," Bob said with exasperation, "Is that you need to treat this journey like a real test of your skills and not an excuse to follow around a man you like. My own mother's already suspicious about your motivations and has been asking questions. I don't like questions. They always somehow become accusations against my awesomeness."

"Why has Marinsa been asking questions?" Kieri demanded a little louder than was necessary or prudent.

Bob's mother Marinsa was the matriarch of the family. Even if Kieri's mother had not fallen to The Darkness ten years ago, there would have been no guarantee that Kieri's mother would have been matriarch simply because she was married to the patriarch. The patriarch and matriarch of an Obari family were not always a mated pair. The patriarch and matriarch were simply the most skilled members of the family.

"Of particular note, in this area, is not only the sign of a skeskin Darkness, but that the plant life seems to be totally unconcerned by a rash striker's presence in the area. The moss and bushes specifically seem almost downright talkative today,"

Galeb said, loud enough for his voice to travel the distance, which must have been a bit of a strain.

None of the Obari seemed to realize that every fourth post was etched with a ruin called 'Amplify'. That Ward gave travelers a heads up about anything lurking in the nearby bushes if they knew enough to recognize the Ward and pause long enough in its proximity to utilize its abilities.

"How the septa? – that man is infuriating sometimes," Kieri hissed between clenched teeth, angry at being lectured. She knew perfectly well that skeskin, small, badger sized Darkness that secreted a viscous substance capable of dissolving all types of organic matter, was not a threat. Skeskin were completely nocturnal and only denned up in rock outcroppings, which there were none close by.

"But he has a point," Bob said, with a grin. "And I told you that my bobwhites didn't give us away."

"Don't try to distract me. What kinds of questions has your mother been asking?" Kieri demanded again.

"The kind of questions one would expect from a matriarch whose unmarried twenty year old niece is continually obsessed with a particular Klynsheimer and whose brother has been complaining about the lack of grandchildren," Bob answered blandly. He didn't add that he reminded his mother of Kieri's behavior every time Marinsa decided to interrogate him about his own pursuits.

Kieri blushed and then muttered that she was not obsessed. Bob just raised an eyebrow. The blush suddenly changed into a flush of anger as Kieri seemed to realize something.

"Bob, why would your mother think that I am obsessed with Galeb?" she asked dangerously. Her low tone seemed to add venom to her words.

"Remember, you're supposed to be imitating moss, Kieri. Moss doesn't get angry," Bob reminded her reasonably. "Think about what Galeb would say about your illusion."

"Now I know that you're hiding something, Bob. Answer my question," Kieri threatened.

"Oh, come on, Kieri, everyone in the camp knows that you go out of your way to be around Galeb," Bob said defensively.

"I see him once a year, Bob. Once a grieshtataing year. Not much camp gossip focused on my doings, usually. Not enough to warrant the term 'obsessive'," Kieri said, remembering at the last moment not to shake her head.

"Yeah, you see him once a year. Without fail. Spend months getting ready for that visit too. If that's not obsessive behavior, I don't know what is," Bob pointed out.

"Marinsa's never cared before," Kieri insisted.

"You didn't go around raising your hemline and guarding his sleep before," Bob said, feigning anger.

"You're not jealous or the over protective cousin, Bob. Don't pretend to be. Kawen might get away with this, but not you. Besides, how would Marinsa know that I guarded his sleep or what exactly I did with my hemline if you didn't tell her, Bob?" Kieri asked, sliding ever so slowly down the tree, as if the moss was separating.

Bob had a very bad feeling that his cousin's hands weren't empty. Kieri wouldn't kill him, but she could very well make him hurt if he got her angry enough. Two chittering squirrels suddenly erupted from where Bob crouched as he retreated faster than Kieri could react.

Galeb was surprised that Kieri and at least two others were following him since he could not recall the last time any of that family group had left their range. Probably Bob and Kawen, since they were her closest cousins. He was surprised and a bit pleased, enjoying the unexpected company. The pleasure was fleeting as he acknowledged that the Obari would probably soon become bored and turn away, seeking entertainment elsewhere, leaving Galeb alone again to wonder idly and a bit jealously if Kieri played with her hemline around other people.

That thought irritated him and he became momentarily resentful for the distracting thoughts. By this point on the patrol Galeb was usually already fading back into the numbness of routine or composing imaginary letters of complaint that he would never send to The Academy. He didn't usually have to be thinking about who else might be getting Kieri's attention.

None of his business, Galeb reminded himself with a shake of his head. Stay on mission; focus on the Patrol. Tomorrow would be the village of Kleidskeiper. Half a day after that would be the way fort at Skaaldsgeiper. Not until he passed those two points would he have to face the loneliness of a solo march. It was three days past Skaaldsgeiper to Runionbalc. Surely by that time Kieri would have turned back and Galeb could lose the misery and find the numbness inside.

Bob held Kieri back when Galeb finished writing the log entry and moved on. He was serious about allowing some greater space between them and admittedly hid from his cousin until her temper cooled. It wasn't his fault that his mother was so easily distracted about her niece's potential love life. Alright, it was Bob's fault for bringing up said love life, but a man had to use any defense possible to distract his mother. Bob had no intention of marrying Esie. Not with the backside he had seen on her. That thing was big enough to be daunting to a skeskin. Of course her top parts more than balanced out the bottom. Poor girl might fall over otherwise, Bob supposed.

But more than anything he wanted Kieri to reflect on what she was doing in regards to the Warder. Bob suspected two things when it came to Galeb's uncanny ability to know when Kieri was near. One, Galeb was just that good. The Warder was always paying attention to his surroundings. Secondly Bob thought that Kieri was intentionally letting Galeb know she was near him. His cousin wanted Galeb's attention focused on her.

Bob could respect the first reason. He absolutely needed to stop the second as it was foolishly dangerous. The fact that Bob considered any behavior foolishly dangerous said a lot about how careless Kieri was being. Bob didn't like taking anything too seriously, which was why he was annoyed that he had to be the one to correct Kieri's behavior. He had better things to be doing like creating bobwhites or finding clever ways to spy on the women's bathing pool.

Of course he had to be a bit serious when it came to Kieri. Bob was increasingly concerned that the Obari existence was not for her. She made mistakes in her preoccupation with the Warder Mage. Mistakes that even Bob found disconcerting. He would be very happy if Kieri found herself tied to Galeb and safely behind his Wards on a regular basis. That way Bob could avoid having to bury the remains of another cousin.

Bob used the excuse of wanting to examine one of the Ward posts that Galeb had recently repaired to stay in the area instead of following immediately after the Warder. Kawen was near by keeping an eye out for any dangers. Kieri was pouting, but watchful as well.

Bob did not know much more than the basics about Wards. He did recognize that Galeb had added an additional ruin, probably to reinforce the resiliency of the post should the skeskin find some way to rub some of its secretions on the wood. Not likely, but it was best to be prepared.

He admired the Ward Post for its craftsmanship like an art lover who admired a piece for its beauty with no true understanding of how the piece was created. He could feel the Ward post's power, see the tightly packed layers of Wards, the oldest carved in and the most recent burned deeply into the wood.

Bob frowned at the newness of the burn marks. He had seen Galeb working on the posts, but had seen no flame or heated metal.   In fact Galeb had not seemed to take the amount of time it should have to create these Wards so meticulously and as tightly packed as the Wards seemed to be on the posts. Hours of work done in minutes. It did not make sense. Hours of work done in minutes...that could explain Galeb's fatigue.

Bob's eyes widened as he realized the implications of his discovery. Whatever Galeb had done was a new technique, not more than a few years old to judge by the weathering of older burn marks on the post. New was not good. Bob wanted to growl in frustration as responsibility suddenly began tugging at him more.

The Klynsheim were already too powerful for Obari tastes. Klynsheim settlers were forever moving into the North Country that had once belonged to the Obari before his people had begun to dwindle. So far there was enough of a balance. The need for Wards slowing the advance and killed off the recklessly foolish. But this new technique could change everything. The work of hours done in minutes. This would mean Klynsheim settlements could expand exponentially.

Bob reminded himself that Galeb was a good man and would not intentionally bring harm to the Obari. But Galeb did seem to pose a threat to the Obari. On the other hand Galeb seemed to care for Kieri and could help keep her safe from foolish behavior. No, Bob needed to know more before reaching a decision before taking any sort of action. He specifically needed to know if Galeb was unique in his talents or if other Warders had developed the same ability. Responsibility sucked.

He prepared a message of air and light, something that he would like to see a Klynsheim try to do, sending a bobwhite winging to the west, back towards the home territory asking for kith, kin, and neighbor to let him know if they had noticed anything new about the Klynsheim Wardings. Bob hoped that there wasn't anything to report.

The Klynsheim Warder's Academy was traditional in its methods; like any organization that was hundreds of years old, it disliked change. Bob wanted Galeb to be an anomaly. He could work with an anomaly, limit the damage, maybe not have to kill the man and break Kieri in the process. No, if Bob killed Galeb he was going to have to kill Kieri as well. Bob was suddenly getting a headache.

Bob was going to have difficulties explaining his request. Ebko in particular would want to know what Bob was up to and if he had discovered a threat to the Family.

Kawen approached Bob, indicating that Kieri was growing impatient to get moving. Kawen was a very easy going kind of guy, never becoming too excited and just seeming to enjoy the moment. He also liked a good scandal and had ratted out Bob's activities at the bathing pool a time or two. A bonus to ratting Bob out was that once the women chased off Bob they never seemed to consider that someone else might be watching them as well. Bob had a few glimpses over the years. Kawen knew every birthmark, scar, and blemish on every woman not closely related to him.

As Kawen moved to turn away he stopped and looked back at the Ward Post, tilting his head slightly and frowning.

"What is it?" Bob asked.

"I never noticed it before," Kawen said, his voice both serious and with a hint of bemusement.

"Noticed what?" asked Bob.

"How much these Wards of Galeb's look like the illusion structures we build. All intertwined and layered. Here I thought that the Warder made that bet with Kieri as an excuse to ogle her when he was actually studying the structures. I don't know whether to admire the guy or be disappointed in him. Either way I've got to give him credit for being inventive. I'm willing to bet that this Ward design is stronger than any of the more traditional Klynsheim designs," Kawen answered, shaking his head of shaggy dark hair before turning his blue eyes to meet Bob's brown ones. "Who would have thought that the day would come when a Klynsheimer would Ward using Obari techniques?"

"Who indeed?" Bob replied, hollowly, waiting to see what else his cousin would say. Galeb's life might be in even more immediate danger than Bob had suspected. He wondered if he should hit Kawen.

On one hand, if he hit him hard enough, Kawen might forget what he saw. On the other hand, if he hit Kawen hard enough, Bob might have to carry him. Choices, choices...

Bob sighed, having to be honest about the kind of person he was. He did want Galeb and Kieri paired. But if Kawen saw Galeb as a threat and wanted that threat eliminated Bob would help him. Family first. Besides, Kawen didn't look light enough to carry. Maybe if Kieri helped him? Hmm...

"Though I can't see the traditionalists among his people being too happy with this kind of work," Kawen said, looking meaningfully at Bob.

Bob could see the thoughts flitting through his cousin's mind and pondered his words. Oh, he hadn't expected Kawen to be reasonable about this discovery. That was a bit of good news. Unless Kawen was trying to lull Bob into a false sense of security before he hit Bob over the head.

"Bob, whatever nonsense you're thinking about, forget about it and think about what I just said," Kawen said, taking a step back from his suddenly suspiciously glaring cousin.

Bob gave Kawen once last glare for good measure and then pondered Kawen's words. The traditionalists would not appreciate any new methodology. The traditionalists would not want this type of work utilized, disparaging it as foreign and untrustworthy. Obari stories about the arrogance of The Academy *were* widespread and truthful. Bob had spread his fair share of them after all. If Bob wasn't trustworthy, then who was?

"It would be a shame to waste such talent when it is not wanted," Bob agreed, trying to feel his cousin out.

"Goes a long way towards explaining how Galeb wound up out here without any prospects of promotion," Kawen added. "I can't see Galeb making too many friends by being inventive."

"I don't suppose that Academy would mind us borrowing such a talent in that case," Bob said, brightly, as if the idea had just occurred to him.

"Oh, I very much suspect that The Academy would mind for no other reason than upholding the principle of the sanctity of The Academy and Klynsheimer unity. Can't very well have Warder Mages taking up with Obari," Kawen pointed out with a snort.

"I don't know about that, Cousin. Galeb is a Warder and he very much does not seem to mind Kieri's company," Bob argued back. "She certainly doesn't mind the idea of the Klynsheimer knowing what she wears under her dress."

"No she doesn't," Kawen agreed, pretending to take a moment to think about the idea. He knew how to manipulate Bob better than anyone. "Might not take that much convincing on our part to get Galeb to take up with the Family. Kieri seems willing enough to show him the way."

"The man respect's his duty too much to give it up so easily," Bob said, disagreeing, hating to suddenly have to present the negative viewpoint. "Can't see him abandoning his patrol. Not without a replacement. He's boringly responsible that way."

"You don't think Kieri can convince him? I thought Kieri was going to strip naked the other night and jump him! You know the thought occurred to her, what with her wandering hem line," Kawen insisted, a bit disgusted about how blatant his cousin became around the Klynsheimer. Mostly because Kieri had been so blatant in front of him. No one wanted to see a relative getting frisky.

"So her hemline's a 'tell' now? Just how many times have you seen Kieri act like that?" Bob demanded, glaring at his cousin. This conversation was getting weird.

"Never and that's my point. Kieri increasingly has no shame when it comes to getting what she wants from that man. Lord knows that nothing else she's tried has worked so far," Kawen shot back getting into the spirit of the argument.

"Are you suggesting we pimp our cousin out to Galeb?" Bob asked, not totally against the idea if it helped the Family. He could always moralize that Kieri was getting what she wanted in the end.

"Do you think that Galeb would have a problem with that?" Kawen asked, raising his eyebrows as if considering the idea.

"Unfortunately he might. Man's got a decent streak a mile long," Bob admitted. "If we get him to join the Family, we're going to have to work on fixing that problem."

"I think you give the Warder too much credit. I thought that he was going to have a seizure when Kieri started asking if he was trying to see under her dress," Kawen argued. "The man was almost beside himself he was so eager. I think that he could be convinced not to protest too much with the right circumstances. Might indeed seek to broaden his horizons."

"Sounds like we have a challenge," Bob said.

"Oh, yes, it definitely sounds like a challenge," Kawen said with a smile. "Don't tell Kieri any of this. She'd kill us."

As if summoned, their cousin appeared at their side, shedding the illusion of a shadow cast by the sun.

"What are you two up to?" Kieri asked, her head scanning the underbrush around, looking for threats, though the deeper they moved eastward, more old growth and less underbrush was present, making the forest almost look like parkland.

"Just discussing your boyfriend," Bob answered.

Kawen shot his cousin a look of surprise. Kieri herself was a bit shocked. No one had openly quantified Galeb and Kieri's relationship before, least of all Kieri and Galeb. While it sounded good to hear someone acknowledge a relationship between them, she would have liked the person doing the acknowledging to be Galeb.

There was also their different heritages to consider. It was not that relationships between Obari and Klynsheim were unheard of or officially frowned upon. It was just in the last hundred years such relationships had become rarer to the point of becoming unexpected and unofficially frowned upon by the Klynsheimers. Klynsheimers who increasingly viewed their Obari cousins as feckless and irresponsible for their refusal to adopt Klynsheimer type government or settlements.

Not to mention that Galeb might want to eventually live in a house. Kieri had never lived in a house before and wasn't sure if she would like it. Oh, my God, she realized.

She was going to have to meet Galeb's parents! Wait...weren't they dead? No, no, she was getting ahead of herself. Maybe. Hopefully not. Better play this casual. No need to encourage her cousins, especially if this was a trick. That resolve lasted up until the moment Kieri opened her mouth.

"He's not my – wait, did Galeb say something to you? Does he think that I am his girlfriend?" asked Kieri, with a hopeful note in her voice and an expression on her face that made her look much younger than her twenty years.

"He hasn't said anything," Bob said solemnly, which should have tipped Kieri off to the fact that her cousin was up to something. "It is more in the way he looks at you."

This was not a total lie. Galeb looked at Kieri with longing or constipation. It was hard to tell sometimes. The Klynsheimer was by no stretch of the imagination smooth when dealing with Kieri.

"The way he looks at me?" Kieri asked, her forehead crinkling. "How does he look at me?

"In a way that ensures that your cousins make certain to keep you well chaperoned," Bob assured her confidently, trying not to snicker.

Kieri blushed and got a stupid grin on her face before scowling at both of her cousins.

"I don't need a chaperone," she insisted. Maybe that was why Galeb was not more forward in taking advantage of Kieri's flirting?

"So following Galeb is all about the test and has nothing to do with wanting to see him again?" Bob asked. Kawen wasn't the only one who knew how to manipulate a cousin. Every time the women moved the bathing pool it was Kieri who unknowingly let Bob know where to find the new location.

"Of course," Kieri insisted, unconsciously twirling some of her hair.

"Then why are you so anxious now that he's out of your sight?"

"I'm not anxious."

"Then why do you keep looking down The Road as if hoping for him to reappear?"

"I'm not," Kieri snapped. "I just want to prove myself in this test, which I can't do if you two insist at staring at a Ward post all day and speculating on my love life."

"A love life, is it now," Bob asked, arching an eyebrow and grinning. This was going to be so easy!

Kieri scowled and then stomped away, heading in the direction of Galeb.

"What are you playing at, Bob?" Kawen asked. "I hoped that we were going to be subtle so she doesn't realize what we're doing."

"Just pushing our dear cousin in the right direction," Bob said. "I don't think that Kieri has the patience for subtlety. Lord knows that Galeb isn't going to pick up on subtle either."

"And what direction would that be?" asked Kawen, trying not to grin. It was so easy to push Bob.

"In the direction that gains our family the services of a very unique Warder Mage and possibly gets our cousin laid."

"Ew."

"No, wait, definitely gets our cousin laid. Yes, definitely."

"I said 'Ew'!" Kawen hissed indignantly.

"Yup, but remember that this is all for a good cause," Bob said sanctimoniously. "Sacrifices must be made."

Chapter 4

Galeb disliked visiting Kleidskeiper. The villagers were happy enough to see him checking on their field, stockade, and household Wards. But overshadowing any interactions with the villagers was the impression that once he was finished with their Wards the villagers were happy to see the back of him heading down The Road.

On one level Galeb understood the villagers' behavior. The people of Kleidskeiper were required by law to provide him room and board, as well as pay a respectable sum for his services. It was not like the villagers had a surplus of wealth or goods lying around to spend on his comfort. The longer he stayed, the more expensive it was for the village.

Not that Galeb ever saw any money or trade goods. The fees were shipped south to the nearest Academy Chapter House at the western end of the Great Trade road. The only time Galeb every saw the fruits of his labor was when he needed repairs to his equipment or new clothing.

That was not entirely true, Galeb reflected. He saw the fruits of his labor every time he saw the villagers who had survived another year on the frontiers along the Trade Road. There was the introspection again. He shook his head in frustration, but this did not help clear his mind.

On another level Galeb had to acknowledge that he bore some responsibility for the villagers' attitudes. He barely spoke to the people, wanting to finish his work and move on to the next task. Not that the people of Kleidskeiper seemed to be open to the idea of conversation. His was an odd, unsettling presence, best kept at a distance. Still, he might try starting up a conversation to see what happened. Might be funny.

What Galeb did not fully comprehend was that the people of Kleidskeiper saw him as a temporary entity that it did not pay to get attached to. Conversation would not be welcome.

Part of this unfriendly regard was that none of the villagers failed to notice Galeb's decline. The last several years every return trip Galeb made was a painful surprise as his presence seemed to remind the villagers that dying could be a tortured, lingering affair and the people resented him for reminding them of such hardships.

The other part of the reason why the villagers didn't like Galeb was that they were imitating the local Way Fort Troopers. None of the Troopers treated Galeb with any respect, so why should the villagers?

What the villagers did not comprehend in turn was that Galeb had similar views on the matter when it came to his attitudes to the Klynsheimers in these parts. He had no idea how to open up to people whom he did not expect to survive very long. Half of the population of the village seemed to be new faces every time he stopped by. Maybe he was being pessimistic but he also didn't see the point.

The idiocy of the situation was that both parties seemed to be waiting for the other side to die and found that waiting an inconvenience.

Galeb was repairing a home Ward near the village center – this was the third time he had to repair the Wardings to this home. The owner, a lazy man, as any man who would not do what was necessary to survive along the Trade Road was in Galeb's mind, still had not repaired his roof sufficiently to prevent the rain water from running down the wall and wearing away at the protections.

Galeb might have been able to work around the man's laziness if he had dared to use any of his light based Wards and weaving techniques like he did on The Road posts. But the villagers would never have accepted such protections even though they were superior to the more traditional single layers of defense that had served the Klynsheim for centuries against The Darkness. No, the villagers wanted simple, bluntly carved and colored ruins and wanted to see him utilizing those techniques.

In a way Galeb should be thankful. The slower, traditional process took less power, giving him more time to rest. But what prevented Galeb from being thankful was the fact that the more time he had to spend in Kleidskeiper the less time he could be somewhere else helping other people.

Galeb knew of four hundred and seventy eight people who had died along the Great Trade Road in the last year alone. Though Galeb had to admit that a fair number of those people had died through their own stupidity, he could not help but see their deaths as preventable with the proper defenses. Which was why, as irritated as he was with the owner of the home, he was still repairing the Wards.

That did not stop him from glaring at the man and the man glaring back. Galeb would lodge yet another complaint with the headman for all the good it would do. He would rather beat the lazy man around the head with one of the rotten boards pretending to be siding, but didn't trust the villagers not to come to the defense of one of their own, even if the man was an idiot who endangered them all.

Galeb had been working on the house for a good half an hour. Before that he had taken only one break since the sun had risen and that had been to stretch his muscles and eat a quick meal. He had taken three apples gifted to him by a thankful grandmother for adding an extra set of Wards around her granddaughter's window and tossed them over the low Ward wall that surrounded the village when no one was looking. He should not have been able to get away with the action without being seen. Another reason why he disliked this particular village. The Kleidskeiper sentries weren't very observant, preferring to see what the village women were up to than watch for encroaching Darkness.

Galeb had tossed the apples in the general direction of Kieri and her cousins, all three of whom were currently masquerading as hay stacks in the one of the small fields surrounding the village. He had noticed the three of them when inspecting the Ward wall.

Kieri was doing a much better job moving with the illusion. The hay stacks even fluttered in the proper direction with the wind. Even so she didn't have a chance of fooling him. No Obari did. Ever since he had gained an understanding of how the Obari constructed their illusions he found himself able to see through them. Not perfectly, more like seeing a person standing in the midst of a fog bank.

In Kieri's case the Wardings that he had woven around her were a dead giveaway. Not that anyone but Galeb would be able to see the Wards when they were not active. Still, the sheer rapture of 'Water flows into the channel' embracing 'Star kisses the Water' like a lover as they circled around Kieri's pretty face was enough to make his heart clench most pleasantly. Or worrisomely. Galeb could not remember the last time he'd had a physical.

He hoped that the Obari enjoyed the apples. No apple trees grew wild in the North Lands and apples were a rare treat for Kieri's people. He just hoped that Kieri or Kawen retrieved the apples and not Bob. Bob had been picking his nose when Galeb last saw them.

Galeb straightened from his work with a groan, stretching the muscles of his back. He was not yet finished with the repairs, but had to stop and re-sharpen his Warding knife. As he pulled out his whetstone, he heard one of the lookouts cry out that riders were approaching from the east. Galeb was surprised that the sentries had heard or seen anything.

Probably a patrol from Skaaldsgeiper. While Galeb was responsible for Warding The Road and villages – Way Forts had their own Warders who visited on a rotating basis – it was up to the Klynsheimer military to drive any Darkness that was too persistent away from the area.

Galeb would like to finish up his work but protocol demanded that he report to any officers he encountered while on patrol. Normally he would have been irritated at the interruption, but he was tired of the lazy bastard who owned this house coming around every few minutes and inspecting the work as if he were an expert at Wards. Galeb definitely wanted to hit the man.

But, Galeb would take the high road so long as doing so got him out of the village faster. In this case Galeb would take a break and share any intelligence that he had on The Darkness, answering any questions the Troopers might have about activity on The Road gladly. Just so long as he didn't have to see the lazy bastard for a few minutes.

Well, he would share most of the activity he had witnessed in the area. Galeb should probably report the presence of the three Obari in the field. He was not going to, but he probably should. Part of Galeb's reasoning was that he did not consider the Obari a threat; the other part was that Galeb was irrationally worried that Kieri would like men in uniform. No – she wouldn't, would she? Better not risk it.

A short patrol rode in through the hastily opened and slowly closed gate. Galeb frowned; the villages needed to handle the gate opening better or they risked allowing in Darkness past the Wards.

Ten Troopers in full plate clattered across the village common, their armor a blunted black to match their horses. All carried lances, short bows, and hand axes. Three war dogs trotted at the troop's heels, their massive bodies heavily muscled and thick with tightly curled coarse hair purpose bred to make it more difficult for fang and claw to penetrate their hides. Galeb watched the men dismount, not recognizing the officer who led the unit. With a short patrol he would have expected a sergeant to be in command, not a captain.

The captain removed his helm, revealing close cropped black hair, a bit uncommon with the Klynsheim who tended more towards lighter browns, a thick mustache, and a face lined from years of campaigning. Anywhere between forty and fifty summers, Galeb guessed. A senior captain; even a stranger sight. Galeb began to feel a little nervous with the irregularity of the meeting. He was suddenly wishing for the monotony of his patrol while at the same time feeling like a coward for desiring a return to the boredom.

Galeb grabbed his pack - even in the village he kept his gear close - taking out his log book. He walked over to the captain, coughing slightly to help his voice. Galeb talked so little when away from friendly people like Kieri and her family that his voice often roughened even more than normal if he was not careful. He ignored the dogs, which were trained only to be aggressive towards The Darkness, and were already sprawled on the ground taking a nap. It was the Troopers that Galeb was not comfortable dealing with due to past experience.

"Itinerant Warder Mage Eielson, reporting as per protocol," Galeb said, standing a little straighter, but not saluting. He was not in the military, as the Troopers in the local Way Forts had reminded him the few times he had offered advice about The Darkness.

The captain looked over Galeb, leaning forward a little to hear what Galeb was saying. With a start Galeb had several sudden revelations. The first was that he was in the midst of a Klynsheim village and still considered himself to be in a dangerous position. Secondly he was wrong; his voice was not stronger when he was among friendly people because that implied he was friendly with more than one person. The long patrol had shrunk his world down to one other person of trust. Lastly Galeb knew the captain; not personally, but by reputation. Every Klynsheimer knew of Captain Ilsbruk, one of the King's Seven.

"A quiet one, Warder Mage," commented Ilsbruk, in a friendly, businesslike manner, though some amusement twinkled in his eyes. Ilsbruk's wife was forever reminding him to appear a bit friendlier if for no other reason that he was scaring his own children.

Ilsbruk took Galeb's log book with a polite 'thank you', also due to his wife's influence, and began glancing through it while his men saw to the horses and dogs.

"Itinerant Warder Mage," Galeb quietly corrected the man. He felt some shame at the correction but had learned to hide the emotion. His insecurities were his own problem.

"You're a bit old to still be an Itinerant," Ilsbruk commented, not looking up from the log book which, the captain had to admit to himself, was impeccably maintained.

Ilsbruk winced slightly realizing that he might have just insulted the man. He could hear his wife chiding him for his thoughtless behavior with a man who had given him no reason. He silently argued back that he was a Captain and one of the Seven and he could talk any way he pleased. As always he lost the battle with his wife's pretend voice.

Galeb was having his own silent conversation.

You're a bit far from the heartlands for one of the Seven, Galeb thought snippily to himself, keeping his face neutral. He had hoped that one of the Seven might be less of an ass than the Way Fort commanders. He shook his head slightly in resignation. Different officer, same attitudes. Galeb decided to just hide behind the formalities and hope for the best.

"My place is not to question but to maintain the Patrol," Galeb said, reciting the mantra that all patrols, whether Trooper or Mage, lived by.   Galeb did not bother saying anything more.

"What is your assigned route?" Ilsbruk asked, trying for friendly again by smiling and then spoiled the attempt by frowning as he noticed the Warder Mage seemed to become more withdrawn as the conversation progressed. The man could at least have the manners to acknowledge the smiling. Ilsbruk worked hard on those smiles.

"The Great Trade Road and all settlements adjacent," Galeb answered succinctly, trying to stay professional so that the conversation could end quickly.

"Be more specific, Itinerant Warder Mage Eielson. The Great Trade Road is four hundred miles long stretching from one end of the forest to its midpoint at the Calzaka River," Ilsbruk commanded brusquely. He would match formality with formality and his wife's inner voice be sep – slightly less persistent.

Frankly Ilsbruk was disappointed in the man. The log book had been the first bright note of professionalism that the Captain had found on the entire miserable road aside from the Ward posts. Ilsbruk had been hoping to talk to someone who actually took their duties seriously.

"I have spoken my Patrol correctly and precisely, Captain," Galeb said tonelessly, reaching into his pack and removing his warrant, which he handed to Ilsbruk.

Galeb knew that he was doing himself no favors by behaving this way, but his mind was closing down his emotions, preparing to face the abuse that he knew would be an eventuality of any interaction in which he was forced to correct an officer.

Ilsbruk's eyes narrowed at what he perceived as impertinence but he took and read the warrant, which stated exactly what the Itinerant Warder Mage had claimed.

"But that's four hundred miles," the Captain protested, any previous irritation obliterated by shock. A Patrol should not have been more than fifty miles at this man's rank.

"My apologies for correcting you, Captain," Galeb said, just as tonelessly. "But The Road does not stop at the Calzaka River – at least not in the last seven years. The Road continues on the other side for another two hundred miles, ever since the discovery of the gold in the Kriegsgru^ta mountains."

"Every section of The Roadway on the other side of the Calzaka is a separate jurisdiction," Ilsbruk said, recovering from his shock, narrowing his eyes, and feeling an irrational sense of triumph at being able to correct the Warder Mage.

"While that may be true for the Military, The Academy warrant makes no such distinction," Galeb explained, not even waiting for Ilsbruk's reaction before commenting drily, "You can imagine my disappointment."

Now where did that come from? both Ilsbruk and Galeb wondered. Ilsbruk was hopeful that maybe there was yet some personality buried in the Warder. Galeb was worried that the Captain might have him struck for impertinence. He'd been beaten once by a Way Fort commander. Wasn't supposed to happen, but it did.

"Your patrol is six hundred miles long?" Ilsbruk asked in disbelief, his jaw dropping in a very unlike 'Captain Ilsbruk of the Seven' manner once the man's reply fully registered. Ilsbruk's wife would have been delighted.

"That is only the length of The Road, Captain. I service the adjacent villages as well," Galeb said, gesturing to the warrant respectfully, trying to do some damage control. The Captain's gauntlets looked like they would hurt if he was struck by them.

Ilsbruk took a closer look at the warrant and then back at the Warder Mage. He did this several times as he tried to regain his composure. He then took the opportunity to take a closer look at the Warder Mage.

Eielson at first appeared tired, but as Ilsbruk looked closer he realized that there were signs of ill health about the man. Exhaustion from dealing with a burden that, to Ilsbruk's knowledge, no Warder Mage of any rank had ever been given was certainly part of the problem. A lack of fresh food might be another. The man's clothing was obviously mended and poor despite clear efforts to maintain it, adding to the overall weathered appearance of the man.

Ilsbruk could hear his wife's voice demanding that he do something to remedy the situation and help the poor man. There was a reason that there was a glut of stray cats at Ilsbruk's home and Ilsbruk had nothing to do with creating that problem. Not that there was much that Ilsbruk could do to help the Warder. The man was technically out of his jurisdiction and under the auspices of The Academy.

Ilsbruk recognized other signs as well now that he was paying more attention to the man's behavior. Eielson's eyes never rested, constantly searching and evaluating his surroundings, looking to identify threats even in a safe zone. His gear was always close at hand, ready if Eielson found the need to flee this place. Most likely Eielson considered the villagers to be a threat. Most likely the Warder Mage felt that everyone was a threat.

"How long have you held this patrol?" Ilsbruk asked gently, suddenly afraid of spooking the man. He only had to read the warrant to know the answer to the question but he wanted to hear the answer from Eielson as if the man's words would make this situation all the more real.

"Eight years," Eielson answered in that too soft, too low voice.

Ilsbruk cursed softly under his breath. Eight years was unheard of. There were rules, procedures and protocols. Eielson should have been rotated back to The Academy headquarters every four years for refresher training and to help teach the new classes of Warders by sharing his experiences.

"When was the last time you went home?" Ilsbruk asked, trying to keep the gentleness in his voice even though he wanted to shout at someone to vent the frustration with this assignment. Eielson was just one more example of the neglect, incompetence, and abuse that the Captain was uncovering along the Great Trade Road while conducting the King's business. Of course, in this case, Eielson was a victim and not the cause of these problems, which was why Ilsbruk could not shout.

"Eight years, Captain," Galeb answered, his tone, if anything, more emotionless. He could tell that Ilsbruk was angry with him as he expected the Captain to be since someone had to take the blame for the screwed up situation and a lowly Itinerant Warder Mage was powerlessly convenient.

Ilsbruk's eyes widened slightly at the response and because he was confused as to why everything he said seemed to push Eielson further away. The Captain suddenly had the absurd wish that his wife was actually here with him. Betney would know what to say to put the Warder Mage at ease.

Thinking of his wife caused Ilsbruk to wince. The thought of not seeing his family for eight years was inconceivable. Ilsbruk was one of the King's Seven and as busy as that position made him, he still made a point of going home several times a year when on deployment. Was the man obsessed with his charge or was he not allowed to go home? Ilsbruk needed to know more about the situation, especially as to how the man's treatment was tied to the abuses Ilsbruk was uncovering on The Road. He tried to be friendly again.

"I apologize for all of the questions, Eielson. I am new to this area and am trying to familiarize myself. The King feels that the frontier has been too long neglected and has commanded me to set things to rights.

"What of the other Warder Mages on your route? I have not encountered any, though I have seen signs of their work on the Ward posts. Which master do you work under? Have their deployments been as long as your own?"

Eielson seemed perplexed by the question as if he did not quite understand what was being asked of him. Ilsbruk was relieved to see some more emotion surfacing at least.

"I have never encountered another Warder Mage on the Patrol other than those assigned to service the Way Forts," Galeb eventually answered, still trying to wrap his head around the idea that Central Command seemed to have no idea about the Warder Mage assignments in the area. He knew that both The Academy and Military jealously guarded their mandates but he assumed that the organizations at least communicated with one another.

"But you have seen the signs," Ilsbruk insisted, gesturing to the Ward wall and beyond to The Road and hoping, with a sinking feeling, that it was perfectly reasonable not to encounter other Warder Mages given the size of the Patrol. Maybe the Mages' progress was staggered to maximize effectiveness, even though Ilsbruk had not seen many signs of effective leadership along the Trade Road.

"No, Captain, I haven't. I've only ever encountered my own Wardings since I took on the Patrol."

"What about maintenance units? Surly you've worked with these units to replace Ward posts when the need arises?"

"Once or twice a year, spare posts are delivered to certain way points. I know that much, since the supply seems to be replenished on a scheduled basis. It is up to me to carry the posts to where they are needed," Galeb explained uncomfortably, knowing what the Captain was going to say next.

"But that's against established Protocols!"

"Work needs doing, Captain. I see to my duty," Galeb said a bit defensively.

"Have you at least alerted your superiors about these flagrant breaches in Protocol?" Ilsbruk asked, uncertain what answer he wanted. If Galeb had not informed his superiors, the man was an idiot and The Academy leadership might be blameless. If Galeb had informed his superiors than he was blameless and Ilsbruk could build a stronger case of abuse against The Academy for the King. Neither outcome was without cost.

"I know my duty," Galeb said, retreating into emotionlessness again, feeling it wise since he could not figure out what the Captain wanted by continuing this conversation. "Every aspect of my patrol is correctly recorded in my log book and reported to local Academy command."

Eielson continued to shock Ilsbruk. Central Command and the King had suspected that The Academy was falsifying records about security on The Road but if what this man said was true the level of negligence was beyond criminal. What game was The Academy playing? Then another thought occurred to Ilsbruk.

"Those Ward posts on The Road are the work of an Itinerant Warder Mage?" Ilsbruk asked in disbelief, realizing too late how condescending the words sounded again. His wife would be so disappointed

"I have held faithful to my Patrol," Galeb confirmed, not taking offense for no other reason than he didn't see the point, not anymore at least.

He just wanted to be done with the conversation so he could go back and finish the repairs and be quit of Kleidskeiper. Too much of The Road still beckoned with need and he really didn't see one of the King's Seven changing that reality for him. He served at the behest of The Academy, not the Military.

Ilsbruk knew that he had bungled things with Eielson again, but for the love of God, conversation with the man seemed to be a full of obstacles, with even innocent questions causing the man to withdraw. The Captain would quite possibly have to add battle fatigue to the list of problems plaguing Eielson.

The Warder seemed lost to his Patrol, too broken by the need to protect his mandate to see the impossibility of his position and the injustice that had been done to him. No, no, the man knew what had been done to him. Ilsbruk could see that in the impatient resignation of the man's posture. It was possible that Eielson held to his Patrol because it was the only thing he trusted anymore.

Ilsbruk was not helping matters by implying that he doubted the man's abilities. As one of the King's Seven, Ilsbruk was very familiar with the skills of the different Master Warder Mages among the Klynsheim. Those Ward posts were no ordinary defense. There were cities in the heartlands that were not half as well Warded and the cities were each serviced by a dozen Warder Mages a piece with full apprentice entourages.

The man was no Itinerant; he was possibly a Ward, the highest rank Warder Mages could aspire to and one that could only be reached through skill and power, not political connection. Not only was the man possibly a Ward, but Eielson might just be Ward of the entire north. Neither the Warders at The Academy Chapter House at the head of The Road nor those assigned to the gold mines seemed to be taking any interests in the northern defenses beyond their front doors.

"You have held faithful; of that I have no doubt, Eielson. Never a report missed, a log not filed, a Ward not maintained," Ilsbruk said kindly, regretting his earlier brusqueness and trying to make amends yet again. Unfortunately he seemed to be having as much luck with the Warder Mage as he did with that one blasted stray cat that kept peeing in his boots back home.

"As you say, Captain. May I go? I need to finish up re-Warding a house before I head out to The Road again," Galeb asked, inclining his head slightly in a gesture of respect. This conversation was the longest he had ever had in the village. Not the most painful conversation though certainly awkward enough as Galeb still had no idea what the Captain seemed to want from him.

"Of course," Ilsbruk said, acknowledging defeat and handing both log and warrant back to the Mage because he had no other answer to give.

Galeb nodded politely and left. As he walked away Ilsbruk noticed the limp and the missing finger. The slight hitch in his movements that hinted at scars beneath the clothing. Based on the man's behavior Ilsbruk was willing to bet that every one of the injuries had been earned in battle without the proper support that the Way Forts were supposed to provide. Why the septa else was a Warder Mage carrying a fighting knife?

Eielson had fought The Darkness alone for eight years. How the man had managed such a feat, the Captain did not know. But what Ilsbruk could clearly see was that Eielson would not survive to see a ninth if the Captain could not find a way to fix this situation.

Kieri, Bob, and Kawen sat leaning up against the wall in complete and utter shock, their apples forgotten. The cousins had slipped closer to the village when they heard the patrol coming and blended themselves in with the wooden palisade to eavesdrop.

Kieri almost did not recognize Galeb's voice as the Captain's conversation with him progressed. She had never heard him so emotionless. Tears began to blur her vision as she heard the answers to so many questions with such painful clarity.

Bob, unusually somber, signaled that they needed to slip away from the village before Kieri completely lost her composure. The Obari moved slowly so as to maintain the shifting illusions that were necessary to see the cousins into the forest and away from the Klynsheim eyes. Once the cousins were secure in a new position the whispered conversation began.

"How does one man Ward six hundred miles?" Kawen asked in disbelief.

"How does one's leaders so abuse a man as to force him to Ward six hundred miles by himself?" Kieri countered, wiping at the tears. She was beyond pissed on Galeb's behalf.

"How does one man last eight years Warding six hundred miles, is the better question," Bob pointed out. No wonder the Mage was so boring.

"Why do this to him?" Kieri asked fiercely. "What has Galeb ever done to deserve this?"

Bob was silent as he pondered this question. He realized the answer at the same time Kawen did as they thought back to Eielson's accounting. Kawen gestured for Bob to answer Kieri's question. Bob acknowledged his cousin's acceptance of his superiority magnanimously. Kawen hit him.

"Because of the gold that the Klynsheim found in the Kriegsgru^ta Mountains," Bob explained as he rubbed his arm. "If The Academy placed a full complement of Warder Mages on The Road there'd be greater accountability; more records on the Trade Route. There'd be a better understanding of just how much gold is being shipped from the mines."

"I'm willing to wager that the amount of gold being reported to the Klynsheim government is significantly less than what's actually being mined. The Academy's being bribed as well as the Military officers at the Way Forts to keep official security low to allow smuggling," Kawen added.

"People are most likely dying because of this neglect," Kieri hissed, horrified by the idea.

"Klynsheimers don't have a proper sense of family," Kawen observed. "They don't care about the deaths of people far from their homes."

"Galeb cares," Kieri said through gritted teeth as if she could make her cousins believe the truth of her words by sheer force of will.

"Galeb's held to his Patrol for eight years," Bob agreed, "There's no doubt that he cares." *Either that or he's an idiot. Probably both.*

"Perhaps he's blinded himself to what needs to be done," Kawen said, sensing an opportunity and hating himself slightly for taking it with Kieri already upset. "Man needs someone to make sure that he's not being taken advantage of, to stand up for him when he can't find the way himself."

"If you're suggesting that we go to that Chapter House at the head of The Road and start smacking the Warder Mages there around, then I'm all in favor," Kieri said, her gaze promising that given the opportunity she would do more than just hit the men.

"No, I'm not suggesting starting a war," Kawen said, a bit shocked. He realized that if given the opportunity Kieri wouldn't be satisfied with only hitting the men.

"What Kawen's saying is that Galeb needs a little representation. Some people – some Family to back him up just enough to ensure that he's not being taken advantage of," Bob said, worried that now that Kawen had given Kieri an idea, she would march off and declare war on The Academy Chapter House.

"He has me," Kieri said defiantly, as if demanding her cousins to acknowledge that fact.

"Never doubted that for a moment," Bob agreed, smiling. He liked the idea of Kieri and Galeb together. Oh, his mother was going to be so distracted that she wouldn't be nagging Bob for a long time to come. He was almost shaking with excitement.

"Through me, he has you two," Kieri continued, following the thought as any Obari would.

"Yes, he would," Bob agreed. "Which is great for Eielson because of my natural awesomeness."

"Which means that you two are going to have to convince my father to accept Galeb," Kieri said, satisfied that she had reached a reasonable conclusion.

"Yes- wait, what?" Bob asked, caught off guard. "Ebko's your father. Why do we have to talk to him?"

"Obviously if I talk to Ebko about this he will try to keep me from seeing Galeb. If you, my cousins, speak for me then I am free to pursue Galeb regardless," Kieri said reasonably.

"We'd also be the one's Ebko would be free to hit if he doesn't like this idea," Kawen protested.

"There is that," Kieri said with a smirk, suddenly feeling a bit better.

Ilsbruk watched the Warder Mage go before turning to find his sergeant and get appraised of the situation in the village. Gorgorin had served with Ilsbruk for ten years and Ilsbruk trusted the man to be about his work and do an exemplary job, which was why Ilsbruk was so angry at the situation that had brought him to the North Country.

Many someones were not performing their duty in this region. He had men in every Way Fort along the western stretch of the trade road trying to figure out the tangled mess that passed for security in the North Lands. The Ward posts along the Great Trade Road had been the only bright spot in this whole sordid affair. Ilsbruk had been happy to see that there were competent Warder Mages in the region. Now that illusion had faded away like an Obari charm, making him angrier.

"Report, Sergeant," Ilsbruk said brusquely when he found Gorgorin near the village well studying the Wards suspiciously. The water source at the last Way Fort had been improperly maintained and become tainted, giving half a hundreds men the ntas, which was why Ilsbruk was currently only traveling with ten Troopers.

Gorgorin looked up and studied his Captain for a moment. Lately Ilsbruk had been acting weird, all smiles and friendliness that seemed as natural as poorly dyed hair. It was refreshing to see his commander's no nonsense demeanor reasserting itself.

"Wards are solidly maintained. Village gate Protocols suck. The villagers are paying their taxes and complaining that there are not enough military patrols in the area. The headman even went

106

so far as to suggest that a Way Fort be built village adjacent," Gorgorin answered.

"What are the villagers' opinions about the Warder Mages servicing the area?" Ilsbruk asked, curious to learn the villagers' perceptions of the situation.

"Confusing, Sir, if I'm honest," Gorgorin said, crinkling his forehead as he frowned. "Headman claims that they only ever see one, and that one looks half dead most of the time."

"Any complaints about the man's work?"

"No, Sir. Folks don't like him, but they don't have any complaint."

"Why don't they like him?" Ilsbruk asked, curious.

"Don't talk much for one. Always seems like he has somewhere else he needs to be. Doesn't socialize or stick around a moment longer than he has to," the Sergeant explained.

Having realized Eielson's burden, Ilsbruk could understand the Warder's behavior.

"Anything else, Sergeant?"

"Nothing worth reporting, Sir."

Ilsbruk gave his Sergeant a knowing look and waited.

Gorgorin looked embarrassed, a little pained even.

"Begging your pardon, Captain, but there was one other comment I overheard. Not polite, just the words of an old, cranky woman sour on life, if you ask me. Headman hushed her right quick afterwards," Gorgorin said, reassuringly.

Ilsbruk raised an eyebrow, waiting for his Sergeant to tell him about those words.

"Woman wanted to know when The Academy was going to send a replacement Mage. Said she was sick of watching the 'tired, chewed up one who was too stupid to realize that he was already dead come around'. Her words, exactly. Like I said, Sir, I think the old woman is just soured on life and wants to make everyone else miserable."

"He's the only Warder for the entire trade road, Sergeant," Ilsbruk said, shaking his head at the casual, though somewhat accurate, cruelty of the old woman's words.

"That can't be right, Sir. That's totally against Protocol, reason, logic, sanity and, nta, grieshtataing decency," Gorgorin said, his eyes wide in disbelief as he smacked a hand against his thigh to emphasize his words.

"The Warder is also ranked 'Itinerant' though he is the one responsible for every one of the Ward posts we've seen," Ilsbruk added. "I suspect that the low rank is meant to keep Eielson from having any authority to change his circumstances."

"Grieshtataing King's right," Gorgorin said softly as all the implications ran through his mind. Gorgorin wasn't a stupid man, which was why he was still a sergeant and not an officer. "This is not just one of his Majesty's conspiracy theories about Academy abuse, is it, Sir? This is actual abuse of power."

"No, Sergeant, this is no conspiracy theory. This is treason," Ilsbruk said, agreeing with Gorgorin's assessment. "The question is just how much is The Academy hiding to feel the need to condemn one man to an impossible Patrol? What justifies weakening our northern border?"

"I thought that we were simply coming up here to stop some gold smuggling," Gorgorin said, at a loss.

"I suspect that we are going to find a lot more than 'some' gold smuggling," Ilsbruk said. "Send a man back to the last way fort with orders for Sergeant Camguten to get the men out of the latrines and headed back to The Academy Chapter House at the head of The Road. I want every log book and report ever filed by Itinerant Warder Mage Eielson in our custody."

Chapter 5

Six weeks saw many miles between Galeb and Ilsbruk's conversation and Galeb had put the man out of his mind. Kieri and her cousins were still following him, which was beginning to confuse Galeb. Why were the Obari so far from their home territory? He would like to ask them but the Obari were trying to avoid notice, acting as if this were one of their tests. If it was one of their tests Galeb hated to disappoint them, but they were failing miserably.

He was approaching Uksaadle, a thriving settlement half way along his patrol. Galeb disliked Uksaadle for different reasons than why he disliked Kleidskeiper. There was a persistently powerful patch of Darkness near Uksaadle, where The Road turned away from the forest. Galeb had wanted to bind back that Darkness for years but had not had the time or opportunity since he was forced to service The Road alone and could not get any of the Way Fort commanders to commit troops. The commanders of the forts to the west and east of the settlement both argued that Uksaadle was the other man's responsibility.

The cousins were sticking to the Warded road, holding the illusions of being Klynsheimers. The Obari had abandoned the forest when they had come across the first Obari warning signs about an evil that lay in these woods. Kawen was in favor of heading back. Bob, having received no messages indicating that other Klynsheim Warders had the same abilities as Galeb and wanting to ignore the questions that Ebko had sent back, was in favor of watching Galeb a little while longer. Kieri was refusing to turn back, determined not to abandon Galeb now that she knew just how alone he was and that these woods held increased dangers for the man. The argument between Kawen and Kieri about proceeding had put the cousins half a day behind Galeb.

The gate at Uksaadle was not as it should be. The Wards were still intact, but the gate hung open, untended, and creating a gap in the protective circle. Galeb reached for a template in his bandolier and pressed it to his quarterstaff, charging the weapon with some extra power before entering the settlement. He loosened the fighting knife in its sheath and triggered 'A Parent's sleepless night', activating the wards around his wrists. At the very least something was about to get a face full of 'The Way is Shut'.

Galeb almost fell to his knees when he entered the village wanting to vomit. Inside of the walls was a story of torment and futile desperation brightly painted across the Ward wall with childlike imagination and skill. The Darkness had not just come, it had lingered.

Galeb clamped down on his suddenly rebellious stomach and began the business of a Trooper. Galeb didn't have the luxury of being a normal Warder Mage. There was a dead village that had to be secured and he was the one who had to deal with the situation.

It was easy to understand what had happened to the settlement. Someone had gotten careless and The Darkness had come hunting. The Klynsheim had realized that the gate was not secured as the first of The Darkness began pouring through the gap and attempted to mount a defense. Galeb gave the dead that much credit.

The first defenders had been overwhelmed, arms torn from bodies, huge chunks of flesh ripped away and then discarded as The Darkness sought to drive deeper into the village. The local militia had rallied, seeking to buy time for the other residents to get into the safety of their homes.

It had been a running battle, fear lying thick upon the stone and wood structures. As the men tried to slow the inevitable, The Darkness had indulged the fighters, tarrying a bit to play. What was left of the militia men was recognizable only because of the scraps of leather armor that held some of their torn and broken bodies together.

Galeb was wrong; that was not the only identifying factor. The faces had been left intact, just no longer attached to the bodies. The skin had been meticulously peeled away from the skulls, creating grotesque parodies of masks that lay perfectly arranged near the village well.

The evidence in the homes was no better. The Darkness had only killed those people caught out in the open. The rest of the settlement had died from dehydration and starvation as they became trapped behind the Wards, knowing that The Darkness waited for them to emerge from their homes. At least two children had tried to make a break for the well. A trail of intestines gave an indication of how successful the younglings had been.

The Darkness was gone now, back to its home since there was no more prey to play with in Uksaadle. Galeb closed the gate, sealing the Wards and slowly collapsed to the ground. Here was the evidence of his greatest fear – his greatest failure – and it broke Galeb like eight years of hardship could not. It didn't matter that none of this tragedy was his fault. His Wards had failed to protect.

Galeb didn't fall apart for long. There was no time for self-pity in the North Country. There was only duty.

Galeb argued with himself that night. He should report the loss of the settlement to the Way Fort commanders. The eastern Way Fort was closer. If he took the time to report the Death of Uksaadle then Kieri and her cousins would be here before he turned back. The Darkness might be waiting for them.

He could double back to the western Way Fort and try to find the Obari on his journey. If the Obari were keeping to the woods there was no guarantee that he would find them. The western commander would not be receptive either. The man would hunker down, refusing to risk Troopers without reinforcement. More time for The Darkness to spread.

No, Galeb would not waste any time trying to convince the Way Fort commanders who'd always refused aid in the past. He had no more patience for excuses and inaction. Kieri was coming. He was a Warder Mage. He would Ward the way.

Chapter 6

As the sun crested the horizon Galeb left the protection of Uksaadle and returned to The Road. He took out his log book and made one final entry before leaving it open on The Road way. Galeb then turned to one of the Wards and activated an emergency sequence.

The Wards were more than just barriers against The Darkness. The Wards were also a primitive communication system designed to aid the common defense. Pulses shot from Ward post to Ward post racing toward The Academy Chapter House far to the west at the start of The Road. From the Chapter House the pulse would relay its way all of the way to the capital along the Ward network. This time tomorrow The Academy headquarters would receive the beacon that a Patrol no longer had its Warder. He was able to send an abbreviated version of his log entry along with the emergency pulse. More impressions than actual words. Just enough to provide meaning. Someday someone needed to find a way to better utilize the capabilities of the network. Klynsheim would benefit greatly with increased communications.

Galeb was at peace with his decision to seek The Darkness alone, though he held some regrets. He would miss Kieri, the thought of whom urged him on. Okay, he was partially at peace. The rest of him was terrified. Galeb left The Road and headed northeast following The Darkness's trail.

The Obari knew that there was something wrong with Uksaadle as they approached the settlement. There were no sounds of humanity. Kieri saw the log book first and ran over to it, recognizing it as Galeb's. All color drained from her face as she read the last entry.

Uksaadle has fallen to a Darkness that dwells northeast of the settlement, as previously reported. I know my duty. I go to Ward The Darkness lest it spread.

Kieri dropped the book with a curse and a wail of despair that was so unlike her that both cousins froze in shock. Before Bob or Kawen could recover, Kieri raced from The Road, wrapping herself tight with illusions that made it difficult to track her progress.

Captain Ilsbruk was in a foul mood as he traveled The Road east in search of the Itinerant Warder Mage. Six weeks of swift and frustrating action had seen the arrest of Way Fort commanders the length of The Road between The Academy Chapter House and where he now rode. Boats were heading upriver to arrest the Way Fort commanders east of the Calzaka River on charges of treason and dereliction of duty.

Ilsbruk rode at the head of three long patrols of men and war dogs fiercely loyal to King and Seven. He would take no risks with either Academy agents or corrupted Troopers trying to silence the Warder Mage before Ilsbruk could get him to the capital. The Itinerant Warder Mage was the last piece of Ilsbruk's investigation that he needed to finalize the case against The Academy.

He had secured Eielson's log books from the Chapter House. There had been attempts to tamper with the logs but the Warder Mage had been clever enough to place small, barely noticeable Wardings on his writings. Every altered section of the log was blatantly obvious shining with its falseness. The true accounting seemed to somehow swim under the altered sections, waiting for a person to focus on it and bring the true writing back into ascendency.

Ilsbruk had never heard of such a Warding being possible and apparently neither had the leadership at the Chapter House or they would have simply destroyed the logs. Based on the indisputable fact that the House Leaders had altered the logs and knowingly left one man to patrol an entire road, thus violating the sacred trust and security of the Klynsheim people, Ilsbruk had the men executed. The House Master had been shocked as his throat was slit; Warder Mages, particularly older ones long separated from actual patrols, always seemed to forget that their Wardings were only designed to work against The Darkness and not against a Trooper's steel.

The remaining Warder Mages in residence readily agreed to begin patrolling The Road as they should have been doing for eight years. Granted that those Warder Mages were all well beyond retirement age; Ilsbruk had arranged the use of several wagons for their travel needs. He also had several Warders who normally saw to Way Fort defenses on the way to see the Trade

Road properly patrolled until more permanent arrangements could be made back at The Academy.

Ilsbruk needed to find Eielson. He had the log books but needed Eielson's testimony to bring greater context to his writings. The day to day minutia of an eight year patrol that was all wrong that the man hadn't thought to write down.

For instance, Ilsbruk had the testimony of a caravan of settlers detailing how Eielson had held a failing Ward Line with nothing but steel and gut wrenching courage. Eielson's description of the event in his own log book was certain to be more prosaic.

Eielson would bolster the King's case against The Academy leadership. Not that the King would wait to confront The Academy. King Sigsrata had waited years to catch The Academy masters in an act of disloyalty, knowing that The Academy's power and arrogance had grown too strong.

Ilsbruk looked at the matter a bit differently. He did not care about the King's vendetta against The Academy. Ilsbruk cared about the treason that was costing Klynsheimer lives.

Ilsbruk reached Uksaadle twenty minutes after the Obari. He found Galeb's log book abandoned on The Road and read the final entry just as Kieri had when she found the book. Ilsbruk did not wail like Kieri had but he certainly cursed just as loudly. He was angry at the thought of losing Eielson's testimony. He was horrified that The Academy's abuse and the corruption of the Military along The Road had cost the lives of an entire settlement. Ilsbruk was enraged at the thought of the loss of a man who, even betrayed by his own people, still offered his life to protect them.

"Sergeant!" Ilsbruk hissed out, trying to master his temper as he glanced at the quiescent Ward posts.

He'd be willing to wager that Eielson had triggered an alert along the Ward Line besides leaving the book behind. The man was too methodical, too professional to have done otherwise. The Warder Mages at the Chapter House must have not learned their lesson well enough and blocked the warning. Probably hoped that Eielson would get himself killed before anyone could come to his aid. Easy way to silence the man without a thought to the repercussions.

Ilsbruk would have to purge the entire place. Stinking vermin!

There was no doubt among any of the men which sergeant Ilsbruk was summoning. Gorgorin road forward his normally impassive face a bit green from what the Troopers had found in the village.

"Reporting, Captain," Gorgorin said crisply, recognizing his Captain's temper and helping Ilsbruk find control through formality.

"I want a communication line in place from The Road along our progress to the northeast. I have no idea how far away we will be going; space for maximum effective range," Ilsbruk snapped. "Riders to the nearest Way Forts to apprise them of the danger and to send reinforcements to the region. Trigger the emergency alert along the Ward Line. Level Three. We need the settlements aware and taking precautions."

Gorgorin knew better than to ask questions. The Captain would explain once the task was done. Gorgorin turned and began to issue the orders, the other sergeants seeing to the details.

Galeb had been right in thinking that increased communications abilities in the Ward Posts would greatly benefit Klynsheim. There had been significant developments in that area over the last eight years. Each Trooper in Ilsbruk's command carried a bundle of quick sticks, Wardings designed to copy and send images along the Ward network. Much more capable than the emergency beacons built into The Road's Ward Posts and purposefully prevented from being used along The Road by The Academy.

The quick sticks had limitations. They were a line of sight system and would require Troopers to consistently fall behind the main group as each stick was placed and aligned. Ilsbruk would just have to see that the men were motivated to move as quickly and efficiently as possible. He would do so without smiles and friendliness.

"First line in place, Captain," Gorgorin came back a few minutes later. Over the sergeant's shoulder Ilsbruk could see the Ward posts shift from a soft buttery yellow to a pulsating red.

"Give me a clear visual on the line," Ilsbruk ordered.

"You heard the Captain," Gorgorin shouted, "Clear the line!"

The Troopers shifted their horses, moving out of the way so that Ilsbruk could see the first quick sticks.

"Troopers of Klynsheim! Troopers of King and Seven," Ilsbruk said, his voice ringing with a clarity earned upon the battlefield as the quick sticks flashed, recording every movement and gesture, translating his voice into written words.

"One man has held the Wards of The Road. One man has fought The Darkness alone for eight years. Ignored by The Academy, disparaged by the men who would dare call themselves Troopers along this Road. One man abandoned by the very people who should have supported him.

"Uksaadle has paid the price for this betrayal. But this Warder Mage, this one man of unparalleled duty, has held true to his mandate. He goes now to face The Darkness, to fight it and to Ward it alone."

The Troopers exchanged uncomfortable looks. Warder Mages did not fight. Rune Wards took too long to fashion to be effective on a shifting battle field.

"We bear the shame of this situation. Not as men but as representatives of the Military that has so failed this region. I will not stand by and let one more death of an innocent be laid before me!" Ilsbruk thundered, scowling with barely suppressed rage.

The Troopers were scowling as well, angry at the failures that they, as part of the Military, were forced to take upon themselves through no fault of their own. Some even saw the Warder Mage's actions as a direct defiance of the established order and as an attempt to bring greater shame down upon them. These men began to shout.

"Mages Ward! Troopers Fight!"

The sergeants called for silence, seeing that Ilsbruk had more to say.

"Mages Ward! Troopers Fight!" acknowledged Ilsbruk. "But here, in this place a Mage is forced to fight because no one would stand with him!"

"We Stand!" shouted the Troopers in protest.

"And yet a Ward Stands Alone!" Ilsbruk countered

The Troopers silenced almost immediately as if Ilsbruk's words struck a physical blow. 'A Ward Stands Alone' was an ancient call to arms from the time of the First Rising, when the newly met Darkness had shattered the old kingdoms. A rallying cry in which Klynsheim had been forged with the blood of Trooper, Soldiers, and Warder fighting side by side as everyone else had fled in panic. In the centuries since the phrase had become a euphemism for the deepest dishonor. Not the dishonor of a man, but the dishonor of an entire nation.

These were Troopers of the King and Seven. Not border guards all too willing to forsake their duty and embrace the corruption sponsored by The Academy for a bit of gold. To these men 'A Ward Stands Alone' was an accusation of utter agony.

Ilsbruk continued, challenging his men and the very King who would receive this message, as his mount danced restlessly beneath him. "The Ward of the North Stands Alone!"

By now every man in Ilsbruk's patrols knew Galeb's story. Every man knew that every defense on The Road that was worth a septa was the doing of one man. To call Galeb 'Ward of the North' was pretentious. It was also accurate.

"Will you bear this shame or will you ride to his aid?" Ilsbruk asked, knowing the answer but having to ask it anyway for the sake of the men.

"We stand with the Ward!" came the reply as shield met lance in deafening pledge.

"Troopers of Klynsheim, The Darkness Rises and the WARD STANDS ALONE!" Ilsbruk roared, challenging the men again.

"WE STAND!   WE STAND!" roared back the Troopers in frustration and growing battle lust. War dogs howled.

"Then for King and Seven, *battle march*!" Ilsbruk commanded, wheeling his horse and leading the way into the forest until the vanguard could take position. Scouts were already on Galeb's trail. Horses cantered nervously and the dogs grinned with feral anticipation.

Chapter 7

The term 'Darkness' was at best a generalization used by both Obari and Klynsheim to describe the myriad of creatures that saw humanity as a particular type of food source. Wolves, lions and bears would eat a human should the opportunity present itself but were not considered Darkness. To be considered Darkness, the predator had to revel in the pain and terror it caused as much as it derived pleasure from its meal.

The Darkness enjoyed the choking screams, the piss filled trousers, the mingled scent of nta and fear. The Darkness played with its food, drawing out the agony. Darkness killed not because it had to but because killing was a form of entertainment.

None of those distinguishing characteristics helped Galeb in the slightest. He tended to hate the impreciseness of the name. 'Darkness' was too vague, a term coined by people who were safe in their cities far from the danger and who had the luxury of being esoteric in their descriptions.

Galeb lived in a world that relied on precision. When he walked The Road or Warded villages, he needed to know exactly what he faced at any one moment so as to present the best possible defense.

The term 'Darkness' was also misleading. While many of the creatures so described were nocturnal not all were so restricted. In fact many of the more intelligent of the nocturnal creatures only hunted at night because it added to the fear their prey felt at being stalked, not because of any aversion to the sun.

As he travelled Galeb looked for signs of what he would be facing. The limited sign in previous years was as telling as the actual marks he now saw upon ground, rock and tree. Whatever had killed Uksaadle used to be very careful, intelligent enough to avoid giving away too much of its presence. Now, with the death of the settlement, The Darkness was arrogant, full of its power, assured that it would go unchallenged.

Skitter marks showed two clawed toes moving in an almost hopping, skipping motion. Kielsgruntara. Insect like creatures fashioned in an almost canine form capable of moving on two and four legs. Mid-sized pack creatures. Not particularly smart, but trainable. Not true nocturnes, though their eyes were light sensitive. Dawn and dusk hunters.

Slashes into bark, deep and a staggering twelve feet up the trees, left the impression that other creatures had almost been drunk on their kills. Coarse hairs, glistening and greasy caught in the slashes. Skrieksgrata and Shaeloman. True nocturnes, dangerous and fiercely intelligent.

Not the Skrieksgrata; the Skrieksgrata were clever at best, more raw muscle and bloodlust. The Skrieksgrata would control the kielsgruntara. The Shaeloman would control the Skrieksgrata.

Shaeloman were manipulators, whispers in the dark that lured and confused. Not physically imposing like the hulking pig-ape like brutes that were the Skrieksgrata. No, the Shaeloman were whipcord thin, snakes sheathed in hair rather than scales. Easily confused for a man in loose clothing at a distance. Hands that held needle like claws that were intended to cut a person apart one thin, agonizing slice at a time, not smash and rend like the Skrieksgrata.

The Darkness had nested near Uksaadle, biding its time, building its resources, waiting for an opportunity. Galeb and The Academy had given The Darkness the opportunity. Yes, a careless

Uksaadle resident or residents had let The Darkness in past the Wards. But it was the Warder Mages' and Military's lack of action that had allowed The Darkness to grow into such a threat in the area.

Galeb should have insisted harder that The Darkness be dealt with when he first became aware of it through village warnings and disappearing travelers. He should have done more, but The Road had always beckoned, there had always been so much other work to do. Now there were no more excuses.

Galeb had no illusions. He would not win this fight. He was already having second thoughts about this course of action. He only hoped to maim The Darkness, weaken the enemy until a greater response force could arrive. The Academy had ignored the needs of the Patrol. No matter how uncaring, The Academy could not, would not ignore the loss of an entire settlement and the Warder who should have protected it.

As fatalistic as Galeb was trying to be in order to hold back his fear, he was not careless. His senses strained, his Wards were active, and he warded the way, establishing fall back points for himself and simple traps, burning the runes into tree and rock where ever he could. The Wardings were draining, but he would rather be prepared than forced to run without anywhere to run to.

He finally found The Darkness' home, reaching a valley well after midday, his Wardings slowing him considerably. The entrance to the valley was blessedly narrow. Galeb stopped and cut several saplings, using his templates to burn Wards along the green wood. He placed the new made Ward posts all along the valley entrance, where there was no good rock or tree to anchor the Wardings. He was not trapping The Darkness, just limiting its movement. Galeb had no doubt that there were other ways in and out of the valley.

The Mage turned away from the valley and looked at his back trail, grabbed his templates and began burning rune Wards into every available surface in the immediate area in a fifty yard ring. Always have a fall - back position; a rule that a Warder lived by.

As Galeb finished his work he returned to study the valley bottom, knowing that The Darkness in the valley was probably watching him in turn. He could see where The Darkness had denned only because the Skrieksgrata had smashed several trees in their blood fueled celebration. Near the right side of the valley, where the ground sloped up the valley walls, kielsgruntara burrows dotted the landscape, shallow depressions easily missed if a person did not know what they were looking at. The Skrieksgrata had tunneled into the rock, creating a den to shield them from the sunlight. The Shaeloman could be anywhere in between the burrow and the den, though the puppet master would be close to control its servants.

A dozen or more kielsgruntara. Four or five Skrieksgrata. Two Shaeloman at the most. An older one and a younger one was definitely possible. Shaeloman did not share authority. Younger ones learned from the older Darkness until they felt strong enough to kill their mentors.

He would have to rely on the arrogance and The Darkness's need to play with its food to get close. The creatures would still be sated from their destruction of Uksaadle. There would be no hurry to kill him.

Galeb would make his stand in the center of the valley, in a large clearing most likely created by Skrieksgrata temper.   He would lay out his light Wards in the earth around him, keeping the Wards hidden until The Darkness triggered them. He would lure the enemy to him, trap as many as possible before they brought him down.

Not the best plan in the world, but Galeb would work with what he had. Galeb wished that he could weave illusions like the Obari. He would have an advantage if The Darkness did not know he was there until too late.

Galeb harvested a half dozen more saplings and prepared them with his templates, to Ward his chosen ground.   He moved quickly, but calmly – he was filled with a rising terror but was doing his best to beat it down - templates tight in his hands and continuing to burn Wards. He was soon pouring with sweat, but did not dare loosen his coat.

The Darkness let him reach the meadow. Galeb was certain of that fact. Still, he would take the favor and try to use it to his advantage. The frail Ward posts were forced into the ground, giving him a little breathing space with which to work.

When Galeb sat down in the middle of the Ward ring and drank deeply from his canteen, he knew that he wasn't standing up for a while. He was exhausted and still had too much work to do before the sun set. The quarter staff was in his lap, Ward marked to the point of shimmering with waves of power. If the staff was broken and Galeb was still holding onto the weapon the backlash might very well kill him before The Darkness had a chance to do so.

As Galeb sat, he burning weaves in the ground around him in an every widening circle. He had to visualize the weaves without using his templates so that The Darkness would not realize what he was doing. This made the process much harder and slower and nowhere near as effective. What he created was a tangle trap maze. Intertwining layers of 'The Way is Shut', 'A Lady's Smile beckons', and 'Turns the Tide'.

As long as the earth wasn't too badly disturbed, the Wards would work. If the ground became too churned up, the protections would be marred and useless.

Galeb was also soaking in the sun. Not figuratively; he was literally infusing sunlight into his wrist Wards, slowly trickling power into the arrays using 'gathers the light'.

The Darkness made him wait, which was the best outcome that Galeb could hope for given the situation. He may even have napped a bit as insanely reckless as that sounded.

The sun was low in the afternoon before the kielsgruntara erupted from their burrows, a few of which had been much further out from main nest than Galeb had expected. There were at least two dozen of the creatures, maybe three. The Darkness skittered, hopped, skipped their way down the valley floor like giddy, gigantic, crickets.

Galeb carefully made certain that none of his buried Wards triggered. He needed the bigger threats to come out and play. So far he would trust his make shift Ward posts to protect his back. Like he had during the Incident, Galeb pulled up his hood and face mask and then stepped into the Ward line and began fighting.

The kielsgruntara shivered with delight when they saw that the Mage was going to be accommodating to their twisted ideas of fun. The Darkness slammed into each other, piling over one another to be the first to reach Galeb, while others ignored him completely and began making runs at his Ward posts, trying to overpower them by sheer number of attacks.

"For King and Seven!" Galeb shouted, figuring in cases like these, a man should shout something. His voice cracked a bit and spoiled the effect.

The quarter staff blazed with light, the wards burned upon its surface triggering with dizzying speed as the Mage laid into The Darkness before him, the kielsgruntara's own impatience giving Galeb the opportunity to strike them down.

"King and Seven!"

Flesh blistered and bone broke under the impacts of wood and Ward.

"King and Seven!"

Wood began to splinter and leather tore as claw and tooth sought purchase.

"King and Seven!

Ward posts shivered, scars pulled and his hip ached as he staggered behind and then back into the Line, the battle before him and the Incident blurring together in his mind. Blood was dripping on both sides.

"King and Seven!"

A Ward post failed as he was slammed back into it as a Darkness leapt and collided with him faster than the stressed Ward Line could react. The kielsgruntara shrieked in agony as the remaining Wards devoured it in thrashing arcs of energy.

"King and Seven!"

The words were weaker, shouted just as defiantly, as Galeb struggled to his feet in his suddenly smaller island of safety and tried to gain his bearings. Blood and sweat threatened to blind him. The kielsgruntara were impatient. He hated to disappoint them, lurching forward, staff thrust forward like a spear.

"King and Seven!"

Bob and Kawen knew that they could not stop Kieri in her single minded determination to reach Galeb. Instead they contented themselves with guarding her back, ensuring that no Darkness caught her by surprise. That was how they stumbled upon the kielsgruntara stalking behind their cousin.

There were only two of the creatures, obviously out hunting in the gloom of the forest. At least the cousins hoped that the creatures were only hunting and not purposefully searching the area for trespassers in their territory. If that was the case, it spoke of a guiding intelligence that neither Bob nor Kawen wanted to consider. Remembrances of the Obari warning signs flashed through the cousins' minds before they separated, each targeting a different animal.

The voice started as the sun fell far enough below the rim of the valley that the clearing was in shadow. Barely heard, tantalizing, enough to distract and fixate. Galeb found the noise irritating more than anything and firmly kept his eyes on the circling kielsgruntara and checking the remaining Ward posts. Both sides were taking a breather, too tired to continue the fight. The Darkness licked their wounds and dragged away their dead to devour the bodies at a safe distance while the Mage bandaged his own wounds. He disappointingly drank the last of his water.

Galeb may have offended the source of the voice by ignoring it because the voice suddenly shifted to overt and clear threats.

A new voice overrode the first one. This voice was older, more confident, more amused than anything. The Shaeloman were making their presence known.

"Such impatience in the young, do you not think, Itinerant Warder Mage?" asked the voice, which seemed to circle the Wards lazily, as sinuous and caressing as the feel of clotted oil. "I have been watching you, Itinerant Warder Mage. Every time that you've passed through this region I've watched you. That's how I knew you would come alone. You just needed a little push, such a little push.

"I've found you so fascinating, so dedicated, so deliciously powerful for one so low ranked. You are a mystery to me, Itinerant Warder Mage. Such an alluring mystery.

"I wanted to meet you, wanted to test you, wanted to *savor* you. But those Wards of yours, Itinerant Warder Mage. Those naughty, naughty Wards kept me from meeting you.

"I tried to reach out to you before now. Little nibbles to attract your interest. The Forester near Eiksritter? The little girl at Margsbatten last year? The pelancorant attack that left you with your limp? That one was my special gift to you.

"Yet you ignored me, Itinerant Warder Mage. Why did you ignore me? Such behavior was so very, very rude that I had to issue you a much better invitation. One that you would appreciate and could not ignore.

"You hated Uksaadle; I know. Such nasty people. I knew that killing them for you would both gain your esteem and bring you to me. Now we are both happy."

The words cut at Galeb. How could he have missed being stalked and manipulated by The Darkness? No, he knew how he had missed the signs. He had been too overwhelmed, too obsessed with his duty to see the more subtle dangers. Another mistake, another failure.

"No thanks for all of my efforts? What about the gifts I left for you at Uksaadle? The masks by the well? I'd hoped that you'd like them since you're always hiding who you really are, Itinerant Warder Mage. A thoughtful gift, no? Something to be treasured, yes? I was so very careful when I pealed the faces away. Not an easy feat, I must tell you. They struggled so, not wanting to give up their masks, so selfish with their screams. But it was worth the sacrifice to be able to give you such a gift. Now you can be whomever you want. I'll not mind so long as it's you under the mask."

Galeb's face twisted in revulsion.

"You don't like my present? This makes me sad, Itinerant Warder Mage. I tried so very hard to find a present that I thought you'd like."

There was genuine grief in the words.

"I would have no presents from such as you," Galeb said, his eyes searching for the source of the voice, his stance defiant.

"Tsk, Itinerant Warder Mage, so very ungrateful after all that I've done for you. I've brought you recognition; I have turned the eyes of your King to the North. For the very first time in your life you are noticed for what you are."

Those words held Galeb's attention despite himself.

"Oh, now I have your interest? Good, *good*. I have waited so long for you to notice me. To challenge me! To finally let me rip the confounding secrets of your existence from your marrow! Such ecstasy. Such exquisite delight we are going to have!

"Your attention truly does bring me such pleasure, Itinerant Warder Mage. I want more of it. I want you focused only on me....ever on *me*.

"Perhaps we will wear masks together, you and I? Forever laughing at the world that cannot see us as we are? What a rich joke that would be!

"But first I would like to see what lies beneath that mask, to see some appreciation for all of my hard work on your behalf. Just give me a little taste of the sweetness that I've given you."

The Shaeloman raced out of the gathering night, swatting the weakened Ward posts aside and raking Galeb's face faster than he could react. The face mask was ripped clean away along with half of the hood. Blood splashed in the wake of torn leather from thin, ragged cuts.

Galeb staggered to the side, blinking back tears and moving the quarter staff back into guard position. A parent's sleepless night stirred the wards around his wrists. He had not wanted to activate them just yet, hoping to draw in the Skrieksgrata first and trap the beasts in the tangle maze.

He shivered when he heard delicate licking noises off to his left and sighs of contented pleasure. The Shaeloman angled around him just out of sight, the voice shifting direction.

"Thank you for that little nibble. I want you to know how much it means to me so that you understand my appreciation.

"I will also tell you what else I have done for you, Itinerant Warder Mage, so you can show gratitude and we can both be on an equal footing so that we can better explore our relationship to our mutual satisfaction.

"Now please do not be overwhelmed by the depth of my devotion. I don't want you thinking that you are unworthy of my attention. I'm hoping that once you understand all that I have done for you, you will not only notice me, but *want me, plead for me, beg* for the touch of my claws upon your flesh."

That definitely sounded sexual. Galeb was mortified. He had the absurd hope that the Shaeloman was at least female.

"The little girl at Margsbatten. Such a nobody as a father. Just a simple draftsman, who drove a wagon. Nobody that anyone would look at twice, which was what made him such a good smuggler.

"Smugglers should not talk. But this one did; grief stricken and knowing how purposefully poorly patrolled The Road east of the river was to allow that smuggling. The poor man was eaten up by guilt knowing that he might have done something to prevent me from gutting his daughter, nibbling on her toes and borrowing her eyes.

"He just had to tell someone what was going on. I ensured that his story reached the right ears. Don't worry, I let those men keep their ears though they were awful tempting."

Galeb flinched. He did not mean to but the 'poorly patrolled' comment got to him.

"Do my words pain you, Itinerant Warder Mage? My apologies if they do. I don't mean to disparage your efforts. No, I speak of the Troopers who turned a blind eye to your struggle and security of The Road. I have nothing but the *utmost* respect for your own efforts. I wouldn't have brought you here otherwise. I wouldn't have lavished so much attention on you."

The Shaeloman actually sounded bothered that it might have hurt Galeb unintentionally.

"So much respect for you, Itinerant Warder Mage. My proud, strong man. I tremble at the thought of the sensation of my claws cutting into your skin as I hold you so close.... I can hardly wait, my need is so great. I don't even want to share you with the youngling."

The kielsgruntara began to circle again, ignoring the broken Ward posts. Galeb glanced towards the nest and could see the Skrieksgrata were stirring from their den, their massive, shuffling shapes emerging into the deepening twilight.

There was a shriek that suddenly pierced the valley air, causing the kielsgruntara to momentarily scatter in panic. The shriek was cut off and the grisly mass of what Galeb assumed was a Shaeloman head landed outside the circle of his Wards.

"No, I don't want to share," the voice said, returning, sounding suddenly jealous. "I want you all to myself with no more Wards between us. I want to feel your body next to mine. I want to hold you gently as your last sobbing breath bubbles from your lips. That is why I have lured *her* here."

There was such frustrated anger in the tone, such pure hate that Galeb stiffened with anger and fear blazing within him as he realized whom the Shaeloman was referring to. No, no, *no*!

"I thought that if I took the burden of The Road from you, you would finally come to me. But that didn't work. You were still distracted by *her*. You could not see me, treasure me, because of *her*.

"I will not share you. You are *MINE!* But we don't have to worry about her any more. No, she was so easy to manipulate. Just the right amount of stress placed upon you and Kieri could not help feeling the need to ease your burden. I put out some Obari warning signs and she could not help but run to your aid.

"In a way she and I are similar. Both so fascinated by you, Itinerant Warder Mage. Both wanting to comfort and cherish you in our own way. I could almost pity her if she didn't want to take you away from me."

The Skrieksgrata were not descending to the valley floor. They were moving off towards the entrance to the valley. The kielsgruntara began to shift away as well, heading for the mouth of the valley and Kieri.

"Your log book was the last piece, Itinerant Warder Mage. That touchingly heroic last entry. What woman could not help but swoon? The poor girl took off to find you as soon as she read it."

Galeb bent with pain, knowing the truth of the Shaeloman's words. He had put Kieri in danger.

"I would like to say that I'm sorry for causing you that last bit of pain, but I'm not. I needed another little nibble before the main course. Don't worry. I'll have plenty of time to make it up to you. I'll share such ecstasy with you, my Itinerant Warder Mage."

Galeb slammed his staff into the ground and activated the buried Wards.

Chapter 8

Bob and Kawen were wrong. There were not two kielsgruntara. As they dispatched the two six more erupted from the ground nearby, their burrows hidden among the tree roots, seeking to bring the Obari down. Bob distracted the beasts with an eruption of flashing stars that momentarily blinded them as Kawen wove an illusion of a deep chasm separating the beasts from the cousins. The kielsgruntara surged around the illusion as the cousins wove camouflaging images around themselves, appearing and disappearing as they struck at The Darkness, sewing confusion among the beasts.

Bobwhites erupted from the ground, whispers surged around the beasts and shadowy image appeared in The Darkness's peripheral vision. Distractions raged around the pack hunters as the cousins desperately stabbed and slashed. Unfortunately the kielsgruntara responded to the illusions by snapping and slashing wildly in every direction, driving the cousins back in their frenzy.

Kieri was attacked as she reached the mouth of the valley, a kielsgruntara leaping for her back but recoiling at the last minute in a blinding flash of power just as her sword licked out in a terrifyingly fast strike, severing the creature's jugular. Bob was staggered by the illusion, which lacked subtlety, but was overwhelmingly effective in its intensity.

Moonlight seemed to gather around Kieri as she danced across the forest floor, dodging another attack with liquid grace. She put her back to a line of Ward posts at the mouth of the valley and soon glowed like the face of the moon, dark and terrible in cold majesty, having achieved in an instant the look that she had been trying to master for years. Bob didn't know what his cousin was thinking. Stealth would better serve them in this fight. There were too many of The Darkness for a direct confrontation.

But, unbelievably, the kielsgruntara were falling back, quivering before Kieri's aura as it crackled and snapped with a frigid power that burned The Darkness from the inside out. While this turn of events was good for Kieri it was more problematic for her cousins. Denied one prey, The Darkness turned their full attention to the others.

Ilsbruk could see the flashes of light in the distance and hear the chittering whines of the kielsgruntara as the Obari battled for their lives. He raised a hand and the three patrols increased their speed as much as they could through the forest. The Captain was grateful for the lack of underbrush as the Troopers, three hundreds strong, surged forward. It was bad enough that their charge was broken up by the trees.

Bob would have shouted for joy at the sight of hundreds of Klynsheim Troopers charging out of the surrounding forest and cutting down the kielsgruntara if he was not so busy trying to avoid being trampled. Once he found a spot of relative safety he looked for Kieri to see if she was safe. He couldn't find any sign of her, which turned out to be fortuitous.

The kielsgruntara scattered under the Klynsheim onslaught and the Troopers spread out in squad pursuit exactly as intended. When the squads were spread out just enough to prevent easy support the trap was sprung. Five Skrieksgrata burst from the trees, smashing everything in their path aside. Trees splintered, rocks shattered and men died.

Gorgorin swore a blue streak as an entire squad went down under the sudden onslaught on their left flank. Skrieksgrata came charging out of the gloom, sending the Troopers into panicked chaos as they turned to meet the new threat.

The Darkness were massive pig apes, with distended jaws and curving claws a foot long. There was nothing elegant in their attacks, just a frenzy of sweeping claws that dismembered. Armor was a minor inconvenience to them.

One man was caught in mid-charge, the right side of his face and body ripped clean away, his horse carrying the rest of the remains away in panic. Another horse had its back broken as a Skrieksgrata slammed down on a Trooper's helm, pulping the man's head and driving his body down into the animal.

So much blood was suddenly splashing about that it felt like it was raining. Heads, arms, stomachs – everything was being torn open and thrown about as the Skrieksgrata ran rampant in blood lust. One horse had its entire head bitten off.

Sergeants and lieutenants bellowed orders as one long patrol surged to meet the Skrieksgrata head on while half a patrol swung around them to catch The Darkness from the rear. The other half a hundreds dropped their lances, dismounted and began firing arrows at the lumbering giants from the shelter of surrounding trees. The remaining hundreds took up guard positions, watching the rear for further attacks.

The Darkness did not disappoint. A full hundred kielsgruntara erupted from the surrounding wood, throwing themselves at the rear guard. Half a hundreds war dogs leapt to meet the charge, beast and kielsgruntara colliding in the air and tumbling to the ground in snapping, growling, chittering hatred. It was hard to tell where Darkness and dog ended as the beasts fought, jaws tearing flesh free in great gouts as claws struggled for purchase.

The Skrieksgrata strode forward to meet the Klynsheim charge, whistling with joy as their claws smashed trees and armor with equal abandon. Gorgorin, racing along with a squad assigned to the head on assault could have sworn one of The Darkness was smashing things blindly as arrows protruded from both eyes. Both shots had required skill but were incredibly, wastefully stupid. Skrieksgrata eye sockets narrowed dramatically, leaving no room for an arrow head to pass by the thick bone of the orbital socket and pierce the brain. Someone was going to get the lashing of a life time before they repeated training. Septa fool should know how to identify the weakness of different Darkness better.

Captain Ilsbruk was in the middle of a maelstrom as his men fought to drive The Darkness back. He stood in the center of it all, dismounted and directing the men to counter each new threat. A few more moments and the flanking force should be in position to pincer the Skrieksgrata that had already downed nearly half a hundreds men.

The quick sticks were aligned and a squad was in position around the terminus relaying information back to Central Command along the Ward Line. The Darkness was Rising; this was no simple threat. The attack demonstrated pre-planning and coordination. Spriegs, Guunt or Shaeloman; any of the three more intelligent Darknesses might be behind this and all were differently dangerous. The Academy's neglect had allowed a threat to fester to the point that the whole frontier might very well be threatened if The Darkness felt ambitious enough.

"'Ware the rear!" came a scream in the distance from the direction of the flanking force.

A wave of excited chirruping overwhelmed the scream.

"They're everywhere!"

"Fall back!"

"Grieshtata-AAHH!"

The Skrieksgrata roared and blunted the charge against them, literally ripping their way through the bodies of the horses and throwing the Troopers against the trees to smash and fall like limp, broken dolls. Hundreds of kielsgruntara poured past them from the direction of the flanking force whom Ilsbruk had to assume were now all dead. Any attempt to retreat would most likely end in failure as well.

"Grieshtata it all!" yelled Ilsbruk. "Hedgehog formation! Rally point is the terminus. Get your backs to each other. Use lances. Drive them back!"

Troopers struggled to close the formation, men being torn apart, kielsgruntara aiming for any chink in the leg armor to bring the desperate Klynsheimers down.

"You heard the Captain!" Gorgorin bellowed, wading through the panicking men, pushing them into position. The sergeant was bathed in the blood of his horse which had saved his life by rearing into the swipe of a claw aimed at his head. "Don't give The Darkness an opening. Lances to the front. Make those septa Skrieksgrata squeal!"

The noise was almost deafening as the line closed and abandoned mounts fought for survival, lashing out with hoof and teeth as they tried to race clear. War dogs snarled or whimpered in pain, as they and The Darkness continued to hunt each other in the deepening twilight.

Ilsbruk nearly threw up as he watched one of the dogs, completely disemboweled trying to drag itself towards the Troopers, its intestines hanging from the ragged wound as it whined. He cursed and ran over to the squad at the terminus and looked squarely at the quick stick, pain and anger flowing through him as his command fought and died around him.

"The Darkness has Risen! Seven miles north east of Uksaadle on the Great Trade Road. The Darkness is Risen!"

Ilsbruk then turned, took his place in the line, gripped his hand axe more firmly and clove the skull of the first kielsgruntara to reach him.

"For King and Seven!" he bellowed in defiance.

He spun in a dance that was far from the smiles and pleasantries that his wife had pleaded with him to learn. The axe whirled in a deadly arc, smashing kielsgruntara to the side, his shield thrust forward to block attacks. He stabbed forward with the axe, the spike that capped the haft above the axe head taking a kielsgruntara in the chest. Here Ilsbruk felt natural, accepted for who he was without the need to coddle to other people's feelings.

Then the world exploded into light.

Chapter 9

The Wards erupted, searing with seeming indomitable power, trapping the kielsgruntara where they stood and preventing them from joining The Darkness already at the head of the valley. The kielsgruntara howled in agony as they fought the Wards. A small victory at least.

"Well done, my darling Itinerant Warder Mage!" the voice crooned seductively, the words caressing the air with heat and lust. "You make me desire you so. But still, you disappoint. Is this the best that you can do? Simple traps?"

Galeb ignored the disturbing words. Kieri was still in danger. His fault. All his fault. He raced for the head of the valley as fast as his limp would allow him. Galeb knew when he crossed the last of his tangle Wards because the voice shrieked in rapturous joy, a shape coming leaping out of the gathering night with sinuous grace.

Galeb did not slow, could not slow. He released a burst of the hoarded sunlight, lighting the air around him and sending The Darkness screaming away from him.

"So playful! You are so good to me," the Shaeloman purred in satisfaction as it recovered from its shock and launched itself at Galeb again.

Galeb let loose another burst but The Darkness was prepared, closing its eyes and lunging at where it knew Galeb's next steps would take him. Galeb blocked with his staff, the embedded Wards flaring with fire, sending the Shaeloman stumbling back, but not before a claw left a burning line across Galeb's chest.

The Shaeloman did not immediately attack, just stood back and watched Galeb, a blurry outline in the night. Galeb kept an eye on The Darkness which allowed him to see the creature raise a single claw to its mouth and lick the blood dripping from the appendage. The Shaeloman shuddered with pleasure.

"So much better than even the first time," The Darkness whispered, as if to keep the moment intimate. "But you have so much more to offer. You're still hiding. Show me the true you. *Please.*"

A sound caused Galeb to look back towards the way he had come. Kielsgruntara came in a tumultuous horde from deeper in the valley. A wave of hundreds all bearing down on him.

"I Ward The Darkness," he whispered, dropping the quarter staff and raising his arms to meet the tide.

The light was everywhere as tree and rock erupted in angry, vicious Wards. Troopers fighting back to back suddenly stood stunned as one of the Skrieksgrata was flunk off its feet into a tree, smashed free, was blasted back by another ward into another tree and then smashed back and forth until The Darkness was literally just a smear of dripping hide.

Kielsgruntara were repulsed, blocked, riven and slaughtered in an orgy of light that brought hope to the failing Troopers. The Darkness fell back in confusion, trying to regroup and find safer ground. Sergeants took advantage of the lull, rallying the survivors to a central point where their numbers could be more telling. Officers looked around, trying to map out the territory of their protections.

Gorgorin limped over to Captain Ilsbruk, who was looking around in shock, his axe drawn back in one hand and his other still gripping the throat of a kielsgruntara that he had strangled, his shield lost somewhere.

"I think that it's dead, Sir," Gorgorin said softly.

Ilsbruk looked at his sergeant in surprise and then glanced at his hand which was locked around The Darkness's crushed windpipe. He dropped the creature with a look of embarrassment.

"How far does the Warding extend?" Ilsbruk asked, lowering his axe and shaking his head.

"Fifty-sixty yards?" Gorgorin answered.

"I think I love that Mage," Ilsbruk said with a goofy grin as the fact that he wasn't about to die yet sunk in.

"Quite fond of the grieshtata myself, Sir," Gorgorin agreed.

"How many men do we have left?" Ilsbruk asked, squashing the grin as he regained control of his emotions.

"Not enough," was Gorgorin's answer.

Then the night erupted in light once again, this time coming from the direction of the valley.

"He might still be alive," Gorgorin said, raising an eyebrow and looking at his captain.

"Extend the terminus. Central Command will need to see everything," Ilsbruk commanded. Only God knew how many more Darkness were in the valley.

The deep Wardings stirred in a twisting, serpentine dance along Galeb's arms. 'Lights the Way' curled around 'Wind whispers in the reeds' to be met by 'leavens the bread' before flowing forth to ravage the first wave of The Darkness in thick tendrils of flame that stuck like tar and burned through kielsgruntara hide.

Galeb spun in place, releasing 'leavens the bread' and replacing it in the configuration with 'spins the top' extending the fire in a swirling wall as the kielsgruntara swarmed around him. The beasts shrieked and shriveled but pushed forward relentless, snapping and slashing. The sheer weight of numbers forced him to stumble back and release the fire.

'The Way is Shut' caressed 'Hammer and the Anvil', smashing deep rents in the enemy line before he could be dragged down. 'Star Kisses the Water' froze blood, causing The Darkness in the rear to trip and tumble over their suddenly immobile counterparts in the front. But it was not enough. The kielsgruntara kept coming, their numbers seeming limitless. He clumsily dodged attacks, lashing out with the Wards. He staggered under tooth and claw before driving The Darkness back. Blood flowed, weakening him further.

"So much better!   But is this all that you are? Is this your true face? *No!* You are still hiding from me! *Show me who you are*!" shrieked the Shaeloman, running at him and slicing his back open before he could turn.

Galeb cursed and slammed 'The Way is Shut' into the ground all around him. He was an idiot. He needed to think – think, septa it! Don't react, be prepared!

The kielsgruntara surged forward to be met with 'Pebble in a pond's' marriage with 'Thunder in the silence', which created air bursts that tossed The Darkness like rag dolls.

"More!" roared the Shaeloman. "You are so close! *Show me who you are!"*

So he called the lightning.

Chapter 10

The Grand Hall was the heart of The Academy, a vast structure designed to house the entirety of the Warders in Residence, from student to master. Debates were held, strategies discussed and lectures presented as the occasion warranted. This time in the evening the Hall was usually empty, as the dinner hour was held almost sacrosanct by The Academy leaders, known collectively as the Twelve. Old men rich in their power, wealth and reputations.

Tonight the Twelve were displeased, summoned by the King to Audience, and so were all of the Warders in Residence. The King had not requested the gathering of all Warders; the Twelve took it upon themselves. Partly because if they were to be denied their dinner, so would everyone else. Partly to demonstrate the Twelve's authority over all Warders. And partly to humble the King; the Twelve were confident that Sigsrata would be shown the fool yet again, his accusations against The Academy false and hollow. This was a game with a long history of Academy victories.

No love was lost between the Twelve and the Klynsheim King. Sigsrata felt that The Academy was trying to usurp his authority – the Twelve most certainly were, feeling that they deserved even greater stature than they already held in Klynsheimer society. The Twelve felt that Sigsrata wronged them by not giving them greater control over Klynsheim. As always, the rest of The Academy was caught in the middle.

Jans Sepsrigga and Obel Jargsin were two such Warders caught in the machinations of their superiors. Both held prestigious enough postings, Sepsrigga assigned to the South Wall of the capital, while Jargsin held a comfortable place in the southeastern quadrant of Ulsbarg, the kingdom's second city and jewel of the Southlands. Both were back at The Academy doing their teaching rotation and falling into old arguments as they waited for the King's arrival.

"I'm just saying that the teaching rotation is fine for some, but I don't need a refresher course," Obel complained, shaking his thick mane of brown hair that was so dark it was almost black, irritation flaring in his blue eyes. "I serve in Ulsbarg, for God's sake. There are twenty three Warders of master level there. What can I learn here that I can't learn back home?"

"Humility, maybe?" Jans suggested, turning her head to take in the room. Her own hair was Just as long as Obel's though tied back in a long braid. Also unlike her friend, her rich brown hair was natural and not the result of a dye job intended to make the other Warder look more exotic.

Both were journeyman Warders, eight years out of training and well on their way to master status. Their postings and connections guaranteed mastery in another year or so. Their clothing, Warder's robes of an elaborately expensive weave and burgundy color reflected their success.

"Who do you keep looking for?" Obel asked, still irritated that Jans refused to recognize the logic of his argument.

"Galeb. I haven't seen him since graduation. He should be here on his teaching rotation," Jans explained.

"Why?" Obel asked, surprised. "Who cares if Galeb is here? It's not like either of us ever associated with him. Wasn't much point, what with his lack of connections and strange ideas about Warding."

What Obel said was true; it wasn't as if either of them had been particularly close to Eielson. The man's fascination with the simple runes hadn't exactly made him the popular choice to be around during their school days. There was nothing fashionable about simplicity and fashionable was the easiest way into the best positions.

"Honestly, Obel, I don't know what you have against Galeb," Jans said in disappointment, still scanning the room.

"Don't play high and mighty with me, Jans. You weren't exactly going out of your way to move in the same circles as him during school either," Obel pointed out.

"No, but I never looked down on him," Jans argued.

"Jans, you didn't have to. You ignored him like everyone else did," Obel said, reminding his friend of the reality of those days.

"I did not – did I? We were all so busy...," Jans said, shaking her head as she tried to remember.

Obel wasn't fooled. He knew perfectly well Jans was trying to rewrite history in her head to make herself look more upstanding. These days Jans was going for the reputation of a benevolent Mage in hopes of finding more supporters and faster advancement.

"You still haven't explained why you are looking for Galeb," Obel reminded her.

"His mother lives near one of the sections I Ward. She's been asking after him. Says that she hasn't seen him in eight years. I certainly don't remember Galeb being that rude. I have no idea why he's avoiding his mother," Jans explained.

"So how is that any of your business?" Obel pressed.

"The man needs to be reminded about the importance of family. His neglect is worrying his mother and needs to stop," Jans said primly.

Oh, now Obel understood. 'Jans the Benevolent' was going to show another Warder Mage the errors of his ways in a very public fashion. Obel felt better knowing that Jans was working an angle.

"You can stop looking now," Obel informed Jans a few minutes later.

"Did you find him? Where is he?" Jans said, straightening and practicing her stern face.

"No, I didn't find Galeb. The King's here," Obel said with a shake of his head.

Everyone in the Hall stood, though the Twelve did so almost languidly, their rich ermine robes and glittering jewels shining in the rune light, intricately carved staves held in each of their hands. These were not subjects greeting their sovereign. These were masters indulging a child. Not that the king could ever be considered a child, no matter how disdainful the Twelve acted towards him.

King Sigsrata was a bear of a man, the image of a fighting King, though no King had need to lead the armies anymore. His face was broad and covered with a massively unruly beard that was at odds with his perfectly groomed hair, kept short in Trooper style. Instead of robes he wore the armor of the General of Patrols, intending to show his support of the Military. The armor was in no way ornate; instead it was utilitarian which made it that much more intimidating. The long hafted axe that Sigsrata carried instead of a scepter added to the overall impression of a hardened Soldier.

The King's Throne sat off to the side of the central dais, flanking the chairs of Twelve, which though they lacked the name, were even more ostentatious than the King's Throne. The Twelve held court in The Academy and were taking every advantage to remind the King of their positions. Normally such disdainful treatment infuriated the King. Tonight, Sigsrata looked almost sedate. Obel wondered if the King was mellowing or just trying another tact with the Warder Leaders.

The King took his seat with the grace of a panther, laying the axe across his lap. Half a hundreds Troopers flanked him. Large for an honor guard, but not unheard of considering the 'warrior king' look Sigsrata cultivated. The King gestured for the Twelve to sit as well, which all of the elder Warders did, somehow making it look as if it were their idea. The Assembly of Warders sat only once their leadership was comfortable.

No one spoke. Sigsrata sat patiently, a bemused expression on his face, watching the Twelve. The Twelve looked back with mixed looks of serenity, superiority, and impatience. It was Coreb, Seventh of the Twelve, and the crankiest of the leadership who broke the silence. He was a gaunt, scarecrow of a man, with little hair on his head and a perpetual scowl on his wrinkled face.

"Your Majesty has summoned us at this unfortunate hour," Coreb pointed out haughtily, baiting the King to lose his temper, "The least that your Majesty can do is address the issue and let us return to our dinners."

The King, once again uncharacteristically, did not take the bait, but smiled.

"My apologies, Warder Coreb," Sigsrata said, his voice a deep rumbling bass. Sigsrata never used the royal 'we', finding it pretentious, even though he sometimes joked that he was big enough to qualify as a 'we'. No one ever laughed at the joke. The King wasn't fat and could wield his great axe easily with one hand. "I sometimes forget how important meals can be to gentlemen of your advanced years."

Coreb scowled at the reminder of his age. A few others of the Twelve did as well. The rest looked serenely condescending, having won too many victories over the King in the past to jeopardize their reputations over a minor insult.

"And yet you continue to dissemble," pointed out Aeub, Sixth of the Twelve. There was more flesh and hair to him than Coreb, but his face was as wrinkled as the Seventh.

One, Two, and Three of the Twelve, also referred to as 'The Three' would never address the King, feeling such an act was beneath them as the most powerful of the governors of The Academy.

The King smiled.

"To the point, then," Sigsrata agreed. "I have come for a bit of conversation."

"What, are your Seven incapable of more than monosyllables?" Coreb demanded snidely. "I imagine trying to converse with them would be most boring."

The King's smile strained for a heartbeat but he returned to smiling benevolently.

"What I wish to discuss is beyond my Seven," the King agreed, "But not because of their intellect. No, I wish to converse about a fascinating Warder that Ilsbruk, one of the Seven, has had the good fortune to meet."

"I thought that Ilsbruk had a wife," Aeub said, raising an eyebrow and trying to make an innuendo that fell a bit flat.

"He does, indeed," agreed the King. "A good woman that he is eager to return to once his business in the North Lands is complete."

Most of the Twelve visibly stiffened. Only The Three remaining impassive.

"We were unaware that Captain Ilsbruk was in the North Lands," Caj, Fifth of the Twelve said a bit nervously. "We were led to believe he was in the East, visiting his family."

Caj was a portly, grandfatherly looking sort with big tufts of gray hair isolated on either side of his head.

"What the septa is going on?" Jans asked Obel, whispering. "I thought that we were in for another one of the King's rages and the Twelve's speeches."

"I don't know, Jans. I've never seen the Twelve nervous," Obel admitted.

The King shifted slightly in his throne, his smile predatory now.

"You were led to believe that Ilsbruk was in the East," the King agreed. "I felt that the Captain needed his privacy and quite a few tongues were cut to ensure that he received it."

There was no missing the menace growing in the King's voice. Everyone knew that the Twelve had spies. So did the King. Apparently the King's spies were the better of the two. Or, more to the point, the King commanded better assassins. Jans didn't doubt from the King's expression that many of the Twelve's spies were face down in their graves.

"You have not asked for the identity of the Warder Mage that Ilsbruk finds so fascinating," the King pointed out, almost purring. "Perhaps because you already know? Though how could you? There must be dozens and dozens of Warder Mages working the North Lands and the Great Trade Road."

Desmond, Twelve of Twelve was looking decidedly green, his fleshy hands gripping his robe tightly.

"Let me tell you the Warder's name so there is no mistake," Sigsrata said, leaning forward slightly. "Galeb Eielson. *Itinerant Mage* Galeb Eielson."

All of the Twelve stiffened.

"I see that you are familiar with the man," the King said, grinning, as he leaned back comfortably in the throne. "He has had quite the career from what I understand. Are you gentleman interested in some conversation now?"

Silence greeted the question and the King looked even more pleased.

Galeb coughed, a gasping, wet, wretched thing as the power ripped through his deep wardings and the valley erupted in terrible arcs of light and ear bleeding claps of thunder. The Darkness before him wailed as the energy coursed through them, their bodies looking purple as every bone was highlighted from the inside out. Scores of kielsgruntara fell burnt and twitching, the stench of feces and sizzled flesh filling the air.

Galeb did not stop. Before the lightning faded he sent a river of fire rolling forth to incinerate the remnants. The flood of Darkness became a trickle and then dried up as the survivors fled in all directions from the Ward wrought destruction.

Galeb felt no pride of victory. He staggered and coughed wetly again, as the Ward arrays around his wrists sputtered and died, spent.

The Shaeloman grinned, its mouth impossibly wide, pride flaring in its yellow, pupil less eyes. The Darkness clapped in glee.

"This," the Shaeloman hissed, striding closer while shaking its head. "This is the true you. No more hiding. No more masks. No more pretenses."

The Shaeloman stopped short of Galeb and cocked its head to the side in puzzlement.

"Why would you ever want to hide something so beautiful?" it asked, gesturing to the carnage that lay in every direction for almost a mile.

Galeb didn't answer. He drew his fighting knife, though his arms protested. He stumbled as The Darkness moved closer and then fell as the Shaeloman kicked his left knee, wrenching it painfully. Galeb rolled as he fell, avoiding two more strikes and came up on one knee, slashing with his fighting knife, catching the Shaeloman in the side with the tip of the blade as The Darkness scored slashes across his hands. The Darkness giggled. Actually giggled at the contact.

"You want to taste my blood? Do you think that it tastes as sweet as yours? Does the thought of tasting me on your lips make you shiver as much as it does me?"

Galeb tried to stand but could not. He grimaced at the pain, holding the knife as tightly as he could with the blood from his hands making the grip uncertain. He could not afford to lose the knife. Kieri was still in danger. Septa, he was in trouble.

"Poor gentle soul, I can see what you're thinking. Yes, you've failed her. I'm certain that she will be disappointed in you," said the Shaeloman as it circled him, its stride sinuous and playful. "But that's because she was never for you. You were meant for me and I'm not disappointed. You've made me *so* happy. Drop your blade and let me make *you* happy. I will peel that mask away from your head and give you any other one that you may want after I get to see the face that matches the man who can kill so spectacularly."

Galeb shuddered. Did the Shaeloman actually think that his face was a mask?

The Shaeloman suddenly stopped pacing and tilted its head listening. Galeb shifted, keeping his guard up and listening as well. Now that he was not running and the Shaeloman was not talking Galeb could hear the sounds of fighting and the battle cries of Klynsheim Troopers.

"Hmmm...this is certainly inconvenient," the Shaeloman admitted. "I didn't think anyone would still be alive up there."

Galeb had just enough time to widen his eyes at the words when the Shaeloman was upon him with a dizzying burst of speed. His knife went flying from his hand as The Darkness backhanded him and then crushed his wrist, the claws sinking deep.

"We really have to be going," the Shaeloman said, grinning. "I'll have to rise to the occasion and resist the temptation to see under that skin until we can be alone."

The grin might have been seductive. Galeb couldn't be sure. He just saw a lot of teeth and a lot of hair.

Galeb reached for another knife. He was backhanded again and the remainder of his weapons were ripped away with a good portion of the coat and shirt. Galeb may have momentarily blacked out because the next thing he knew he was being dragged across the ground.

"How in God's name is Galeb still ranked an Itinerant?" Obel asked in disbelief and perhaps a little too loudly since a more senior Warder nearby glared at him.

Considering the sudden absurdity of the situation Obel glared back. Jans hushed him, wanting to hear what the King had to say.

The Twelve were silent. The King quirked an eyebrow and filled the silence.

"Imagine Ilsbruk's surprise upon meeting Itinerant Warder Mage Eielson," the King rumbled. "A man dressed as a pauper despite his station. Scarred, battered and blooded in battle."

Whispers were growing around the Hall. Warders did not fight. The idea was a bit revolting.

"I believe that we have an image of the man," the King said waiving a hand, "Taken from the Ward Lines of the Great Trade Road."

One of his guards walked forward with a quick stick, the wards glowing dully in a loop, indicating stored information. Coreb stood indignantly at the sight of the quick stick and the King's words.

"The Ward Network is the purview of The Academy. No information is to be taken from the Network without Academy knowledge and approval," Coreb thundered, slamming his staff into the marble dais. It was hard to tell what made Coreb angrier – the fact that the King had information taken from the Ward Network or the fact that a Mage had obviously helped the King to do it. Most likely the later.

"Normally your words would be true, Coreb," the King agreed, his eyes filling with molten anger as he leaned forward. "But Treason gives me every right!"

There was now open shouting at the accusation among the Warders. The Twelve did not try to stop the outrage from building. They silently encouraged it, reminding the King of who ruled in this Hall.

The King did not try to silence the shouting either. He didn't have to. Three hundreds of Troopers and Infantry poured into the Hall from every entrance, crossbows knocked and ready as they took aim at the jeering Warders showing support for the Twelve. Silence suddenly seemed more than prudent.

"You would attack Warders of the Realm?" asked Sevrug, First of the Twelve, his words ringing in condemnation as he deigned to talk to the King.

Sevrug was a tall man, balding, but with a long, immaculate beard. His every movement indicated grace and refinement. Of a similar age as the other members of the Twelve, his face seemed oddly youthful and serene in comparison.

"I would stop treason," the King countered, still seated and leaning back now, almost relaxed. "I would also come prepared. I am not an idiot. I have learned from our previous encounters how this bunch dances to your tune. I simply offer a caution to everyone present"

"We are Warders of the Realm!" shouted Coreb, slamming his staff against the marble again.

"You are a traitor to the Realm," snapped the King.

"Evidence!" demanded one brave soul in the crowd.

Obel and Jans exchanged looks, neither one willing to speak. Like most Warders assigned to cities neither one was willing to risk their necks. Theirs was a comfortable existence, not one prone to acts of heroism.

"Of course," agreed the King, all calm and confident, his anger leashed behind hooded eyes once again. "I assume that you would recognize doctored log books, falsified reports, bribery and corruption of Military personnel and a few assassinations as evidence, all of which will be presented at trial of course."

The King paused, looking over at the Trooper who was trying to activate the quick stick. The Hall had a projection system, the entire wall behind the dais of the Twelve an elaborate Warding designed to show word and image. The Trooper was unfortunately not familiar with how the system worked. The man looked at the King and shrugged sheepishly.

"Oh for God's sake," Jans said, pushing Obel out of the way and descending to the dais. She could read the room well enough to know that the Twelve's time was up barring a miracle and she might want to try and ingratiate herself to the King.

The Trooper was pushed out of the way as well, though he grumbled more than Obel had at the same treatment. Jans had the quick stick active and interfacing with the Warding panel shortly thereafter. She turned and curtsied to the King, who nodded his thanks before returning to her place at Obel's side. More than a few of the Twelve's closest supporters glared at her.

Jans was unconcerned. The Troopers were taking note of the glares and officers were being informed. More than the Twelve would fall tonight if the King's accusations were proven true.

An image began to appear on the Warding panel much like a pen and ink drawing. Obel and Jans barely recognized Eielson, the image showing him walking from one Ward post to another. The King's description was both accurate and incomplete.

Where there should have been a well-kept man dressed in Warder robes was instead a gaunt figure dressed in battered leathers and armed with a quarter staff and fighting knife. The face was the worst, eyes haunted, the exhaustion clear to everyone, with faintly visible scars along his jawline. Obel, Jans, and Galeb were the same age.   Galeb looked at least a decade older.

Jans strode down streets with dignity and poise. Obel sauntered with an arrogant gate. Eielson limped, his movements stiff and pained.

"My God," Jans said, her face paling. "What happened to him?"

"Here is clear evidence of treachery and treason," the King said, showing sympathy as he looked at the image. "Itinerant Warder Mage Galeb Eielson, who, by your own records, is accounted as weak and unworthy of promotion; a nobody who is kept in service through the generosity of The Academy."

"Galeb was never weak," Obel hissed, offended despite himself. "Stupidly obsessed with simple Wardings, but never weak."

"Answer me this, Twelve of The Academy," Sigsrata challenged. "If Itinerant Warder Mage Galeb Eielson is such a charity case why was he charged with warding the entire Great Trade Road by himself?"

 Mages turned to each other in shock at the accusation before looking for the Twelve to deny the King's claim. The Twelve were ominously silent.

The King stood now, grasping the haft of his axe, as he strode closer to the Twelve.

"Eight years that man has held the entire Northern defensive Ward Line of Klynsheim by himself!" Sigsrata roared, his rage in full evidence now as he pointed at the image. "Six hundred miles of Wards!"

There was stunned silence among the Warders. Treason was bad enough. But this – this was a betrayal of the trust of a Warder. It was a sad reflection on The Academy and a sign of the Twelve's poisoning influence that the betrayal bothered the Warders more than the thought of treason.

"How much gold did you receive for betraying our nation?" the King suddenly demanded. "How many lives were lost because you wanted to keep the Trade Road weakened so that you could smuggle a few more ounces?"

"The Military shares responsibility for the defense of The Road," Aeub pointed out weakly. "You cannot lay blame for smuggling solely at the feet of The Academy."

Other members of the Twelve glared at Aeub, his comment all but admitting guilt.

"I do not lay blame at the feet of The Academy. I lay blame at the feet of the Twelve," the King said, correcting the Sixth of the Twelve deceptively mildly, though no one was fooled by his sudden shift in tone. "Though I do agree with you, Warder Aeub. The Military does share some blame. Every Way Fort commander along The Road has either been arrested or executed. Ilsbruk has been busy gathering *so* much evidence."

A few Warders, all known loyalists of the Twelve tried to bluff their way past the Troopers at the exits. The rats were trying to abandon a sinking ship. Oleb thought the movement premature until legates pushed into the Hall, bearing sworn testimonials and began reading, the full power of the Klynsheim courts, which by law both Academy and King were accountable too, behind every word. The King had not been bragging. The Twelve had many witnesses to their crimes, in arrogance thinking that they were above suspicion and reproach. Way Fort commanders, smugglers, mine owners, even Academy Chapter House staff – all brought witness to the Twelve's crimes.

The Troopers shackled the Warders trying to escape the room and dragged them away. The King was bringing The Academy to heal and the leadership was going to be purged.

Sigsrata stood in triumph, his stern countenance marred by a bit of gloating.

"What say you in your defense?" the King demanded of the Twelve as the legates continued to read testimonies.

Some of the Twelve were shrunken upon their chairs, old men suddenly frightened as the implications of the legates' words were hammered home. Others still sat defiant, unwilling to show the least bit of concern to the King who they still felt was beneath them.

"Trooper, Soldier and Warder," the King said softly, his voice becoming very serious, the gloating erased from his features. "Defenders of the people. Not above the people, no one group better than the other. We all live to serve, not to be served."

"Noble words from a King whose life is as privileged as our own," Sevrug spat.

"True," Sigsrata agreed. "But I know my place. King, Military, Academy, Justicers. Four pillars of the land. Not one. Though I should point out that 'King' is first on that list."

The First of the Twelve opened his mouth to give a bitter retort but the King was no longer paying attention to him. Instead Sigsrata was staring so rigidly at the Warding Panel behind the Twelve that the King's muscles bulged from his neck. Sevrug turned in mounting horror to look at the panel, almost as if he knew what he would see there.

An emergency message came in from Itinerant Mage Eielson. The message was in the old style, more pictures and impressions than clear words. The meaning might have been clear enough even if another message did not override the first one. This second message was in the modern style, words clearly formed upon the panel.

Jebup, one of the King's Seven, a small, dark, lithe man with a well-oiled van dyke, ran into the room and saluted the King.

"Dispatches from Ilsbruk, Your Majesty. I apologize for the delay. We had them redirected from Central Command and getting the systems to integrate properly took some time. Mostly because some Warders were trying to block the messages on this end. They have been executed for endangerment of the Realm's defense."

Muttered words of fear and outrage rippled through the assemblage at those words.

Image joined the words on the display and Jens and Obel could clearly see a Trooper holding up a Warder's log book. The words in the journal seared through the hearts of both Trooper, Soldier and Warder alike as the King's words about Eielson's service became much more than an abstraction. Even the legates stilled, their testimonials paling next to the Warder Mage's log entry.

Uksaadle has fallen to a Darkness that dwells northeast of the settlement, as previously reported. I know my duty. I go to Ward The Darkness lest it spread.

"Warders do not fight," Obel said, shaking his head in disbelief. He was horrified as much by the idea of Eielson fighting as he was by the phrase 'as previously reported' and the fact that an entire settlement was lost.

"How do I tell his mother that Galeb's dead?" Jans asked, clearly distressed.

"That's what you're worried about now?" Obel demanded incredulously. "The Twelve have betrayed Klynsheim, The Academy is being held in the Hall under threat of death and an entire settlement has been lost to The Darkness. Out of all of that you focus on the need to tell Eielson's mother that her son idiotically went off to fight The Darkness by himself and was killed?"

Jans slapped him hard across the face. A nearby Trooper watched approvingly.

"Have you heard nothing?" Jans spat angrily. "Galeb fought The Darkness for eight years! By himself! No one who should have helped him did a septaed thing and in the end he was forced to continue to face The Darkness alone! He did his duty!"

Oleb put his hand to his stinging cheek in astonishment. Not at the slap or the speech. No. He was astonished that Jans seemed to be sincere in her anger. The Mages around them shifted away, torn between watching the argument and the message playing out on the Warding Panel. Oleb ignored Jans' anger and went back to watching the messages.

An image of Ilsbruk and the words 'A Ward Stands Alone' burned into everyone's eyes and the Troopers and Soldiers glared accusingly at the Warders, angry grumbles becoming more audible. The King looked to be actually crying, his hands gripping his great axe so tightly his knuckles were white.

The panel blanked for a moment and then a new image took shape. Ilsbruk appeared again, seeming to shout silently into the quick stick he was facing. Behind him were glimpses of struggling and dying Troopers as a Skrieksgrata smashed them down.

The Darkness has Risen! Seven miles north east of Uksaadle on the Great Trade Road. The Darkness is Risen!

The King screamed in fury and turned on the Twelve, cleaving Sevrug from head to crotch. The old Warders scrambled to escape the King's wrath, some trying to fend off the great axe with their staffs while others tried to flee. Most died by the King's axe bloody and broken in all their finery, their bodies strewn across the dais. Coreb was felled by a bolt when he tried to club Sigsrata from behind as the King beheaded Aeub.

"THE DARKNESS HAS RISEN!" roared the King. "Troopers and Soldiers arrest the rest of the conspirators!"

Twelve loyalists were dragged out of the Hall quickly and efficiently. A quarter of the Hall had been emptied.

"The rest of you," the King said, rounding on the Warder Mages still in the Hall. "Klynsheim has been betrayed and The Darkness has taken advantage. Tomorrow I go to see to the Ward Line in the North Lands. You are all coming with me. A Ward Stands Alone. I will not see his sacrifice be for nothing! Go, prepare for travel."

Pandemonium erupted in the Hall as Warders and students fled to their rooms under the watchful eyes of Troopers. Three more hundreds of Soldiers were spread out through The Academy and would form the heart of the force that would march with the King on the morrow. Tonight the Military made certain that no Warder sought to shirk their duty.

Chapter 11

Kieri was through the Wards and racing down to the valley floor as soon as she killed the kielsgruntara. She followed the flaring light at the center of the valley, knowing that if there was trouble, Galeb was certainly at the heart of it. But he was no fighter; Kieri could beat him blind folded on his best day. Her heart clenched at the thought.

Kieri tried to move faster, but Galeb wasn't making it easy for her. Kieri was forced to take shelter as the valley center erupted in a boiling inferno. When Kieri blinked her eyes clear, she caught glimpses of Galeb standing defiant before a host of kielsgruntara, the air around the Mage crackling with impossible energies.

Kieri froze in shock at the sight, trying to reconcile the Galeb she knew with the man hurtling The Darkness back, sending their bodies tumbling battered and broken. Then the lightning came followed by another fire storm and Kieri fell to the ground, whimpering in terror at the devastation Galeb wrought.

In the sudden silence that followed, Kieri didn't know whether to feel relief or dread, but worry pushed Kieri to her feet. Kieri slowed her movements, gathering the night around herself, moving not so much as a shadow, but more like an extension of the night air.

Her heart nearly stopped when she realized that several minutes had passed without a single flare of a new Ward. She headed in the direction of the last Ward that she had glimpsed and almost walked headlong in to The Darkness that was mincing its way unconcernedly toward the left valley wall. Kieri did not know who was more surprised, her or The Darkness. Both reacted swiftly, sword blocking claw strike. Kieri twisted away, moving to dodge the claws of the second hand which never lashed out.

Kieri was momentarily confused as to why the creature was fighting one handed until she noticed that The Darkness's other hand was clutching the forearm of a collapsed figure. The Darkness was dragging the body of a man – no, The Darkness was dragging Galeb! Kieri swept her blade in a dizzying attack that The Darkness dodged with patient grace, never once relinquishing its hold on the Mage.

When The Darkness spoke, Kieri was so surprised by the words that she stopped in mid attack. The words were matter of fact, almost sanguine.

"As you can see, the Itinerant Warder Mage and I are quite happy together. Since you did not take the first hint and die as I hoped you would, please take this piece of advice to heart. The Itinerant Warder Mage is mine. Go find your own plaything."

Kieri ground her teeth together in a feral snarl, and rebalanced herself.

"Galeb is not yours to take," she spat out, rage and - was that jealousy? - filling her voice.

"You will not speak his name!" The Darkness shrieked, indignant. "His name is for me. All for me.... I do not even speak his name. Not until he begs me to. I cannot wait until he pleads for me to say his name...."

The Darkness seemed to hug itself, as if the thought made it swoon with anticipation. Kieri was stunned by the tender, almost girlish mannerism. This was wrong, all wrong. It was as if the creature was infatuated with Galeb.

Kieri had the ludicrous thought that she hoped Galeb had not been leading The Darkness on. She almost giggled at the image of Galeb flirting with whatever this thing before her was. It was too dark to see it clearly. But then her eyes were drawn to Galeb's body and the silly thoughts stilled.

"No," Kieri countered softly. "He's mine."

She thrust with her sword as she spoke, reigniting the fight. The Darkness did not dodge the attack. It simply lifted Galeb's body and used him to block the thrust. Kieri watched in horror as the tip of her sword pierced the Klynsheimer's shoulder.

"There, I have let you have a taste of him as well. Be satisfied with it and get out of our way," The Darkness said, its voice the same, calm sibilance as it dropped Galeb's body back to the ground. "No?"

The beast let go of Galeb and crossed the distance between them with eye blurring speed, its claws reaching past the guard of Kieri's sword. That was when all septa broke loose.

Galeb's calculations were off. The Wards that he had bound around Kieri were not four feet out from her body. They were three. As the Shaeloman's hands passed the threshold of the Wards', molten ribbons of light flashed into existence. The burning reds and orange-whites of a forge fire flowed around the Obari woman as the Ward symbols thrummed with the ferocious intensity of a man maddened to desperation. The Shaeloman screamed in agony as the Wards tore at its body, hurtling it away to smash and tumble to a stop in the distance.

The Wards rippled and swam about Kieri, cooling to a white magnificence of fresh driven snow. Rivers of runes, intricately woven in skeins of cool perfection. Kieri was astounded and mesmerized by the Wards that seemed to be forever shifting, forever dancing around her, their colors changing with aching subtleties. The purest silver whites of a midnight moon reflecting off of a snow field flowed into the haughtily cold power of the stars. Diamonds glittered and sparked throwing off image of cold fire and deep lakes. All of it gathered around her with a terrible might that caused the very air to shiver and warp away from the Ward's luminance.

Kieri should have been terrified, but, somehow the Wards seemed to convey a gentle comfort and feeling of safety that Kieri only ever felt around Galeb. As she looked at herself bathed in the Ward light, Kieri briefly wondered if this was how Galeb thought of her. The Shaeloman's – Kieri now knew what it was; she had had a good enough look when the Wards flared to life and set some of its hair on fire – words broke her reverie.

"I could be jealous right now that the Itinerant Warder Mage has given you such a wondrous gift but I refuse to see it that way. No, this is not a gift for you. This is a gift for me. A wondrous challenge meant to wet my passion for him. He really is the dearest man," the Shaeloman said, stalking closer and looking at Galeb's body tenderly even as its fur continued to smoke from the cold heat of the Wardings.

Kieri shifted her position and stood over Galeb's body.

"He is not for you," Kieri said, throwing the creatures' words back at it. "He is mine and you shall not have him."

'You are a fool if you think that you can keep him, Obari," the Shaeloman said mockingly before launching another attack. "But to be fair, I will let you try."

The Wards crackled around Kieri, becoming colder, clearer, and sharper, hissing as all warmth was bled from the air. Kieri smiled.

"You will be disappointed," she promised, gliding forward, her sword poised and ready.

Bob and Kawen found themselves a place to stand against the madness of The Darkness and the Wardings that had shifted the tide of battle. The place happened to be under a dead fall well clear of the fighting and just inside the Valley. Both were wrapped in darkness and doing their best imitations of rocks.

Bob still had his spear, gripping the weapon tightly. There were makeshift bandages on his neck, arm, and leg and he was a little wild eyed. Kawen was in better shape though he was down to a knife and what might have been the lower half of a spear shaft. It was hard to tell and Bob was afraid to ask. Kawen had this maniacal gleam in his eyes and looked ready to stab or beat anything larger than a mouse.

Both men were staring down into the valley where they could just make out their cousin in the night. The fact that Kieri seemed to be glowing was admittedly beneficial to identifying her position.

"That's not natural," Kawen eventually hissed.

"An illusion is an illusion," Bob tried to say casually. The tremor in his voice ruined the effect. "I've made bobwhites that were more realistic."

"That's not an illusion, Bob. Kieri is actually glowing," Kawen said, barely suppressing a hysterical giggle.

"She's fighting something," Bob pointed out helpfully. "Should we go help her?

Both men winced as the light surrounding their cousin flared brighter and The Darkness was smashed backwards.

"She seems to be doing alright on her own," Kawen pointed out. "I'd hate to distract her."

"That's a good point, Kawen," Bob agreed, nestling in a little deeper.

Chapter 12

Obel just wanted to leave the Assembly Hall. Jans had a different idea, moving back down the stairs to where the King still stood in front of the Ward Panel as image continued to form and then fade. Mostly image of Troopers fighting and dying. Obel followed Jans, having no real idea why other than the vague thought that Jans was good at sniffing out opportunity.

Blood covered Sigsrata, dripping from his great axe and from his clothing though he didn't seem to notice. Jebup was standing nearby, glancing at his King as the member of the Seven issued orders to a continuous line of messengers and officers. Ward Law was being enacted, the kingdom being put in a state of emergency. Already the warning bells could be heard tolling, calling the people to their neighborhood assembly points to hear the news and prepare for the coming conflict.

Scenes continued to play across the Warding Panel. Troopers died and Ilsbruk strangled a kielsgruntara. Than The Darkness seemed to suddenly shrink back as small bunches of light flared across the scene.

"What am I seeing?" the King demanded, barely glancing at Jans as she stopped a respectful distance away.

Jans studied the image but it was Obel who answered, being first to recognize the meaning of the light.

"Wardings," Obel explained, sounding a little condescending, which was normal for him. "Where ever the Troopers are fighting, the area just went active with Wardings."

"Then there is hope yet," the King said softly. "I didn't look forward to telling Betney that her husband was dead."

"Eielson's Wardings, but the look of it," Jans explained, studying the image more closely. "His style always favored the more basic runes."

"Whose else's would they be, Warder Mage?" the King asked, quirking an eyebrow. "Didn't you hear me say earlier that Eielson was the only Mage working the Line?"

"Of course, Your Majesty," Jans said, embarrassed and apologizing, looking away and then looking back with a sick look on her face.

Troopers were gathering the heads of the Twelve, putting the loose ones in a sack and separating the few still attached with efficient sawing motions. The heads would be taken to Traitor's Square and allowed to rot in full view of the public.

"What do you want, Warder Mage....?"

"Journeyman Mage Jans Sepsrigga," Jans said, introducing herself with a curtsey.

"Journeyman Mage Obel Jargsin," Obel said, introducing himself though the King had not asked him his name.

"What do you want?" the King demanded, turning his attention back to the panel.

"To be of service," Jans said, trying to seem as sincere as possible.

The King was not fooled. He knew that Jans was just looking to secure her position.

"Warders were better once," the King said, sadly, as he shook his head. "We were all better once. The quick stick just shifted its vantage. I thought that I saw a valley, but now all I see is this...? What am I looking at now?"

Jans glanced at the panel ready to give an answer and froze, unsure of what was happening. The inky image on the panel seemed to be...roiling. Almost as if what was being recorded by the quick stick was overwhelming the ability of the Ward network to handle and interpret.

Obel was frowning next to her. Jans knew that her friend had many faults but his mind was quick and his reasoning usually flawless. Seeing him confounded was almost funny, though Jans did not dare laugh in the King's presence. She could still hear the blood dripping off of the axe and hitting the floor.

Whatever was wrong with the display seemed to resolve itself because the panel cleared, a new image forming. No longer was there a scene of desperate Troopers or unexpected Wardings blossoming to life. Instead there was a solitary figure as if seen from a distance.

"Eielson," the King muttered, recognizing the Mage first.

"Oh my God," Jans breathed, her eyes widening in disbelief and horror.

"The Ward stands alone," Obel breathed, shaking his head incredulous, not a trace of his usual arrogance in his words.

Much of the scene was black, with only a small area around Eielson in light. Not surprising since it was night. All around Eielson, at the edges of whatever was illuminating his position moved kielsgruntara. Dozens of The Darkness pushing forward to overwhelm the Mage.

Then...then the impossible. The blackness of the panel faded away revealing hundreds of kielsgruntara, not attacking, but dying. Stylized lightning rippled across The Darkness, tearing huge holes in the heaving mass of the beasts.

"His hands. Look at his hands!" hissed Obel, pointing wildly.

"What?" Jans asked in confusion, tearing her eyes away from the destruction.

"Explain," demanded Sigsrata, his gaze darting over the scene.

"Wards. I don't know how, Your Majesty. There are Wards flaring all around his hands.   Dozens of Wards all at once."

"That one there," breathed Jans, pointing. Now that she knew what she was looking for the runes were easier to identify. "That's 'Petting a Cat in Wool'. And the one next to it is 'Fevers the Air'. I can't tell what the other ones are...."

"What kind of name is 'Petting a Cat in Wool'?" asked the King, perplexed.

"A child's rune, Your Majesty," Jans explained. "One of the first Wards taught to students. The name is meant to help young children understand both the purpose of the rune and maintain interest in their studies. Eielson was always fascinated with the basic Wards. He claimed that they had more potential than simple introductory teachings."

"He may have been right," Obel admitted, though he wasn't happy at the admission.

"What does the Ward accomplish?" asked the King.

"It creates static," Obel answered with a grunt. "A way of showing new students that the energy of the Wards can come from anywhere."

The lightning was replaced with fire and all three momentarily turned away from the carnage.

"Can anyone else do this?" the King asked, gesturing with the great axe, which caused both Mages to wince as drops of blood flew through the air.

"I- we don't even know what Eielson *is* doing," Jans said, shaking her head.

The King opened his mouth to ask another question but stopped as they witnessed Eielson's fall to the Shaeloman.

"A Ward Stood Alone," the King snarled, tears once again in his eyes. "You will not speak of what you saw here until we can unravel Eielson's secrets. In the meantime, you are both attached to my service personally. I fear there is much that you will need to explain to me once we reach the Ward Line."

Obel quirked an eyebrow, too wrapped up in trying to puzzle out Eielson's abilities to feel much at the Mage's death. Jans just shook her head.

"He deserved better," Jans said softly, shaking her head. No Mage deserved to die alone beyond the Wards.

"He died as he lived," Sigsrata acknowledged, clenching his jaw. "In service alone, with no one or nothing to support him. The old woman was right... This is a shame that I will not forget, forgive, or see repeated."

Jans looked at her King. The man's feelings were genuine, his pain raw. She had only ever seen Sigsrata as an object of belittlement by the Twelve. For the first time Jans wondered what the King was really like and if the civilians saw the King as the Twelve had or as someone better.

"What old woman, Your Majesty?" Jans asked, curious.

"One of the villages along the Ward Line that Ilsbruk visited," The King explained. "An old woman there wanted to know when a new Warder Mage was going to be sent. She was tired of watching 'a broken man who was too stupid to realize that he was already dead' or something like that."

Jans pondered the King's words and tried to imagine what Galeb must have been like to have warranted such a harsh opinion. She couldn't; her life had never been particularly difficult. But there was something that she could do for Eielson.

"His mother lives in the city in South Wall Quarter," Jans informed the King, somehow realizing that Sigsrata would like to know.

"I would see her know of her son's deeds, but all I can offer her is a missive and a medal since I have to head to the Ward Line. Cold comfort," the King said, closing his eyes in frustration.

"She will also have any accumulated pay," Obel said pragmatically. "It didn't look like Eielson spent much of it."

"You are an ass," hissed Jans, flushing in anger. "A man dies and all you can think about is his pay?"

"We are all who we are, Jans," said Obel, with a shrug, still staring at the Warding panel as if it would give up the secret to Eielson's abilities. "You aren't a saint either."

"There is no accumulated pay," Sigsrata said, shaking his head and spitting in the general direction of the Twelve's bodies. "That miserable lot ensured that Eielson never had a dime. The Chapter House records were full of the excuses for why his pay was continually docked."

"That's not right!" Jans yelled, insulted, truthfully more for herself than Eielson. Fair compensation was a Warder's right.

"Don't be naïve," Obel snapped. "No pay meant that Eielson's position was that much weaker. He was more controllable with fewer means to protest his situation."

"Never again," the King swore softly, turning to call for scribe. Medals and commendation would be issued as swiftly as possible. There was also the matter of informing the populace that the Twelve were dead and branded traitors.

Chapter 13

The Shaeloman did not erupt in anger and blindly attack as Kieri had hoped. Instead it threw back its head and laughed, the sound full of desire and admiration.

"I can understand your obsession with the Itinerant Warder Mage," the Shaeloman said companionably as the laughter died. "His endless surprises are quite endearing. His uniqueness is mesmerizing. What other man could weave Wards of light around another being? What other Warder Mage would have the audacity to be so innovative? He makes me dizzy with delight every time he does something like this. Blessed is the day when fortune brought him to the North Country and into my life."

Kieri had never heard of a Darkness acting this way.

The attacks, when they came, were probing, methodical, as the Shaeloman tested the Wardings. Kieri met each attack that she could with blade and Ward, driving the creature back. The air was filled with the popping crackles of energy and the unnerving sound of claw scratching across steel. The smell of burnt hair assaulted Kieri's lungs as she took deeper breaths to keep up with The Darkness's assault.

Her jaw clenched in determination as she danced the blade's edge all around The Darkness, trying to find an opening and being frustrated again and again. Sweat was beginning to pour from her skin and she clenched her teeth tighter, wanting to hurt the creature.

They were almost a hundred yards away from Galeb before Kieri realized what The Darkness was doing. She cursed as she turned to run back to his side, depending on the Wardings to protect her. She had faith in Galeb and she would have to have faith in his workings.

Everything fell apart in that moment. Two Skrieksgrata, unnoticed by Kieri up until this point, were lumbering into position to prevent her return to Galeb's side. Galeb chose that moment to stagger to his feet and limp directly into the Skrieksgrata's path. Kieri and the Shaeloman both screamed at the same time, horror shredding the word ragged.

"NO!"

Get up. Get up NOW!

The words hammered in Galeb's mind as he rolled onto his side, wracked in pain and watched the Skrieksgrata lumbering down the from the forest, having abandoned their attack on the Troopers. They were making their way towards where Kieri was fighting the Shaeloman, surrounded by the coldest, crispest moonlight of the Wards.

My Queen in winter.

The thought brought a smile to Galeb's mouth. He always loved Kieri's moonlit illusions. The smile faded into a rictus of pain as he forced himself to stand. Something was broken inside of him. But he didn't dare give into the pain.

All around him was the destruction that his deep weavings had wrought, but in the end, those Wards were overwhelmed by use. The Wardings that he had woven around Kieri were still shining bright, but would they withstand the repeated attacks of a Shaeloman and two Skrieksgrata? He couldn't risk it.

He did not walk; he staggered towards The Darkness, trying to gather a shred of power into him so that he could shape a Ward, any Ward. His body protested but his mind pushed, trying to draw in enough energy.

Please, Please, Please!

Galeb begged and his body became wracked with spasms, overwrought. He fell to his knees and almost passed out. Somehow he staggered back upright, swaying with effort, blood and sweat pouring off of him in pink rivulets.

Please, just one more Warding.

He raised his arms, the limbs rigid with spasms, motes of light forming between his hands. There was only one Ward that he could focus on, his first and favorite. He poured every ounce of himself left into the shaping hoping it would be enough. Galeb screamed as the Ward solidified, feeling as if the rune was tearing itself free from his skin, like jagged glass squeezing through every pore.

The Skrieksgrata collided with 'The Way is Shut'. For a moment the air seemed to shudder in trepidation before ripping open with a roar of light and sound unmatched by Galeb's screaming.

Kieri and the Shaeloman watched horrified as Warder and Darkness collided. The concussive blast sent a wave of air buffeting over them. The Skrieksgrata hurtled backwards, bones shattered in their arms and chest, crashing into the earth with deep thuds.

Galeb flew through the air as well, smashing into the earth before cartwheeling air born again and falling back to the ground in a rolling, limp tumble nearly fifty yards from where he had been standing.

Bob and Kawen materialized from the night, striking at the dazed and wounded pig apes, stabbing with spear and knife in frenzied determination. If Kieri was not mistaken, Kawen was screaming in terror as he plunged a knife repeatedly in a Skrieksgrata's throat. Bob was simply flailing desperately with his spear stabbing the ground as much as the beast he was attacking.

The Shaeloman sighed, looked at the Obari men's antics, and then glanced at the head of the valley, shaking its head in disappointment. Troopers could be seen emerging from the tree line, glancing hesitantly into the valley.

"My lovely boy puts his heart and soul into crafting his Wards. There was no appreciation among the villagers. While I found Uksaadle's death throes so thrilling I was also angry on his behalf," admitted the Shaeloman. "He took so much time and effort to ensure the safety of those people and they did not even bother to secure their gate properly. It was like using a priceless porcelain vase as a chamber pot."

The Shaeloman shrugged, shaking its head at the absurdity of the villagers' behavior before turning to face Kieri head on, a tall, lithe figure of hair, claw, and fangs.

"I don't have the luxury of time to fight you for him this night. We'd be interrupted long before I managed to find a hole in those Wards. The Itinerant Warder Mage is also badly hurt. I would not see him die yet and do not have the luxury of caring for him.

"I'll allow you to keep him for me for a time. Nurse him back to health, but do no more than that. He is *mine* and I will be coming to reclaim him."

The creature stepped back, howled, and then spun away and loped off into the night, disappearing from sight. The Wards around Kieri slowly dimmed and faded as the threat faded into the distance. Kieri ran over to Galeb, falling to her knees as she tried to assess his wounds.

"Just what have you been doing to warrant such horrific attention?" she asked him and then added, "It better not be your girlfriend."

A spasming laugh greeted Kieri's statement and for a brief moment Galeb's eyes met hers.

"You stabbed me," Galeb said accusingly.

The man had at least one broken arm, two broken legs, and countless other wounds and he would have to fixate on one minor puncture.

"I didn't do it on purpose," Kieri scowled. "Besides, you're lucky that's all I did to you. You warded me without a single 'by your leave'!"

188

"Beautiful, aren't they," Galeb grunted, coughing with a deep rattle in his chest. "I wanted them to compliment you."

"So you think I'm beautiful?" Kieri smiled, trying to hide her fear. Galeb was injured so badly. She wasn't certain that she could help him.

Galeb didn't answer. He was unconscious, which was probably a blessing

"Septa it!" Kieri shrieked. "You could have at least answered the question!"

Chapter 14

Captain Ilsbruk sat astride a horse, one of a dozen or so that the Troopers had managed to round up, the job made harder by the lightning that had sundered the night and the blast of air that had surged briefly through the trees. He was surveying the small valley where so much death had come from. Troopers streamed by him, moving out in search patterns to flush out any remaining Darkness, not that he was expecting the men to find any. The Darkness could have destroyed his command but chose not to, disappearing into the night as suddenly as they had attacked. He wouldn't even still be here himself if he didn't need to find the Mage.

He had lost nearly two hundreds of men. Eighty horses. Thirty war dogs. The worst losses in decades. Reinforcements were starting to trickle in from the nearest Way Forts. Ilsbruk didn't know if he should be bitter that the Troopers arrived too late to help in the fight or relieved that the men had been spared the slaughter.

As he gazed out over the valley floor he watched twisting bands of light shining through the night and could hear the cries of more kielsgruntara panicking as they fought to break free from the Wards entrapping them. Ilsbruk was unsure what those Wards were exactly or how they had been fashioned. Either The Academy was hiding abilities or The Academy leadership had no true understanding of their own Warders' potential. One was potentially treasonous, the other was a sign of stupidity. All the more reason why he needed to find the Mage.

The Captain eventually descended into the valley after giving Gorgorin orders to study those Wards closely before they faded – if they faded - and to dispatch The Darkness trapped within. Ilsbruk was surrounded by a guard of about twenty, searching the night for threats and hoping to find none.

The Captain rode through the valley slowly, lit by Ward and flickering fire, his horse snorting at the smell of charred flesh and churned earth. He was seeking a moment to clear his head and make sense of the attack when he stumbled across an Obari woman tending to an unconscious Eielson.

The Mage was mass of torn and broken parts. Ilsbruk might have been daunted by the sheer number of wounds if he had not recently seen Troopers and horses brutalized by Skrieksgrata. Which reminded him. Two very freaked out Obari men were hiding nearby, if the reports were to be believed. There were certainly two Skrieksgrata corpses that looked like they had been more mauled in blind panic than purposely slain. Best to be cautious.

As the Captain dismounted and walked over to the Warder and Obari, signaling for someone to find a corpsman, if there were any still alive, to attend to the Warder Mage, he was surprised by the Obari woman's words.

"I've had quite enough of people trying to take Galeb away from me tonight, Klynsheimer. I am in no mood to let you try if that is your intent," the young woman said, slowly standing and assuming a fighting stance, her sword pointed meaningfully at Ilsbruk.

Ilsbruk looked at the Obari, shocked to see that there did not seem to be a shred of illusion clinging to her, glanced at Galeb, and then looked back at the Obari woman, quirking an eyebrow. Eielson still had a few surprises in him.

"Are you married?" he asked politely.

"Not yet," she answered cautiously, quirking an eyebrow at him in return, a subtle challenge.

"Does he know that?"

"He will when he wakes up," the Obari said matter-of-factly. "Though there seems to be some disagreement as to who will have him."

"I can assure you that I have no such designs," Ilsbruk joked, smiling.

"I wasn't talking about you, Klynsheimer. There's a particularly possessive Shaeloman out in the dark somewhere who made it very clear that she would be coming back for him," the Obari woman explained. "And you really shouldn't try to smile. It doesn't look right on you."

"How do you know it's a she?" Ilsbruk asked, turning towards several men and appraising them of the danger. He chose to ignore the comment about his smiles.

The men rode off, raising the alarm, appraising the others of the specific threat. More Troopers replaced the men, doubling the guard around the immediate area. Not that there were that many Troopers to spare. A corpsman approached, but made no move to go to the Warder Mage, instead eyeing the Obari's sword cautiously. There were plenty of other wounded who needed the corpsman's help. He would rather not waste his time if the woman was intent on stabbing him.

"I don't. I just prefer to hope that it is a female based on the way it was acting," explained the woman, deadpan.

"Oh, that is gross," Ilsbruk said, shuddering.

"You have no idea," the woman said, grimacing. "Is that corpsman of yours going to stand their all night staring at me or is he going to help patch up Galeb? He's bleeding from several areas and if I tear any more cloth away from my dress for bandages this whole situation is going to get a whole lot more indecent than it needs to be."

"He is waiting for you to put your sword away," Ilsbruk explained. "And I should point out that if you are worried about decency you shouldn't be standing so that Eielson can look right up your dress when he wakes up."

"I know. Why do you think I am standing here," said the woman with a grin, shifting her stance slightly wider. "I don't mind him seeing under my dress, just you lot."

Ilsbruk laughed, shaking his head. "My name is Captain Ilsbruk," he offered.

"Kieri Sonovonol," she answered with a dip of her head, as she sheathed her sword. She glanced back at the Mage, worry clear upon her face. "He's hurt badly. I'll kill you if you bring him more harm."

The corpsman hesitated again until Ilsbruk waived him forward impatiently.

"I don't mean him any harm," Ilsbruk said reassuringly.

The earlier grin that had played across the Obari's face was not even a ghost of a memory as she looked him in the eye.

Something overwhelmingly defiant stood in its place, fickle and unforgiving.

"You mean him no harm? I'm to trust your word when clearly Galeb didn't?"

Ilsbruk scowled at the accusation. He had done nothing to break trust with the Mage and said so. Kieri twisted her lips in a mocking smile.

"Galeb decided to confront The Darkness alone. Why did he do that, Klynsheimer Captain of the Seven? Tell me what would drive a Mage to leave the Wards and face The Darkness on its own terms when The Road is full of Way Forts? Why didn't Galeb seek the assistance of Troopers?"

"He knew his duty. Clearly the threat couldn't wait," Ilsbruk began, , barely registering the fact that the Obari knew his rank, hating the words as soon as they left his mouth. He had a fair idea why Eielson had not sought aid from the Way Forts but was unwilling to discuss the failings of The Road security with an Obari.

"Warders don't fight!   Isn't that what you Klynsheimers believe? Isn't that what you Troopers always claim?" Kieri hissed through clenched teeth, her gaze condemning Ilsbruk.

"That's true," Ilsbruk agreed, carefully reigning in his own temper. His men had fought and died upon this ground. They deserved no accusations. But he knew that it was important to let Kieri have her say and he found himself unwilling to continue with the lie he had started to speak.

"Then why did he fight? Answer me, Captain of the Seven! Why did I have to teach Galeb the knife? Why did my cousins have to teach him the staff? Why did Galeb have to stand here getting carved up by a Shaeloman?" Kieri demanded, shaking in her anger. "You are his People! How could you do this to him?!"

Ilsbruk clenched his jaw, letting the questions and accusations wash over him.

"*We* did nothing but come to Eielson's aid," Ilsbruk pointed out, quirking an eyebrow and daring the Obari woman to challenge this claim. "Hundreds of my men were killed or wounded battling The Darkness. Do not lay the failures of others, however disgraceful those failures may be, on these men."

Ilsbruk had not wanted to discuss the failings of Road security but the Obari woman seemed determined to drag it out of him.

"Perhaps not," Kieri acknowledged, noting the restrained anger in Ilsbruk's face and words. "But answer me one last question, Captain of the Seven."

"What?" Ilsbruk asked impatiently, wondering what blame the Obari would seek to lay upon his men this time.

"If your men are so true to their purpose, to their duty, why does Galeb fear them so much that he found facing The Darkness alone preferable to seeking their help?" Kieri asked softly.

Nta. Nta. Nta. He did not want to be having this discussion and certainly did not like the idea that the Obari were apparently well aware of how bad the defenses on The Road had degraded. Ilsbruk was also concerned; just what had the Way Forts done to the Mage to make him afraid of all Troopers? He hadn't been able to ferret out that information during his investigations.

"How can a man who did this," Ilsbruk asked, trying to distract away from the woman's question as he gestured to the mass of dead Darkness littering the valley, backlit by smoldering fires, "be afraid?"

Kieri looked to where Ilsbruk gestured and then gave him a pitying look.

"How couldn't he be afraid?" she asked, so softly Ilsbruk had to strain to hear her. "This was not some heroic stand, Captain Ilsbruk of the Seven.   This was desperation."

Ilsbruk looked at the unconscious Mage being tended by the corpsman. The corpsman looked anything but confident the more he examined the Mage's injuries with the help of two other Troopers. Ilsbruk thought back to his first meeting with Eielson and looked again at the burnt and splintered Darkness.

Desperation. He would have said reckless courage and rampant stupidity. He wouldn't have considered desperation. Now he wasn't so certain. A thought occurred to him.

"Were you travelling with the Mage?" Ilsbruk asked, turning to face Kieri again.

"No," the Obari woman said, shaking her head. "We were following behind, half a day at most."

"He cares for you?" he asked.

"He is mine," Kieri said defiantly through clenched teeth, daring Ilsbruk to challenge her claim. "He is also my friend."

"I have travelled this Road, Sonovonol, from one end to the other," Ilsbruk said, with a sigh, placing his hands behind his back in parade rest. "You are the first and only person among everyone I have spoken to who would claim friendship with the Mage."

"Then everyone you've spoken to are fools," Kieri said defensively, looking at Galeb, and jerking her eyes away as she took in the enormity of his wounds.

"Perhaps," Ilsbruk acknowledged. "But I wouldn't be surprised if you're the only one to claim friendship because you are, in fact, his only friend."

The idea did not sit well with Ilsbruk, but there it was. Eight years of service and the Mage probably only had one person who would mourn his passing, which might be sooner than was convenient by the bleak look on the corpsman's face. The corpsman seemed to be running out of splints for all of the broken bones.

"He has *me*," Kieri whispered fiercely, tears in her eyes. "I'm all he needs."

"As you said," Ilsbruk said, acknowledging Kieri's words and hating himself for what he said next. "This was an act of desperation. Eielson has one person who cares about him in the entire world and that person is following a half day behind him, walking towards a mass of Darkness. What would you have done in his place?"

"So this is my fault?!" Kieri demanded, whirling to face Ilsbruk, anger, pain and uncertainty clear upon her face.

"No," Ilsbruk assured her. "This is not your fault. The Darkness should never have been able to gather here in such numbers.

"But it was and Eielson was faced with an impossible decision. He did what he felt he needed to do to save you."

"He can't die," Kieri said, tears pooling in her eyes.

"No," Ilsbruk agreed, but with a mild correction, "We can't afford to have him die."

The corpsman jerked slightly at these words, looked at Eielson's body then at Ilsbruk and back again at the Mage. The man was making no promises.

"Nor can we afford to stay here," Ilsbruk said gently. "The Darkness chose to go, we didn't drive it away. It will be back."

"The Shaeloman said it would be coming back for Galeb," Kieri said, wiping at the tears angrily.

"In that, the Ward has done us no favors," Ilsbruk said, shaking his head.

"It isn't Galeb's fault!" Kieri said fiercely, staring up at Ilsbruk, daring him to lay blame upon Eielson.

"No, Eielson didn't bring this Darkness," Ilsbruk said, reminding the Obari woman that he already agreed with her. "But he has challenged it. The Shaeloman is already interested in the Mage. Other Darkness will learn of what happened here and come looking to pit themselves against Eielson. The Darkness loves a challenge."

"The Darkness has Risen," Gorgorin said in agreement, as he walked up, cleaning his hand axe. The reminder was chilling.

"There is also that," Ilsbruk agreed.

The attack had been too calculated, too coordinated to be a single event. History gave warning; when The Darkness Rose it was never a singular attack, but a campaign. The Darkness would throw itself against Klynsheimer defenses until sated and satisfied with the destruction.

"How soon before we can move him?" Ilsbruk asked the corpsman.

The other wounded were being put on make shift travois. Eielson would receive the same treatment. Not ideal but the best that they could do until the Troopers managed to bring up some wagons.

The corpsman ran a hand through his hair and then jerked his head to the side, asking the Captain to join him a few feet away, out of ear shot of Kieri.

"Begging your pardon, Sir," the corpsman said, running another hand through his hair. The man was young, on the short side, but with crow's feet at the corners of his eyes and a face that looked like seriousness was not its normal expression. "But we probably shouldn't be moving him at all."

Ilsbruk nodded his understanding and lifted an eyebrow, indicating that he wanted further elaboration as to the problem.

The corpsman looked away and then looked at Ilsbruk from the corner of his eyes as he decided how exactly to explain the situation. He sighed and then launched into his explanation full force.

"Both legs are broken, the right one in multiple locations. Right wrist is broken as well. Left arm broken and dislocated from the shoulder. There are deep slashes across his back and cuts and bite marks across the Mage's hands, legs, torso and face. His ribs seem to be miraculously intact, but his breathing doesn't sound right," the corpsman said, looking away again.

"What else?" Ilsbruk asked, knowing that there was more from the corpsman's attitude.

The man swallowed nervously, but nodded acknowledgement of the question.

"Scars pretty much everywhere, Sir. The Mage has seen a lot of fighting. Years of it if I had to guess. It's not right, the man shouldn't have - sorry, Sir, not my place," the corpsman said shaking his head and raising a hand in apology before continuing. "I'm not certain all of those wounds healed properly. Especially his right hip; it took a lot of trauma at one point. That I can tell didn't heal right. It might have been re-damaged during this fight. I don't have the skills to tell."

"Were any of the old wounds properly treated?" Ilsbruk asked, dreading the fact that he was almost certain that he knew the answer.

"Treated, yes, probably by the Mage himself by the looks of things. Not properly, though," the corpsman said, swallowing nervously again.

Eielson should have received proper medical care at any of the Way Forts. Obviously the man had avoided doing so either by choice or...more likely was refused treatment. Every time Ilsbruk thought that he was gaining an understanding of how deeply the corruption and neglect went on The Road, there always seemed to be more waiting to be discovered.

"Sir," the corpsman started to speak, stopped, coughed, and then tried again. Obviously the man was deeply troubled by something he had found on Eielson's body.

"Speak," Ilsbruk commanded, growing impatient.

"Yes, Sir," the corpsman said, straightening and coughing nervously one last time. "Not all of the scars are Darkness wrought. The Mage was beaten pretty badly at one point by a swagger stick."

Ilsbruk closed his eyes and cursed softly, but viciously. A swagger stick was a punishment device employed by the Military to impose discipline. Basically a one inch thick rod of wood that would be beaten into the back of a man tied to a post for severe transgressions. Not a punishment to be used on a Mage who undoubtedly did not deserve punishment of any kind.

Ilsbruk suddenly had an answer to the Obari woman's question of why Eielson had asked her and her folk to teach him how to fight. Why Eielson had not sought help from the Way Forts when Uksaadle fell. Why the Mage had been so withdrawn when he first met Ilsbruk.

"We have to move him," Ilsbruk said, returning to the matter at hand. Everything else would have to wait.

"I know, Sir, but it's not a good idea. The Mage's body can't take being jostled about right now. He needs better treatment than I can give him," the corpsman said plaintively.

"We don't have a choice. The Darkness will return and we dare not face it here, exposed beyond the Ward Line," Ilsbruk said, shaking his own head. "Patch him up the best that you can. We'll carry him out on a stretcher. Reduce the movement to a minimum. Hopefully we can get wagons before moving him too far."

"Yes, Sir," the corpsman said, acknowledging the order and moving back to the Mage to double check his stitching and look for any other wounds that he might have missed.

Kieri was no longer watching the corpsman work. She was staring at Ilsbruk, silently judging him and all his People.

Chapter 15

The first bells that had pierced the night air of the capital had roused a suddenly panicked people from their beds or revelry to gather in the local muster points to hear the news that all Klynsheimers had feared since the founding of the kingdom. The bells were enough to inform everyone that The Darkness threatened; people desperately wanted to know where and in what numbers.

King's Speakers had been slow in coming, well over two hours since the bells had begun ringing until the first of the bright blue liveried men stepped up to the speaking blocks in the center of the lamp lit squares. The crowds hushed as the Speakers, all men chosen for their deep, carrying voices, unfurled proclamations from the King. Every proclamation bore a black and red ribbon, signifying the dreadful importance of the news.

Tynes Bottom Square, in the second section wall side of the fourth quadrant of the South Wall, was no different. People stood in rapt attention as Koring, King's Speaker and local son stood proudly and began to speak, his voice echoing off the walls of the surrounding buildings.

"People of Klynsheim, be aware that on this day, Second day of Second Week of Fourth Month of the Summer Season, Ward Law is in full effect!"

"Tell us something we don't know!" shouted a voice in the crowd.

There were a few half-hearted laughs that were quickly hushed. Koring glanced at the crowd in annoyance, saw his Aunt

Corinne gesturing for him to continue and prepared to do so. Koring liked his aunt – a small, worn woman who ran a modest tap room and had nothing but support for all her kin. Not that her kin always appreciated her efforts. His selfish cousin for one....

"The Darkness has Risen along the Northern Ward Line, also known as the Great Trade Road," Koring called out as the crowd listened now with rapt attention. "The settlement Uksaadle has fallen and the King now musters an army to march to secure the rest of the Ward Line."

Cries of disbelief and horror rippled through the crowd.

"Attend!" Koring bellowed.

"Attend!" cried his three assistants.

"Attend!" Koring cried one last time, as was ritual for importing the next bit of news. "Let all hear and Truth be known! On this Second day of the Second Week of the Fourth Month of the Summer Season the leadership of the Warders' Academy, also known as the Twelve, have been charged with fifty three accounts of smuggling, twenty three accounts of corruption of Military officers, one count of willful neglect against the security of the realm and one count of treason against the Klynsheim people!"

Shouting erupted at the accusations

"Attend!" Koring and his associates cried, eventually silencing the tumult. "Be it known that the Twelve willfully weakened the Northern defenses and that neglect led to the death of an entire settlement..."

The speech was a good one, probably the best one ever written with such short notice. Koring himself was in fine form, from his neatly pressed uniform that was admittedly starting to bulge a bit tightly in the middle, to his stylishly cut sandy hair and perfectly curled mustache. People hung on his every word and he loved it. He could have done with a better topic, but beggars couldn't be choosers...

He was only interrupted twice more. Once with the announcement that the King had executed the Twelve. Equal grumbles about that one, some in favor and some against. The other time was when he announced that the heads of the Twelve were being mounted in Traitor's Square, their possessions forfeit, their families fined and their lives placed upon Restriction. Fourth Quadrant was working class and enjoyed when the rich got a bit of a comeuppance; the people cheering loudly at the announcement.

Business finished, Koring turned to descend the block and leave the square. A single bell toll stopped him in mid stride. The Mourning Bell was ringing, a dreadfully pure, unmistakable sound. Someone important had died and the bell surely wasn't ringing for the Twelve. The crowd, which had also begun to disperse froze and came back into the square, looking to see if Koring had more news.

He didn't. He looked at his assistants in confusion and they shook their heads. They were as confused as he was.

Then a drum sounded low in the distance, growing louder. The crowd parted as a Military Speaker, with full escort of assistants, drummers, and banner men, their banners furled, approached through the crowd. The Military Speaker was dressed in gleams of gold wrought red over a uniform of black. The man walked ram rod straight, a bit older than Koring, with dustings of silver in his hair. His uniform was also snug, not from a growing waist line but from being expertly tailored to the man's muscular frame. His face was impassively stern, his gray eyes flashing in the lamp light.

"Always have to make an entrance, don't you Geb," Koring said with a slightly mocking smile as he approached his rival. All Military and King's Speakers were rivals, some more good naturedly than others.

Instead of rising to the bait, Geb glanced over to Koring with a look of compassion in his eyes. Koring's eyes widened in surprise at the unexpected emotion.

"Go find your aunt, Koring," Geb said softly.

"What's going on, Geb?" Koring asked confused.

"Just...just go find your aunt," Geb repeated, shaking his head slightly as he marched up to the speaker's block, the banner men and assistants flanking him. There was more than a bit of troubled emotion on the Military Speaker's face, as if what he was about to impart affected him greatly.

The drummer continued to maintain an easy beat, softening it as the Speaker looked out over the crowd. The Mourning Bell pealed one last time before silencing.

"People of Klynsheim!" Geb began, his voice rolling over the crowd in the sudden silence, his arms raised over his head.

Koring could not help but admire Geb's skill as he made his way through the crowd, looking for his aunt with a growing sense of unease.

"Attend now and hear the Reading of the Roll of Honor for a fallen Son of Klynsheim," Geb continued, his hands now folded in front of him in reverence, his gaze fierce as it swept over the crowd.

Koring froze mid-stride and glanced towards the block in surprise. There hadn't been a Reading in over ten years, not since the Old Queen died.

"Honor him, in word and deed. Value him for duty and loyalty. Mourn him, for we are lessened. Remember him, for we are lost."

Geb actually choked on the last words before gathering himself.

Koring wanted to admire a bit of theater, but almost suspected that the choking hadn't been faked.

"Hear now. Know now. Far to the north beyond the districts of the Caping Bow, far from Noble's Deep and Kering Way, upon the Great Trade Road of the Northern Ward Line Ilsbruk of the Seven a Warder Mage found.

"'Fair thee met', did Ilsbruk say, 'Where does thou walk upon this day?' 'Upon The Road', the Warder Mage did reply, 'Six hundred miles ere I end my days'."

"Six hundred miles for one man!" called out an assistant.

"Six hundred miles to Ward and ware!" another roared.

"Six hundred miles upon the battle line, with fighting knife and staff held high between The Darkness bold and Klynsheim hold."

Disbelief rippled through the crowd at the impossibility of a Mage fighting. Shock and a growing sense of outrage followed in its wake as people tried to comprehend the sheer amount of Warding laid at the feet of one man.

"Ilsbruk now, of noted frown, sought word and wisdom on the truth of such a fate," Geb spoke, "So throughout The Road from Fort to Free Hold he did ask, 'Does anyone know the Mage?'"

"'He crossed the line at Wissing Wild, while mothers wailed and held their child, where Ward Post sputtered and grown men shuddered', one traveler swore," called out the first assistant.

"'A dead man walks upon the path, broken down and beaten wrath', claimed another," called the second, his voice not quite matured to the point where it fully carried.

"Stories high and tales far low did Ilsbruk hear upon The Road," Geb said softly, "but not a tale about another Mage. Only one to Ward the way. Only one to walk the way, only one to hold The Darkness at bay."

The crowd might have rippled with outrage before, but now was frozen in shock at the magnitude of such a betrayal.

"One constant with every witness; One truth born by all," Geb cried out.

"He held!" An assistant cried out.

"He held!" echoed another.

"HE HELD!" all of the assistants shouted in unison.

"Eight years HE HELD THE LINE!" Geb roared out, raising a hand and clenching his fist in genuine anger – either that or he was an even better speaker than Koring had ever bothered to credit the man.

One of the banner bearers slammed his pole into the ground, unfurling the stylized drawing of a Mage. Koring wasn't certain, but he thought that the banners were the same ones that were used in the schools to help young children learn about The Darkness.

"One Mage alone to walk and defend six hundred miles of Wards!" Geb thundered, as the crowd gasped.

Another banner bearer thudded his pole into the flagstones, unfurling a picture of a Ward post. Koring, dawning comprehension and dread filling him, was now trying to desperately make his way through the crowd to his aunt's side.

"One Mage walked The Road alone, abused and neglected by order of the Twelve. One Mage Warded The Road alone, by fiat of the Twelve. One Mage to hold and heal, one Mage to counter Darkness Zeal. One Mage held true to duty while Academy and corrupted Way Forts never stopped to wonder, as greedily they plunder, no concern about the Ward Line breaking asunder," Geb's eyes flashed as the drummer gradually began to increase the tempo.

Geb's voice began to soften again, drawing the crowd closer as they strained to hear his words.

"One Mage walked The Road alone to Uksaadle, where Darkness wrought battle left only carrion crows to feast upon the bodies. One Mage who saw The Darkness clear. One Mage left alone to conquer his fear. One Mage left with but a single choice, while foolish Twelve, greedy Twelve, counting coins, rejoice."

She had been near the center. Koring was now pushing people aside furiously, not bothering to offer apology.

Geb's voice may have started out soft, but roared to another crescendo as the words left his mouth.

"One Mage with no Trooper to aid him because of the scheming of the Twelve. One Mage with no companions to share his burden by the betrayal of the Twelve. A Ward who could have turned away, to wail and moan. Instead, a WARD STOOD ALONE!"

The crowd erupted, a maelstrom of emotion. Geb paused, letting the anger grow as if waiting for a signal. It came with the Mourning Bell, one brief ripple of sound piercing the night air that silenced everyone.

"One Mage, one Ward left to face The Darkness lest every settlement along the Northern Ward Line fall into blood and horror," Geb said, softly yet again as the last note of the bell shattered the air.

Geb paused to swallow, genuinely seeming to be shaken by the news he was imparting. Koring was almost to his aunt, he could see her just ahead in the throng of people.

"So we honor him. So we know him. So we remember him. Blood and Iron!" Geb called out, raising his right fist in salute.

Right fists thrust into the air, thousands took up the call.

"Blood and Iron! BLOOD AND IRON! KLYNSHEIM! KLYNSHEIM!"

"Hear now, the man we honor!" Geb cried, silencing the tumult. "Ward Galeb Eielson! The Ward Who Stood Alone against The Darkness!"

The remaining two banner bearers thudded their poles into the flagstones, unfurling image of Skrieksgrata and kielsgruntara. Koring could hear the keening wail of his aunt just as he broke through the last of the men.

"Alone in the night, near far Uksaadle Ward Eielson met The Darkness in battle, Wardings raging as Darkness roared and rattled. On they came as the Ward stood defiant, calm in his Wards reliant. With tooth and claw, the Wards The Darkness rake, yet against the Ward twas The Darkness that did break.

"The Ward stood alone, though some hoped not for long, for upon The Road Ilsbruk came with Trooper and dog, seeking Mage and finding page, a Warder's last words of honor and duty."

"'Uksaadle has fallen to a Darkness that dwells northeast of the settlement, as previously reported. I know my duty. I go to Ward The Darkness lest it spread'," recited one of the assistants, providing the Mage's final testimony.

The words were utterly septaing. If the Twelve weren't already dead, the crowd might have run riot and torn the Mage leaders apart with their bare hands.

Geb let the crowd thunder for a few moments before raising his arm again, as the banner men slammed their poles into the flagstones, silencing the crowd once more. Koring watched Geb's mastery over the crowd with envy as he continued to hold his aunt.

Geb straightened even more, swept his gaze across the crowd and began speaking again.

"'A Ward Stands Alone!' did Ilsbruk rage while Trooper growled and war dog howled, before marching to Eielson's aid.

"The Mage's path did Trooper and war dog follow, until they came upon a Darkened hollow. The Mage, in battle dear, they could hear, and with throats ringing clear, the Troopers surged ahead. But Darkness hides and Darkness bides, waiting with tooth filled grin.

"Eielson and Ilsbruk in forest fair, found The Darkness Rising, fighting Mage in Valley low, and Trooper in tree field row."

There wasn't a sound; you couldn't even hear a single breath as the crowd gazed fixedly upon Geb and his assistants, straining to hear every word. Aunt Corinne sobbed soundlessly into Koring's chest. His aunt may have had no contact with his cousin in years but she still loved her son dearly.

"The battles raged in fury and fire, battle cries and wounded dire. 'To the Ward!' Ilsbruk cried. 'To the Ward' the Troopers aspired; but Darkness wants and Darkness haunts and never sees a Klynsheim wish transpired.

"The Mage stood alone, wielding Ward and fighting forward, sending Darkness shrinking back while Troopers fell to Skrieksgrata hack. Lance and shield, helm and axe, all seeking to close the gap, but the Rising too well built the trap."

"Eielson knew the end; Eielson with every heartbeat still urged to defend. Eight years upon the six hundred mile; eight years to know how The Darkness defile. Eight years to plan and create and learn how to use The Darkness' hate, setting his own trap, with himself as bait.

"But no trap or plan the first touch of battle survives. Troopers' pain and Troopers' wain, left the Mage a choice; fight on while Troopers fall or answer his own conscience's call.

"The Ward Stood Alone and decided to fall, raising his power in one last call, coaxing the Wards away to fall under Ilsbruk's sway, leaving himself open to The Darkness."

Geb allowed another silence to fall, looked down, his arms crossed in supplication, a voiceless prayer falling from his lips. When he looked up again, his words were oddly gentle.

"A Ward stood alone against the enemies of Klynsheim and died so that his People might live and so we Honor him."

Koring gathered his aunt into a tighter embrace before she collapsed to the ground sobbing. Galeb was her only child, the last of her immediate family with her husband long dead in a stupid, drunken brawl.

Geb stepped off of the block, looking suddenly old and drained. His assistants moved forward, calling out the Honors.

"Ward Eielson's name to the Wall of Righteousness, by King's command!"

"Ward Eielson's name to the Wall of Immaculate Duty, by King's command!"

"Ward Eielson's name to the Wall of Heroes, by King's command!"

"Ward Eielson's name to the Wall of the Fallen, by the Seven's command!"

"Ward Eielson's name to the Wall of Battle, by Trooper acclamation!"

"Ward Eielson's name to the Righteous Man by Church decree!"

Koring bitterly noted that The Academy offered no cold comfort for his cousin's lost life. He barely noticed as the men began to shift around him, some moving forward as a call was made for men to honor Galeb's memory by mustering to the King's infantry to fight in the expected conflict.

Chapter 16

Galeb tried to regain consciousness several times but the pain usually drove him back under. He had glimpses of memory; remembered being carried on a stretcher, the shift to a wagon, but not much more than that other than fleeting impressions of light and darkness. Once he woke up screaming as broken bones were wrenched and panicked voices talked about pulled stitches and blood, but a cloth was shoved over his face and he fell back in a chemical haze.

He was still on a wagon when he finally mustered enough strength to remain awake despite pain and fatigue. Galeb could see the white canvas cover stretched taut over the hoops of the wagon frame. He was bound to a stretcher, unable to move his arms and legs. He was aware of his own smell and a desperate thirst.

Galeb's mind began to work over the possibilities of his situation as the long Patrol had taught him. He knew he was hurt. The bindings may have been to hold him steady and keep him from disturbing his wounds. Galeb might also be a prisoner, held accountable for any number of crimes the Twelve might lay at his feet to cover up their own failures with the loss of Uksaadle.

Captain Ilsbruk had mentioned weeks ago that he was tasked by the King to see to the defenses of The Road. Galeb might be the last piece needed to be dealt with; either he was relieved honorably or he was a last embarrassment that needed to be removed. There was no love lost between The Academy and the King, though Galeb had never supported the Twelve's politics for obvious reasons.

There was also the Shaeloman to consider; all of the pain and destruction the creature had wrought to bring him to the valley. Galeb doubted that anyone had been able to kill it, which meant that the Shaeloman would continue with its obsession, bringing more death.

The Darkness had Risen and Galeb had met it head on, a thought that had Galeb grimacing in remembered fear. He'd challenged The Darkness – had no choice – and it would be coming now in greater numbers. His fault in the end and how the King and Twelve would view that particular information could go either way.

Then there was Kieri. He'd put her in danger, intentional or not. The Shaeloman wanted her dead, saw her as an obstacle in its obsession with Galeb.

There were choices that needed to be made. Hard choices that frankly sickened Galeb. But first he had to see to Kieri. She was nearby. He could feel his Wards, though he doubted that he had the strength to power a single new Ward if his life depended on it.

Breathing hurt, like something was clawing at his insides. His muscles didn't feel much better.

"Galeb? Are you awake?" Kieri asked softly, as she climbed into the wagon bed.

He tried to speak but only a grating noise came out of his throat. Kieri crawled forward with a water skin, trickling some water into his mouth. Galeb swallowed gratefully.

"You don't know how glad I am to see you awake, Galeb," Kieri said, her face creased with worry as she ran a hand gently over his face. "It's been weeks..."

She was so beautiful... Nearly dying was making him maudlin...or more willing to acknowledge what he had resisted for so long.

Galeb tried to speak again, swallowed a few more dribbles of water, and then managed a croaking hush, Kieri having to lean close to hear his words.

"Where?" he asked, trying to add to the information so he could plan accordingly.

"We're on The Road, heading west, about a week from my family's range," Kieri answered. "You should rest, Galeb. Don't worry about where we are. Just focus on healing."

"Softer. Not...so loud," Galeb instructed, not wanting to attract too much attention. Attention was never good, especially with no firm plan in place.

Kieri moved closer, touching her forehead to Galeb's and kissed him gently, smiling warmly, though the worry hadn't left her eyes.

"You scared me so much, Galeb. You wouldn't wake up and your wounds...you were hurt so badly," Kieri said, her words a feathery touch as she spoke softly. There were tears in her eyes.

Galeb watched her, trying to convey his regrets for making her worry, even though he knew that having such regrets was ridiculous. He would love to just watch her, but couldn't afford to waste any time.

"Why...am...I tied up?" he managed with a slight wheeze.

"You have so many broken bones, the healers don't want you moving unnecessarily. And then you pulled your stitches and began bleeding again. Everyone thought tying you down was the best way to keep you from hurting yourself further. I don't think untying you is a good idea."

"You need to...untie me," Galeb insisted.

"But-."

"Just one hand. ...Feel like...prisoner."

"You're not a prisoner," Kieri said, frowning.

"Still feel...like it. Just one hand," Galeb continued to insist.

"Don't make me regret this," Kieri grumbled, reaching over and untying his left hand.

"Thank you. Now...you...have to...go, Kieri," Galeb said. He didn't like the way that he kept wheezing. Hard to breathe. Getting harder to think.

Kieri scowled angrily, gently, but firmly placing her hands on either side of his face.

"I'm not going anywhere, Galeb. You are mine and I am yours. Face it, Mage, you aren't getting rid of me."

"Not...safe," he wheezed.

"We are protected by the Wards of The Road, Galeb, under full escort of nearly a hundreds Troopers led by Ilsbruk of the Seven. We're as safe as we can be from The Darkness and that bitch Shaeloman," Kieri explained reasonably. She wanted to hug Galeb fiercely and then shake him for making stupid suggestions.

She was never leaving him again and he had better get used to the idea.

"Not worried...bout Darkness. Not...the threat. Well...not immediate threat," Galeb tried to explain.

"Galeb, Ilsbruk isn't a threat. He and his men saved you. They don't mean you any harm."

"Kieri...listen...to me. You saw what I...what I...what I did. What...I...am capable of...doing," Galeb insisted, swallowing with the difficulty of breathing and talking.

There was an unmistakable flash of fear in her eyes. Kieri knew exactly what he was talking about.

"Just because you do something new – scary new, I'll admit – doesn't mean that Ilsbruk would want to hurt you. For God's sake, Galeb, you saved his men's lives with your Wardings as much as he saved your life. You saved my life," Kieri whispered, kissing him again.

Galeb had to admit that the kisses were distracting. He had to focus.

"Doesn't matter...Kieri. When the Twelve...hear about...it they will want control," Galeb said, pleading for Kieri to understand. He needed her to understand. Talking hurt so much.

"Twelve will do...anything to get that control. Will hurt you."

"I can take care of myself," Kieri said fiercely. "And no bunch of old men are taking you from me."

"Will find a way," Galeb insisted. "If not them...then King will want me...controlled."

Galeb knew The Academy well. The Twelve despised different, unorthodox behavior. Even if that were not a factor, the Twelve would see him as a threat to their power. He also knew too much. He would most likely be silenced and Kieri along with him if he could not convince her to leave. The King might do it himself if he thought that Galeb's techniques could be used to increase the power of the Twelve.

"You are being ridiculous," Kieri said, scowling again.

"Then why...am I in a covered...wagon?"

"To keep the sun from burning you, you septa fool. You're hurt bad enough without adding sunburn to it," Kieri said with a snort before looking a bit thoughtful. "Though I also think to keep anyone from seeing you. Ilsbruk wants you taken as safely and swiftly to the King as possible. I think that he expects threats against you. Probably from the Twelve."

Galeb watched Kieri as he absorbed her words. Kieri seemed to understand the threat posed by the Twelve. She did not seem to see the King as a threat. To an Obari, it would be standard practice to report to the Patriarch. Kieri might very well view the king as a type of Patriarch and not as the leader of a nation who would have no trouble doing away with someone in the name of political expediency.

"Kieri, what is an...easy way Mages recharge energy needed to...give life to Wards?" Galeb finally asked her.

"Sunlight...," Kieri said, her eyes going wide as she looked at the canvas, suddenly re-evaluating its purpose. "No, you can't be right."

Kieri was finally understanding and Galeb was grateful. He did not have a lot of energy left in him.

"Kieri, you've got...to...go," Galeb insisted again.

"I'm not leaving you," Kieri hissed angrily, eyes locked on Galeb once again. All hope that she would listen to reason gone.

"Not just...about me. You need to warn...Family. Get them south of...Ward Line. Darkness Risen."

He was not above using her Family against her if doing so kept Kieri safe.

"Bob and Kawen are taking care of that," Kieri said smugly.

"You're here...alone?"

Kieri's eyes narrowed and an angry gleam came into her eyes.

"Are you implying that I can't take care of myself?" she demanded.

"No...just wish you had...someone...to watch your back," he answered truthfully.

"I have you," Kieri said with utter confidence.

Kieri was not going to leave and Galeb was too weak to keep arguing. A growing part of him did not want to see her go. Regret for wasted years struggled in his mind, but he squashed it ruthlessly. He held to his duties. Galeb would do what he must when the time came. Now...now he had to sleep.

Chapter 17

TeraUsuat was a city that held onto the ulceritic glory of its past while steadfastly ignoring the putrescence of its decay. The City, as it was known to its inhabitants since in their minds there was only one city worth knowing, sprawled across a concentric ring of hills that upheld three rings of massive fortifications. Fifteen other rings lay shattered in the outer districts of the hills giving testament to a once great people. The Darkness ruled those areas with the arrogance of conquerors.

The remaining walls stood not only as a defense, but as a testament to the rigid age based social structure that allowed TeraUsuat's citizens to continue to cling to their tired existence. The outer walls were manned by the young and unmarried, fewer each year as the population declined. The inner walls were manned by the families, with the inner most ring home to the elderly and leaders of the city.

As in all things, the young felt the greatest burdens, having to hold off continued assaults by The Darkness against the walls of a city that they did not particularly hold a fondness for or devotion to. No, it was the elderly who refused to relinquish a once proud civilization, caught in the delusional memories of a past long dead, killed by tooth, claw, spike and talon. The City was their home, their only link to their own tattered youth and the elderly refused to give up the little that they had left no matter the cost.

The families were caught in the middle, simply concerned with keeping their children safe until their time upon the walls came due. Every passing year tightened the families' connection with the city as comforting familiarity slowly morphed into the dangerous obsession of the elderly. Age was ever the trap that bound the people to TeraUsuat.

Like all of the peoples that dwelt upon these lands there was a simple truth that defined each culture. The Obari avoided The Darkness, the Klynsheim confronted The Darkness and the Usatchi of TeraUsuat accommodated it with all of the horrid realities that statement implied.

TeraUsuat had been the farthest northern human settlement when The Darkness first crossed the Barrier Mountains. A shining jewel unmatched by their southerly cousins, humbling all who walked Usatchi lands. The power, majesty and arrogance of the Usatchi civilization was what had tempted The Darkness.

Generations of Usatchi warriors had made the journey into the Tundra lands of the North beyond the Mountains to pit themselves against the creatures there to prove their worth. None had ever thought to consider that The Darkness would follow these same warriors south in search of their own prey. Thus the First Rising of The Darkness had caught the Usatchi unawares and eroded away their civilization in a ceaseless tide of nta drenched fear.

The Usatchi hadn't inadvertently lured a few monsters out of the Tundra. The Usatchi had unleashed an entire carefully balanced and incredibly hostile ecosystem upon the lands South below the Mountains. Like many invasive species, there were no native animals capable of stopping the invaders and the Usatchi lands had become bathed in blood.

In desperation the Usatchi had guided The Darkness south to feast upon Klynsheimer and Obari flesh. The Obari kingdoms, home to a peaceful, scattered and thoughtful people fell quickly.

But the Klynsheimer, with lands of iron and will, died by degrees, Trooper, Soldier and Mage putting up a fierce resistance, mauling The Darkness and unwittingly luring even more creatures south.

The death throes of the old kingdoms kept The Darkness distracted and allowed the Usatchi to muster their resources and survive another day. Over time turning The Darkness toward the Southlands evolved from a matter of survival to a matter of policy aided by the Usatchi's own brand of magic.

The Usatchi were skin walkers, able to take the hide of a Darkness and bond with it, becoming the creature for a time. The Usatchi used the skill to manipulate The Darkness, shift its attention in other directions, and give TeraUsuat a little more time to fester in its decrepit sense of superiority.

No one was certain how many of the Usatchi had the ability to skin walk. The elders kept the walkers to a minimum lest the population see a way to abandon the City. A simple brand upon the shoulder unlocked the magic. A brand that faded with every walk and had to be replenished. A brand that was held by the elders.

The old wanted to remain. The young wanted to go anywhere that did not stink of self-sacrifice and the stubborn blindness to the reality of the situation. This blindness was established by the Usatchi King during the First Rising. That King had refused to abandon his capital and flee to Klynsheimer lines, whom he considered beneath him. The same king who had sacrificed half of his people to build the massive defensive walls rather than flee to the safety of the Southlands.

The elders celebrated that king. The young cursed him.

Jesia Ulbrms was among the young Usatchi and one of the few granted the privilege to Skin Walk and enjoy a bit of freedom. She had just returned to the city after an extended Walk that had encompassed elder business and her own.

Extended Walks were dangerous for the Skin Walker. The longer the Walker wore the hide of The Darkness, the more characteristics of The Darkness the Walker took on. Walkers were occasionally lost that way, which might be another reason why the elders kept strict controls over who was allowed to Walk.

Jesia's brother Abrms was a perfect example. He often Walked in the hide of a Skrieksgrata and had become more brutish over the years, occasionally walking on his fists even when not wearing a skin.

Jesia was meeting with her brother in one of the hundreds of chambers in the outer wall section of the City. There were many such rooms lying abandoned and unused as the population dwindled. In truth, barely half of the dwellings in the outer ring were occupied.

Jesia was typical of her race, skin a dusky reddish brown, ears narrow and slightly pointed with no lobe. The assumption was that the close association with The Darkness over the centuries had wrought changes in the Usatchi. The elders just claimed that the Usatchi's drastically different physical appearance from their southern cousins was a sign of their races superiority.

Jesia's eyes were deep brown and almond shaped, but turned up at the corners, her face delicate, and her hair a lustrous black that hung from a thick pony tail bound at regular intervals with thick cord. Jesia's build was almost waif like, in sharp contrast to her brother who seemed a towering mass of muscle, with an ugly, perpetually scowling, face.

"How did the Walk go?" her brother asked, his voice a gravelly grunt. "Is everything prepared for the Culling?"

The Culling was held whenever the pressure of The Darkness on the walls of TeraUsuat became too great. The Darkness were lured southward with the promises of blood and flesh, challenge and battle.

The only organization that The Darkness recognized was that forged through sheer power of will. The stronger Darkness dominated the weaker Darkness. The weaker Darkness sought to overwhelm the stronger Darkness. Life was a series of dominance challenges. The Culling offered the ultimate opportunities to prove dominance by crushing powerful foes.

"Better than we had hoped, Abrms," Jesia said, smiling brilliantly and bouncing around with nervous energy, each move sinuous, "Though I think that my Shaeloman hide is ruined."

"The elders won't be pleased," Abrms grunted, moving around the room and scraping his fingernails along the stone, imagining his claws gouging out the rock. "We can't afford to attract too much attention. Nothing about this Cull is sanctioned."

Jesia and Abrms were operating rogue, she had to admit. The need for a Cull was not yet pressing, but she and her brother were initiating one none the less. A large group of the young were hoping that with The Darkness distracted they could make a break from the City and escape their purgatorial existence. A lot of planning had gone into this move and Jesia was nervous, but not worried. The elders would not know of their schemes until it was far too late. All involved were committed through common desperation.

"I've already replaced the skin, thank you," Jesia said snidely. "I killed that pup that was hanging around me. Took enough of its hide to make a new skin. The elders will never know the difference.

"Besides, it was so worth it."

Jesia giggled and did a little happy pirouette around the room.

"Abrms, he is so magnificent!" she crooned, hugging herself as she spun. "So amazingly powerful and handsome. Definitely handsome. And mine, all mine!"

Abrms watched his sister with some amusement as she sighed 'mine' again in utter contentment. Shaeloman were definitely obsessive Darkness and his sister had internalized that value to perfection.

"So the Mage will help us when we escape south?" Abrms asked, tilting his head as he flexed his fists, imagining the power of such movement when he Walked. "I can't believe being set up to start a Culling would sit well with the man."

"That's because you don't know him like I do. He'll welcome me with open arms and beg to help me as he utters his devotion. I made quite the impression on him and I can promise you that he will not be forgetting me any time soon," Jesia said with smug satisfaction and a swish of her hips. She suddenly frowned. "Though he would not show me his true face. I was so close before being interrupted."

Jesia kicked the ground petulantly.

Abrms thought about correcting his sister's twisted belief that Klynsheimers and Obari were simply Usatchi Skin Walking but discarded the idea. He had argued with Jesia enough on that topic. At this point he no longer cared what Jesia believed so long as she continued to advance their plans.

Of more immediate concern was the meaning of his sister's statements that she had made quite the impression. Jesia's words could have many meanings depending on whether or not you viewed them from a Usatchi or Darkness perspective. Since either interpretation was equally as likely, Abrms did wonder if his sister was becoming quite mad.

"So you've met the man and got him to stir up The Darkness. Is everything else in place?" he asked, trying to refocus Jesia on the task at hand.

"Oh don't be such a worrier, Abrms, really. Of course everything else is in place. My Mage was full of delicious surprises and I made certain that enough Darkness escaped his wrath to ensure that word will spread among the Elites that a Mage of the Old World walks the lands again."

"The man held a Ward Line alone for eight years, Jesia. I'm certain that the Mage has many hidden talents to have survived that long. His power's the whole reason we have centered our plans around him," Abrms said drily, resisting the urge to lift his fists above his head and smash down on the stone flooring for the sheer joy of movement. "But calling him a Mage of the Old World is a bit much, don't you think?"

"You wouldn't say that if you had seen him, Abrms. I could scarce believe my eyes. The Mage bore Wardings of light and air all around him. He took the fight to The Darkness and burned them like the Old Ones did during the First Rising. It was so...so...stimulating!" Jesia said hopping a few steps with her arms and head thrown back, a huge grin upon her face.

"I would like to see the Mage, Sister. I seem to recall you bringing him here was part of the plan. It will do us no good to escape the City only to fall to The Darkness beyond these walls. We need his Wardings," Abrms barked, tired of his sister's prancing.

Jesia stopped and pouted before glaring at her brother.

"There were complications," she admitted in a quiet mutter.

"What kind of complications?" Abrms asked, glaring at his sister. If she had lost control again....

"Some bitch Obari woman seemed to think that the Mage was hers," Jesia said with a scowl, crossing her arms. "As if he would aim his gaze so low."

"Why didn't you just kill her?" Abrms asked, surprised. It was unlike his sister to show restraint towards a rival.

"I tried. She was Warded. It was spectacularly inconvenient," Jesia answered with a pout.

"What do you mean 'she was Warded'?" Abrms asked, narrowing his eyes as he sought to find meaning in Jesia's words.

"The Mage warded her, literally and truly. A vast network of Wards floated around her. I've never heard of the like. It was those Wards that ruined the Shaeloman skin," Jesia said begrudgingly, opening and closing her hands randomly in the air as if mimicking Wards.

"The Mage can Ward people?" Abrms asked, scarce believing his ears, his eyes widening in wonder.

"I tell you that *my* Mage fought The Darkness directly, wielding Wards around his body and you scarce bat an eye. I tell you that *my* Mage warded *another* woman and you are amazed," Jesia said, shaking her head in mild disgust. "You could at least indulge my jealousy for pity's sake."

"The Mage being able to shape Wards around himself is one thing. Being able to shape Wards around other people is an entirely different matter. This particular ability is exactly what we need to escape this prison and never fear The Darkness again," Abrms explained excitedly.

"While you may have a very valid point, Brother, it does not change the fact that the Mage isn't here and most likely will not be for some time," Jesia snarled in annoyance.

"You were supposed to bring him with you. Never mind. You will have to go back and get him," Abrms urged. "You haven't reported to the elders yet. They probably don't even realize that you've returned. Our people were working the gate. Word won't have spread."

"There is another problem," Jesia admitted embarrassedly.

"What did you do?" Abrms growled, scowling.

"I may have gotten a little carried away," Jesia said, refusing to meet his eye and running a toe over the ground nervously.

"Define 'little'," Abrms said, his eyes mere slits that failed to disguise his anger.

"He will recover, Abrms," said Jesia in a huff before adding "Eventually."

"Septa it, Jesia," Abrms thundered, truly wishing that he wore his skin and could rage appropriately. "We don't have time for your vague notions of 'eventually'. You may have destroyed our only chance to flee this tomb."

"There is still plenty of time left to us," Jesia countered. "The Spriegs won't move south until the Guunt do. The Guunt don't do anything quickly. Not to mention that the Shaeloman will sew mischief and discord wherever they can, further slowing any advance on the Ward line."

The Guunt, Shaeloman and Spriegs made up the most common types of Elites, Darkness with true, recognizable intelligence. The Guunt were mountainous, giants of iron and stone, with bat like faces and ears, massive arms and short, but heavily muscled legs, causing The Darkness to move like an ape. Undeniably savage, brutally cunning and battle hungry. Unless distracted the Guunt normally warred among themselves for dominance, killing any Darkness that wandered into the midst of one of the giants' disputes.

Motivated, the Guunt drove all other Darkness before them, pushing The Darkness into a tide of forms all filled with terror and hate.

The Spriegs were like large earthbound squid, their massive brain sacks giving them the ability to control any creature they touched and injected with their venom. The name 'Spriegs' was a corruption of 'sprigs', a nickname once given to all the creatures under a Spriegs' control. The possessed had growths that erupted from their foreheads, resembling the sprigs of a tree.

Abrms spun away from his sister, his face distorted with a feral snarl. He didn't want to wait. He wanted to be free now! He wanted to roam in his skin without limits. His sister was...his sister was...control. He needed to be in control. Just a little while longer. He couldn't give into the rage. Not yet. Not yet, even though he so dearly wanted to.

Abrms turned to look at his sister. Jesia wasn't paying him the least bit of attention. She was thrusting her stomach out, mimicking being pregnant and rubbing it, giggling. He shook his head and stalked away. There was nothing more to be done until The Darkness began to move.

Chapter 18

Ilsbruk was worried. He should be seeing to the defense of the kingdom, commanding one of the base camps being established all along the Northern Ward Line. He should be overseeing the construction of defensive fall back points, supply caches and organizing patrol routes.

Instead he was traveling the Trade Road by King's command. Yes, he was inspecting Way Fort defenses - again. Yes, he was technically in charge of ensuring that the Warder Mages inspected and reinforced Eielson's Ward Line. Not that the Mages were having much luck with that task. Eielson's Ward posts were intricately layered to the point that most of the Mages were unwilling to even touch the posts for fear of damaging them. Instead the Mages were building a secondary line behind the first.

But that was not Ilsbruk's primary purpose. Ilsbruk's primary task was lying in a heavily guarded wagon that was to be delivered to the King. A positive was that Eielson had finally woken. There had been a time where there had been every doubt that the Mage would ever wake up. But a negative was that the man was not saying much more than monosyllables to anyone who wasn't Obari. Not that Ilsbruk could ask any of the questions that he wanted to in order to satisfy his own curiosity. He was under King's command that no one was to discuss Eielson's unique abilities.

Then there was the Obari woman. Ilsbruk had thought that he and Sonovonol had reached an understanding of sorts. Now she watched his Troopers with suspicion the few times that she left Eielson's side.

Her cousins had also disappeared and Sonovonol seemed to be waiting for their return. What that return would entail bothered Ilsbruk as well. Everything was in movement and unsettled.

Ilsbruk sighed. At least there weren't any caravans to slow the march today, as there had been over the past weeks. All of the settlements along the Ward Line were being evacuated in anticipation of the next Darkness assault. When there weren't caravans of frightened and bitter settlers there were columns of volunteers answering the King's call to arms. By abandoning the settlements, most of the settlers were losing everything they had. Many of the young men had entered the King's infantry as a means to earn enough money to start over.

Duty did attract more than a few; Eielson's story tugged at something deep in every Klynsheimer and the enlistment rolls had filled rapidly. Ilsbruk should be happy, but he was slightly ashamed at the untruths that continued to be spouted in Eielson's 'memory'. To the Kingdom the Mage was dead; the King wanted that belief to remain until he had Eielson secured and everyone had a better idea of what Eielson had done.

The Academy was still in the process of being purged of the Twelve's influence; there were likely some who would strike out at Eielson whether out of fear, anger, hate or a belief in upholding traditions. Though Ilsbruk hated to admit it, there were probably still some allies of the Twelve in the Military that might want Eielson silenced as well. The man had borne witness to some of the worst abuses of the Twelve.

So 'dead' the man remained and under strict escort and secrecy, which was the whole point of keeping the Mage sealed away in a covered wagon. The fewer people who knew about Eielson's whereabouts the better.

Which was a big part of the Captain's worry, but not the only problem. Something did not feel right. There had been a building tension all day. He could see it in his own men as they road westward. Furtive glances along the tree line on all sides – another problem that needed to be rectified. The trees should have been cut back a hundred feet on both sides of The Road. Crews were working on fixing this problem but is was a slow process.

The Troopers were fingering weapons and muttering amongst themselves as if waiting for an unidentified doom to settle on the unit. Ilsbruk's own hands were tight on the reins. It was almost a blessed relief when the attack came.

A creaking noise was the only warning the Klynsheimers had before trees from the surrounding wood crashed to the earth in front of and behind the column in a deafening explosion of tree limbs and leaves. The trap was perfectly executed. The Troopers were penned in with no room to maneuver, horses rearing and spooked.

"Dismount!" Gorgorin bellowed, not even bothering to wait for an officer's command. It was a sound decision; the men would just be bigger targets sitting on top their horses.

The attack was not Darkness based. The trees never would have pierced the Ward Line if that were the case. Who did that leave as a threat?

Conspirators against King and Eielson was a likely answer, which would likely mean men armed with bows. The horses would provide some cover for the Troopers at least.

The Troopers searched their surrounds for threats muttering to themselves. No one made any move toward the downed trees. There was no way the Troopers were moving such large obstacles without a lot of time and help.

Shadows were flitting through the wood half glimpsed and terrifying. Whispers that seemed to be just on the edge of hearing could be detected rising to a fever pitch of insanity until you tried to focus on the words and then there was silence, leaving a man doubting his own sanity. Feelings of menace and threat seemed to pulse in the air, skittering like spiders up a man's backbone. Not on the outside, but like the spiders were underneath the skin, picking their way over muscle and bone. It was so unreal and driving the men quickly towards panic. In that moment Ilsbruk knew what he faced and turned to glance at the wagon with a bitter curse.

"Obari!" Ilsbruk called out the warning. "Secure the wagon!"

"Why the grieshtata would Obari be attacking us, Sir?" Gorgorin asked, perplexed, as he kept his mount between him and any likely areas of attack, trying to move closer to Ilsbruk so that he wouldn't have to shout.

"Why the septa has everything gone to nta for us these past few weeks? The Mage. They want the Mage," Ilsbruk said with certainty.

"Maybe we should let them have him," Gorgorin said seriously. "Woman's attached to him so bad that her kin would risk war with us, it might be the smart thing to let him go for the time being."

Ilsbruk stared at his sergeant.

"Who the bloody septa are you?" Ilsbruk demanded, shifting his axe. "Gorgorin would never consider breaking King's orders."

Gorgorin looked sheepish for a moment before melting away into light and shadow.

"Ware illusions!" Ilsbruk warned, shifting to look intently at his men.

"No nta!" barked the real Gorgorin from somewhere deeper in the press of Troopers.

"Someone poke the Sergeant and make certain that he's real," Ilsbruk ordered, a grin tugging at his mouth at the sergeant's comment.

"You move that finger one inch closer, Boy, and I'm going to feed it to you," the real Gorgorin warned an unseen Trooper with gruff menace in his voice.

"I suppose that is you then, Sergeant," Ilsbruk said with a laugh.

"Who else the grieshtata would I be?" Gorgorin complained.

"A few moments ago you were an illusion," Ilsbruk explained, as another thought struck him. "Sergeant, check the men who secured the wagon. Make certain they are Klynsheim!"

Darkness descended like a hand clamped to his eyes. Troopers called out in shock and growing panic as they all seemed to be suddenly blinded.

"Can't see a septaed thing!" one Trooper called hysterically. "God help me I can't see."

"But we can see you, Klynsheimers," a deep, rich voice, dripping with menace said, his voice resonating all around the

Troopers, causing more men to call out in growing panic. "Let us take the Mage peacefully and your sight will be restored to you."

Ilsbruk whipped his head around, trying to locate the speaker. As he did, Ilsbruk could see for a moment before The Darkness reasserted itself over his eyes.

"Move your heads," Ilsbruk ordered. "Keep moving. The Obari can't keep the illusion over our eyes if we keep moving!"

"Well that sucks," said a familiar voice.

"Shut up, Bob," the deep voice said in annoyance.

Sonovonol's cousin. Ilsbruk knew that he recognized the voice.

"Why?" demanded Bob. "It's not like we're being subtle. I wanted to just sneak in and avoid all of the dramatics. But that wasn't good enough. No, we had to get all grandiose – which, believe me, I'm flattered that you felt that this plan had to be grandiose to complement my awesomeness – OUCH!"

Ilsbruk was having some success keeping his vision clear, though he was growing a bit dizzy shaking his head around and moving in random jerky movements. He might just throw up if he had to continue this ridiculous maneuver.

"You take the Mage and it's an act of war, Patriarch," Ilsbruk warned, adding the title because it was a good bet that this raid wouldn't happen without the permission of a matriarch or patriarch.

"Only if you make it so, Captain of the Seven," the Patriarch said gently. The man clearly didn't want any more fuss than necessary. Which was odd considering that Bob was right about this operation being too dramatic.

"Captain, these being Obari tricks, maybe the trees aren't real," Gorgorin reasoned. "Maybe we get mounted and ride out of this."

"If they can blind us they can blind the horses. Even if they don't the horse aren't going to charge downed trees, real or illusion. Probably have trip wires laid out just in case," Ilsbruk said, rejecting the idea.

"That would have been a good idea," Bob said thoughtfully.

"Shut up, Bob!" the Patriarch thundered. "I swear there's something wrong with you!"

"I killed a Skrieksgrata," Bob answered, as if that explained everything.

There seemed to be some quiet arguing and then a few thuds, followed by some mild cursing and then the sound of someone stomping away sulkily.

"You are interfering with King's business," Ilsbruk warned through clenched teeth, trying to reason with the Obari, as he stilled his movement. He was definitely going to throw up.

"Your King's got plenty of Warder Mages. We only want this one," the Patriarch reasoned. "Besides, Eielson's more ours than yours. Has been for years now."

While there was no denying that Eielson was some sort of cultural hybrid, Ilsbruk refused to even acknowledge the point.

"He has none like this one," Ilsbruk muttered to himself as he fought down the nausea before saying louder, "The Mage is bound for the South lands by King's Command. You have no claim upon this man."

"Unfortunately I can't counter that argument," the Patriarch admitted.

There was silence for a moment.

"Kieri?" called out the Patriarch eventually.

"Yes, Patriarch?" she called back from somewhere nearby that was definitely not in the wagon.

"You love Eielson?"

"Yes, Patriarch," Sonovonol answered, equal parts delight and irritation in her voice. She obviously thought that the answer to the question was ridiculously apparent.

"You want him?"

"Of course I do!" Sonovonol snapped angrily, affronted that anyone would question her commitment.

"Calm down, Girl," the Patriarch commanded, obviously displeased with the Obari woman's show of temper. "It's not like the Family isn't risking nta all doing this for you."

"Then stop asking stupid questions," Sonovonol shot back, clearly unwilling to let the Patriarch have the last word.

"If you haven't noticed we are holding nearly a hundreds of nauseous and increasingly pissed off Troopers in thrall," another, older, authoritative woman's voice snapped out. "If you two would quit arguing and get to the point it would be much appreciated."

"You tell 'em, Mom!"

"Shut up, Bob!" the woman thundered, before muttering. "I swear I didn't drop him on his head that much when he was a child."

"Dad did a couple of times," Bob admitted. "Though killing a Skrieksgrata didn't help either."

Ilsbruk didn't know whether to laugh, curse or throw up. He really wanted to throw up.

"Now if *you* two don't mind, I would like to hurry this along," the Patriarch grumbled.

"Don't grumble at me," warned the woman. "I'm Matriarch of this family, Ebko."

"And I'm Patriarch," Ebko rumbled. "If we are done having a pissing contest I would like to finish this up."

"Fine," grumbled the Matriarch, "Though you are the one holding everything up by arguing."

"Good," Ebko said, choosing to ignore the last comment before turning his full attention back to the problem at hand. "Eielson!"

"Yes?" answered a weak voiced Eielson.

"You love Kieri?"

There was a hesitation as Eielson was probably drawing a troubled breath from the sounds of it.

"Yes," eventually came the answer.

"You want her?" asked Ebko impatiently and maybe a little blasé, as if he was trying to hide annoyance at asking these questions.

"Do you have to make it sound like you are giving away a slab of meat?" Sonovonol complained angrily.

"This is not the time to find fault with me, Girl!" the Patriarch thundered. "So help me, God, Eielson, you better say yes or I am going to beat you to death with Bob."

"What did I do?" Bob asked, offended.

"Shut up!" Ebko yelled through clenched teeth.

"I will not be foisted off on a man because you threatened him!" Kieri shouted just as loudly. "Besides, Galeb's hurt bad enough without getting Bob smeared all over him."

"Hey!" Bob shouted indignantly.

Eielson tried to say something but was being drowned out by the bickering Obari.

Ward light suddenly rippled through the air, catching everyone by surprise. A deep, painful rasping sound could be heard in the sudden silence.

"Galeb," Sonovonol's voice sounding almost shrill, "You shouldn't be standing!"

"Feels good," Eielson said, his quiet voice strained.

"Really?" Bob asked doubtfully.

"No, not really, Bob. Hurts...a lot," Eielson admitted.

"If he reinjures himself, I am not being held accountable," the Corpsman said to no one in particular.

"Eielson! Answer the question," snapped Ebko.

"What was the question?" Eielson said weakly, like he was about to faint.

"Do not let him fall!" warned the Corpsman.

"Do you want Kieri?" Ebko said through clenched teeth.

"I suppose," Eielson said, trying to be funny since this whole situation seemed absurd to him. He needed time to think and was being given none. He didn't have enough information to plan accordingly. He hurt everywhere and it was hard to focus.

"You suppose? You SUPPOSE?" Sonovonol shrieked in outrage.

"He's trying to be funny," Ebko said with a mournful sigh as if he felt that the world was conspiring to make his life more difficult.

"He really shouldn't do that," Bob said helpfully. "He's not really good at that sort of thing. Almost as bad at it as the Captain is at smiling."

"I should let you fall," Kieri threatened Eielson angrily.

"Do not let him fall!" warned the Corpsman plaintively yet again. "Does anyone here understand the importance of not letting the Mage fall?"

"I need a clearer answer," Ebko said.

"I – ouch!" Eielson said.

"Oh stop being a baby. All I did was poke you," Kieri said, still disgruntled over Eielson's earlier attempt at humor.

"Don't poke him either," the Corpsman warned.

"I'll poke whomever I want to," Kieri said, sullenly, not liking being corrected and frustrated over this whole situation, which in her mind should have been a simple snatch and grab, not a debate.

"Will you all be quiet and let the man answer," Ebko ordered.

"Yes," said Eielson. "And I think that I would like to lie down now."

"Finally!" growled the Patriarch. "We have a claim of blood, Captain of the Seven. Much as I hate to say it Kieri and Eielson are bound."

"What do you mean 'bound'?" Ilsbruk demanded.

"Married," Ebko clarified.

"But there was no ceremony," Ilsbruk said, perplexed.

"Yes there was," Ebko insisted as if he was talking to a simpleton. "She said yes and so did he."

"But there was no priest or special blessings," Ilsbruk insisted.

"Thank God, no. Who's got the time for that kind of nonsense?" Ebko asked with a laugh.

"But...but...that's-," Ilsbruk was at a loss for words.

"That's Obari tradition, Captain," Eielson said from somewhere much closer to the ground than he had been.

"You still cannot take him," Ilsbruk said angrily, running a hand through his hair in frustration and immediately regretting it as the movement caused his insides to heave. He threw up quickly and violently.

"We have claim and we have reason," Ebko said calmly, once Ilsbruk stopped vomiting.

"Even if you do, it will change nothing but make you more enemies," Ilsbruk insisted, wiping his mouth on the back of his hand and wishing he could see well enough to find his canteen which was strapped to his saddle.

"The Darkness has Risen, Captain of the Seven. I think that you have enough enemies to worry about without adding us to your list," the Matriarch said reasonably.

"As do you, Matriarch," Ilsbruk pointed out. "Where would you go that The Darkness would not threaten? If you are hoping to rely on the Mage to help, you can see that he's a long way from being functional. Can you hide from The Darkness long enough to allow him to recover?"

"What do you suggest we do?" the Matriarch asked reasonably.

Ilsbruk did not like the sudden idea that popped into his mind, but with The Darkness Rising, the Kingdom could use allies. Eielson had loyalty to his duty. That loyalty could be used to bind the Obari to the Kingdom's defense as scouts at least and another weapon as best. There was a way to turn this whole mess into an advantage

"Come South with us. Enter Klynsheim as guests," Ilsbruk suggested.

"You would welcome all of us into your kingdom?" the matriarch asked skeptically.

"Define 'all of us'," Ilsbruk requested suspiciously.

"Define 'guests'," the Matriarch countered.

Ilsbruk decided to humor her with honesty in hopes that the Matriarch would answer his question.

"Allies in the fight against The Darkness," Ilsbruk said.

"Ours is not your ways, Klynsheimer," the Matriarch warned. "We will not face The Darkness in the battle line."

Ilsbruk laughed.

"Do you think that you will have a choice, Matriarch? Remember whom you have bound your family to. When Eielson could in good conscience have turned away from Uksaadle and let someone else deal with the problem he chose to do battle. *Battle*, Matriarch. Eielson met The Darkness head on. Do you really think that he will turn aside and let others fight in the upcoming war without him?"

"I will not let him come to harm," hissed Sonovonol, then corrected herself. "Further harm. And his name is 'Sonovonol' now."

"You are admitting that you will have no choice but to be in the fight," Ilsbruk insisted with a shake of his head. "Your husband will fight because he must. Because deep down that is who he *is*. You will not keep *him* from the battle lines and he will drag *you* in after him."

Ilsbruk didn't add that he strongly suspected Eielson would fight because deep down that was all Eielson knew how to do. Eight years had worn away every other option the man might have once been able to understand.

"But I am not asking you to fight in the battle line," Ilsbruk explained. "Your talents don't lie in that direction. I was thinking more along the lines of distractions and scouts."

"We could do that," the Matriarch said thoughtfully. "We accept your offer of guest right."

The Darkness and downed trees faded away as if it had never been, leaving Troopers blinking rapidly in the sunlight and very angry.

"Remount!" Gorgorin snapped, getting the Troopers moving before they had a chance to act on their anger. "Captain's extended guest right and you lot better remember it."

Gorgorin turned to remount himself and found Sonovonol's cousin Bob standing nearby staring up at him with an odd smile on his face. Gorgorin glared at the man. Bob smiled even broader.

"I killed a Skrieksgrata," Bob offered, a manic gleam in his eyes. "You are going to have to do better than that if you are trying to intimidate me."

Gorgorin scowled and then glanced back to make sure that all of the Troopers were mounting up and that Eielson was being helped back into the wagon. Obari were pouring onto The Road behind him. Lots and lots of Obari.

"How many of you lot are there?" Gorgorin asked, his mouth slightly agape.

"Seventeen families so far," Bob said with a shrug.

"So far?"

"Yeah. Who the septa wants to be north of the Ward Line with The Darkness Risen?" Bob said, looking at Gorgorin as if the answer should have been obvious. "Besides I killed a Skrieksgrata. I don't ever want to do that again. Only thing worse would be seeing Esie's butt again. "

Bob shivered as he walked away leaving Gorgorin to wonder just how unhinged Bob had become after his fight with

The Darkness. Gorgorin was also morbidly curious to see who 'Esie' was to inspire that much fear in a man.

Ilsbruk looked back at the Obari Matriarch before mounting himself.

The woman was similar in looks to Sonovonol, though her face was a bit more raw boned and worn with age. Her hair also hung longer and thicker. Standing nearby was the Patriarch who looked close enough in looks to possibly be the Matriarch's brother. However, that was where the similarity ended.

The Matriarch was slight with well-toned muscle. The Patriarch was slightly shorter than Ilsbruk, but massively muscled, making him seem almost squat. He carried a great axe, one to rival the king's and was scowling in the direction of the wagon. Short, shaggy hair made the man look even fiercer.

Ilsbruk turned his full attention back to the Matriarch. He had to try to give her fair warning. To make her understand the situation.

"You don't understand what you are getting into," Ilsbruk warned the Matriarch, shaking his head sadly. "You don't understand what he is becoming. What the King will need him to become."

The Matriarch gave the Captain an appraising look before arching a brow, crossing her arms over her chest and shaking her head at him pityingly.

"We know better what Galeb Sonovonol is than you ever will, Captain of the Seven. Who do you think he came to when you lot abandoned him to the Patrol? We understand perfectly what he has *always been*. We just have more hope than you Klynsheimers."

The Matriarch then glanced towards the wagon, looked towards her brother, and said with a grin:

"The one you should be worrying about is my niece."

"Oh?" Ilsbruk asked, assuming that the woman meant Sonovonol.

"Yes. Kieri has been after that man for years. Now she has him right where she's always wanted him - flat on his back - and he's too injured for her to take advantage," the Matriarch said. "Kieri is bound to be quite irritable at the moment."

Her brother glared at his sister and stomped off angrily. The Matriarch laughed.

"Ah it is going to be such a good day," she mused. "I can't wait until Kieri is pregnant. Her father is going to be chewing on his axe at the thought of just how that happened."

"He doesn't like Eielson?" Ilsbruk asked.

"Sonovonol, Captain of the Seven. There is no more Eielson. But to answer your question, no more than any father likes the thought of his daughter with a man."

Ilsbruk frowned. He had three daughters under the age of seven. Come to think of it, Betney's father glared at him the first three years of their marriage. He wondered if any of his little girls were open to the idea of joining a nunnery.

Kieri was beaming when she was not fussing over him. Galeb was shocked at the events that had just transpired. He had not intended to marry Kieri – not that he was against the idea, he just needed to get Kieri far away from the danger that was swirling around him. But his mouth had different ideas than his brain and he had spoken his agreement before his brain could interfere. Or maybe he had a moment of clarity and understood that he was better with Kieri than without her. He also might have been a little afraid of being hit if he said no. Kieri didn't look like she would have forgiven a rejection.

Why now? He kept coming back to that thought. Almost dying might have something to do with it, but was not the only reason. Besides, he tried not to think about the agony that had ripped through him with that final Warding. Felt like his soul was being torn from his body.

Galeb could only think that he felt lighter somehow. He wasn't even focusing on the Ward Line...much. Not that he could do anything about maintaining the Line despite the fact that a part of him was feeling guilty about not at least trying. He was doing his best to ignore the guilt; other Warders were charged with its maintenance now.

Galeb had also seen how tense the situation was between the Troopers and Obari. He could easily see the situation spiraling out of control. Galeb had coldly looked at the possibilities and decided that agreeing to the marriage was the best way to handle the immediate situation.

The marriage also gained him allies. He would need allies in the coming fight; he was not referring to The Darkness. Why was he overthinking this? He hated that he couldn't just be happy.

Kieri was worried. She was doing her best to hide it, but she couldn't help but bite her lip when Galeb wasn't watching. Kieri finally had what she had been chasing for years and she wasn't happy. Well...no. She was happy. Deliriously so. But she was also unhappy because she didn't understand why Galeb had so readily agreed to the marriage after years of putting her off.

He was acting odd. No, Galeb was odd. He always had been. But he had been frighteningly odd ever since the battle. Half dead, delirious with fever, his body broken and on more than one occasion the Mage had tried to slip away into the night, crawling and ignoring the grinding of broken bone.

Twice they had found him trying to walk his old Patrol, shuffling and stumbling miserably about his duty. Kieri had been able to talk him back to the wagon under the gaze of the Troopers. The Klynsheimers had watched with barely concealed pity. All except Ilsbruk. The Captain's eyes had burned with anger.

The last time had been the worst. If it hadn't been for the pulled stitches and the blood trail they might not have found where he had hidden himself. The Klynsheimers had been amazed by the tiny refuge where they found Galeb alongside The Road.

Kieri had been proud of his skill right up until the moment she realized that Galeb was trying to get into a fighting stance and looking like Death itself had come for him and he would meet it standing. The sheer amount of fatalism in his eyes had been heart wrenching.

Ilsbruk had had enough at that point and ordered him bound. Kieri hadn't exactly lied about why Galeb had been tied up. She wanted to tell him the truth but since he didn't seem to remember the incidents it seemed better not to worry him any more than was necessary.

Her family was not helping. Her aunt was making comments about what Kieri should be doing with her new husband whenever her father was within ear shot. Ebko was scowling. A lot. Kawen wasn't speaking; hadn't said a word since the valley. Bob...was being Bob. A slightly freaked out version of Bob, but still Bob.

The other families were watching cautiously. A great deal had been made about Galeb. The term 'Old One' had been used quite liberally. There were expectations now.

It had been so long since there had been a fighting Mage that the Klynsheimers themselves had forgotten about their existence. No surprise there; no fighting Mages had survived the shattering of the ancient kingdoms. Death in battle or the overemphasis on creating defensive wardings had either killed those Mages or driven them into obsolescence.

But the Obari remembered. The Obari knew what Galeb had become and would use him as their shield. Kieri hated that fact.

Ilsbruk had been wrong when he warned her aunt that there would be nothing the Obari could do to keep Galeb from seeking out the battle line when The Darkness came. The Captain of the Seven had believed that the Obari would try to stop Galeb; the Families had no such intention. When the time came, the Families would push Galeb into that battle line. Kieri had made that possible.

She had lied to Ilsbruk about keeping Galeb from harm, but did not feel guilty deceiving the Klynsheimer. But Kieri should be honest with Galeb. She wanted to be, but she was afraid of driving him away. No. Galeb would stay with her. Kieri knew that. She just didn't want to admit that she was willing to sacrifice him for her Family. She wouldn't even hesitate and she would be at his side when she did it. Still didn't make it right.

Chapter 19

The trees of the Great Forest shifted like the waves of the ocean as The Darkness gathered and headed south. There was no cohesion to the movement. Simply masses of creatures all moving in the same direction. South towards the Challenger. South towards blood and flesh.

Spriegs, many limbs dancing in the air, serenely drove their thralls before them, seeking to add to their growing collection of minions. Guunt walked with towering menace, supremely confident as the trees bowed before their terrible weight. Packs of lesser Darkness either fled before the giants or danced at their heels, eager for the scraps of their betters. Shaeloman glided along the edges, alternately aiding and hindering the exodus as the whim took them, their own followers adding to the sheer numbers heading for Klynsheim.

There were no hurried steps among The Darkness. The time surrounding a Rising was to be relished, drawn out in its exquisite promise. Besides, The Darkness had to eat and hunted each other with a driving will, further hindering progress.

Kiesh was no ordinary Guunt. He stood head and shoulders above his brethren, massive shoulders and broad chest for even his kind. His brutish, bat like face hid an intelligence that had led to the domination of a massive force of Darkness that better resembled an army than the usual hordes that served Elites.

Kiesh's forces reflected careful consideration and purpose, unlike the ever greedy Spriegs who gobbled up the servitude of as many mind slaves as was physically possible for the squid like beings. The Spriegs' greed always led to solidification and death, the malleable flesh of the Spriegs hardening to a leathery stone like consistency as the effort to dominate dehydrated the beings.

No, Kiesh was very selective, each being under his domination carefully chosen for a specific purpose. Twelve Guunt served under him, helping keep in thrall the lesser Darkness. Over a hundred Skrieksgrata lumbered in the wake of the Guunt. A full herd of Ulanimani hammered the earth with their hooves, their tri-horns wicked and deadly. Threshers by the score, their humanoid sized bodies belying the strength in their flexible limbs and the bone and flesh whips that extended over their clawed hands. Kielsgruntara by the hundreds completed his compliment.

Every one of The Darkness served several purposes. Some were scouts, others shock troops, some like cavalry, but all food, though only the Guunt dared eat the Ulanimani. The minerals imbedded in the Ulanhimani's hide were particularly relished by the Guunt, adding to the resiliency of their iron and stone hides.

Kiesh wanted to be the first to meet the Challenger but knew that he had intense competition. At least seventeen different Spriegs were moving their puppets south. The Shaeloman as well had their resources. One was even thought to have enticed an entire pride of Korskiq into service. Kiesh was mostly unconcerned. The Korskiq were notoriously fickle, the toothed serpents as likely to make the journey as turn back to the north to bask in the Tundra winds.

Kiesh paused to watch his minions move south, ripping a tree from the ground and using it as a make shift back scratcher. His creatures moved in a long line, purposefully driving lesser Darkness from the ground and pushing them forward towards the human defenses. These lesser Darkness would be his skirmish line, probing the defenses and revealing to him the best place to attack.

Soon, soon he would meet this Challenger and grind him into dust. Then he would take his remnants back north to hammer upon the walls of that cursed city. He tired of its continued survival and was insulted by the existence of the Skin Walkers. Kiesh often suspected that all Shaeloman were really Usatchi Skin Walkers. It was the only explanation for how annoying the Shaeloman tended to be. That thought had Kiesh scowling and the tree shattered in his grip.

The Darkness owned all of the land that they cared to claim. It was time that the humans were reminded of this fact.

Kiesh threw his head back and roared, the sound deep enough to resonate through bone and flesh. His forces quickened their pace.

Perhaps he would stay awhile in the South Lands after all. The humans were said to be filled with iron rich blood. Kiesh shuddered at the thought of eating human flesh. There would be no satisfying crunch with the humans' squishy bodies. Perhaps if he pulped them like a fruit? Yes, he could definitely squeeze the iron out of their bodies, drinking it. That would be less disgusting.

Kiesh ambled over to the Ulanimani herd and snatched up a straggler, biting down with relish. The Ulanimani bellowed in terror as its body crumbled beneath the Guunt's anvil like teeth. Bits of stone fell from his mouth, clattering along his hide. Kiesh looked thoughtful as he stared south. Maybe if he just dug a pit and had the Skrieksgrata drain the humans into it?

Chapter 20

At midday another hundreds of Troopers met Ilsbruk's party, merging in to increase the escort. The reason for the additional security was that the King had come. Sigsrata had grown impatient to meet his terrifyingly wondrous new Mage as he referred to Eielson. The King rode with Ilsbruk for a while before making his way back to the wagon where Galeb sat, his healing body granting him that blessing.

The Mage was much improved and yet still frail enough not to be allowed more than short, slow walks with much assistance. Old injuries were complicating the healing of more recent hurts just as the corpsman had feared.

Sigsrata had brought with him his two Journeyman Warder Mages as Obel and Jans were now commonly viewed by others. The seemingly close relationship with the King had both advantages and disadvantages, since other Warders were either jealous or viewed the two as traitors to The Academy. Obel and Jans were wary around the first group and dismissive of the second. Every day fewer and fewer Mages were willing to associate themselves with the old policies of the Twelve.

Obel and Jans were both hanging back within sight, both glancing at the wagon in eager anticipation. Obel wanted to interrogate Eielson badly; Jans was looking for potential political maneuvering. Given what Ilsbruk had told the King about Eielson, Sigsrata did not trust either Mage to not make a mess of the situation and had to forbid Obel and Jans to talk to Eielson until Sigsrata himself had a chance to meet with 'his most loyal Mage'.

This was the official line that Sigsrata was establishing to both tie Galeb closer to the crown and to capitalize on Galeb's notoriety. When the King was ready to declare Galeb miraculously among the living Sigsrata wanted the Mage to be firmly associated with the monarchy and not the Academy.

"What is your assessment of Eielson?" the King asked as softly as was possible for him, once the Troopers had given the two men some space.

Ilsbruk glanced up at his king. Sigsrata was an enormous man and the horse required to bear his weight was a massive brute.

"Physically he's a wreck. I've seen seasoned veterans with fewer scars, your Majesty. Even when he's recovered I doubt he would be able to move swiftly. Bones are healing but there are too many old injuries that didn't heal right complicating matters," Ilsbruk answered.

"I'm not interested in having the man stand in a battle line," Sigsrata said drily. "I could do without the drill sergeant assessment. I want your assessment of the Mage. Tell me about the man."

"Yes, your Majesty," Ilsbruk said with an understanding nod.

"And cut out the 'Majesty' crap," Sigsrata grumbled. "We both know who I am without you trying to stroke my ego."

"Yes, Sir," Ilsbruk acknowledged, with a quick grin that faded as he pondered the answer to the King's question. When he finally answered, he did so with a scowl.

"The man's broken, Sir. Have no doubt about that. Eielson's broken in a way that isn't going to ever heal. He's twisted up inside like one of those trees you see growing on cliffs, stunted, stubborn, and unyielding once he's made up his mind.

"We had to tie him down to keep him from wandering away even when he was in pain bad enough that he should have passed out."

"Where was he going?" Sigsrata asked, scrunching up his face as he tried to imagine what could possibly drive a man to such actions.

"His Patrol. He was trying to walk the Ward Line," Ilsbruk explained. "Tore a strip of leather and tied it into his mouth to bite down on to deal with the pain and keep from crying out."

The King grunted in surprise.

"Could use more like him then," Sigsrata said with a twist of his lips as he digested this information and tried to find a positive spin. "Lord knows that the Twelve have encouraged laziness and neglect in the Warders."

Ilsbruk started to nod agreement and then shook his head.

"No, Sir. This is not a man loyal to his duty. This is a man trying to hold on to the only thing that makes sense to him. He tries to walk the Line because that is all he can think to do."

"Can't be that bad," the King said, skeptically.

"He sees us all as the enemy, Sir," Ilsbruk tried to explain. "Eielson has this way of looking at you like he's waiting for you to attack him. Not like he's scared so much as resigned to that inevitability and is determining the best reaction to the threat."

"He's had reason," the King said, shaking his head, disgust rising once again at what the Twelve had wrought.

"Perhaps," Ilsbruk, acknowledged, "But the last time he slipped away before we tied him down...was worse than usual. Still have no idea how he slipped away like that; just gone before anyone noticed. Must be some Obari trick he learned...

"We wouldn't have found him if he hadn't left a blood trail from broken stitches. We tracked him to a hidden shelter of sorts, fully warded and not easily seen just on the edge of the Ward Line. When Troopers went in after him he tried to fight. Knew right enough who had come for him and he was still going to fight. We weren't to be trusted; he's lumped every Klynsheimer along the Ward Line in with the Twelve.

"Told him that the Twelve are dead and gone. I don't think that Eielson really believes us. He sure didn't that night. If it wasn't for the Obari woman, I don't know how we would have gotten him out of there without further injury.

"I've had the men looking since then. There are similar shelters all along the Ward Line. A few show signs of old blood."

"He's had to go to ground before," the King said, clenching his teeth in anger.

"Septaed disgrace the way he's been treated," Ilsbruk said, equally angrily. "Point is, Sir, he's like an injured war dog. No telling who or what he's going to snap at."

"He responds to the Obari," Sigsrata said, more of a statement then real question.

"Yes, Sir. Kieri Sonovonol or Kieri Eielson now, I suppose. I'm not really sure about Obari customs," Ilsbruk admitted.

"Galeb Sonovonol," Bob supplied, somehow appearing next to where the King and Ilsbruk rode. "Obari men take the name of the family that they marry into."

The man carried his spear over his shoulder and acted like it was perfectly natural for him to enter a conversation with a king.

"You would be?" Sigsrata inquired, raising an eyebrow at the strange man.

"Bob," answered Bob with a grin that did not reach his eyes. A disturbing gleam rested in those eyes that had Sigsrata looking away for a moment.

"I killed a Skrieksgrata," Bob explained, nodding politely as if the King's uneasiness was understandable given that fact.

"Well that explains everything, doesn't it?" Sigsrata said, slightly baffled.

"No, not everything, but a lot, I suppose," Bob said thoughtfully. "I'm handling it a lot better than Kawen is. Even got a few women interested in me now."

"Kawen?"

"My cousin. He killed a Skrieksgrata too. Didn't take it as well. Of course we were both freaked out by Galeb blowing up all sorts of things at that point, I suppose," Bob said, scratching his head. "Didn't help that there were Klynsheimers being ripped apart by The Darkness all over the place either. Could hardly take a step without stepping on something squishy."

Bob shuddered at that statement, as he became momentarily lost in the memories. Sigsrata looked at Ilsbruk, who shrugged. Bob was Bob. Ilsbruk had learned that it was best to accept the man as he was, which was decidedly less than normal but understandably so. Ilsbruk didn't want to remember that desperate fight himself.

"I was worried that I was going to have to kill Galeb," Bob admitted when he struggled free from the memories.

Both Ilsbruk and Sigsrata stiffened at the comment.

"I knew that he was different in a way that was going to give you Klynsheimers another advantage over us. Too many of your settlements pushing into Obari ranges as it was without adding new skills to your Warders.

"But that was before the valley," Bob explained, almost apologetically. "Before I really understood what he is."

"What is he, Bob?" asked Ilsbruk carefully. Bob was increasingly erratic.

"*Death*," Bob said with a harsh sobbing laugh, staring at both men. "I realized that going after Galeb Sonovonol was pointless. I mean, seriously, how can you kill Death?"

The Obari shook his head and wandered away, blending into the shadows as he wrapped illusion around himself.

"That was certainly uncomfortable," Sigsrata finally said.

"Bob's just another concern I have about Eielson," Ilsbruk admitted.

"Which is what, exactly?" Sigsrata asked, raising an eyebrow. "All you seem to have about that man is concerns."

"It's my duty to have concerns," Ilsbruk said with a twist of his lips. "Eielson's broken; seems anyone who spends enough time around him breaks as well."

"You make him sound like a threat," the King said.

"Because he is," Ilsbruk said, "That's what I've been trying to explain to you, Sir. Eielson's a threat to everyone around him because he can't see anything beyond Warding The Darkness. He goes after that duty with a mindless devotion regardless of collateral damage. People aren't as important as maintaining the Wardings."

"Sort of his job, Ils," Sigsrata pointed out patiently. Every one of the Seven were chosen for different skills. Ilsbruk's particular skill lay in over analyzing situations and people, uncovering every possible motive and threat. This skill was the very reason Ilsbruk had been given the task of evaluating the defenses of the Great Northern Trade Road. It was just a pity that the man could not relax a bit more.

"I know, Sir, but his single-mindedness is the problem. Our entire strategy when dealing with The Darkness is to Ward, but not provoke. Without realizing what he was doing Eielson definitely provoked and we are all going to have septa to pay for it."

"The death of Uksaadle was the provocation," Sigsrata disagreed. "You going after the Mage was the provocation. The Twelve's neglect was the provocation. The septa foolish carelessness of the settlers in not maintaining their defenses was the provocation. In my thinking, Eielson was the least of the problem."

"Perhaps," Ilsbruk conceded, running a hand through his hair. "But we have to make the man see more than the fight or he's going to keep repeating the Valley. The Darkness won't stop coming if he flings himself headlong at every threat. We have to teach him a measured response."

Sigsrata was silent for a few moments thinking on Ilsbruk's words. While the King knew that Ilsbruk had some valid points he also knew that some of Ilsbruk's concern over the situation stemmed from the raw display of power that the Mage had demonstrated. A rather unorthodox display that the Captain was struggling to quantify and categorize in the grand scheme of the nation's defense.

Tempering. Yes, Sigsrata liked the analogy. The Mage just needed some tempering like any good blade. Despite the propaganda of the Twelve over the years, Sigsrata did possess a rather keen brain and was well educated, though he didn't flaunt the fact.

"He trusts the Obari woman," Sigsrata pointed out when he finally spoke. "Use her to reign him in."

"Yes he does," Ilsbruk agreed, blowing out a breath. "She's another problem. We can't trust her motivations."

"You're not supposed to trust other people's motivations," Sigsrata pointed out with a grin. "You're supposed to be suspicious of everyone's motivations."

Ilsbruk snorted. "I'm always suspicious on your behalf, Sir. In this case, it's more worry about how healthy a relationship those two have with each other. Sonovonol's devoted to him; I can't deny that. Eielson...he's...desperate."

"Strange choice of words, Ils," the King said giving him a sidelong glance. Well, more of a look down and sidelong glance.

Ilsbruk tilted his head in acknowledgement.

"Doesn't make it any less accurate. The Ward held the patrol for eight years alone. In that whole time I figure he only trusted one person. He only cared about one person. Man's centered his life on Kieri Sonovonol."

"Is he so different from you and Betney?" Sigsrata asked, surprisingly Ilsbruk. It was the King who ensured that Ilsbruk and Betney met and married. He was rather proud of that match. The Captain got the support and love he desperately needed and Sigsrata got the biggest War Dog kennel in the Kingdom firmly tied to his House.

"In some ways, no," Ilsbruk admitted, "in others, greatly so. If I were to lose Betney, God forbid, I would grieve deeply, bury myself in my duty and see to my children. If Eielson were to lose his wife, I fear that last bit of feeling in him would be gone. He would be fully gutted, hollow and nothing would stand between him and Warding The Darkness."

"He is a Mage, Ils," the King admonished, "He's supposed to Ward The Darkness."

"What Eielson did in the Valley is going to bring The Darkness down upon us in an even greater Rising. But what he did there was restrained in defense of Kieri Sonovonol among other things by all accounts. Imagine what he would do without restraint and the Rising that would bring," Ilsbruk argued. "He might possibly see the world burn without a thought as to the repercussions of that action."

"You're getting dramatic," Sigsrata said with a faint smile, "but I take your point. Best keep the woman safe."

"Better said than done. Sonovonol isn't going to leave Eielson's side especially if it means fighting at his side," Ilsbruk said glumly. "I know. I've tried to convince her otherwise; I think Eielson's even tried. Woman's stubborn."

"A good match to reign him in then," Sigsrata said with a grunt. He approved of strong willed women as much as he approved of his Queen taking extended visits with her relatives. Both were often sorely needed in much greater supply.

"Not as good as it could be. Sonovonol's devoted to him but she's also using him. The whole ambush on The Road and sudden marriage to Eielson was an obvious set up to get the Obari safe passage into our lands.

"She's Obari; Sonovonol's always going to put the needs of her Family and people above Eielson. She may love him, and for his sake I really hope she does, but he's still Klynsheimer. An outsider.

"If he realizes that his marriage is just another means of using him to advance the goals of others...he might not recover from such a misfortune," Ilsbruk said worriedly.

"My own marriage was forged to advance the goals of others," Sigsrata pointed out wryly. "I got used to the idea."

"But you knew that going in, Sir," Ilsbruk said. "Eielson may not be as understanding."

"I don't think you give the man enough credit," Sigsrata said with a shake of his head. "He walked a solo Patrol for eight years. He's fought The Darkness and survived. The Mage is neither blind nor foolish."

"As you say, Sir. But consider that the man has been used and abused that entire time. What would such a man do if he found the one person whom he believed to have done neither was just as bad as everyone else who'd failed him over the years?" Ilsbruk asked.

"Given what I have learned of the man, he would bury the pain and Walk the Line," Sigsrata said. "He would return to the one thing he's always been able to rely on and as you said in a lot of ways the only thing he seems to understand. A sad existence, but one that doesn't pose the threat you fear."

"The Ward deserves better," Ilsbruk said with a shake of his head, as if doing so could clear away the things that the Captain did not like about the world.

"And we finally come to the heart of the matter," the King said, nodding in satisfaction. "The Twelve died for what they did to him."

"Begging your pardon, Sir, but I can give septa all for what happened to the Twelve. Their deaths don't make up for what Eielson's gone through. What no servant of Klynsheim should ever have had to bear as a burden and yet we're going to continue using him."

"Ils, the man's a weapon. Like you are a weapon. Like I am a weapon. We fight The Darkness. What we 'deserve' doesn't factor into the calculations," Sigsrata said regretfully.

"What if I feel that Eielson's done enough?" Ilsbruk asked, looking the King in the eye. "What if I felt that the best thing we could do for him was to send him South. Let him train Mages in his ways, but keep him from the fight?"

"He will die on the field of battle, Ils, not in the halls of The Academy," Sigsrata said with a determined shake of his head. "Even if we could safely send him to The Academy, which I doubt, he would seek the fight rather than have others fight for him. I'm sorry. I am. My feelings don't change the fact that I will wring out every last drop of usefulness from the Ward as I can for the good of the kingdom."

"Still not right," Ilsbruk grimaced.

"It is my burden to bear as King," Sigsrata said. "The man is too useful to let him molder in the halls of The Academy."

"Sometimes you're a bastard, Sir."

"No, I'm always a bastard, Ils. Comes with being the King."

The two men rode quietly for a brief time before Ilsbruk broke the silence

"You believe that Eielson will not survive?"

"No more than you do, Ils. No more than you do. Man's a fighting Mage," the King said with a tone of regret. "We don't have many of those walking around for a reason."

"Do you think that any of the ancients had Eielson's skills?"

"I don't know but I want to doubt it, Ils. If the ancients could wield such power how did The Darkness overwhelm the old kingdoms? How did none of them survive the First Rising?" Sigsrata said with a shake of his head. "At least I hope that none of the ancient Mages had Eielson's abilities. If they did and still fell, what hope do we have?"

"There's hope," Ilsbruk suggested cautiously.

"You're getting maudlin, Ils," Sigsrata said with a teasing smile that was an attempt to break the growing sense of melancholy.

"There's hope," Ilsbruk insisted, sounding almost desperate to have the king agree with him.

"Betney's been good for you, Ils," the King said with another smile, ending the conversation.

Chapter 21

The column halted for the night at a Way Point adjacent to a Way Fort, the large defensive structure straddling the Road, ready to seal off the trade route in either direction should a section of the Line be breached. Galeb was relieved to find that he was being given a tent. He was heartedly sick of the wagon. Kieri made certain that the tent was comfortable and Galeb had water to bath before hurrying off to see to her Family and the other Obari. Galeb was trying to figure out if Kieri's Obari sensibilities drove her into the nightly gatherings that Galeb was thankful to have an excuse to avoid or if she was uncomfortable around so many Klynsheimers. He hoped that she wasn't trying to avoid him. Not that he'd blame Kieri if she was; he still slept more than he'd like. Galeb couldn't imagine it was too thrilling to sit around watching your husband sleep most of the day away.

Galeb did not immediately enter the tent. Under the watchful eyes of the corpsman – Galeb really needed to ask the man his name – he alternately stood in place or walked slowly, both activities having him pouring in sweat. He hated feeling so weak, but this wasn't the first time he'd had to build back his strength and endurance. Still he was grateful to be allowed to clean up afterward and to retire to the tent, which, like the wagon, was under the watchful eyes of Klynsheimer Troopers who did not even bother to hide the fact that they were assigned to make certain that he didn't wander off. A bit of a surprise was the dozen or so Obari who, wrapped in their illusions, watched both the Klynsheimers and Galeb.

Kawen - silent, traumatized Kawen - gave a bow of acknowledgement. Galeb noticed the red dyed left shoulder of

Kawen's tunic. When he looked closely he noticed that all of the Obari watching him had the same red dyed shoulder on their clothing. Apparently Galeb had some permanently assigned guardians. He wasn't happy with the revelation.

He was used to risking himself; Galeb could deal with looking out for himself. It was enough of an adjustment realizing that he put Kieri at risk, let alone a vast number of other people. Not that he could ever stop Kieri from walking with him; the woman always had been stubborn. Not that he wanted to be separated from Kieri. Life had just been a lot less complicated when he'd been on his own. He was never going to be alone again; he knew Obari culture well enough to understand that truth. Still, it wasn't an easy adjustment.

Galeb paused at the tent flap, straightened up and looked out into the growing darkness beyond the Ward Line with a sudden feeling of intense longing. He wanted to be walking the Line, away from the people who all seemed to want something from him. He wasn't stupid. Galeb knew that everyone in the encampment saw him as a means to an end.

Absurdly he missed the freedom from complications that his Patrol had given him. He shook his head and entered the tent. As much as he missed that freedom, Galeb also wished that Kieri was here with him, to hold him as he lay on the blankets. Something felt off, almost like there was a slight tremor under his skin. He shook his head again trying to rid himself of the feeling.

Jesia smiled from the shadows of cathedral oak, the massive roots forming arches that hid her quite well. She stood motionless but wanted to dance with joy. Her Mage had looked right at her! Eielson knew she was near and had sought her out!

Soon, my love. Soon. Jesia smiled wider. As soon as the party reached the terminus of the Ward Line she would have her man. Fool Klynsheimer seemed to forget the one weakness of fixed defenses. They were unmovable and could be broken simply by going around them.

Galeb paused as his eyes adjusted to The Darkness of the tent. The King sat on a camp stool in the corner watching him. He bowed his head and waited, showing proper deference. The King seemed amused.

"Proper deference from a Warder Mage. I had forgotten what that looked like," Sigsrata admitted.

Galeb, as was his habit, remained quiet. Intellectually he knew that the King was not here to do harm. Instinctively he was already preparing to step back and melt into the night. He hated the feeling but after all of these years authority figures still meant danger to him.

"Ward of the North, they call you, Mage Eielson," Sigsrata said, choosing to ignore how uncomfortable Galeb obviously felt. Both because he didn't think trying to put Eielson at ease would do any good and because his purposes did not require Galeb to be more comfortable. "Not entirely accurate, I think. The Obari have been heard referring to you as an 'Old One'. Any idea what that means?"

"No, Your Majesty," Galeb said, his voice its normal harsh softness.

"You might want to ask your wife," Sigsrata suggested, leaning back and making himself a bit more comfortable on the stool. "Titles come with expectations."

"I live to serve, Your Majesty. I am a Warder. That is all the title I need," Galeb said, wishing that the King would leave. He was having a hard time holding back the panicked nervousness. Absurdly he wished that he had his fighting knife. Kieri had the weapon and wasn't giving it back to him until he was healed enough to wield it.

"No, I don't think so, Eielson. You are definitely not a Warder," Sigsrata said with a shake of his head. "A Warder carves runes into defenses. A Warder doesn't take the fight to The Darkness. I don't know what you are, but you are no Warder. The Twelve were fools to waste your potential."

"I understand that the Twelve have paid for their mistakes," Galeb said, wincing slightly at the tone of satisfaction that crept into his voice.

"Children make mistakes, Eielson. What the Twelve did were not mistakes," Sigsrata said harshly. "But enough of the

Twelve. They are dead. You are not and it is you I need to learn more about."

"As it pleases Your Majesty," Galeb said with another dip of his head.

Sigsrata sighed. Eielson should stand proud and powerful. He needed Eielson to stand proud and powerful. Instead he got an anti-social cripple. He did not have the time or inclination to baby the man.

"Tell me, Eielson, when you faced The Darkness in the Valley were you afraid?" the King asked.

"Terrified," admitted Galeb.

"Never admit that," Sigsrata snapped pointing an accusing finger at Galeb. "Troopers can admit fear. They are but men. You are not a man anymore. You are a symbol of hope, defiance, and power. The men will look to see how you react to The Darkness. They need to see confidence or they will break. If they break, their deaths will be your fault."

"But, Your Majesty, I'm just-."

"You are the *Ward of the North*," Sigsrata said harshly. "You are the *Ward who stood Alone and survived*. Nothing else matters when it comes time to stand in the battle line.

"Understand this, Ward. I have mustered the largest army that Klynsheim has seen in centuries and I do not think that all that serried steel will be enough against the Rising. For every veteran I have, I have twenty new recruits who barely know one end of a bill from another. Even among the veterans, none have experience with what is coming.

"You though, have stood against The Darkness on its own ground and thrown it back. That one fact makes it very important that you stand as an example."

"Your Majesty seems to forget that I fell to The Darkness and only survived because my Wife and Captain Ilsbruk saved me," Galeb said, heat in his own tone.

"A bit of fire, Eielson? Good. You fell, yes, I know that you fell. But you got back up. You kept fighting."

"I didn't -."

Sigsrata cut off Galeb's words with a slashing gesture of his hand and then picked up a quick stick from where it lay on the ground near him. Attached to the stick was a slate, rune inscribed to turn the stone into a viewer of sorts.

"Do you know what your wife has been doing many of the nights she spends with her people? No? She has been telling the Obari stories. She has been showing them this," Sigsrata said, activating the stick with a calculated precision that showed the King was still uncomfortable using the tools.

The image were of Kieri shaping an illusion. The illusion was an image of Galeb's final Warding in the Valley. 'The Way is Shut' burned in the night air, massive and terrible in its intent. Galeb shuddered in remembered pain at the titanic collision between the Skrieksgrata and the Warding.

"Wondrous memories the Obari have; great attention to detail. Sonovonol doesn't tell stories and show these image because her people lack entertainment. The Families are afraid and need reassurance that they will be safe in the South. So

Sonovonol shows her people you. A man half dead who still manages to stand and Ward no matter the cost to himself.

"My Mage advisors tell me that the Ward you used should not have been so powerful or so large. But it was both, despite its simple nature. You seem to do the impossible, Eielson."

"I'm just a Mage," Galeb protested. A voice inside of his head was screaming at him not to be noticed; to slip away.

"Have you heard nothing?" Sigsrata demanded, truly angry. "You are not 'just' anything. You lost that right to be 'just a Mage' at the Valley. Everyone watches you now. You have to be more."

"What if I can't be more?" Galeb asked plaintively.

Sigsrata sighed, letting go of his anger and understanding that nothing in Eielson's life had prepared the man for the role he needed to assume.

"Tell me this, Eielson, how did you survive eight years of Warding six hundred miles of Road?"

"By enduring," Galeb answered honestly.

"Then you can endure what I am asking of you as well," Sigsrata said, standing and gesturing with the quick stick. "Your duty demands no less."

"Duty," Galeb whispered.

"Yes, I know you understand duty," Sigsrata said, moving to leave the tent. "Hold to your duty."

Galeb stood unmoving for several minutes after the King left, a sense of familiar hopelessness seizing him. Duty. Yes, he knew those chains very well. He turned to face the Ward Line, feeling the pulse of every protection like a second heartbeat. The yearning grew to be almost unbearable, a siren song beckoning him back to the simplicity of the familiar. He had to clench his fists and breathe deeply. Around his arms the Wards stirred to life, reforming, reenergizing, and pulsing with a power stronger than his body as without thinking he added to their complexity, desperate to find something to hold him here.

Jans stood staring down Obel a few yards from Eielson's tent. Now that the King had had his interview with Eielson, Obel was all for barreling into the tent and begin interrogating Galeb about his techniques. Jans was explaining how bad an idea that was to Obel who was stubbornly refusing to listen.

"What do you want me to do, Jans? Walk in there and mother him? Be sweet and supportive? That's your tactic, not mine," Obel argued, smoothing out his beard in irritation. Obel was quite proud of the beard. He felt it gave him a sense of age and wisdom.

"There is nothing wrong with being sweet and supportive, Obel. After everything the man's been through I don't think a barrage of cold and calculated questions is the right approach," Jans argued back.

"Seriously, Jans? You've seen what the man can do. More importantly you've seen how willing he is to fight and how well he fares in combat. We need to understand his techniques before the idiot gets himself killed once and for all.

"We're lucky he's still alive, for God's sake. There is no time for niceties. We need to learn as much as we can as fast as we can and now is the time to do that. Especially with the barbarian woman away visiting her kin. We don't need her distracting Eielson."

"Oh, I'm certain that Eielson will be more than willing to cooperate if you explain to him such impeccable logic," Jans said mockingly. "Just tell the man that we're pressed for time because he has a death wish and his wife is inconveniently foreign. I imagine that explanation will go over quite well."

"You two do know that my husband isn't deaf? Banged up, I'll admit, but not deaf," Kieri asked, shaking her head at the two Mages, her hands on her hips, as she walked up to the tent. "For that matter, I'm sure that half the camp heard your argument.

Obel turned his head to put the Obari woman in her place and stopped, tilting his head in puzzlement. Kieri glared at the Mage who was now blatantly staring at her.

"You do realize that I'm married?" Kieri asked in disgust. "Contrary to any misguided fantasies that you might be having Obari are monogamous."

"What?" Obel said with a start. "Why would you think that I would desire you?"

The Mage gestured at Kieri from head to toe, indicating that he found her more than wanting.

Kieri's eyes narrowed further in anger.

"Brilliant, Obel. Alienate the one woman who has a great deal of influence over Eielson," Jans said, scowling at Obel before turning to Kieri and smiling. "Really, my dear, you are quite lovely despite what my idiot colleague thinks."

"Of course," Obel said, with a cough as he realized that Jans had a point. "Quite lovely in a...in a...savage, unrefined kind of way, I suppose. Bathe a bit more, get some better clothes, I'm sure that you would be...er...lovely?"

As sad as it was that Obel had to borrow Jans own compliment it was very clear that there was no sincerity in his words. Kieri was also highly offended by the statement that she needed to bathe more often. The Mage obviously couldn't tell the difference between a tan and dirt.

Kieri straightened to her full height, admittedly a few inches short of Jans, and looked cold and imperious. Shadow and moonlight gathered around her in cold authority, turning the woman into the very vision of a dangerous eldritch being whose hand was stroking the hilt of a terrible weapon.

"Could you stop that," Obel said with an impatient wave of his hand. "You're blocking my sight of the Wardings."

The illusion faded with a start.

"You can see them?" she asked Obel in surprise.

"What are you talking about?" Jans demanded.

"Yes and I'm talking about Wardings," Obel explained. "Eielson's woven hundreds...no thousands of Wardings around this woman. I'm trying to ascertain how he's done it."

"This 'woman' has a name," Kieri snapped. As much as she loved Galeb she had little patience for his ill-mannered people. "And his name is Galeb Sonovonol."

Jans tilted her head trying to see what Obel was talking about. As much as she hated to admit it, Obel's skill outweighed her own in detecting subtle Wardings.

"Are you certain?" she asked in mild frustration.

"Of course I'm certain," Obel said offended. "They are well hidden, but there is a bit of roughness I would expect from someone like Eielson. The man always went for the simple, never understanding the truly intricate. I'm amazed that he was able to craft something of such complexity as what I'm seeing. Here, let me pour some power into them. Maybe deactivate a Ward or two and you will be able to see what I'm talking about."

Obel reached out a hand intending to do just that. Kieri took a step back, her hand going to her sword at the audacity of the man who thought he would tinker with something that Galeb had created specifically for her. It felt like a violation of her very being.

"I wouldn't do that," snapped a voice, low, harsh and soft, but full of awful command.

Galeb was standing in the entrance to the tent, as straight as he was able to, his eyes flat and dangerous. Golden light swam around his arms.

Jans gasped.

"What?" Obel said, lowering his hand and turning to look at Eielson. He winced at the sight.

"Oh, Good God," Jans hissed under her breath, equally as taken aback by Eielson's appearance as Obel. They had both seen images of him but neither were prepared for the ravages of an eight year Patrol and a desperate battle. Of course, she was focused on his appearance. Obel was focused on the Wards wrapping themselves around the man.

"You Klynsheimers are strange," Kieri said with a forced laugh. "It's just Galeb Sonovonol."

She looked dismissively at the two Mages. Yes Galeb was a bit worse for wear but to her he was the same man that he always had been, albeit a bit frustrating. The man was supposed to be taking it easy, not staring down Mages and weaving Wardings.

"No, it's not," Bob said from somewhere in the evening gloom. "He stopped being 'just Galeb Sonovonol' in the Valley."

"Shut up, Bob," Kieri said in frustration. Problem was that she agreed with Bob. As much as she loved Galeb he had scared her a bit ever since he'd called down the lightning. She was doing her best to ignore the Wardings that increasingly looked to be swarming around his arms like a bunch of enraged insects.

"Why is everyone trying to silence me? Is it envy?" Bob demanded.

Jans' eyebrows rose at the question and she smirked a bit in disbelief.

"Bob...," Kieri growled in warning.

"Yeah, thanks for letting everyone know who I am. Saves some time. Did anyone mention that I killed a Skrieksgrata?"

"Bob!"

"Did you really kill a Skrieksgrata?" Jans asked, morbidly curious as she looked around the night, trying to find Bob.

"Yes, I did," Bob said, his voice going all funny deep, in a way that Kieri imagined Bob thought was smooth. "Would you like to talk about it? Maybe somewhere clothing optional?"

"Um...no," Jans said, disbelief at the offer clearly written across her face.

"But I killed a Skrieksgrata."

"Yes, you keep saying that," Jans agreed.

"Why shouldn't I touch the Wards around your woman?" Obel demanded, interrupting the conversation. "I know my craft beyond well."

Obel was impressed by what he was seeing. However, he was determined not to seem too impressed and focused on somehow lessening Galeb's status so that the men would be on more equal ground.

Both Jans and Kieri glared at Obel because of the 'woman' comment. He made Sonovonol sound like a mistress or whore.

"Not well enough to not tinker with what you don't understand," Galeb said, his features harsh and stern. "I can assure you that any attempt to manipulate those Wardings around my *wife* would end quite badly for you. I know my type of crafting far more intimately than you ever will, Jargsin. I seem to remember you and Sepsrigga being quite dismissive of my experimentations back at The Academy so I doubt that you've changed your area of study since then."

"That was a long time ago," Jans said, trying to be conciliatory. "What you have managed to accomplish here in the

North is simply amazing. We only want to understand these techniques of yours and determine how they can best help Klynsheim."

"I wrote a treatise," Galeb said flatly. "It was sent to The Academy as per protocols. I suggest you read it before trying to tamper with my Wardings. What are simple runes by themselves become incredibly intricate – incredibly sensitive - in combination. I wouldn't recommend tinkering with them until you understand the underlying theory. Particularly since the basis of what I do is founded upon eight years of experiences that you lack and a quite extensive study of Obari illusion crafting.

Jans winced at the reminder of Galeb's experiences along the Ward Line. Obel simply rolled his eyes. Kieri grinned saucily, running a hand down her side suggestively when he mentioned 'studying'.

"And here I thought that all of those years you were just staring at my body," Kieri giggled.

Galeb smiled warmly at her before staring stonily again at the two Mages.

"If you figured out how to do this," Obel said trying to reestablish his position after being thoroughly chastised as if he were a second year student and gesturing vaguely in the direction of Galeb and Kieri's wards, "I'm certain that I can figure it out."

"Good luck with that," Galeb said, raising an eyebrow before turning to Kieri with a smile. "Why don't we leave these two to use their apparently impressive minds to uncover all sorts of interesting facts about Warding? I for one feel like cuddling."

Kieri smiled and then smiled even more broadly when Galeb waggled his eyebrows suggestively. She moved into the tent with languid grace, drawing her husband in after her. The tent flap billowed slightly as she tied the flap shut.

"Well that went well," Jans said sarcastically.

Obel was standing still, looking incredulous at having been dismissed so casually, his mouth working but no words coming out.

"He-he just insulted me," Obel finally managed to say.

"You think? People tend to take offense when you talk down to them and insult their wives," Jans pointed out.

"I have a mind to walk into that tent and -!"

"I have a sword," Kieri called through the fabric. "You come in here and you'll find out how well I can use it."

"She wouldn't!"

"She would," Galeb advised. "Kieri once faced down a Shaeloman with obsessive tendencies that thought to get between the two of us. I hardly think that she would see you as a challenge. Now if you don't mind I am trying to 'cuddle' with my wife."

"Wait-what? Are you suggesting that your-? That's just ill mannered!" Obel objected trying to sound morally superior and win at least one victory in this encounter. He wasn't used to being dismissed so easily.

"When did you turn into such a prude?" Jans asked arching a brow, enjoying Obel being put in his place for once.

"I am not a prude. I simply don't condone turning 'cuddling' into a spectator sport by announcing to all and sundry that I am engaging in such activities."

"Then why are you still outside of our tent?" Kieri asked, laughter filling her voice.

"I- this is not the end of the discussion, Eielson. We will be talking more when you remember how to act in a more civilized manner," Obel promised sounding like a shrill school marm.

"What has gotten into you?" Jans laughing in disbelief. "Is this the arrogant and mighty Obel Jargsin?"

"Shut up," Obel snapped as he stalked away. "Don't forget that he basically called you an idiot as well."

"No," Jans said, "Eielson didn't call me an idiot. He correctly pointed out that we don't know enough about his techniques to alter his Wardings."

"Shut up," Obel repeated over his shoulder.

"Don't take offense," Bob said to Jans from somewhere to her left. "People tell me to shut up all of the time. Don't mean anything by it. Since you seem to be free at the moment could I perhaps show you to the women's bathing area?"

"Oh, your *Bob*, aren't you?" Jans asked, looking around for the man and realizing that she knew more about Bob than he thought. "Your mother already talked to me about you and bathing areas. Considering that I don't get my thrills by having strange men watch me bathe, I'll decline. Besides I need to see about obtaining a book."

"Are you sure? I killed a Skrieksgrata," Bob offered, as if that entitled him to some special consideration.

"I seem to recall that Eielson slew hundreds of Darkness," Jans pointed out. "You don't see me throwing myself at him."

"I don't share," Kieri called from inside the tent in a voice that was filled with warning.

"See, he's taken. I am quite available," offered Bob hopefully.

"No thank you, Bob," Jans said moving away. "You might want to work on a better technique for wooing women."

"I don't know," Bob reflected. "It's bound to work eventually."

Chapter 22

The Wards were screaming. At least that was how it felt to Galeb as he lurched upright from a sound sleep. His head was pounding and his heart was spasming in his chest. Thunder echoed through the night as lightning clove the sky. Rain began in a soft patter and then came down in a torrent.

He struggled up, disentangling himself from a protesting Kieri who was already reaching for her clothes and sword. She called for him to wait, but as soon as he had his breeches on he was out of the tent.

Galeb stood in the rain, barefoot and shirtless for a moment, staring north of the Line. He walked towards the posts whose color was already turning from a warm gentle yellow glow to an ominous red. Troopers were beginning to call out warnings in the Way Fort. Sure enough the Obari had also stirred.

At first he could not see the source of the disturbance until he stepped almost into the Line itself. Then he noticed the small shapes, barely bigger than rats, throwing themselves by the hundreds at a single Ward post. Melgort, vermin-like Darkness who tended to clean up the messes left by the bigger Darkness.

Melgort were scavengers; they should not be attacking the Line. But the melgort were attacking the Line and while one or two small bodies posed no real threat to the defenses, hundreds were going to cause a certain amount of stress.

Galeb ignored the melgort; they were a distraction at best and a nuisance at worst. Something else was out there waiting beyond the Ward Line. Something that could drive the melgort into a reckless frenzy.

There, near a copse of cathedral oaks, was a bunch of vines moving against the direction of the wind. A lightning flash gave him a quick, strobing vision of the Spriegs commanding its diminutive thralls. The Spriegs was a juvenile, small, with a bloated head barely four feet around.

Such a relatively weak creature attacking the Ward Line didn't make sense. It couldn't hope to breach the Line unless.... Galeb hurried over as best he could to reach the Ward post being attacked.

"Galeb, what's wrong?" Kieri asked, running up to join him.

Troopers assigned as his escort were gathering around with lanterns as well as a few Obari with the red shoulder patches. The Obari blended in with the rain and night, largely unnoticed by the Klynsheimers.

He didn't answer. Instead he called the Wards to life around his arms and crafted 'Lights the Way', sending the rune slashing into the ground and trees near the Spriegs, revealing The Darkness. It hurt to do so; the distance was greater than he expected and his body was none too happy with the exertion.

Arbalests on the Way Fort walls opened up, sending bolts at the Spriegs which was weaving away in a frantic attempt to avoid the attacks while maintaining control of its thralls.

"Nta!" Kieri cursed before noticing that Galeb was hurrying away towards the Ward post being attacked. "What's going on?"

It was as Galeb had feared. Someone had defaced the Ward post under assault. A few quick sloppy slashes across the

Ward faces. Without the redundancies that Galeb placed on all of his Wardings the post already would have failed.

"Kieri, I need tools. A file and fine grit," Galeb said, clenching his teeth in anger.

"Move aside, Eielson," Obel said, tools in hand as he and Jans hurried over. "Unless you think that I'm incapable of removing fouled Wards?"

Galeb twisted his lips in distaste before noticing the King's presence and immediately adopting a more withdrawn demeanor, the voices in his head warning him to avoid notice, avoid provoking a reaction. The King watched Galeb for a moment and Galeb knew that the King was taking in the sight of all the scars, particularly the ones on his back. Galeb took the look as a rebuke and reminder of what the King could order done if Galeb caused trouble. He swallowed bitterness and stood back, giving Obel plenty of room to effect the first steps of repair.

Sigsrata was shocked. It was one thing to hear Ilsbruk's report on the beating Eielson had endured, it was another to see the sheer mass of scar tissue on the man's back. The Mage noticed Sigsrata's appraisal and backed away from the lantern light, the expression on the man's face guarded before the night and rain obscured him. For a moment the King had an uneasy feeling that Eielson was expecting another beating and was going to run – well limp away. He remembered Ils comment that the Mage was broken; attitudes were going to have to change.

Obel was filing away the worst of the damage and Jans was applying grit to smooth out the roughness. Both Warders worked quickly and efficiently, doing their best to ignore the broken melgort bodies that fell away from the Ward Line and the multitude of melgort that took their place.

"Did you see his back?" Obel asked Jans, never taking his eyes off the task at hand.

"How could I miss it?" Jans hissed, her mouth pinched in a scowl.

"What do you think he did to deserve a beating like that?" he asked.

"If it were anyone but Galeb would you even be asking that question?" Jans spit out.

"What do you mean?" Obel asked, arching a brow.

"You assume that Galeb deserved the beating. Would you assume that any other Warder deserved to be beaten?" Jans demanded, the motions of her hands not reflecting the anger in her voice.

Obel had the decency to think about the question before answering.

"Probably not," he admitted.

"Then why do you assume Galeb deserved the beating?"

"Why else would he be beaten? Those scars aren't the result of a few swipes across the back. That's the result of a very methodical and purposeful flogging."

Jans shot Obel a look to clearly communicate that he was being an idiot for still insisting that Galeb had deserved the punishment.

"Eielson was blameless," Sigsrata said, interrupting the two Mages. The King's hair and beard were sodden messes plastered to his face. "As near as we can determine the Twelve ordered the beating when Eielson started to question his Patrol. It was a way to silence him without the need to replace him."

"It took over a month for Galeb to recover," Kieri explained from where she stood nearby, fury filling every word. The Obari woman had the sense to be wearing a cloak. "The Troopers who did it threw him over a horse, and carried him miles away from their patrol area and dumped him on The Road. By the time we found him Galeb had crawled over a mile trying to reach our range. His back was covered in blood and flies.

"Even after all of that, as soon as he could stand up without pulling open his wounds Galeb went back to his Patrol."

There was only the sound of grit, file and rain for a moment before Kieri spoke again.

"How he does not hate you people I will never understand. I will have to hate you enough for the both of us."

The Obari walked away, her hand on the hilt of her sword, using the occasional lightning burst to find her husband in the gloom. Other Obari eyes remained to watch in judgement.

"This was purposeful sabotage," Obel said idly, giving voice to what everyone already knew. "Do you think the Obari did it?"

"Journeyman, you are perhaps brilliant when it comes to studying Wardings. In everything else I despair that you are an idiot," Sigsrata commented drily. "It's best not to speculate openly about possible enemies in their hearing."

Jesia smiled her Shaeloman grin, all teeth and glee, satisfied with a good night's work. Let the Klynsheimers see how unworthy they were to be near her Mage. Let them see every bit of pain carved into Eielson's skin and know shame.

Let her Mage see the doubt on the faces of his countrymen. Let him hear their speculations and realize that he did not belong among the Klynsheimers.

Kieri did not return to the tent long. She knew that Galeb would not be there and only paused to grab him a cloak. Nor did she have to seek him out. Her kin let her know that he waited just outside the encampment, lost in his thoughts and inspecting the Ward Line for any additional damage.

She gently pulled him away from the Line and put the cloak on him before holding him close in silent comfort.

"That was purposeful sabotage," Galeb said into her hair as he breathed in deeply.

"What else would it be?" Kieri said sarcastically.

"But it was sloppy, barely mischievous, not a real threat," Galeb said confused.

"A message?" Kieri speculated.

"Probably, but from whom? Supporters of the Twelve, people unhappy with the King? That crazy Shaeloman?"

"All Shaeloman are crazy," Kieri pointed out. "Besides, no Darkness would have been able to pierce the Line."

"Unless it coerced someone to do the dirty work for it," Galeb pointed out. "Shaeloman are manipulators."

"'Her' work, not 'It'" Kieri reminded Galeb with a grin, as she pulled back and looked him in the eyes.

"I prefer 'it'," Galeb said with a shudder.

"I don't think you get a say in picking its gender," Kieri teased.

"I don't think you would find this so funny if it was obsessed with you," Galeb said, scowling.

"No," Kieri agreed smiling. "I have my man. Like I told that ass of a Mage, we Obari are monogamous."

NO! Jesia mentally shrieked in outrage. *He is not your man! He is mine! Mine! You cannot have him!*

She turned away with rage boiling inside of her. Jesia should never have wasted her time with that child Spriegs. What had seemed like a good bit of fun had soured. That bitch Obari was causing Jesia anguish. Time to return the favor.

Her Mage was being naughty. It was time to remind him not to trifle with her affections.

Chapter 23

Three days later Troopers were racing down the Line as Ward Posts began to flash amber. The amber color was an emergency code, signifying multiple Ward Post failures beyond the Line's ability to compensate. The lights began to blink, creating a ripple effect leading westward, indicating the direction of the failure.

Galeb took the emergency in stride, actually preparing his equipment as he fell into a routine honed by years of solo action. Kieri looked at what Galeb was doing, glanced towards the Ward Posts, shook her head, grabbed him by the ear and twisted until he looked her in the eye with a scowl on his face. She gently told him to let others handle the emergency, reminding him that he no longer held a solo Patrol. Kieri refrained from pointing out that Galeb was in no shape to deal with such an emergency, since his fastest speed was still a hobble. She let him hold onto his pride with a loving smile and a kiss.

Ilsbruk's reaction to the emergency was to roll his eyes and scowl at the Ward Line as if it were conspiring against him. Sergeant Gorgorin cursed as a matter of habit, not putting much bite into the muttered 'grieshtata'. In the sergeant's opinion there was far too much excitement to be found in Eielson's presence and he should in no way be surprised that yet another disaster presented itself. The King looked at the Ward Line as if he it were personally insulting him before called out commands.

"Jargsin and Sepsrigga with the advance party under Ilsbruk," Sigsrata ordered. "The rest form up around Eielson's wagon. This emergency reeks of a trap and I don't want us caught unaware."

"Sepsrigga," Galeb called from the wagon, his voice its usual rasp. He couldn't remember a time when his voice was stronger. "Look for 'the Cat's Smile'. I have bolt holes all along the Ward Line. Get yourself and Jargsin to safety if an attack comes."

Jans smiled in thanks and Obel muttered 'Of course you do', before turning their horses to join Ilsbruk and the Troopers gathering around the Captain.

The Klynsheimers were not the only ones preparing. Illusions flowed around the Obari, some fading from sight, while others seemed to become bigger, more powerful. Feelings of threat and menace filled the air. The Klynsheimers didn't notice that their own forms seemed suddenly more intimidating, lending a feeling of strength to the defense. The number of Troopers suddenly doubled.

The Obari hoped that whatever enemy they faced would either be too intimidated by the Klynsheimers or at least attack the southerners first, giving the Obari time to withdraw. The bulk of the Families began retreating back in the direction of the nearest Way point while only the strongest warriors remained to help guard Galeb.

Ilsbruk led a hundreds away while the remaining escort advanced cautiously. Kieri fingered the hilt of her sword after handing Galeb his fighting knife. He took the weapon, tucked it into his belt and went back to carving a staff from a tree limb a helpful Obari had gotten him the day before.

The staff was a new idea, not containing any defensive Wards. Instead an intricate array of 'Gathers the Light' and

'Leavens the Bread that would fill the staff with energy allowing it to flow down a twisting path from tip to butt and back again in a slow procession. The idea was that this method would allow the accumulation of more power than a staff or post this size could normally handle, keeping the energy moving along a loop so that no one part of the staff bore too much energy at one time.

Normal Ward Posts had to constantly discharge energy throughout the Ward Network or risk overloading. With this new design Galeb would theoretically be able to allow a greater amount of power to accumulate before discharge became necessary.

Galeb had had a lot of time to think while healing, particularly about the limits he faced in battle and how if he'd had more power at his disposal he might not have fallen so quickly. Galeb couldn't channel more power through his body. The craft didn't work that way. Physical limits kept his body from burning itself out. But if he could find a suitable storage medium to tap into, drawing power through and from it instead of himself, he would be only shaping the power, not directly channeling it. Galeb should be able to double or possibly triple his Warding time. At least he hoped so. Galeb was going to be awfully disappointed if all he succeeded in doing was allow himself to craft for two or three seconds longer.

Or blew himself up; that probably would be more disappointing and painful. Galeb was fairly certain that Kieri would be mad. Maybe; she might just laugh at him. It was hard to tell with women.

The only problem was that the staff would take a while to fully charge. The flow of energy needed to be slow so as not to overwhelm the wood.

As Galeb carved – he didn't want to trust such intricate work to burning with light Wards just yet – he wondered if what he was making was the original purpose of the staves that the Twelve had once carried. If a practical tool had become a simple ornament over time. Galeb was under no delusion that he was some genius that had just created a whole new method of Warding. He figured that he was just rediscovering old ideas. He felt better thinking that way. Otherwise he was recklessly experimenting and just might be creating something that really was going to blow up in his hands. Hmmm...best to make certain Kieri wasn't too close when he tried this out.

He suddenly noticed that the inside of the wagon was getting brighter. He looked up and saw Kieri's Wards were becoming visible. Galeb paused for an instant to reflect on how beautiful she looked Ward lit. Then he realized how big the danger had to be for her Wards to already have activated.

His eyes widened at the realization and then a thought struck him. Maybe he could tweak the Wards into some sort of early warning system. Hmmm...no, concentrate on the immediate problem. Galeb opened his mouth to give warning. Okay, he tried calling out a warning, but his voice lacked the volume, cracking long before the required level was reached.

"Darkness comes!" Kieri yelled for him, patting him on the shoulder as she did so.

Galeb scowled at the gesture, knowing the Kieri meant for it to be comforting, but not liking it in the least.

"Cut the horses loose," Galeb ordered, standing and tearing the cover from the wagon.

"Just because we're married doesn't mean you can order me around," Kieri said, scowling, hands on her hips.

"Cut the horses loose, please," Galeb revised.

"That's better, I suppose," Kieri said, still annoyed, moving out of the wagon and releasing the horses that would only be an encumbrance in an attack.

Finally free of the tarp, Galeb stood tall on the wagon bed, golden light racing up and down his arms as his own Wardings came to life.

"Get behind the wagon," he said, his voice suddenly powerful and commanding, light glowing around him as if a second sun had descended to the earth. Galeb raised his hands and slammed 'The Way is Shut' into the ground a dozen yards in front of the wagon, burning the ward into the earth. For good measure he reinforced the Wards with the 'Roots run deep'.

Galeb wasn't happy with the Wards. Using the soil as a medium was a fool's game under any other circumstances. A single scuff or a bit of rain was enough to mar the Wards into uselessness. Desperation; always desperation. It was just like back in the Valley. It had been a miracle that his tangle trap had even worked.

"A bit much, don't you think, Bob?" Galeb asked, looking down at himself when he was finished.

"I'm doing the voice," Bob said dismissively, sitting on the back of the wagon. "Kawen's working on the light, though I wouldn't thank him. Whatever is coming is going to be focused on you."

"And yet you're sitting right behind me," Galeb pointed out.

"Better chance of not being hit by whatever insanity you're about to unleash," Bob replied laconically.

"We need to form a battle line in front of the wagon," Sigsrata argued. "There isn't enough room on The Road for the horses to maneuver."

"Agreed, Your Majesty," Galeb acknowledged, fighting down the urge not to argue. He was entering battle. No time for hesitation. "Best to form it behind my Wardings until we know what comes."

Sigsrata scowled, giving Galeb a look that indicated the King wasn't an idiot and began calling out orders. A mass of Troopers bearing lances moved to the front of the wagon, forming up just short of the Wards. Archers moved to the rear, bows knocked and ready. The rest gathered up the horses and walked them clear.

Galeb was contemplating a third layer of Wards when The Darkness came charging down the path.

Ever present kielsgruntara, though a small enough pack. Lumbering in the wake of the creatures were Grass Titans.

If you ever wondered what the preferred prey of a Skrieksgrata was, it was the Grass Titan. Massively muscled, cloven hooved, standing on two enormous haunches, barrel chested, arms thick as a Skrieksgrata's thigh, elongated snout and antlers that would give a moose pause.

A head and shoulders bigger than a Skrieksgrata, Grass Titans were vegetarians, but ferociously territorial. The animals did not tolerate any other creatures in their presence. Given that the Titans were prey animals that bit of xenophobia was understandable. More than likely the kielsgruntara were not proceeding the Titans, but running away from the massive beasts.

The ground shook under the Titans' stride – Grass Titans out-massed Skrieksgrata by at least two to one and none of that mass was fat. There were three of the beasts, one buck and two doe. It was easy enough to distinguish the two genders for obvious reasons.

"Don't worry, Love, you've no need to feel envious," Kieri said with a straight face as she gestured towards the buck. "It wouldn't be a fair comparison."

"I wasn't making any comparisons until you said something," Galeb said drily.

"I don't know about Eielson, but *I* have nothing to be envious about," the King said with a grin, winking at Kieri

The King laughed at the sudden look of speculation on Kieri's face and the look of annoyance on Galeb's face as he poked his wife in the shoulder.

"What?" Kieri demanded equally annoyed at being poked.

"You're mentally undressing the King," Galeb complained.

"What? No, I'm not," she argued. "I'm just wondering how threatened the man must feel to have to make that comment. He's obviously not as secure as you are."

"Right…," Galeb said in disbelief.

"Hey!" Sigsrata protested, offended.

Kieri laughed at both of the men.

The King scowled and then cursed when he looked closer at the Titans. There was crumpled armor dangling from one of the does' antlers. It was not a comforting thought to wonder where the rest of the Trooper had gotten to since the scrap of armor was not empty.

"Betney's going to kill me if Ils is hurt," Sigsrata grumbled.

Archers began to loose arrows at the beasts, though the Titans didn't seem to notice the pricks until one lucky archer hit one of the does in the eye. The Titan fell to the earth bawling in pain, thrashing in agony. The buck bellowed and rage and charged forward with greater speed.

The kielsgruntara hit Galeb's Wardings first, slamming to a halt with the sound of splintering bone. Those Darkness that survived the impact were quickly ground into paste by the enraged buck. The Wards buckled under the impact, barely holding.

"If you are going to do something suitably impressive now would be the time," Sigsrata suggested, wincing at the clash of Titan and Ward.

"I have an idea," Galeb admitted.

"I don't think I am going to like this," Bob muttered before saying louder, "I think we are in too confined an area for lighting or fire."

"I know. Anyone have any sling stones?" Galeb asked.

Both Bob and Kieri looked at Galeb like he was an idiot. Obari children and most adults had slings because they were an effective hunting weapon. That said, the chances of someone having a stone was rather high. Galeb had stones in his hands quickly.

Galeb burned 'the Conflicted Lovers' into the stones. He then took aim at the buck's head and burned the same rune into its forehead as it slammed its antlers into the energy barrier before being repulsed yet again, enraging the animal even further.

"Get ready," Galeb said, "This is either going to be impressive or stupefying."

Kieri shook her head at the comment, her sword out and Wards burning with cool malice as she prepared to protect her husband from whatever risk he was about to take. Galeb grinned at her, mostly to hide his nervousness and fear, and then threw the stones at the buck.

'The Conflicted Lovers' was a teaching Ward, designed to emphasize to young students the importance of choosing Wards that were mutually supportive, enhancing a group of Wards harmoniously. 'The Conflicted Lovers' was a Ward that constantly attracted and repelled itself, each repulse increasing the intensity of the attraction. In other words, it was a very disharmonious rune.

The stones that flew at the buck slammed into its forehead, connecting with the rune burned there before repelling and then slamming back into place. The result was a constant assault on the Titan's forehead, leading everyone to wonder what would break first, the stones' or the creature's skull.

The buck stumbled backwards, trying to swat the stones away. The remaining doe tried to help, snatching the stones in her massive hands. The result of this was not what the doe intended. Instead of stopping the attraction, the stones in her hands continued their momentum. The result was that the doe's fist slammed into the buck's forehead. The doe bawled in surprise and the buck cried out in pain, backhanding the doe in desperation to stop the female from hitting him. Soon both Titans were fighting, antlers tangling, hooves and fists smashing, while the stones continued to pummel the buck's forehead.

"That is the most ridiculous fight that I have ever seen," Sigsrata said, his mouth hanging open in disbelief before laughing hysterically.

Bob, Galeb and the King winced in unison as the doe kicked the buck in the groin.

"That a girl!" Kieri called out encouragingly, laughing and pumping a fist in support of the female Titan.

The buck kicked out as it fell, catching the doe in the chest and sending the creature flying through the air. The Ward posts kept the Titan from crashing clear, instead bouncing it twice before it landed in a cloud of dirt on The Road.

The buck stood, admittedly hunching a bit, and threw its head back, bellowing its anger. This turned out to be a poor decision as the doe leapt out of the dirt cloud and caught the male in the throat with her antlers, tearing skin and muscle away in a gout of blood and flesh.

"That, boys, is why women always win!" Kieri laughed. "Stupid men always too full of themselves."

Sigsrata and Galeb exchanged a look.

"I'd sleep with a knife handy if you ever piss her off," the King advised.

"Pffft," Kieri said dismissively, waving her hand at the two men. "As if Galeb could take me in a fight."

"Thanks, Love," Galeb said, twisting his lips.

Kieri just beamed at him.

The King laughed.

"There is still one Titan left," Bob pointed out. "In case you've forgotten."

The doe was pacing back and forth, stopping to stomp the dead buck occasionally. The stones were helping, continuing to batter the buck's skull with jarring thumps.

"I'll leave that up to Your Majesty," Galeb said, reinforcing his impromptu Ward Line.

Arrows caught the doe's attention and she proceeded to pound on the Ward Line. The King stood just on the safe side of the line and lashed out with his axe, hamstringing the Titan. Troopers moved up with lances to finish it off.

The doe bawled in agony, reaching out and snatching up several of the lances, dragging men over the Ward Line. The Troopers tried to let go and fall back, but the Titan lashed out with swipes of her massive hands, pinning them to the earth and crushing their armor until their bones snapped, blood pouring out of the men's mouths.

Sigsrata roared in outrage, seeming like he was going to outshout the Titan. He raised his axe and strode forward. Troopers moved to stop him but fell back at his glare.

"I don't think that's a good idea," Bob said.

Without thinking Galeb flung his hand forward, burning wards into the axe head so fast that his vision blurred. 'Wind in the trees' wrapped around 'Hammer hardens steel'. 'Hand hones the blade' embraced 'First rays of the sun'. The axe suddenly thrummed with power, though the King took no notice, crossing the Line with purposeful steps that quickly increased in speed as he hurtled himself at the wounded Titan.

The doe smashed a fist at Sigsrata, but he dodged aside with more grace than a man his size should be capable of performing. As he moved, the King spun, the axe cleaving the doe's extended arm. The blow would have normally driven deep. The Ward wrought weapon not only tore the arm from the Titan's body but smashed the animal backwards stunning the doe.

Monopolizing on the doe's surprise, the King followed up with two crushing blows to its other arm and chest. Blood fountained, bathing the King and causing him to roar louder, the axe rising and falling as he dismembered the beast.

"King Bloody fist!" one Trooper shouted in salute.

"King Blood shanks!" yelled another.

"King and Seven!" shouted even more.

Sigsrata didn't seem to hear the acclaim. He grimly advanced on the other doe which lay still breathing heavily and mewling softly, the arrow still embedded in its eye. Sigsrata raised his axe, bloody drops spraying off of its edges. One blow took off the suffering Titan's head. He turned and strode back towards the Troopers.

"I want the antlers," he ordered as he passed the Troopers before stopping to glare in barely contained rage at Galeb. "Don't you dare to *ever* Ward my weapons! I will live and die by my own hand!"

"And I will Ward," Galeb said, stepping in front of Kieri in case the King meant violence, which was why the arrow struck him instead of his wife.

Galeb slowly sunk to his knees, his eyes wide in disbelief, his mouth working and only tortured breaths coming out, the arrow quivering high in his chest. From an impossible distance he could hear Kieri screaming in shock and anger, trying to shield his body from further strikes. Bob wove darkness around the pair, while Obari slammed disorienting illusions into the forest.

Sigsrata ducked behind the wagon, looking for an enemy to slay. Troopers rushed forward with shields, trying to protect the King and occupants of the wagon. The corpsman was blindly trying to climb into the wagon and see to yet another wound cursing about ill lucked Mages.

A Shaeloman came crashing out of the wood, screaming in frantic rage, battering at the Ward Line.

"NOOOO!" Jesia screamed.

He wasn't supposed to get hurt. Not again. Jesia had been so careful. She whimpered, her hand reaching out to him as he crumpled.

Everything had been going so well. Destroying the Ward Posts had been easy; all she'd needed was a little anger and a hand axe. Finding the hunter risking his life for some exotic Darkness pelts had not been too difficult either. There were always idiots who thought that they were invincible right up until the moment death confronted them with a grin. Then the men's confidence evaporated and they were willing to do anything to breath a few minutes longer. Sometimes Jesia was accommodating. Usually she ended up killing them since their bodies were regrettably fragile. In this case it was easy enough to convince the hunter to become an assassin. Unfortunately the man had just proven himself to be an incompetent assassin.

Jesia turned on the hunter in incandescent fury. The filthy man still knelt with his bow, another arrow nocked, looking for his target. She grabbed him by the throat lifting him off the ground. The man struggled trying to alternately beat her with the bow and stab her with the arrow. Jesia shook the man as she began to scream at him.

"You had one task. One! Shoot the girl! Does my Mage look like a girl? I can assure you that he deliciously does not! And yet you confused the two of them. How can you confuse the two of them? One has breasts and the other doesn't! How could you shoot my Mage?!"

It was right about this moment that Jesia realized that man's head was flopping impossibly backwards because she had torn out his throat and shredded most of his neck muscles. Jesia rolled her eyes and tossed the body aside and began pacing, filled with angst, running her hands over her head.

She had never meant to hurt her Mage. She was just trying to kill that interfering Obari bitch, standing on top of the wagon, presenting such a tempting target. He had to understand that she never meant to hurt him. He would understand. Yes, he would forgive her. Jesia would make him understand.

Jesia just had to get to him. All would be well once her Mage realized the Obari was supposed to die, not him. Never him. He would forgive her then.

The Ward line repulsed Jesia, preventing her from coming to her Mage's aid. She howled in frustration, slashing at the Wards which blasted her back. Illusions strobed in front of her so disorienting that she wanted to vomit. Then realization hit. The Ward Line could not distinguish between her and a real Darkness.

With a triumphant laugh Jesia tore off her skin and ran towards the Ward Line, which was no longer an obstacle. Jesia would reach her man and apologize making him understand that he never had to fear her. Maybe then he would trust her enough to shed his own skin. Jesia shivered in delight at the thought.

Sigsrata gaped in horrified disbelief as the Shaeloman ripped free of its skin and a young – albeit strangely dressed and featured – woman emerged, running for the wagon. Troopers grabbed her as she ran and the woman shrieked, clawing at them and fighting free before being tackled and held down.

"Let me go!" the woman screamed, obviously stronger than she looked as she almost broke free of the Troopers again. "I have to get to him. He needs to know that I am here for him!"

"Who?" demanded Sigsrata looking in the direction of the wagon, "Eielson?"

"Don't you say his name!" spat the woman angrily, her eyes filled with outrage. "You're not worthy enough to say his name!"

Sigsrata looked indignantly at the woman in turn but did not have time to express his exact opinion of who was and was not worthy. Sonovonol leapt from The Darkness covered wagon, her face twisted full of hate and her sword drawn, stalking forward with a warrior's grace and a murderer's intent.

"I don't recognize your form, but I'd never forget that voice," Kieri demanded, her voice a ragged promise of death. "Didn't you hurt him badly enough at the Valley? Weren't you pleased with breaking his body?"

"You have to let me go! He needs me!" sobbed Jesia, ignoring Kieri and kicking at the Troopers holding her.

"Yes, let her go," Kieri agreed, her eyes burning and her face lit by a merciless grin as she held her sword ready, promising that blood would be spilled.

The Troopers looked at Sonovonol uncertainly, more than a bit disconcerted by the two women, neither of whom they felt was particularly sane at this moment.

"Hold fast," Sigsrata commanded, moving forward to interpose himself. The King knew what he had seen. He had seen a Shaeloman unable to cross the Wards transform into a girl who could. He needed the strange woman alive until he could understand exactly what kind of creature she was and how the woman used her abilities. The idea of Darkness shape changers was beyond unsettling.

Kieri easily dodged around the King.

"Move aside," she demanded of the Troopers.

"You'll not kill this woman," Sigsrata commanded.

"You are no king of mine, Klynsheimer," Kieri spat. "I don't obey your orders."

"As if she could kill me," Jesia said mockingly, hanging limp in the Troopers' arms and then breaking free of the Troopers who had relaxed their holds, thinking the strange woman had ceased to fight.

Kieri lunged forward, her sword point just missing Jesia as she spun aside, leaping for the wagon. Sigsrata's hands shot out, almost too quick to follow, one grasping Jesia by the ankle and slamming her to the ground in a wide arc, the other grabbing Kieri's sword arm and holding it still.

"I said that the woman was to be held!" Sigsrata roared at the Troopers who'd lost their grips on Jesia before turning to Kieri who was struggling to break his grip on her sword arm. "And I told you to leave the woman be!"

Jesia lay on the ground stunned and gasping like a fish, the wind knocked out of her lungs. Kieri let go of her sword, latched her free hand on Sigsrata's arm, leapt up, kicking him soundly across the face, and then landed while attempting to twist his arm and free herself.

Sigsrata shook his head like a startled bear before lifting Kieri up in the air by one arm.

"My wife has hit me harder, Sonovonol, with the same result. You will be still."

Kieri glared at the King, before acknowledging that she wasn't going to break free. Then she smiled, gathering illusions in another attack until her father spoke.

"Leave be, daughter. You have a husband to see to. You can kill the crazy woman later," Ebko said, shaking his head at what he considered to be foolishness. Kieri needed to prioritize.

At the reminder of Galeb's injuries, Kieri's face fell and she looked desperately at the wagon. Sigsrata let her go.

"No," Jesia mewled, raising a hand weakly towards the wagon. "He needs me, not you."

"I don't think so," Sigsrata said with a shake of his head. "I suspect that you have caused enough trouble for Eielson."

"DO NOT SAY HIS NAME!" screamed Jesia, struggling to break free of his hold.

Sigsrata slammed her into the ground again.

"You are aware that hurts?" Jesia pouted as she shook her head clear again.

"I imagine so," the Kings said drily, arching a brow. "But I can't seem to muster much concern for a Darkness."

"I'm not a Darkness," Jesia said, glaring at the King in annoyance.

"Then do you care to explain why you seemed to look an awful lot like a Shaeloman a few moments ago? Oh, not to mention the fact that Sonovonol seems to have fought you in the Valley near Uksaadle?" Sigsrata inquired, his brows arched in disbelief of Jesia's claim.

"Not particularly," admitted Jesia, who was altering her plans. The elders were not going to be pleased, but considering that Jesia and her brother were plotting to betray them anyway, she couldn't muster too much concern. In the end the goal remained the same. Get her Mage to her people. She was just going to have to be a more up front with her methods. Jesia would worry about betraying this annoyingly strong king later. "Though I will answer your questions with some conditions."

"Oh?" inquired Sigsrata curiously, the grim set of his jaws implying that he would as soon beat the answers out of her as make a bargain with Jesia.

"No need to threaten, Klynsheimer King," Jesia chided with a giggle. "I can assure you that I am well versed with pain and that no amount of torture will get me to speak any truths that I do not wish to share."

Sigsrata didn't particularly want to torture the woman and agreed that the woman seemed to be unhinged enough that she might actually enjoy pain. Still, he couldn't help but think that the crazy woman was challenging him.

"What kind of conditions are you suggesting?" He asked, still holding onto the woman's leg while Troopers bound her hands behind her back.

"I will answer your questions as long as I get what I want," Jesia said, no longer resisting the Troopers and trying to smile winningly.

The smile looked more than a bit deranged with far too many teeth showing.

"What do you want?" Sigsrata asked. "Death, destruction? Mass chaos? Isn't that what Shaeloman want?"

"I'm not a Shaeloman!" Jesia hissed, anger flaring across her face before the disturbing smile returned. "What is it with you

Southerners and your refusal to acknowledge the skins we all wear?"

"What are you talking about," Sigsrata demanded, letting Jesia's leg drop and wiping his hand on his thigh as if fearing that the woman was afflicted with some sort of disease.

"Oh come on, you can drop the act. That Shaeloman skin was just a mask, like the one you're wearing," Jesia snorted.

"This is my face," Sigsrata said, running a hand along his cheek in confusion.

"Yeah, right. Like you look in any way human. You Southerners and your games," Jesia tittered. "It's okay if you don't want to show me what you really look like. All that matters is that one day my Mage will show me his true face."

Jesia's face suddenly looked all dreamy as she sighed.

"So...you want me to show you Eies-your Mage's true face?" Sigsrata asked skeptically.

"Of course not," Jesia said with a snort of disdain as if she felt that the King was acting purposefully stupid. "Only he can show me his true face. I have to earn that right. No cheating."

"Then what do you want?"

"Time," Jesia said with a genuinely warm smile. "Time with my Mage. That's all I want. I want to hold him, let him know that I am his, as he is mine."

"NO!" Kieri yelled from inside the wagon. The tarp was back in place and Bob's illusion had been dispelled.

"That's not your choice!" Jesia shouted back. "He's my Mage!"

"He's my husband!" Kieri growled angrily.

"A minor inconvenience," Jesia yelled defiantly.

"I'll show you-!"Kieri yelled, moving inside the wagon, with the unmistakable sound of a sword being pulled from its sheath.

"Stop yelling in my face!" Galeb croaked.

"You're awake!" Kieri said in relief, putting her sword away and reversing direction.

"I'm here, my Love!" called Jesia.

"Please tell me that's not the Shaeloman," Galeb said, his voice full of worry. "And would someone please take the arrow out of my chest."

"We have to be careful," explained the corpsman. "The arrow struck you at an angle and it looks like it didn't penetrate too far into the muscle but we have to ensure that isn't any damage that we can't yet see. You're also weak enough as it is, without adding another wound."

"I'd have the arrow out already if I was by myself," complained Galeb.

"Explains why you look like something that a kielsgruntara's been chewing on," muttered the corpsman.

"I've had that happen. Don't recommend it," Galeb said deadpan.

"I imagine that you have," the corpsman said shaking his head. "That what happened to your voice?"

"No," Galeb said, reluctant to discuss it. His voice was worn by the years and abuse, mostly human, not Darkness.

"So, is that the Shaeloman?" Galeb asked again, wanting to change the subject.

"Yes and no," Kieri said, trying to explain.

"Oh, I suppose that's a little bit better," Galeb admitted when he found out that Jesia was humanish.

"How is it better that you have another woman obsessing over you?" Kieri demanded frostily.

"At least it's a woman and not a Darkness," Galeb said, as if that explained everything.

"You do realize that this woman is probably responsible for the arrow the corpsman is trying to pull out of your chest?" Kieri asked.

"It's not my fault," Jesia insisted, struggling to sit up. "Stupid hunter was supposed to kill the Obari bitch who keeps trying to come between us. Don't worry, I killed him."

The reassuring look Jesia gave the man hidden in the wagon didn't reassure anyone. The look was made all the creepier by the earnest desire for approval clearly written across the woman's face.

Sigsrata looked between his prisoner and the wagon in surprisingly bemused disbelief.

"How is that supposed to make me feel better?" Galeb rasped.

"Well, obviously the man can't shoot you with another arrow," Jesia explained carefully. Though I suppose that I'm going to have to find another way to kill the Obari brat. We can talk about that later. You might have some ideas about the best way to kill her."

"You are not going to touch her!" Ebko and Galeb shouted at the same time. Well, Ebko shouted at least. The big Obari was standing nearby watching Jesia with his axe held ready to cut the strange woman down if necessary.

"Why? Do you want to kill her yourself? Are you going to make her death a present for me?" Jesia asked Galeb gleefully, excited by the idea.

"Someone's going to die," muttered Kieri darkly.

"Yes, you," Jesia said, shaking her head in disappointment. "Haven't you been paying attention?"

Galeb tried to pat Kieri's hand reassuringly but the corpsman decided to pull the arrow while the Mage was distracted. Galeb gave a strangled cry before passing out, his body having had enough of being abused.

"I think he's milking it for the sympathy," Bob commented, staring down at the unconscious Mage.

"I'll grant you supervised visits in exchange for information," Sigsrata said, ignoring Bob and watching the woman warily as Sonovonol was distracted helping the corpsman sew up and bandage Eielson's latest injuries. Bob was offering helpful tips that were only annoying everyone more.

"How long will each visit be?" Jesia asked.

"Ten minutes for every question answered completely and satisfactorily."

"Fifteen," Jesia countered.

"Agreed."

There was a lot of protesting from certain parties. Jesia just smiled triumphantly.

"What's your first question? I'm eager to see my Mage."

Chapter 24

Ilsbruk returned as darkness was setting in. The Captain was missing several horses and over two dozen men. Ilsbruk looked exhausted, his armor dented and blood splattered. As soon as he saw his men settled he reported to the King, who sat outside is tent inside the Way Point, which was larger than most. Another day would see the group at the end of the Ward Line, at The Academy Chapter House. This close to the end of the Line, Way Points were designed to accommodate groups heading in both directions.

Ilsbruk settled into a camp stool next to the King, sighing in contentment to be off of his feet. He'd had a long day chasing down kielsgruntara after the initial rampage of the Grass Titans. Eielson's bolt holes had saved both Mages' lives and Jans and Obel had replaced the damaged Ward posts, securing the Line.

Both men took turns exchanging information with the ease of long familiarity. Ilsbruk giving his sovereign a report and Sigsrata informing his trusted subordinate of his extensive questioning of Jesia.

"You look like nta, Ils," Sigsrata commented once enough information had been exchanged.

"We can't all slay Grass Titans single handedly," Ils said with a grunt.

"I am quite skilled," Sigsrata said with false modesty.

"Is it wise to keep our new guest?" Ilsbruk asked, looking at his King out of the corner of his eyes.

"Seemed the best thing to do. We can't afford to let Eielson keep getting attacked. Man's a bit piss poor at keeping himself safe, despite his abilities," Sigsrata said with a shrug.

"You really thing that this is a good idea?"

"Woman knows things that we need to know ourselves, Ils. A city of shape shifters? Can you imagine?"

"You do realize, Sir, that this woman is most likely responsible for the destruction of Uksaadle?"

"I've granted the woman – Jesia's her name, by the way – visits with Eielson. I did not grant her clemency. She will pay for her crimes once her usefulness is at an end."

"Just so, Sir. Just so. I'm tired of losing men to her...efforts," Ilsbruk said, shaking his head angrily.

"To those who've served," the King said, raising his hand in salute.

"To those who've fought," Ilsbruk agreed, raising his hand in salute.

"To those who've fallen," both men finished in unison.

"Enough sadness," Sigsrata said, shaking his head and reaching down to pick up a cup and drinking deeply. "We will have more than enough of that soon. Let's look forward to some fun. You should have seen Sonovonol's face when she found out that Jesia earned several hours in visitations."

"I'm certain that the Obari is overjoyed that you are letting a twisted murderess cozy up to her husband," Ilsbruk said wryly.

"Not so much," Sigsrata said with another twist of his lips.

"It's going to get worse, isn't it, Sir?"

"So very much so, Ils. If half of what that woman claims is coming down on us is true the kingdom is going to be bled white," the King said with a grimace.

"All thanks to this city of shape changers," Ils said angrily, kicking out and scowling.

"No. All thanks to a city of shape changers and the Twelve. We cannot forget our own people's involvement in this mess," growled Sigsrata, his hands clenching.

"True," Ilsbruk said. "Still-."

"You're not sleeping with us!" came a shriek from further in the camp.

"I don't want to sleep with you!" came an answering shriek of outrage. "I just want to sleep with him!"

"Get out!"

"I'm allowed to be here! I answered questions. I have *hours* of time granted to me and I choose to use them cuddling up to my Mage!"

"Not now you don't! Bob! Stop laughing!"

"I feel bad for Eielson," Ilsbruk said with a shake of his head.

"What? Having two women fighting over him?" the King asked, arching a brow. "Yes, I pity the man."

"Seriously?" Ilsbruk looked at Sigsrata with a shake of his head. "One's a pissed off and reasonably jealous Obari woman and the other is an insane woman from a city whose entire foreign policy seem be based on sending nightmares in the general direction of their neighbors."

"Have you met my wife?" Sigsrata said with a shudder. "That Mage is in a state of bliss compared to my own marriage."

"The insane woman's idea of foreplay is to nearly kill Eielson," Ilsbruk pointed out.

"Could be worse. My wife decided to cook me dinner on our last anniversary."

"How is that worse?"

"Ils, the dogs wouldn't even touch that food. I hid some of it in a potted plant. The plant died," the King said plaintively.

"You're just happy that it's Eielson in this mess and not you," Ilsbruk accused his King.

"Of course I am. Aside from Jesia's admittedly homicidal tendencies, I find her arguments with Sonovonol to be very entertaining," Sigsrata admitted with a grin. "Besides, the Obari challenged me in front of the men. I wasn't going to forgive that offense easily."

"My daughter is irrational when it comes to her husband. It can be amusing to play on her insecurities, but will you be laughing when the Guunt descend upon us?" Ebko asked, moving out of The Darkness and settling by the King's fire with a grunt. The man looked as if his sleep had been rudely interrupted.

"No," said the King, humor fading from his face, and glancing solemnly into the night sky. "But I will be facing them, so I'll enjoy laughter while I can."

"We can't do this, Obel," Jans said with a shake of her head, gesturing to the book that she'd been reading for the better part of a day.

"I know what you mean," Obel said, pointing to the book dismissively. "I've tried reading it myself. A child could have done a better job writing. Truly, the man was educated for the better part of fifteen years and he can barely string two sentences together. It's embarrassing."

"What? No, well, yes, the writing is simplistic, but that's not what I mean. Eielson's ideas are clear enough. It's just I don't think that we can duplicate them," Jans said. "His techniques require a complete mental shift in the way in which we Ward. I don't think any veteran Mages are capable of making that shift."

"If Eielson can Ward differently, then I'm certain that I can figure the methodology out," Obel said, experimenting with carving several simple Wards.

"Really, Obel?" Jans said in disbelief. "From everything I can put together, Eielson can only Ward differently because of intense study of Obari techniques as well as desperately crazy improvisation."

"He's done the hard work. We just build off of his efforts," Obel said with a shrug. "I hate to admit it but the man does have some good ideas."

Jans gave Obel a measuring look.

"While it's admirable of you to admit that Eielson is skilled, such 'praise' doesn't guarantee that you will able to replicate his efforts."

"Most won't be able to master his techniques," Obel admitted. "But that's not what I'm talking about. We don't have the time to try to fully replicate Eielson's Warding structures. I don't even know where to begin with his 'light' structures, let alone 'Deep Wardings'. The man must be more than a little insane even to try those types of Wardings.

"I'm referring to his doctrine of using combinations of simpler Wardings on the posts instead of more intricate single Wardings. His combinations take half of the time to carve and seem just as effective, if not more so in certain groupings. There is room for improvement, but I am going to suggest to the King that all camp Wardings be shifted to Eielson's configurations."

Jans looked at Obel in surprise.

"What? I can acknowledge a good idea when I see one," Obel said, taking offense.

"That is awfully big of you," Jans acknowledged.

"Thank you. Once I tweak Eielson's admittedly sloppy methodologies, I should be able to write quite the treatise. There may even be a permanent professorship in it for me,"

"And there is the Obel I know," Jans said disapprovingly. "You're going to steal Eielson's ideas."

"No, I am going to improve his ideas and then offer to teach them to all who are interested," Obel corrected. "Any misconceptions about the origins of those ideas are not my fault or concern."

"You're a bastard," Jans pointed out.

"I'm a product of The Academy," Obel pointed out.

Galeb smiled grimly as he overheard his two fellow Mages arguing. He was walking quietly towards the latrines, both Kieri and Jesia having walked off in separate huffs and acting like this was all his fault. Why, he had no idea. It wasn't like he was encouraging Jesia's attentions. Galeb shuddered at the thought.

He'd rather be back in his tent, curled up with Kieri. That would ease the aches and pains. But no, he was out here, skulking towards the cesspits. He moved his shoulder gingerly, grateful that the arrow hadn't driven deep and annoyed at yet another nagging injury.

The latrines, neat outhouses in a row, were located at the back of the way point, just a few feet short of where the Ward posts ended, which were perfect for his purposes since no one wanted to be either that close to the Ward Line or downwind of the latrines. A cesspit was a cesspit no matter how you dressed it up.

He stopped just short of the latrines and turned to look back at the camp with a sigh, deep regret welling up in his chest. At least Kieri had made it easier to sneak away. At least physically. Well, maybe not physically. He was going to hate this walk.

Still, it was not only better this way, but necessary. Bob and Kawen were waiting for him, wrapped in illusion, having taken over the watch the Obari insisted on keeping around him now that he was part of the Family.

"Is everything ready, Bob?" Galeb asked, thankful for once that his voice was naturally quiet.

Bob emerged from the night, a smile upon his lips and a contented gleam in his eyes.

"*I* killed a Skrieksgrata," Bob boasted, though there was a slight quaver in his voice. "Of course I'm ready."

"Bob, everyone knows you killed a Skrieksgrata. You don't need to keep reminding people."

"Well, I *did* kill one; that has to be worth something," Bob complained, and then muttered, "And saying it reminds me that it's dead and I'm still alive."

Kawen flinched at those words and shuddered before nodding his agreement.

"Well, to business. I'm glad that you're doing this," Bob said, gesturing grandly and disturbingly with his spear. Bob didn't seem bothered by Kawen and Galeb's sudden need to duck. "I was suspicious when you gave in so easily to the marriage; didn't seem like you. You always seemed too stubborn to do the right thing; probably why you're such a good match for Kieri. But now, now I understand. This is what I expected from you. Very sneaky."

"I killed a lot more than a Skrieksgrata, Bob. That changes a man," Galeb argued. He was as affected by the Battle of the Valley as Bob and Kawen. He'd come to terms with the fact that as long as Kieri wanted him he was a fool to deny her. Galeb didn't need another regret in his life.

Which was why Galeb was leaving, going to meet The Darkness before the Rising had a chance to reach the Ward Line. Jesia's descriptions of what was coming, as well as her certainty that the worst of the elites wouldn't bother attacking the line, but simply go around it, had made the decision easier. No matter what defense the King mounted it would not be enough in the short amount of time that Klynsheim had left before the advance elements of The Darkness arrived. The Darkness had to be drawn away, buying time to craft better defenses and giving Galeb a chance to weaken the Rising as much as he could before he fell to it.

This was his fault after all.

Galeb nodded to Bob, glancing back briefly towards the camp, sad as he thought of Kieri. He seemed to have lost the ability to wall away such thoughts and focus only on his duty.

"You're doing the right thing, Galeb Sonovonol," Kawen said, grabbing Galeb's arm gently and looking him in the eyes, the ever present fear that had been in Kawen's eyes ever since the Valley almost giving Kawen's words an odd sense of solemnity. "You are drawing danger away from the Family. This is a good death."

Bob snorted, muttering that 'Death' could not die.

Galeb ignored Bob's comment and walked closer to the cousins, examining the illusion wrapped horses with burgeoning packs full of food and a Warder's supplies instead of saying anything. As much as he'd hated his duty over the years it was familiar and after weeks of feeling off balance he craved that familiarity. He understood it when nothing else had seemed to make sense around him.

"I won't need all of this food," Galeb said, noticing just how many supplies the cousins had been able to pilfer.

"We are going with you," Kawen explained. "You need to find a place to stand. No offense, Galeb, but you are too crippled to make it on your own. We'll get you where you need to go. We have a need to protect the Family as much as you do."

"I can't-," Galeb began to protest.

"Enough," Kawen interrupted gently, though his eyes were fever bright. "This is a good death. After...after the Valley going with you scares me less than trying to act normal. I – we need to embrace our fear lest it conquers us and we become useless. We have no regrets."

"I regret that there isn't a woman's bathing pool here," Bob argued, before frowning when both Galeb and Kawen looked at him in disbelief. Bob rolled his eyes before speaking again. "We need to get moving, which means that you need to get up on a horse."

"I don't know how to ride," Galeb admitted, looking at the one horse that was saddled.

"Well, you're certainly not walking," Bob observed. "You can figure it out as we go."

Galeb looked very uncertain.

"We need to hurry. If Kieri catches us there is going to be septa to pay," Kawen urged. "We'll tie you into the saddle if need be."

"You're assuming that 'Kieri' is too stupid to realize when her husband and cousins are plotting," Kieri whispered harshly as she let the illusion that she was holding near one of the horses fall away.

All three men gaped in shock. Kieri raised an eyebrow, shaking her head in disappointment at the three men.

"Did you think that I wouldn't notice you two having hushed conversations? Or the supplies that you were stealing? Oh, and Husband? I've figured out that you can see through our illusions. You can't see through a horse. That's how I snuck up on you."

Galeb's mouth gaped even wider as he tried to figure out how Kieri had known what he was thinking. Kieri strode over to Galeb, closed his mouth, leaned up, and kissed him before grabbing an ear and twisting it.

"We are married, Galeb. Did you mean it when you pledged yourself to me?"

"Yes," Galeb said, twisting as he tried to free his ear and grimacing with pain.

"Good," Kieri said, twisting harder. "You don't lie to me. Ever."

"Kieri -."

"Keeping secrets is lying," Kieri insisted.

"But -."

"Where you go, I go," Kieri said, letting go of his ear, with a gentle smile that didn't match the anger in her eyes. "Now get on that horse before that horrid woman finds us."

For good measure Kieri smacked Galeb upside the head.

Galeb wisely chose not to argue, given where Kieri might hit him next. Getting on the horse proved difficult. Galeb lacked the flexibility to mount easily. Kieri and Kawen exchanged a look and before Galeb could protest they pushed him up and then tied him into the saddle.

Slipping out of the way point proved slow considering that the group had to avoid other Obari and Klynsheimer sentries. Kieri and her cousins were sweating profusely maintaining the illusions. Galeb thought that she looked cute in a sweat soaked sort of way. He mentioned that to her once they were clear of the camp and heading east. Kieri wasn't flattered, pulling back several hairs that were plastered to her face and muttering about 'stupid men'.

Bob didn't help when he questioned whether or not Galeb's eyesight was failing because there was no way Kieri looked anything but sweat stained.

"Where are we heading?" Kawen asked as Kieri briefly chased Bob around with promises of greater pain if he didn't stop running.

"Ten miles further up the line there is a grove of cathedral oaks that will make for a good Ward Point. The trees' mass and support roots will be sturdy enough Ward Posts and there's also a creek fed pool for water," Galeb explained.

"The Berinal Family women's bathing pool," Bob said, perking up as he jogged past, still evading Kieri. "I know that place pretty well."

Kieri gave her cousin a look of disgust as she chased after him. Kawen just looked thoughtful. Galeb focused on trying to get comfortable in the saddle with little success.

Chapter 25

Kiesh sat huddled in a council of war with his fellow Guunt. While Kiesh preferred honest combat he was not above using spies, a role for which some of the smaller Darkness were well suited. He was well aware that the Mage had separated himself from his previous group and taken a small band a short distance away. Kiesh was also aware that a large human army was mustering near the edge of the Ward Line. This was the direction in which Kiesh's growing army had been heading in until this news reached him.

Some of his Guunt wanted to change direction and head for the Mage that had challenged The Darkness. Others wanted to maintain the direction of their march either because they wanted to try themselves against a human army, something no Guunt living had ever done or because it would be hard to turn the growing tide of Darkness Kiesh commanded.

Kiesh looked over at Omkarl, a smaller Guunt, but one who had more intelligence than many of his fellows. Omkarl was sitting quietly, watching as he always did, letting the more dominant Guunt argue, which involved as much fighting as it did actual talking. Guunt were born of iron and stone and were suitably rough, feeling that fists were as convincing as a well-structured argument.

"Speak," Kiesh said to Omkarl, as he reached over and smashed the Guunt who'd been speaking into the earth, ending that one's argument.

"Take both," Omkarl said, shifting warily as he watched the other Guunt for attacks.

"Why?" asked Kiesh, his grin full of jagged pleasure.

"Because both challenge us by their existence. By taking one and then moving to the other we invite others to take our battle from us. We are Guunt; both Mage and army belong to us. To let others dispute this fact successfully invites disrespect. Disrespect leads to unworthy fights that are beneath us."

"Why else?" Kiesh demanded.

"Because this Mage seeks to make us come to him. We do not let him dictate where we walk."

"Good," Kiesh said approvingly before lashing out and slamming Omkarl from the ragged circle of Guunt. It would not do for the youngling, barely ripped from the mountain of his birth a century ago to feel too valued. "We choose the ground upon which we battle, not this Mage."

"Good!" roared Kiesh again, smashing the ground.

The other Guunt caught their leader's excitement and smashed the ground in turn.

"Margul," Kiesh said, turning to one of the most massive of the other Guunt, which still left Margul well short of Kiesh's might, "You will take a group and destroy the Mage. We will continue to this army and feast on their iron!"

Margul took the order and lurched away, his eyes lingering on Kiesh, barely contained rage in his eyes. There was nothing unusual in this; all Guunt had rage in their eyes. Margul would kill Kiesh if he was able, which was also to be expected. Kiesh took no offense. He would take the challenge gladly when it came. But not today.

Several days later and not nearly far enough to the south of the Guunt horde Sigsrata stood at the edge of his grand encampment looking north as the sun set. Warded fighting lines extended like wings on either side of the main encampment. Ten thousand men settled in for the night while Obari sentries roamed the perimeter and scouted the distance for miles around. Exhausted young Journeyman Mages and even apprentices trudged around the camp adding last minute changes to the defenses or carving replacement posts.

Obel and Jans, under Sigsrata's authority, had organized the Warder Mages into quick reaction groups, focusing on reinforcing and replacing Wardings with only the most basic Wards, utilizing Eielson's doctrine. Convincing the Warder Mages to accept these more basic forms had been a near titanic struggle, with only the youngest Mages embracing these forms over the more fanciful traditional Wardings. The older Mages had refused to stop using their treasured and overly complicated Wardings even after a series of drills under combat conditions proved that the ornate style was too time intensive. One hundred percent of the traditional Mages 'died' in the drills as opposed to fifty percent of those using the basic Wardings.

Obel and Jans' relative youth had not helped convince the traditionalists, many of whom felt that they should be in charge of the Warder detachments. Not even the King's authority had quelled all of the dissent. If Sigsrata hadn't needed the Mages in the upcoming fight he would have had a few executed as an example. As it was he'd sent the worst of the trouble makers south to continue working on a secondary emergency Ward Line.

Sigsrata personally commanded the Western end of the Great Northern Road. Eight thousand infantry and two thousand cavalry at his command, as well as a thousand war dogs. Beninup, Captain of the Seven, commanded the mountain garrisons on the Eastern end of the Ward Line with five thousand infantry. Ekriq of the Seven commanded a center force below the Trade Road, in a position to reinforce the Line, Beninup, or Sigsrata as needed. Six thousand Troopers waited upon the command to march. Ilsbruk commanded the Ward Line itself, every Way Fort fully manned, with two thousand Troopers as a quick reaction force ready to repel any assaults on the Line and effect repairs.

Sigsrata needed the Ward Line to hold. As long as the Line held The Darkness would be funneled in two directions. Assaulting the mountain garrisons seemed less likely since the approaches out of the North were little better than goat paths. No, it was far more likely for The Darkness to head west, which meant that the King's army would face the brunt of the attacks.

Eielson and his wife had slipped away well over a week ago. The shape shifting woman had become crazed when she realized that the Mage was gone and had to be restrained. Sigsrata's reaction was more sedate. He was angered by Eielson's leaving without permission and yet he understood the motivation and supported it. Eielson was going to draw as much of The Darkness to him as possible. None of the Obari had been the least bit surprised, seeing Eielson as acting to protect his Family. Whatever the motivation, any lessening of forces arrayed against the King's army was welcome.

Sigsrata approved of Eielson's brash action of another reason. As powerful as the man was, Eielson was a loner. The man fought as an individual, with no mind to the greater flow of battle. That lack of understanding might have caused more problems than benefits.

A few more weeks would see an additional thirty thousand infantry out of the Southern-most lands. That infantry, like their more Northerly brethren were getting training as they marched, which meant that their quality was dubious at best. Klynsheim would bleed. But that was as need be; Klynsheim would meet The Darkness with blood and iron.

As Sigsrata felt the sun set on his left he saw another sun rise to the northeast. He did not need the scouts or the cries of the men to tell him that The Darkness had found Eielson's group. The Darkness would be coming for Sigsrata's army soon. He could not allow the men to become fearful.

"Behold!" Sigsrata shouted, gesturing with his great axe, "The Northern Ward has engaged the enemy! Hail the Ward! Death to The Darkness!"

The men, needing to believe in the strength of Mage, Soldier, and Trooper took up the call with their sergeants' urging.

"Hail the Ward! Death to The Darkness!"

Chapter 26

Every bone and muscle Galeb possessed seemed to ache.
Days of Warding the Cathedral oak and preparing traps had worn
upon him until fatigue seemed an ever present friend. Though he
didn't want to admit as much, Galeb was out of shape. His recent
injuries and the weeks away from the Ward Line had lessened him.
Still, a perverse part of himself enjoyed the aches and fatigue since
they reminded him of a time when he only had to worry about the
occasional Darkness incursion, not a full - fledged Rising.

But as tired as Galeb was, he had to admit that the area and
the work that he'd done were good. Cathedral oaks were a non-
competitive species. This meant that there was no other plant
growth around the small grove for nearly a hundreds of yards in all
directions making it difficult for any Darkness to sneak up on them.
The grove was actually a single massive tree, the arching support
roots towering nearly twenty feet in the air on their own, spreading
out in a thirty foot radius around the central trunk. The pool of
water was sheltered under the support roots, fed by a creek that
meandered amongst the supports, nourishing the greedy tree.

Defensive and offensive Wards adorned both supports and
the central trunk. Interspersed were arrays of 'Gathers the Light'.
The last thing that Galeb wanted was another night battle where
he couldn't see the enemy until they were right on top of him.
Gathers the Light was linked to 'amplify', lighting the surrounding
ground for well over a hundreds of yards.

The traps were spaced far from the oak, consisting of Ward
etched stones. Every spare moment had been put into preparing
these defenses, a feat that would have been impossible without

the staff. The staff worked so well that Galeb had carved a second one and started on a third, the process streamlined now that Galeb knew what Wards did and did not have to be included in the preparation. Light Wards sped up the process even more, though he still had to hand carve the most precise of the Wardings.

Kieri was still suspicious about why Galeb had his eyes closed when he first used the staff. He had answered her questions with a quick lie about needing to concentrate more the first time that he used it. Galeb wouldn't admit that he half expected the staff to explode. When Kieri asked him how flinching fit into the need to concentrate Galeb tried to creatively distract her. Kieri had happily let the matter drop at the time but was like a dog with a bone. She kept bringing the question back up at the most random times, trying to catch him off guard and get Galeb to admit that he was being reckless.

Well, the staff worked so Galeb was technically no longer being reckless. Not that he had time to be indulgent even if he wanted to be a little reckless. While awake Galeb Warded; Bob and Kieri saw to the placement of the traps, which could be left active or triggered when needed.

Kawen had helped Galeb angle his defenses, commenting on how a Skrieksgrata had been pulped when different Wards continuously slammed the beast into trees during the battle of the Valley. When Galeb had looked at the man in surprise Kawen had realized that the Mage had no idea what he was talking about and that the effect had not been deliberate. Galeb didn't even try and pretend otherwise. Mages, even one such as himself, primarily built barriers - walls of Wards - their thinking was rather linear on the subject. As was Kieri in her continual campaign to admit that Galeb had been experimenting with the staffs.

Galeb had wanted to protest every time Kieri brought the subject up, but wisely kept his mouth shut when Kawen created an illusion of him at the time he had first activated the staff. Seeing a life sized version of yourself, eyes clenched shut, a slight panicky look on your face, and flinching stilled Galeb's argument. Sometimes it really was unfortunate that Obari had perfect memories and eyes for detail.

Everyone took turns preparing supplies, gathering healing herbs, stimulant plants to help keep them alert longer and protecting their water supply which The Darkness might try to foul. Part of the pool was separated from the rest by mounding in stones, dividing it as best they could from the creek that flowed into the pool. Water skins were filled and wood laid by.

Kieri was the group's early warning system. Her protections glowing whenever a Darkness neared their location, which was surprisingly rare given that a Rising was occurring. The consensus was that the beasts were either attacking somewhere else or massing for a more brutal assault. Neither thought was comforting to anyone but Bob. Bob was quite happy at the thought of The Darkness attacking anywhere where he was not present.

Their luck didn't hold longer than a week. The light of the day was fading fast when The Darkness arrived, a spike strider triggering one of the traps farther out from the camp. The stone exploded in a blast of heat and light killing the beast and giving the four enough warning. Galeb triggered 'Gathers the Light', pushing back the gathering gloom and revealing the spike striders massing for an attack.

A few modifications ensured that Kieri's wards flared to life bathing her in cold white light even before the spike strider's pack mates rushed forward and entered the detection range of her Wards. Before Kieri could demand to know if he was experimenting again, Galeb triggered his own Wardings, golden light dancing along his arms, chest and lower back. He still hadn't found the time to extend his Wardings into a full body covering and his legs were unprotected. Kieri was quite critical of that fact. Kawen just laughed, saying that the lack of Wardings made his legs look scrawny and mismatched with the rest of his body.

Galeb huffed, trying to pretend that he was unaffected by the comment and then muttered a slight curse as he grabbed a cloak and threw it around his shoulders, drawing the hood up and casting his face in shadow, while covering most of his legs from view. He was not being vain. He was not. Galeb cursed again and grabbed up the first of his staves, making the connection that he needed to draw the power out and through the wood instead of himself. His other hand began to make a coaxing gesture as he pulled energy forth.

Kawen and Bob faded into the night, seeking to attract no notice to themselves. Galeb had discovered that while channeling the energy from the staffs greatly extended his ability to Ward, it took quite a bit more concentration then usual to guide the energy from the staffs into the Wardings. Instead of drawing the energy through himself, Galeb had to focus on keeping it separate, monitor the rate at which the staff was being drained, and fashion the energy into Wardings. This left him with very little focus with which to direct attacks. Kawen and Bob would act as spotters, directing his efforts, while sewing confusion among the enemy with well-placed illusion. Kieri would guard Galeb's back, which was fortuitous since she refused to leave his side. She stood next to him, sword drawn, waiting for the attack to hit the first of the defenses.

The spike striders, fully fifty strong, milled at the edge of the light. Not being nocturnes, the light did not bother them overly much. The Darkness hesitated because the light represented a power that the animals were reluctant to tangle with because the sheer amount of area illuminated was a bit staggering.

The striders looked to their alpha – The Darkness's quills were a ruddier red than the others and there was less white on its coat. The spike strider glared at the Mage with slitted eyes, growling deep in its throat before rattling its quills in a display of pure aggression.

The alpha weighed its options as it decided whether or not to attack. It was proud of the pack it had mastered and was loath to waste the pack's strength on a foolish attack. The Mage before him seemed strong. The Guunt commanding this attack was known to be strong, ruthless and unforgiving like all of its kind. Certainty trumped speculation and the alpha bunched his muscles, leaping forward, the pack surging around him.

The alpha had heard that the Mage was a gnarled, scarred thing; the man before the alpha did not seem crippled, standing tall and powerful as he held a glowing staff aloft in one hand and pointed his other hand forward in a fist. The illusion was of Kieri's crafting. As for herself, the strider saw an otherworldly queen encased in a nimbus of terrible promise, sword held ready, seeming to cleave the very air asunder with every movement.

There was something about that cold light that almost caused the alpha's steps to falter. The woman's Wards did not seem to merely threaten; the Wards seemed eager to inflict unending pain to any being who dared challenge them. The alpha was Darkness; power, pain and hostility were part of its existence. But the sheer malice emanating from those Wards was overwhelming.

The alpha felt a twinge of uncertainty at the sight, shook his quills harder in order to reaffirm his aggression and ran harder towards the humans, drool filling his mouth at anticipation of the first bite.

Rather than wait for the striders to hit the first of the Wardings, Galeb breathed in deeply and then sent a roiling wave of fire at the beasts, a battle cry erupting from his lips as the words of the King echoed in his ears. Be afraid, but never show it; do not admit to the fear. Stand strong so others will stand strong with you.

As he unleashed the flame Galeb caught a glimpse of Kieri out of the corner of his eye and a rage erupted from his soul. His wife should not be here. His wife should not be standing at his side facing The Darkness.

Galeb just wanted to keep Kieri safe. He'd always wanted to just keep Kieri safe. It was a clawing need inside of him, desperate and agonizing more so because he was the one putting Kieri in danger.

Galeb poured power into the flames, Ward combinations buzzing like hornets around his arms moving so fast that they seemed to be never ending streaks of light. Galeb didn't want to hurt the spike striders. He wanted to scour them out of existence. He wanted to watch the flesh crackle and split away from their bones. Galeb didn't even realize when his battle cry turned into an inarticulate snarl of rage.

Bob watched the Mage with disquiet sensing the maddened need pouring off of the man in waves and nodded slightly to himself. Kieri bathed her husband in an illusion showing Galeb as a powerful Mage, defiant in the face of the enemy. That illusion was wrong. Galeb wasn't just a man – he was Death and Bob altered the illusion to reflect the reality of what he saw whenever he looked at the Mage.

The cloak darkened until it was the rotting black of a midnight cave, the ground around Galeb suddenly glittering with ice as if the Mage's mere presence was sucking the warmth out of the earth. Every tendon and muscle in Galeb's hands seemed to stand out in stark relief, eldritch power draped over cadaverous bones. Bob finished by tinting the fire a snarling, snapping cancerous black that drove the spike striders into a sudden panic. The pack tried to break off its mad rush, but the fire smashed into the massed flesh, turning the beasts into staggering stick figures outlined in nightmarish flame. Maybe twenty escaped, fleeing back into the underbrush, Galeb cursing in frustration that any of The Darkness had avoided his attack and took a step forward before Kieri restrained him.

"Less power, Husband," Kieri warned Galeb, trying to mask her disquiet at Bob's illusion. "Use only enough to kill. Rely on the defenses to hold them back if The Darkness presses too close. This will not be a quick fight."

"It broke the charge," Galeb pointed out, a bit irritated by the criticism and shocked by the anger inside of him that seemed to be only growing worse as it warred with the fear. She shouldn't be here. He couldn't.... *Please* God....

"And wasted energy needlessly," Kieri continued reasonably. "Striders were not going to break through your Wardings. Ration your strength."

Galeb wanted to argue but realized that Kieri was right. He needed more control. He needed to ensure that he had enough strength to protect her even though he knew that Kieri could take care of herself. His thoughts were a tangled mess.

"I love you," he said.

Kieri smiled gently, pleased, but her eyes continued to scan the dark beyond the Warded area, waiting for what would come next. Focusing on The Darkness was important and better than dwelling on the gleam of desperate madness in her husband's eyes as he destroyed the enemy.

The next attack was more than an hour in coming and came from all sides at once. A horrendous roar that seemed to shake the trees heralded the assault. Leaves certainly fell, browned by the advanced season. The night would be chill. Galeb doubted he'd have time to feel cold.

The roar was apparently for the striders' benefit, driving the remaining pack members back into an attack from the same direction. At the same time kielsgruntara chittered out from the left in a solid line, running full out, their feet hammering into the ground and raising a discordant racket.

Perinwen, child sized Darkness with overly large eyes, hairless red bodies, blunt tipped claws, and mouths that distended into razor sharp grins, came from the right, leaping over one another in their eagerness to reach the humans. Perinwen were single mindedly stupid creatures and seemed to be brawling with each other as much as wanting to kill the humans.

Traps exploded in earsplitting shrieks of sundered stone. The Warded cathedral oak hummed as power coursed through its trunk and supporting arches. Lights of every color flashed to life, repelling or killing The Darkness that moved into range. Raw power blanketed the area and Galeb found himself reveling in the destruction. He wanted to kill them all until he wasn't afraid any more. Until he could stop having the nightmares of Kieri dying.

"I hope that you and Bob didn't set any of those traps too close," Galeb said, suddenly wincing as another stone exploded and a thought occurred to him, bringing him back to himself. "The energies won't affect us, but flying stone chips can."

"Mind what you're doing, Husband," Kieri snapped, as discomfited by the attacks as Galeb. "Bob and I know what we're doing."

Galeb wisely kept his mouth shut, watching the destruction instead.

The cousins took advantage of the sudden chaos to craft illusions that funneled the spike striders right into the path of the perinwen. The Darkness momentarily forgot the humans as the spike striders, maddened by fear and angry at the beasts suddenly blocking their path, impaled the perinwen and went into death roles. The perinwen shrieked in outrage – the sound like an actual baby's scream – and tried to overwhelm the spike striders and tear them to pieces, which did not turn out very well. As said, the perinwen were quite stupid.

This left only the kielsgruntara as a threat. Since Bob and Kawen were focused on their funneling illusion, Kieri called out the best places for Galeb to strike.

Galeb, remembering Kieri's warning, tried a different approach, merging 'Draws the line', 'Burns bright' and 'Cuts the stone'. A narrow line of energy twenty feet long and barely an inch wide collided with the kielsgruntara, dismembering the creatures into a pile of heaving body parts as suddenly limbless beasts crashed to the earth amidst a rain of steaming blood, intestines and various other body parts in a jigsaw of mismatched viscera.

"That is disgusting," was Kieri's only comment as she covered her mouth with a hand.

Bob threw up somewhere in the shadows of the trees. It looked that Kieri was only avoiding doing the same through sheer force of will. Galeb kept his mind apart, cursing again that some of The Darkness had escaped. He wasn't doing well enough! He shook his head in frustration and focused back on the task at hand. He decided to experiment a bit and superheated the air in the struggling mass of spike strider and perinwen, using the liquid in the creatures' own bodies to flash cook the beasts. Surprisingly superheating the air took a lot less energy than generating actual flame. Galeb would have to investigate why when he had more time.

The smell had Bob throwing up again. Kieri gagged a bit but held on, looking at her husband and noticing his grim, yet slightly manic expression and grew even more worried.

Galeb was starting to pant a bit at the rapid fire Wardings. He was disconcerted at how rapidly the first staff was depleting. There had not been enough time to fully recharge the staves after warding the oak. He hoped that he had enough power left in it to kill whatever had roared earlier. It had sounded disconcertingly big.

Margul watched the failed attack, unbothered by the carnage. He had sent the least of his forces against the Mage, testing the man's defenses, mapping out traps and watching as different Wardings activated to protect the humans who sheltered in the grove. Satisfied, he directed the next attack, indicating what areas The Darkness should avoid.

More perinwen surged forward. They were fit only for a distraction. Margul slammed his fist into the ground, commanding the main attacking force to begin a flanking maneuver. Flickering blue-black shapes wrapped in tattered shadows moved stealthily through the wood, seeming to appear and disappear at will. Every sighting of the creatures was of where they had been, not where they were.

Margul grinned in anticipation. Let's see how the Mage dealt with Bael Wights.

"One o'clock!" yelled Bob his voice holding a hint of hysteria.

Sweating fiercely, Galeb sent out a thin stream of light in the indicated direction, using the same Wardings that he had used to kill the kielsgruntara earlier. The Mage was hoping that he could at least wound the Bael Wights with a broad attack since he could not seem to touch them with more focused attacks. Not that he was having much luck this way either.

The attack missed, as another Bael Wight, all flickering gray-green rather than the blue-black Galeb had seen so far, with horribly huge clawed hands, and a glowing white face that seemed a caricature of a human skull grafted over a head of darkness tore at the Wardings. The Wight shrieked insanely, wobbling black tendrils at the edges of skull, the sound not audible but somehow clawing its way around the inside of Galeb's head.

The Wight was repulsed, but unharmed. The general Wardings that repulsed The Darkness were effective enough but the Wards designed to actually kill could not seem to focus on the creatures. Galeb didn't know if the Wights were simply moving too fast for the Wards to lock on to or, more disturbingly, most of the offensive style Wards had no effect on the Wights.

The Academy's only input on the subject during Galeb's years of education had been that Bael Wights were a seldom seen

Darkness and best opposed by generalized repelling Wards until the Wights lost interest. Not very helpful especially since the Wights seemed uninterested in ceasing their assault any time soon. The attack had already been going on for the better part of three hours.

The Wights had caught the group unaware. Galeb had been focused on another attack by perinwen. By the time any of them realized that there were Bael Wights attacking, the creatures were past the traps and hitting the main Wards.

They were in trouble and it was Galeb's fault. Hadn't he learned in the Valley to pay attention to his entire surroundings? Why did he keep messing up?

The Bael Wights were keeping a steady pressure on the Wards and keeping Galeb focused on them. Other types of Darkness took advantage of this and pressed the Wards from different directions. The central trunk of cathedral oak was an enormous medium, having the necessary mass to take the stress of opposing forces being placed on the Wards, but it was only a matter of time before some of the support roots gave way, weakening the defenses and allowing the Wights that much closer.

The pounding waves of fear that the Wights were emanating wasn't helping matters. It was becoming increasingly hard to think. Kieri was the only one who seemed largely unaffected, which was not surprising considering that she was completely surrounded by personal Wardings.

Galeb decided to try something new even though he was pretty certain that it would completely drain the staff. Different ranged attacks in quick succession might reveal a weakness or score a lucky blow. He was feeling a little desperate at this point.

"Everyone look in a different direction. I'm going to try something. Watch the Wights for a reaction."

"What kind of reaction?" asked Kieri.

"Any sort of reaction. Nothing seems to be working so I'm making this up as I go."

He gathered his focus and sent small motes of flame through the air in every direction at once. The motes exploded randomly in gouts of flame. Galeb followed up this assault with a wave of frost, followed by a final curtain of flame. The energy from the staff sputtered and died, utterly spent. Steam rose through the air, eerily lit by the Ward light and creating a small fog bank.

"Anything?" Galeb asked, having seen nothing on his side of the grove.

"Nothing," Kieri said sharply. "It would have been easier if you'd told me specifically what you were hoping to see."

Galeb gritted his teeth.

"Nothing," Kawen agreed, his voice sounding nervous.

"Huh...," said Bob.

"What do you mean, 'huh'?" asked Kieri before Galeb had a chance to do so.

"Well, remember that time when you had that conversation with your husband about your dress?" Bob asked in reply.

"Which time?" Galeb asked.

"Right after she failed to trick you with one of her illusions."

"Which time?" Galeb asked again, earning a glare from Kieri.

"Get to the point, Bob!" snapped Kieri.

"It was the time Galeb Sonovonol mentioned that you weren't matching your movements perfectly with the illusionary dress and he could see your real dress underneath," Bob explained helpfully. "I just saw something that was like that time."

"More information, Bob," Kieri demanded, gritting her teeth in frustration. She knew that this was Bob's way of processing what he had seen but it didn't make it any less frustrating.

"A Bael Wight wasn't moving right through the steam. It's almost as if it isn't really there. Kind of like an illusion," Bob explained.

"Pretty effective illusion," muttered Kawen, watching another Wight Clash with the Wards.

Galeb sat down because he was tired, sweat soaked, sore and frustrated. He tried to think through Bob's observation. He had never heard of a truly solid illusion. It was possible, he supposed. Wards created solid effects so why not a hardened illusion? Galeb had no idea how such a thing could be created but had to admit that it was at least possible.

But what if it was not an illusion? What if it was more than that? What if the Wight had the ability to make itself insubstantial? No. That wasn't right. If a Bael Wight could make itself insubstantial it should be able to pass through solid objects and the Wights hadn't done that.

Galeb was back to the idea that the Wights' forms could be illusionary based. Possible given that the Obari had illusion based magic. Given that possibility, how were they doing it? No...it didn't matter how the Wights were creating the illusions. What

349

mattered was if the attacking Wights were actually illusionary – hardened light or whatever. If the Bael Wights were illusions then they had to be projected from somewhere. That was the key – he hoped.

Galeb slowly stood and retrieved the second staff, wiped sweat away from his face, and turned to Kieri.

"What's the maximum range for a guided Obari illusion?"

There was a huge difference between a constantly maintained illusion and the kind of sendings, like Bob's birds, that were used to convey messages. Sendings were extremely limited in their functionality, while guided illusions were eminently adaptable. That difference was a closely guarded secret; no outsiders were supposed to know about the sendings. If Galeb wasn't married to Kieri, he wouldn't even have known – theoretically. Galeb had been well aware of the sendings for years – there wasn't a lot he missed when it came to magic and Bob had been particularly careless one time. Bob always argued that Galeb had always been Kieri's so there was no harm in Galeb knowing the secret. Even so, the cousins had sworn Galeb to secrecy, sworn never to tell Ebko, and thumped Bob repeatedly for the mistake.

Kieri thought about this before answering "About fifty yards. Why?"

Galeb didn't answer her, already focused on the problem at hand and running calculations in his head based on Kieri's information. Galeb considered that the Bael Wights seemed to be powerful, looked at areas that the actual Wights might be hiding in while casting illusions and came up with a three tiered attack, modifying the earlier Warding combination that had slaughtered the kielsgruntara. Galeb sent ripples of burning light at three different heights pulsing outward, pouring power into the ripples, pushing everything the second staff had in it in an attempt to reach a maximum range of one hundred and fifty yards. He hit something.

Shrieks of pain echoed through the night. The Bael Wights collapsed in on themselves as many somethings suddenly keened in pain.

Margul cursed the useless grubs. A little singeing and the Wights burrowed deep, afraid, abandoning their projections. Cowards.

The Guunt marshalled his remaining forces and ordered an all-out attack on three sides. Wasteful, but the Wards were already stressed. He just needed to break them now.

The Darkness surged forward, hammering at the Wards. Margul began ripping up trees and boulders, hurling them at the fourth side of the Wards.

The cacophony was deafening, the Wards nearly blinding as the oak shuddered under the combined attack that seemed to have gone on forever, just not long enough for dawn to arrive. Thunderous booms echoed every time a boulder smashed apart against the Wards. Tree trunks snapped and splintered as they were repelled. Darkness of a dozen types chittered, whistled, screamed, howled, mewled and cackled as they attacked the Wards in an enraged frenzy.

Galeb and the Obari watched in stunned awe at the attack. Galeb tried to reinforce the Wardings wherever he could. Kieri and her cousins wove illusions in a constant stream as they tried to drive The Darkness away from the Wards. But there was too much pressure, too many attacks.

First one of the support roots crumbled, followed by two more in rapid succession. The group stumbled back as The Darkness pressed forward. Three more roots splintered and fell apart. It was too much, too fast.

No one saw what kind of Darkness was responsible, but as the group stumbled back, Kawen wasn't fast enough and his left arm was ripped off just above the elbow in a gout of blood and tattered flesh. Kawen screamed as Bob pulled him back towards the ever tightening protection of the Wards.

Kieri took a guard position, her Wards and sword lashing out, driving the beasts back. Bob frantically tore free some fabric from his tunic and used it to make a tourniquet on Kawen's arm. Galeb looked in shock as he stumbled to help Bob.

Kawen was still screaming in agony. Kieri's jaw was tight as she forced herself to focus on the threat in front of her even though she desperately wanted to see how badly Kawen was hurt. Galeb just saw blood. Blood soaking the ground. Blood splashed on Bob. Blood dripping from Kieri. Blood on Kieri....

Galeb's mind went blank. He stood, his expression and thoughts stilled in a terrible rictus. Something had torn inside of him with his final Warding in the Battle of the Valley. A gaping hole had been left that Galeb had thought healed. He was wrong; oh, so wrong.

An emptiness reared up inside of him, devouring, rampaging and raging. From that ever expanding hollowness poured power, deep and molten.   Galeb ripped the power from the remaining traps and wove it into the wellspring inside of him. A wind rose, ruffling Kieri's hair and then ripping the cloak from Galeb before expanding outward and coalescing around every splinter of stone and wood littering the ground, raising up the debris in a lazy swirl that began to increase in speed exponentially as it flowed around the oak in a tightly bound loop. The loop generated more power that Galeb funneled back into the winds, raising a wall of air, a tornado locked in place. Kawen's screams became drowned out as the wind roared, the stone and wood splinters keening in the air.

"Galeb – what the septa are you-?" Kieri began to ask, blinking to clear her eyes as dust filled the air.

"You will be safe," Galeb said softly, pushing her back towards her cousins and the shelter afforded by the main trunk before striding forward. He would scour the world of every last piece of life if he had to in order to keep her safe.

"Galeb!" Kieri screamed, her eyes wide in shock as she watched him step clear of the faltering protections of the Wards, the wind preventing her from following.

Galeb didn't hear her. He was passed hearing. Passed fear. Passed anger and rage. He was a void at the center of building power.

The stone and wood shards became brutal weapons as they were driven by the wind into the attacking Darkness. The projectiles smashed, cut, broke and splinted flesh and bone, turning the air into a seething pink mass that drowned out even the loudest scream of the dying.

Galeb was drenched in sweat, the effort to maintain the Warding flirting on the edge of overwhelming, his vision tunneled and flashes of random light flitting across his sight. But he held the Warding together, building its power as it built his own.

Power to augment Wardings could come from anywhere. This was one of the first lessons taught at The Academy. Static from a bit of wool rubbed together to brighten a light. Sun soaked Ward Posts to feed the Line. Wind generating massive amounts of energy as it revolved in a frenzy around a central point.

Galeb was killing The Darkness but at the same time generating tremendous amounts of energy that allowed him to keep killing Darkness. He was building power to counter power. Galeb had to admit that it was a bit intoxicating. The thought was fleeting, falling away into the emptiness inside of him that only seemed to have expanded.

Galeb smiled grimly when the Guunt stepped free of the trees, roaring in challenge, uncaring of the wind or its dead minions. When the Guunt charged, Galeb was already stepping forward to meet it.

Margul panted as he watched the destruction of his forces. Not in anger or fear, but in anticipation. The power before him was a staggeringly worthy challenge that would fill his fellow

Guunt with jealousy. Kiesh may be dominant but could not boast a kill such as this. Margul roared in thanks to the Creator.

Margul saw the Mage step forward amidst the destruction and felt satisfaction settle into every pore of his being. Here, here was a child of stone and iron. Not a pathetic child of the Shaeloman, like the Skin Walkers or a cowardly child of the Wight's like the Obari. No, here was a child of the Guunt. A proud product of the magics that The Darkness had poured into their prey when they'd marched South from the homelands a millennium ago in hopes of creating a stronger prey; a prey worthy of the Rising.

Margul stepped forward from the trees so that the Mage had the honor of beholding his death. The Guunt raised his arms and smashed the ground in challenge before roaring again and charging the Mage to help the man find his glorious ending.

The amount of energy being generated by the funnel was enormous, crackling all along its length. Galeb took this energy and focused it into a single point. Lightning sundered the air in a horrific boom, flowing to a point just in front of Galeb's outstretched hands and then bursting towards the charging Guunt.

Margul leaped to the side, but Galeb had anticipated this, forking the lightning into the possible directions the Guunt might take. As soon as one of the forks struck Margul, the rest of the lightning leaped back into the stream and poured into the creature.

Guunt were iron and stone. This wasn't simply an expression that the beasts used to describe their strength. Unfortunately for the Guunt, iron was a good conductor.

Margul's charge faltered and the monster crashed to the earth in a rictus of pain as energy sparked and snapped through his body. The Guunt spasmed uncontrollably as the iron in his body not only channeled the lightning but melted under the assault as the stone split and cracked, falling off of his body in small avalanches.

Margul tried to roar his defiance. He tried to claw his way toward the Mage but could not. Too much of the Guunt's body was falling away. Margul felt a bit of disappointment at not killing the Mage, but the satisfaction overrode the disappointment. This was a good death; a worthy death and so much like a quickening that Margul felt a bit of pleasure mingled with regret now. He would have liked to ride upon the Great North winds on wings of flame.

Galeb watched dispassionately as molten iron poured out of the Guunt's eye and ear sockets.   He thought that destroying the beast would fill him with satisfaction. Kieri would be safe. He was wrong.

Most likely because he knew that she wouldn't be safe. No one would be safe. The Darkness would never allow it.

Something flowed into him – he wasn't certain what; in fact he barely noticed, too caught up in his thoughts. An alienness coursed through his being, filling and altering the emptiness. Power surged, deeper, more ancient, and so very, very savage only to be confronted and twisted by Galeb's equally powerful sense of duty. If the two opposing forces inside of him were sentient, they would have been awfully confused.

He sighed, releasing the lightning, collapsing the funnel of air and pouring every last ounce of its generated energy outwards in a broad line extending north and south of their current position. It was a simple Warding that he wrought – The Way is Shut – but on a massive scale, not even bothering to contemplate the improbable nature of his action. Something whispered in his mind not to worry; such power was his natural birthright since the day he'd been ripped from the rock and stone.

At the last moment he decided to blend in two other Wards. 'Twilight's Satisfaction' and 'Purpose lost'. Galeb burned the Warding into the ground for over a mile in both directions, blood pouring from his nose and ears unnoticed. He smiled again as the Warded area filled with the gentle gleam of a setting sun. The light was welcoming, serving no other purpose, unlike the other two Wards designed to either repel Darkness or send The Darkness away in confusion.

A thought occurred to Galeb. He was certain that it wasn't his by the alien feel of the idea. But since the thought seemed as natural as it was alien, he listened, analyzed the idea, and peered at the earth beneath his feet.

The Warding on the surface flared brighter and then sunk into the ground, twisting and turning upon itself, rooting deep in the soil.

Satisfied with his work, Galeb turned to face Kieri, who was suddenly running towards him, and collapsed with a soft wheeze.

As he lay upon the ground, Galeb wondered why he couldn't come up with these ideas sooner. The power tap that had been the wind funnel was so much more effective than the staves. Why did he always have to be so desperate before a better solution presented itself?

Then the pain hit as every muscle in his body locked up and spasmed. Molten fire seemed to be suddenly burning in his veins. Galeb wanted to scream but he couldn't. He suddenly remembered that feeling of something rushing into him as he killed the Guunt and realized that he should have been a lot more concerned by the sensation and the alien thoughts.

Chapter 27

The expression 'there are few things scarier' is an often overused phrase in Sigsrata's opinion. He'd even used the phrase himself more than once to describe one of his wife's moods. Somehow, as the King stood on his observation platform and stared at the oncoming horde of Darkness, Sigsrata felt that he might never use the phrase again. Nothing in his, or any man's experience, was more terrifying than watching an oncoming Rising.

The King had known what to expect intellectually. The Obari scouts had been streaming in for days bringing in reports of numbers and types. The Obari were good at what they did and not prone to exaggeration. At this point Sigsrata glumly wished that the Obari had exaggerated.

The fodder came first, minor Darkness herded forward by their fear of the greater mass that came behind. Pelgs, garmuts, irkanish mostly. Humanoid creatures waist high to a man and only distinguishable at a distance by their pelts and faces.

Pelgs were a bushy reddish-brown, with round faces, no noses and round ears that stuck out on either sides of their heads. Small arms and legs made them seem to waddle when Pelgs walked upright. 'Roly-poly' was a cute descriptor until you saw the creatures run impossibly fast on all fours and then split open to reveal the horror beneath. Their bodies were a deception. The entire torso split open to reveal a mouth full of rows of teeth. Pelgs raced at their prey, leapt, and used their mouths to latch onto their victims. The teeth were hooked to make it near impossible for victims to tear free. The saliva of a pelg prevented clotting, allowing the creatures to drain prey dry of their blood, leaving an empty husk behind.

Garmuts were grayish, with lank fur and thinner limbs. The garmuts were very agile and good climbers, with three fingered hands with hook like claws that allowed them to hold onto a tree limb before dropping down on top of victims. Centered on the garmuts' faces were long, strong, sharp bills, like a stork or cranes'. Once garmuts grabbed their prey, they used their bills to stab into flesh, wounding and injecting an acid that dissolved flesh into a sludge that the garmuts lapped up with their delicate tongues.

Irkanish were extremely well muscled, being twice as strong as a man, preferring to smash their victims or bite them with their thick fangs. Black furred, beady eyed, and snub nosed the animals were bruisers and brawlers. No poison, no hooked teeth. Just brute strength.

Pike Striders, large spiders the size of a horse, with frail looking, spindly limbs that held the insects almost twenty feet above the other Darkness. The Striders minced among the milling garmuts, irkanish, and pelgs, occasionally dipping down to eat one. The combined mass of what was essentially the vanguard of a greater force seemed to cover the plains as the creatures emerged from the distant tree line heading for the Klynsheimer encampment, many glancing fearfully behind them.

The Klynsheimer forces were already moving into position. The army was anchored by the Ward Line on the right, which turned away from the forest more than two miles distant and ended at the old Academy Chapter House which now was at the center of the main encampment. Spreading out from the Ward Line, the encampment was surrounded by layers of Ward posts, slightly thinner than those of the Ward Line. Fighting positions, known as 'wings' swept out from either side of the main encampment, allowing Soldiers and Troopers to fight the enemy from behind a bit of safety by forming behind and between the posts.

The central encampment was further reinforced by an earthen rampart and lay slightly back from the wings. The wings were positioned to funnel The Darkness in towards the center allowing all three sides to hammer at the enemy in a cross fire of bows, sling, arbalest and engine fire without worrying about striking their own lines. The left wing was anchored by a massive array of Wardings, all of simple designs – Obel had taken to the suggestions of Galeb's book like a fish to water, 'improved' every one of the ideas in the book and taken as much credit as was feasible.

Theoretically The Darkness could simply walk past the army and head further south. There was nothing for several miles west of the Ward Line except open plains that terminated in foot hills and then mountains. The Ward Line had never been extended over the plain due to costs as well as the fact that Darkness didn't like the open plains whether they be nocturnes or not. The Darkness preferred the cool shadows of the forests and had never before shown interest in crossing the open ground.

Doctrine also indicated that The Darkness wouldn't ignore the army but throw itself against the humans in an orgy of blood and death. Just in case doctrine was wrong, the strongest Obari illusionists were ready to redirect the beasts back.

If that didn't work, war dogs were already out on the plain, hidden in the deeper grasses, waiting to intercept The Darkness or harry the enemy depending on need. Handlers stood on their own observation towers, horns ready to relay commands.

A secondary encampment lay several miles behind the main lines with a thousand Troopers, horse archers skilled in hit and run tactics. Beyond that lay the Warded towns and cities of Klynsheim that very well may become islands of safety. Sigsrata had done all he could to prepare his men. Now came the test of those preparations.

It was midmorning, the air hanging chill, hinting at rain in the not so far future. Sigsrata turned away from watching The Darkness and instead observed his forces array themselves for battle. All around him on the platform staff officers milled about seeing to last minute preparations and consulting with runners and communications flagmen.

The infantry was made up of mostly bill men, their seven foot long weapons topped by a foot long thin spear point. Below the points were steel axe heads that had a blade that curved into two points along the front and which terminated along the back into a six inch hooks. The men were armored with open faced bell helms, steel cuirasses, greaves, and large rectangular shields that could be interlocked to form a shield wall or phalanx. Two small, stiff, colored flags were attached to shoulders of each man, allowing general officers to know the exact locations of each unit. The billmen stood in three ranks deep at the front of the wings, ready to repel the enemy, the front most rank with shields grounded to form yet another barrier. Arbalests waited in fighting platforms in the center of the wings, allowing them an unobstructed view of the enemy. Surrounding the arbalests were bowmen who would volley fire into the massed ranks of The Darkness when the time came.

In addition to the arbalests and archers the main encampment housed trebuchets, mangonels and torsion screws.

The torsion screws were the most complex of the engines, designed not to launch a stone aloft, but along a horizontal trajectory. The arm of a screw was mounted perpendicular to the center post, terminating in a basket in which a fifty to eighty pound stone was secured by clamps. The basket was rotated to face outward instead of up. The screw was wound tight and when released the central column spun at very high rates of speed. The crew operating the torsion screw pulled a lever, releasing the clamps and the stone flew outward on a flat trajectory to smash into anything in its way. Operating a torsion screw took extreme skill, particularly when it came to aiming the stone's release.

Sigsrata watched the advancing tide, before looking over his men – veteran Soldiers in the front ranks, green recruits to the rear. Mages hurrying to check replacement posts and emergency supplies. Water runners, grooms, corpsman – every one of them full of nervous energy and fear.

There was a lot of Darkness out there – a lot of mass that would stress the Ward Posts and the men would have to pick up the slack. The Posts were defensive in nature only. No offensive Wards. There wasn't the time or manpower to produce both, let alone maintain both style of Wards over such a broad front. The Soldiers and Troopers would be the offense and he needed them confident, assured in their strength.

"Mangonels only – twenty pound shot. Elevate the torsion screws but restrain fire until commanded otherwise. Arbalests to refrain – there's nothing big enough out there yet to require their use. Archers to volley three times and then use relieving fire only," Sigsrata said, his words calm and relaxed.

Communications officers raised flags and began to relay the commands.

"Let them come," Sigsrata suddenly growled. "We are Klynsheim; we are blood and iron! The Darkness seems to have forgotten this lesson. Sound the *slynkomper* so that we may remind them."

Drums began to play, a deep bass that resonated over the plain. Troopers and Soldiers answered the first notes by hammering on their shields, altering the tune. The new song, the *klynshipin* – the defiance- let the enemy know what the Klynsheimers were – men of blood and iron. A wall between The Darkness and their people.

"Let us greet our guests," Sigsrata said to an artillery officer, smiling grimly.

The order was conveyed. Sharp cracks were heard as throwing arms slammed into leather wrapped beams, releasing stones aloft as the dozen mangonels unloaded. Stones tumbled in the air before crashing down into the ranks of pelgs, garmuts, and irkanish. The stones bounced when they hit, careening down through the horde, opening up aisles of broken bodies. One stone squashed a Pike Strider flat, ejecting green fluid from the pulped body that seemed to infuriate the irkanish and garmuts. It was hard to tell with the pelgs – their faces were only facsimile decoys, incapable of true movement.

It would have been a nice piece of poetry to say that the arrow volleys darkened the sky. Nice, but inaccurate. Thousands of arrows lofted up to hiss through the air as they fell upon the front edges of The Darkness. Thousands, but not nearly enough.

Darkness crumbled to the ground in waves, silent and dead or wounded or bellowing. The following ranks ignored the carnage and surged forward, trampling the fallen or having a bit of an opportunistic snack. Some enterprising Irkanish even snatched up bodies and hurled them at the Klynsheim ranks. Nothing seemed capable of stopping the rampaging horde.

With collective hisses that sounded like a dry husk rattling in the wind, The Darkness surged forward the last few feet to collide with the Ward Posts and the bills of the waiting infantry.

Galeb dreamed of molten blood coursing through his veins. Guunt bodies falling in showers of stone, releasing Kraalsbriekans to dance upon the northern winds, uncaring of the struggling creatures below as they beat their fifty foot wide wings with gentle strokes. Understanding began to fill Galeb to accompany the thrumming power that was swelling to fill the void within him. He seemed to be on the verge of a great epiphany when suddenly he felt like he was drowning and jerked awake to find out that he was indeed drowning – well near enough for there not to be much of a difference.

Kieri had him in the middle of the pool and kept dunking him under the water despite his sudden and numerous protests. Galeb was beating at her arms, trying to break her grip, but couldn't find the leverage. Just what had he done to make her want to kill him?

"I'm not trying to kill you, you idiot. Your body's burning up," Kieri snapped at him, dunking him again. "I'm trying to cool you down."

He must have spoken that last bit allowed.

Galeb weighed the options before him. Possibly become injured due to some strange overheating or definitely drown under Kieri's ministrations. He thought about it, realized that yes, he felt a little warm, but not too bad. On the other hand he couldn't very well breathe under water. He started beating more furiously at Kieri's hold.

"Fine!" Kieri said, letting him go and wading out of the pool while rubbing her arms. "That hurts, you know."

"Well drowning isn't much fun either," Galeb muttered when he managed to sit up and catch his breath.

"I wasn't drowning you," Kieri said indignantly.

"Could have fooled me," Galeb muttered again, standing on shaky legs. He felt heavy. Not lethargic, but almost as if he had gained mass. Must be the water drenching his cloths.

Now that he wasn't drowning his mind cleared and then: *Enemies! Threat! Defend!* overwhelmed his thoughts and sent him staggering forward, his arms out and ready to Ward as his head whipped around looking for Darkness.

He had to keep Kieri safe. Blood...so much blood.... The Wards roiled to life around his body, new combinations snapping into being. The Wards no longer flowed golden around his body but snapped the red-white of the forge fire, thrumming with menace. Let The Darkness come. Let The Darkness challenge him. He would rend them all!

Kieri stepped back from her husband, her eyes wide in shock. Galeb practically vibrated with power and he'd just...growled? Galeb didn't growl. Galeb didn't look this terrifying.

Something else was wrong. Kieri narrowed her eyes as she continued to examine Galeb. He was standing taller, straighter, no longer hunched and twisted by his injuries. He moved like a predator, graceful and threatening. He was also bigger, looking like at least thirty pounds of muscle had been added to his slight frame.

The best course of action was to calm Galeb down and soothe him.

"What did you do?" Kieri demanded, hands on her hips, scowling at her husband.

Galeb's head whipped around, looking at Kieri, the menace on his face slowly slipping into confusion.

"Why do you always assume that I've done something?" Galeb asked, shaking his head before he seemed to remember something and then went back into full predator mode.

"Don't you look away, Galeb Sonovonol. I want to know what you did!"

Galeb looked at Kieri again, confusion once again replacing the dangerous look.

"I don't know what you're talking about."

"Don't know what I'm talking about?" Kieri hissed. "Oh, I don't know, maybe the fact that you seem taller, more muscled – deliciously so, I might add – and moving as smoothly as a swan. Granted, a monstrous swan, but a swan none the less."

"A swan? What?"

"You should have gone with 'bobwhite'," Bob called out from the other side of the tree. "Bobwhites are much more majestic."

"Stay out of this, Bob," Kieri warned.

"I'm just saying he'd probably understand you analogy better if you'd used a bobwhite."

"Bob!"

"Should you be yelling?" Galeb hissed, looking for more threats.

"At this point I don't think it matters. The Darkness won't come near whatever you've done to this place," Kieri said, glaring at the tree as if her wrathful gaze could penetrate the tree and strike Bob down.

"What I've done...?"

Galeb looked around the twilight landscape and shook his head, looking closer. Memories began to surface.

"Huh," Galeb said.

"Huh? Huh? That's all you've got to say for yourself?" Kieri said, poking the air as if it were Galeb's chest.

"How's Kawen?" Galeb asked as he trudged out of the water. He realized that he wasn't wearing clothes just as his foot found dry ground. He thought about being embarrassed but decided that he was too tired. Galeb looked at Kieri hopefully but she was disappointingly still fully dressed.

Kieri noticed Galeb's look and smiled, pleased before looking angrily at Galeb and frowned.

"He's unconscious, thankfully. Bob managed to cauterize the wound and bind it with some herbs that prevent infection," Kieri said. "I'm still waiting for you to explain yourself. What did you do?

"What do you mean?" Galeb said, still a bit confused.

"Husband, trust me when I say that I know what your body looks like," Kieri said, quirking a smile before licking her lips. "You are different."

"What?" Galeb asked, looking down at himself. To his mind he just looked the way he was supposed to look.

"Weren't you listening? You're moving smoother too," Kieri said, licking her lips again, as appreciation argued with concern. "Like you used to before the hip injury. Like a swan."

"Bobwhite!" Bob insisted.

Kieri ignored her cousin.

"Come here, I want to feel your skin."

"This is hardly the place to be groping me," Galeb said, raising an eyebrow. "At least let's find some privacy first."

"Are you flirting with me?" Kieri asked, pleasantly surprised. "Whatever this change is I like it. Maybe. If it doesn't mean something is about to go wrong. Just get over hear. There's something strange about your skin."

"You just want to touch me," Galeb said with a smile as he walked towards Kieri, feeling more at ease than he could ever remember.

"Always, Love, but that's not the point," Kieri said with a grin. "Someone is quite confident today."

"I feel good," Galeb admitted. "Tired, but good."

Kieri ran her hands over his arms and back, her smile turning into a slight frown.

"Your skin is...thicker...not rougher, but...harder?" she said, confusion in her words. "Hotter too. Not as hot as it was when I dunked you in the pool, but hotter than it should be. Are you sure you're okay?"

"I feel fine," Galeb assured his wife.

"Galeb, what happened to you?"

"I'm not sure. When I killed the Guunt something seemed to rush into me."

"I killed a Skrieksgrata!" Bob called out.

"Not the same, Bob," Kieri snapped, tired of the interruptions.

"You kill a Skrieksgrata and then you can be critical," Bob grumbled.

"A Guunt is a lot bigger than a Skrieksgrata," Kieri stated through clenched teeth, offended on Galeb's behalf.

"All I see is a pile of crumbled rock," Bob shot back. "For all we know Galeb Sonovonol passed out while trying to artfully arrange some stone and mucked it up."

"What? Of all the ridiculous.... And even if he had been arranging stone, why would he muck it up?" Kieri demanded, her face turning red.

"Have you met the man?" Bob asked, too mildly.

"Have I? I married him! I know him quite intimately, thank you! I've explored every inch!"

"Yuck, thanks for the image," Bob grumbled.

"Idiot," Kieri grumbled, turning her attention back to Galeb and licking her lips. "Though I wouldn't mind getting reacquainted."

Galeb grinned.

Kieri's eyes seemed to lose focus for a bit before she shook her head, seeming to remember something.

"Wait. Something 'rushed into you'? From the Guunt? You're not going to turn into Darkness, are you?"

Kieri was only half kidding and she became momentarily distracted again when Galeb shrugged his shoulders. She might have even growled a bit or maybe purred. It was hard to tell.

Galeb frowned and thought about it for a moment.

"No?" he finally said.

"That's not very reassuring," Kieri complained, trying to clear her head again and glaring at her husband with a mixture of fondness and exasperation.

"Best that I can do," Galeb admitted. "But I do have an idea."

"Oh, you have an idea. How comforting."

Galeb tried to glare at his wife's sarcasm but grunted instead. He also noticed that Kieri was running her hands over his back quite possessively.

"I suppose that it's not," he admitted. "Anyway, I was having a dream before someone tried to drown me."

"I was not trying to drown you! I was saving your life. You were burning up!"

Kieri was a bit annoyed at the accusation but that didn't deter her hands.

"Okay...matter of perspective, I assume," Galeb said with another shrug.

"I'll give you a matter of perspective," Kieri threatened once her thoughts unscrambled. The man really had to stop shrugging and moving all of those yummy muscles.

"If you're going to try drowning me again I must insist that you take your clothes off first. Fair play and all."

Kieri gaped at him for a moment before laughing.

"Oh, I like this new you. We can get naked after you explain this idea."

"I'm already naked."

"Yes, and I'm enjoying the sight. Now explain your idea so that I can show you how much I'm enjoying seeing you naked."

"I'm not enjoying seeing him naked," Bob chimed in.

"Shut up, Bob!" Kieri said, weaving an illusion of tall, thick bushes between the pool and the tree.

"Thank you!" Bob said. "It's not dignified for Death to be walking around without clothes on. Ruins one's reputation, I suspect."

"Good to see that Bob's still crazy as ever," Galeb said with a shake of his head.

"Yeah," Kieri said softly, looking away for a moment and rubbing absently at an arm.

"What is it?" asked Galeb, embracing Kieri, hoping to comfort her. He'd seen the momentary flash of fear across her face.

Kieri definitely purred this time. He heard the sound quite clearly as she snuggled in to his body.

"Galeb, you didn't see yourself when you did...this," Kieri said, moving away just enough to gesture towards the carnage that surrounded the area. "I've never seen so much power. It was frightening and your expression was so cold. I don't know, it was just terrifying. If I didn't have my Wards I don't know if I could have kept Kawen and Bob safe."

"I'm sorry," Galeb said, placing a finger under her chin and tilting her head up so that she looked at him. He kissed her gently on the lips, trying to not remember the emptiness that he'd felt at the moment he'd raised the wind and slaughtered The Darkness.

Kieri didn't allow the kiss to stay gentle for very long, only breaking away when they both needed to breathe.

"So, I'm still waiting to hear this idea of yours," Kieri said eventually.

"Oh, yeah. Guunts are a transitional Darkness."

"What?" Kieri asked, surprised. Whatever she had expected her husband to say, it wasn't this.

"You know how frogs start out as tadpoles?"

"Yes," Kieri said, arching an eyebrow impatiently.

"Guunts are tadpoles."

"So what's the frog?"

"Kraalsbriekans, I think. Guunts are stone and iron. As the Guunt gain in mass they reach a critical point where the sheer amount of weight creates pressure that quickens the iron in their bodies. The process is slow; the iron becomes molten gradually, transforming the Guunt into a Kraalsbriekan. The process has to be slow, giving the Guunt's body time to adjust. When I killed the Guunt, I liquefied the iron too quickly for a metamorphoses to occur. There was power released – part of the abortive transformation process I imagine – and I think I kind of, I don't know, soaked it up."

Kieri was staring up at him as if he had three heads.

"What part did I lose you at?" he asked uncertainly.

Kieri smacked him upside the head.

"I understood the explanation, Galeb," she growled at him. "I'm trying to process the idea of you soaking up Guunt...stuff."

"That sounds disgusting," Galeb protested. "Let's not refer to whatever happened as me 'soaking up Guunt stuff.'"

Kieri giggled before frowning.

"Yeah, that does sound disgusting. So what does this all mean – assuming that you're right? You're still human, aren't you?"

"I suppose so," Galeb said, thoughtfully.

"You suppose?"

"Look, I'm still trying to process this as much as you are. Three months ago I was a worn out Itinerant Mage exiled to an endless duty. Now I'm doing things no Mage has ever done in recent memory, have talked to the King, possibly pissed him off, have a homicidal shape changer obsessed with me and...and it's a lot to take in."

"You also married me," Kieri reminded Galeb. "It's not been all bad."

"No," Galeb admitted with a smile.

"And you definitely pissed off the King, which was why he allowed you to head off on your own."

"The King knew that I was going to slip away?"

"Husband, you're not subtle. The King saw what you were doing as necessarily stupid and permitted it. He was also mad at you so if you suffered a bit in your attempt to draw off some of The Darkness, Sigsrata was okay with that. Besides, how blind do you think my people are? We weren't slipping past them no matter how good our illusions were crafted."

"You could have told me this sooner," Galeb said, mildly annoyed. "If what you say is true, why go through the whole elaborate process of sneaking away?"

"You and the boys worked so hard on your escape that I didn't want to disappoint you."

Galeb looked at his wife suspiciously.

"What else have you been keeping from me?"

"I'm pregnant," Kieri said.

"What?" Galeb said, his mouth gaping like a fish out of water.

Kieri laughed deeply.

"Oh, your face! No, I'm not pregnant. But I'm going to be eventually and you better handle it better than you are now," Kieri said, her laughter slowly fading with the final words. There was clear warning in her voice.

"I'm not keeping anything else from you."

"I thought it was funny," Bob supplied.

"Thanks," Galeb said, trying to be angry, but failing. He'd been manipulated most of his life. Why should now be any different?

"You're welcome," Bob said.

Kieri saw the thoughts upon her husband's face and hugged him. Galeb was very good at closing off his expressions with everyone else but her.

"No more secrets," she promised.

A few moments passed as they held each other.

"You're still clothed," Galeb observed finally.

"I'm certain that I can remedy that situation," Kieri said, her voice becoming sultry.

Kieri was asleep, snuggled in their blankets. Galeb had woken, too warm and looking for relief. Kieri had mumbled in her sleep, trying to snuggle closer but Galeb managed to extricate himself without waking her.

The air was pleasantly chilly, Galeb's breathe steaming with every exhale as he closed his eyes and smiled, stretching muscles that hadn't felt this loose in years. It could have been a gentle spring day instead of mid fall. Warm enough to walk about in shirt sleeves, not something that Galeb generally did in the North Country.

Looking down Galeb noticed Kieri shiver for a moment before nestling deeper in the blankets. He arched a brow suddenly wondering if it was unseasonably warm or maybe, just maybe, it was his own internal temperature that made it feel so warm. Guunt apparently burned hot.

The Mage contemplated his transformation, wondering if he should be more concerned. But he felt normal, as if his body was exactly the way it was supposed to be. He stretched again, feeling the old scars pull a little but not nearly as bad as they once had. Galeb's hip didn't ache and his movements were almost graceful. No, it felt good not to be a crippled wreck.

Deciding to indulge in walking normally, Galeb strolled out of the camp, glancing down to examine his new Warding. Galeb liked the twilight he'd entwined in the Warding. It was a gentle light, reminding him of summers on the tundra.

He nudged it a little, made some minor changes, and marveled at the ease in which the earth accepted the runes. The Guunt were of the earth – there must be some sympathetic relationship that made infusing Wards into the ground easier.

Galeb certainly had never heard of any other Mage being able to do more than carve temporary Wards into the dirt like he'd done in the Valley and then again on the Road.

At the thought, some of the Guunt Margul's thoughts skittered around his mind, not intrusive, not dominating, just there to be used before they faded. Another perception to guide Galeb's craft. Those thoughts were tugging him in a particular direction.

Galeb looked northeast, uncertain what drew him until he thought of Jesia. Her city – her people lay in that direction. Galeb frowned, thinking over the Rising that Jesia's people had brought down upon the Southlands. Not the first time either if the strange woman's words were to be believed.

The Mage glanced south towards the Ward Line and then again at the Warding he'd embedded into the ground. Huh, he wasn't wearing boots. He shrugged and twisted his lips, contemplating the Warding, still fascinated by what he'd done. It was as if every time he became concerned about his appearance, the thoughts drifted away as if unimportant.

Galeb glanced back at the camp before his eyes looked down at the Warded path again. Not much different than The Road really. This was familiar. This was safe. In some ways it was like coming home.

He turned to look towards the north again, in the direction of the shape changer's city. Those people had gifted the South with a rising. Be a shame not to return the favor.

The winds began to gather around him, slowly churning, building up power. Galeb would need it. He had a long way to Ward and a lot of Darkness to attract.

Kieri woke up angry. Mostly because her husband wasn't lying next to her and it was cold. Galeb's body was like a comfortable camp fire. She was partially angry because when asked, Bob told her that Galeb had wandered off over an hour ago looking 'purposefully distracted' – whatever that meant.

She was contemplating beating Bob for not stopping Galeb when she was distracted by an event and a realization. The event was a flash on the horizon and a rustle of wind. The light on the horizon stabilized into a matching glow to the twilight lighting up their own area. Galeb was Warding.

The realization was that if she hurt Bob, Kieri would have to stay and tend to Kawen. She loved her cousin but Bob was more than capable of taking care of Kawen, allowing Kieri to pursue her husband. Besides, the only other choice was to murder Bob and then she'd also have to dispose of a body.

"Bob, I'm going after Galeb. When we get back I am going to hit you," Kieri promised.

"We'll be here," Bob responded cheerfully. "I don't think that Kawen's in any shape to move and there are enough herbs and other medicinal plants in the area that should help him. The best part is that Galeb Sonovonol has Warded a wide swath around us. No concern about being attacked."

Kieri looked about the strange twilight not as confident as Bob. But she had to admit that there was something about this newly Warded area that was immensely comforting. Kieri had slept deeper than she normally did in the Wild.

The Obari woman shook her head, remembering to be angry with her husband who had the worst habit of wandering off without her. Kieri was of a mind to box his ears, stomp his foot and then kiss him until he passed out from lack of air. Firmly resolved on that course of action she set out, quickly realizing that there was more than just the feeling of comfort that the path exuded.

The ground was easy to navigate, smoother, with less obstacles to trip a person. Not quite designed, as a Klynsheimer road, not quite an Obari track. More like a combination of the two, but on a massive scale.

Even so it was several hours before Kieri caught up to Galeb. It helped that she had moved quickly while Galeb seemed content to amble along his path. Still the distance was unexpected. Kieri accounted it to Galeb having a bigger stride and more stamina than he used to possess.

When she finally found him, Galeb was standing in the middle of a new section of Warding, his eyes closed and his short hair ruffled by the whirl wind that stood tamed at a safe enough distance. He looked almost serene until Kieri noticed that his eyes were not closed, but slitted and the Mage was using every one of his senses to keep alert for danger. Whatever changes had been wrought in the man he was still safely paranoid.

Kieri noticed that her husband was both shirtless and bootless and while she admired the view, she was still irritated that once again she was chasing after him and he was half naked. To make his state of undress even more irritating was that he had a shirt, choosing to carry it in his hands rather than wear it.

"I'm heading to the city of the shape shifters," Galeb explained, anticipating Kieri's question.

That was not her question. Kieri had been about to demand to know why Galeb seemed suddenly incapable of dressing himself properly. Not the most pertinent question but Kieri was angry and distracted. Galeb had a lot of muscles moving under his bare skin and the twilight seemed to highlight every single one of them. Of all the changes, the muscles were the easiest to get used to.

Kieri shook her head and tried to focus on what Galeb had said. It took two more head shakes but she managed to concentrate.

"Without me," Kieri said, hurt in her voice. "Leaving me to wonder if whatever changed you was causing harm."

"I'm sorry," Galeb said. "I tasted the north wind and felt a longing for home. I didn't intend to wander so far; I just couldn't seem to resist Warding just a little further."

"Galeb," Kieri said slowly, "Your home is to the south. You've never been this far north before. We're also almost ten miles from the camp."

Galeb seemed to consider her words and then shrugged. "Must have been thinking of Margul then."

"Who's 'Margul'?" Kieri asked, uncertain if she wanted an answer to the question.

"The Guunt I killed," Galeb explained. "Some of his thoughts seem tangled up in here."

Galeb gestured vaguely to his head before frowning.

"No, not thoughts. More like impressions, I guess."

"That's not any more comforting," Kieri said with a frown of her own, hugging herself.

"No, I guess not," Galeb said with a worried chuckle.

Kieri didn't comment, momentarily distracted by the insistent breeze tossing her hair about wildly. She was glad for the distraction. Kieri didn't want to think about her husband running around acting like a Guunt. No matter how much stronger he looked, there was no way he could physically go toe to toe with most Darkness.

"You still left me," Kieri said eventually, giving up on her hair.

"I know," Galeb said regretfully. "I started Warding and kind of got lost in it."

"Like on The Road," Kieri said, "That always took you away from me."

"But always brought me back again," Galeb said with a gentle smile.

Kieri was not mollified.

"No, you're right. The Road always took me away from you," Galeb admitted, "and I let it, like I was doing just now."

"Is there an apology somewhere in that statement?" Kieri asked, trying to not be sad or angry.

"Kieri, I'm standing here on this new 'road' barefoot, with no boots, cloak, jacket, pack, food, or water," Galeb said, walking closer to her and drawing her into a tight embrace that she grudgingly allowed. "You came after me fully equipped."

"I assume you're trying to make a point?"

"I'm admitting that I'd be lost without you. I need you because I love you and...I need you to save me from myself."

Kieri hugged him back, her grip almost painful.

"You are a handful," Kieri admitted, shaking her head in mock regret. "Always trying to wander off and get yourself into trouble. Can we head back now?"

Galeb breathed in the scent of Kieri's hair, his eyes watching the shadows among the trees for any hint of danger, as his ears strained to hear any sound that did not belong. The hearing part should have been difficult over the sound being generated by the whirlwind, but his hearing and eyes had sharpened. Galeb had the distinctly uneasy feeling that bright sunlight was going to be painful and that the twilight Ward was about more than an aesthetic choice.

"I can't go back," Galeb said after a moment. "I need to go to Jesia's city."

Kieri pulled back a little, looking up into his face.

"You're not going to help that crazy woman are you?" she demanded indignantly.

"Yes and no," Galeb admitted, letting Kieri go when she pulled away and crossed her arms, waiting for his explanation. Kieri quirked an eyebrow impatiently. Her foot began to tap.

"Yes, I am going to help some of Jesia's people. Inadvertently, I suppose."

"Keep explaining, Husband," Kieri said, now clenching her teeth.

"The Darkness is attracted to me – to the power I wield," Galeb explained. "If I head back south, The Darkness will only follow me there. But if I head north, towards this city, Warding along the way, I'm bound to draw at least some of The Darkness after me."

"Awfully full of your own importance," Kieri said acidly.

"Kieri," Galeb laughed bitterly, "I've spent most of my life being unimportant and worked hard to seem even more unimportant because no matter what I did, harm found me. If I could make all of this go away, I would, but I can't. If I have to be 'important' the least I can do with that importance is to use it to draw danger away from our People and send it back to the people who deserve it – the shape shifters."

"You're going to -?"

"I'm going to bring the Rising back to where it belongs," Galeb said grimly. "Let this city that has led to the deaths of so many of our People reap the rewards of its actions."

"You'll be bringing death down upon those people," Kieri cautioned.

"The shape shifters are not Family. They are not Klynsheimers," Galeb said, unmoved.

"No, they're not," Kieri agreed. "I just want to make certain that you understand what you're doing."

"I do. Are you bothered by my intentions?"

Kieri laughed, though there was no humor in the sound.

"Not too much," Kieri admitted. "I'm not concerned about preserving a civilization that gave birth to an insane woman with a fondness of dressing up like a Shaeloman. I'm concerned about what taking this course of action will do to you."

"I'll be fine," Galeb assured Kieri.

"I love that you believe that," Kieri said, raising up a hand to cup his cheek gently.

"I'll endure," Galeb amended.

"Yes, you are good at enduring," Kieri agreed. "But after this is done I want you to do more than endure. You have a life with me."

"I know," Galeb said with a slight smile.

"Good, because I'm going to keep reminding you," Kieri said.

"I wouldn't have it any other way."

Kieri smiled, boxed his ears, stomped his foot and then kissed him until she was in danger of passing out herself.

"Just so long as you know that you don't have any choice in the matter," Kieri said once she'd caught her breath.

Galeb snorted.

"How long is it going to take us to get to this city?" Kieri asked, turning away and appraising the area. She noticed that Galeb's Wardings didn't follow a straight line. There were detours for rougher terrain, water sources and edible plants that she and her cousins had taught the Klynsheimer to recognize. "We'll need to forage after a few days."

"Weeks," Galeb admitted. "Depending on terrain I'll be able to Ward up to five or so miles a day starting tomorrow. I've been lucky so far; the ground's been mostly dirt. We're heading into rockier country and its going to be harder to imbed the Warding."

"Maintaining the power sump -," Galeb paused to point in the direction of the whirlwind, "is also going to be a problem since it takes a bit of concentration to maintain. I'm not sure that I can do it in my sleep."

"You're not going to try and maintain control over a whirlwind in your sleep," Kieri warned him.

"But it takes a lot of effort to build the power sump."

Kieri gave him a look.

"No, I suppose I won't," Galeb acknowledged and then muttered, as if Kieri hadn't heard him the first time, "That means rebuilding the power sump every day. It takes time to build up enough energy to feed the Warding I'm crafting."

"It didn't take you long to build up energy when you killed the Guunt."

Galeb nodded.

"True, but what I'm doing here is designed to be a bit more...persistently stubborn, I suppose you'd say. I'm looking for these Wards to not only link to one another, but to sustain each other against The Darkness for years if necessary. I'm essentially building an entirely new Ward Line by myself without the benefit of Ward posts. I'm embedding the Warding into the very earth. It's kind of tricky."

"Truly," Kieri said drily. "You come up with the strangest, most spectacularly ambitious ideas."

Galeb blushed in embarrassment.

"What?" Kieri asked, sensing that Galeb's embarrassment had nothing to do with the compliment that she'd given him. Especially since she hadn't really meant the words as a compliment.

"It's not really my idea. It's...Marguls'...sort of," Galeb explained, gesturing vaguely.

"A dead Guunt is telling you how to Ward?" Kieri asked in disbelief.

"Not so much telling me. It's more of showing me the way."

"Yes, because that makes more sense."

"Guunt are iron and stone, born of mountains."

"Aren't you being poetic?"

"Kieri! I'm trying to explain," Galeb said in exasperation. "Guunt are literally born of mountains. Their bodies are ripped from iron rich stone by other Guunt. The Guunt pour a bit of their essence into the stone, making connections and not only kindling life, but sustaining it. Seeing how it was done gave me the idea about how to Ward this path directly into the earth."

"So...you're not actually making Guunt when you do this, are you?" Kieri asked, disturbed by the notion. "Because if you're being unfaithful to me with the earth, I'm not alright with that."

Galeb just stared at Kieri. Kieri burst out laughing, punching him lightly on the arm.

"At least get dressed," Kieri said, turning away and handing him his boots.

Galeb got dressed, declining a coat or cloak even though the air was cold enough for Kieri to have bundled herself against the chill.

"I only brought one bed roll," Kieri said once Galeb was finished.

"That's okay," Galeb said, "I don't really feel the cold."

"Galeb...I only brought one bed roll," Kieri said, trying again, enunciating every word slowly.

"Yeah, I heard-oh...."

"We're alone for the first time and we will be taking advantage of that fact. A lot," Kieri said, just in case Galeb was still being obtuse. "So hurry up and get back to Warding. I for one can't wait to set up camp."

Kieri walked past Galeb with a smug grin on her face and a bounce in her step. Galeb looked thoughtful for a moment, grinned stupidly, and then composed his face and went back to the task at hand.

Chapter 28

Parsons had planned to give his family and fellow villagers a chance at a new life by settling in the North Country. The Southern Lords had been squeezing the rents more and more every year, pushing out the small farmers in favor of more enclosures and larger scale farms. Added to that an increasing population and the need to divide the free lands among more and more siblings...life in the South had just gotten to be impossible.

Everyone had been filled with such hope. Yeah, the brutal reality of the North Country had hit Parson's people hard, but they'd learned from their mistakes. Now none of it mattered.

Everyone had lost pretty much everything they owned under orders of a forced evacuation. The settlers had nowhere to go. At least the Military had been willing to buy their wagons so that folks had some coin. Not that it would last long. Prices had already risen dramatically, what with the need to support the war effort.

Enlisting had seemed the only option open to Parson's family – they needed coin to send to their families in the refugee camps. Which explained why Parsons was standing in formation waiting for his officer to blow his whistle signaling the changing of positions. This would be the third change of the day, with the second rank replacing the first, the third the second, and the first falling back behind the other two. The maneuver required skill to be executed properly. Parson's unit managed it well enough given the amount of time that they'd trained, which meant that the movements were sloppy at best.

Ikthin and Klyde were in the line with him, further down. He could hear them joking as they tried to hide their fear. Korin had more brains and was working as an engineering assistant on one of the trebuchets. Fancy title for a guy who helped load the rocks into the weapons. Orin was a decent hand with a bow and was farther back in their fighting wing with the other archers. Sharni, not wanting to be separated from her brothers, was dressed as a man and working as a water runner, toting buckets that were passed up and down the lines of the third rank. There had been quite a fight over that, but as usual, Sharni won.

Parsons wished that she hadn't. In all of the heroic stories he'd heard growing up no one ever spoke about the smells. Metal, wood, sweat, blood, piss, nta – every smell blended together into an almighty reek. The noise – God! How he wasn't deaf he couldn't understand. He wished he was deaf; the sound of claws skittering off of shield faces was so nightmarish that Parsons wanted to whimper.

The officer, an eager young lieutenant, looked up and down his platoon line and blew his whistle shrilly. Parsons gripped his bill and shield tighter and began edging forward as the front rank stepped into the gaps between second and third rank Soldiers. The new front rank locked and grounded shields, while Parson's line slung their shields over their backs and began stabbing and slashing at The Darkness over the front ranks' heads.

Already the men in the rear were calling for water.

His arms ached. Ached from thrusting. Ached from slashing. Ached from the impact of the weapon into the bodies of The Darkness. Ached from just trying to hold seven feet of wood and steel steady. Blasted bill was heavy.

The Ward posts popped and crackled as they repelled the garmuts, irkanish, and pelgs that kept battering at the defenses. The creatures fought with a desperate rage, leaping and hurling themselves at the Klynsheimers without a thought to their own safety. An unending storm tossed tide trying to drag the men down; an inhuman insanity that refused to acknowledge the barriers before them.

Magic didn't stop them. Steel didn't stop them. Parsons was starting to think that even death wouldn't stop The Darkness as he stabbed the same garmut a third time.

Though The Darkness did die...eventually, which you would think would create another problem. Dead Darkness mounded up all along the line, leaving a person to think that the dead would hinder The Darkness's progress. It didn't; at least not for long. Whenever the fallen Darkness became too inconvenient to climb or hurtle, the bodies were simply dragged away and then heaped in mounds further back along the plain. The mounds allowed any beast wanting a snack to help themselves. The Darkness didn't seem to be too picky about what they ate, either. There were constant heaving movements along the mounds as various creatures feasted.

Parsons' hands and arms grumbled in protest. The bill's thrusting point was already caked with filth and he'd taken time to clean it a bit during the last rest. Men cursed around him, while the front rank grunted as claws and teeth battered shields that pushed The Darkness back when the Wards were too hard pressed. The skittering sound was driving Parsons mad.

Sergeants roamed up and down the line, calling encouragement, cursing stupidity and correcting stances. The call of 'Blood and Iron!' was ever present, occasionally overshadowed by the 'crack' of catapults firing into the horde. Mage squads under heavy guard raced up and down the line, checking the posts and making repairs. Parsons' heart seized in his chest every time he saw the Mages fitting a new post because that meant another one had failed.

It should have been cold but Parsons just felt so hot, sweat threatening to overwhelm the band in the helmet and spill into his eyes.

The cry of 'Auger! Auger!' indicating that a post was failing and the Mage squads were frantically drilling a new hole and putting in a replacement snapped through the air. Parsons cursed. A man in the front rank got distracted by the call and edged his shield too far out. An irkanish grabbed the shield and dragged the screaming Soldier clear of the Ward Line.

A garmut impaled the careless Soldier through the neck, silencing the scream while other irkanish grabbed the bills of two men who'd tried to help the fallen Soldier. The men had been stabbing wildly and over extending, presenting the beasts with more than just the sharpened bill head and allowed them to grasp unprotected wood. One of the men had the sense to let go of his weapon before it was too late. The other man was dragged clear and torn apart, blood splattering all over the front rank. The beasts made a show of it, throwing intestines and organs at the shield wall.

Parsons winced as something hot and sticky splattered across his cheek, cursed weakly, and moved to close the gap in his line under the command of the sergeants. The maneuver was even more sloppy than usual since the man next to him was throwing up.

The two men weren't the first to die that day in their unit – far from it. Of course, the Troopers had had it worse. Twice The Darkness had become so frenzied not even arrow volleys or engine strikes were enough to drive them back.

The Troopers had charged out in thundering waves to break the pressure. Pelgs turned out to be very skilled at killing a horse while garmuts were good at taking down riders. Nearly a third of the second charge lay dead upon the field, a few bones and broken armor all that was left of the men. Parsons could still hear the screams...

It was so overcast that it seemed that night was almost upon them, which probably favored The Darkness. Parsons wished that it would rain just to settle the choking dust that was being churned up by the fighting. Maybe rain would even force The Darkness to retreat.

He grimaced, cursed again and went back to stabbing at The Darkness. A pelg was trying to eat the bill head, ignoring the metal that cut its flesh. Parson let go of the weapon rather than be dragged over the Line by the weight of the beast. A sergeant cursed him for losing the weapon, praised him for not trying to hold on and then thrust another bill into his hand. There was still a lot of killing left to do, the sergeant informed him before smacking Parsons' helmet and moving away.

Kiesh watched the weakest of his forces batter themselves upon the Klynsheimer's entrenched position. Threshers kept driving the small beasts forward to test defenses and allowing Kiesh to watch how the Klynsheimers reacted to threats. In particular, Kiesh watched the timing – how often and how long it took for the ranks to shift positions and how long it took the war engines to reload. When the weakest of the human units were on the front lines. How quickly the Mages reacted to faltering Wards. When he was convinced he understood enough Kiesh turned to his fellow Guunt and grunted.

"Drive the Ulanimani forward. Herd them towards the position farthest from the Warded Road. They are weakest there along the edge closest to the center."

The other Guunt grinned in anticipation and moved to obey.

The panicking garmuts, irkanish and pelgs was the first indication that Parsons had that something worse was coming. The Darkness streamed away, heading around the westernmost fighting wing. Horns sounded from inside the main encampment with its seeming forest of observation platforms. War dogs leapt up from their prone positions in the grass and went on the attack with fierce howls, dragging down The Darkness and trying to turn them back. The dogs were armored along their chests and necks, giving the animals some protection as they tangled with The

Darkness, claws gouging and teeth snapping in vicious sprays of blood.

It looked like an earthquake had struck the plain as the grass thrashed wildly under the impact of battling animals. Most of the fighting was invisible, trails appearing in the tall grass as dog and Darkness maneuvered, the occasional blood tipped blades of grass.

Cavalry issued forth to give support to the war dogs who were doing pretty well against the irkanish and garmuts, but steadfastly avoiding the pelgs.

The thundering shaking of the ground was the next indication of a deeper threat. Parsons couldn't see what it was since he was currently in the front rank, kneeling behind a grounded shield. Men behind him began to scream in panic while the sergeants shouted the screamers down and called for the men to stiffen their lines.

Parsons could see his lieutenant chewing his lip as he looked from the Ward Posts, no few of which had been replaced or were in the process of being replaced, and then at the oncoming threat. The man shook his head and then stood straighter as he reached a decision.

"Fifth company, form phalanx!" the Lieutenant ordered.

The sergeants looked questioningly at the officer. Considering that the captain was dead, the victim of a mistimed arrow strike, the Lieutenant had command.

"There's no way we are going to be able to stand up to that!" the Lieutenant pointed and shouted, angry that his order was not yet being obeyed. "If we run deeper into the wing, we'll still be overwhelmed. Our only hope is to form phalanx and charge forward clear of the line. We get clear and fight our way to the center lines. Some of us might survive that way. None of us are going to survive if we stand in a big bloody stupid line and let the beasts plow over us! Form phalanx!"

Parsons knew it was bad even as he stood and moved into the phalanx formation that the sergeants were now pushing the men into. He could hear the torsion screws firing, the high pitched whine as they spun. Arbalests were also being cranked and readied. He still wasn't prepared for the sight that greeted him across the plain.

Ulanimani – hundreds of Ulanimani, tri horns lowered - were charging full tilt towards his position. The ground wasn't shaking now – it was groaning under the massed weight. Behind the Ulanimani was a greater nightmare – nearly a dozen Guunt were loping behind The Darkness urging the beasts on.

Other units were copying Fifth Company forming phalanxes and charging out until there were four columns of men curving away from their previous positions. The archers were already running back towards the main encampment. The Mage squads had obviously also decided that the position was untenable because they were running away as fast as their robes would allow, leaving a jumble of scattered posts and tools behind.

It was a simple matter of mass; there was too much heading towards the Ward Line to withstand the pressure. It didn't help matters that the Ulanimani were being concentrated on a narrow front for maximum impact. The Line was going to fail spectacularly.

It was only the farthest phalanx that couldn't get clear. The formation seemed to blow apart as the Ulanimani caught the Soldiers in their first turn, hitting the phalanx broad side and sending men flying into the air before trampling them into a sanguine mud that clung unnoticed to the beasts' flanks.

Some Ulanimani began to fall, struck by arbalest bolts, smashed aside by the torsion springs, or tripping over the shattered phalanx. Most continued onward, colliding with the far edge of the Ward line in a titanic impact that threw many of the fleeing archers off of their feet.

Dozens of Ulanimani crumbled into broken piles of rock under the combined pressure of the Wards and their fellow beasts pressing behind them. Large snapping sounds, like bone being pulverized filled the air as Ward posts crumbled in cascading failures. The entire edge failed as the Ulanimani continued their charge, now smashing into the Line at an angle, driving deeper into the defenses.

Archers were panicking as they pushed and shoved one another to get clear. Arbalest towers began to topple as the Ulanimani rammed into the supports. Screaming. There was so much screaming. Parsons tried to ignore all of this as his unit pushed on, moving at disciplined speed towards the center. Most of the men were praying in one manner or another at this point.

The Guunt hooted and roared, running around the plain in glee as they watched the defenses crumble. Two Guunt decided to destroy the third phalanx and began to tear it apart with broad, lazy strokes of their massive limbs. Some Soldiers tried to fight back to no effect, their bills scraping along the Guunts' tough hide with a tortured sound but not penetrating. Others tried to run. Most just died.

"Eighty pound shot! Septa your lazy hide, move man!" ordered Engineering Sergeant Aikskrig, a salt and pepper dwarf of a man with a temper to match his bristling mustache and beard.

Korin groaned as he and his loading partner placed an eighty pound stone into the carrying cradle and hurried over to the trebuchet Aikskrig had named 'Marta' in honor of his wife. The Sergeant claimed that the trebuchet's wide supports reminded him of his sweet wife's tree trunk sized hips and the throwing arm was as good as Marta's, which was apparently deadly with crockery at twenty paces.

Korin didn't mind the work – mostly - but he'd already been working as a shot porter helping bring up supplies to the mangonel crews. It was the repetition of carrying the weights that made the stones seem heavier every time you moved another one.

"Men are dying you stupid slugs!" Aikskrig bellowed, impatient to let Marta do her work.

Korin looked up in alarm at that shout. The engine park was on a slight rise in the central encampment, deep enough in the defenses to be protected, but close enough to have a wide range of fire. Even so Korin couldn't see what was going on at the front lines.

He and his partner placed the stone in the sling and then hurried clear. Aikskrig was not a patient man and had been known to release the counterweight before the crew was clear.

The counter weight fell almost ponderously, raising the throwing arm and snapping the sling forward with violent force. The stone sailed clear, a dark streak across the sky. All around other trebuchets were firing or adjusting their aim under the direction of the engineering officers.

"What the septa are you waiting for?" Aikskrig bellowed as the throwing arm was being lowered back into position. "Another eighty pound shot!"

The Guunt gave up their game and ignored the other two phalanxes as the torsion screws and trebuchets began firing for effect, eighty pound shot slamming into the monsters with terrific speed. Booming cracks filled the air every time a shot struck one of the Guunt. The Guunt laughed at first until two screw shots slammed one of the Guunt backwards, leaving two large cracks in its hide. The monster stumbled back and the biggest septa Guunt that anyone had ever seen strode forward and killed it for showing weakness. The Guunt roared and Threshers came charging over the plain in their thousands, heading for the phalanxes while Skrieksgrata hooted and whistled their way towards the shattered fighting wing, intent on bringing down the rest of the Ward Posts.

The Guunt ambled away unconcerned, ignoring the rest of the shot falling around them.

Sigsrata watched his left wing collapse in disbelief but was already running down the platform as his staff officers shouted commands, shifting arbalests to strike at the Ulanimani rampaging through the faltering lines. If the Ulanimani continued their charge they could lose more than just the left flank.

Sigsrata ran in full armor, his Guard around him and his great axe held ready, the runes etched in its blade shining defiantly. The King led the counter charge because he had to rally the men, had to show them that The Darkness weren't unstoppable, and because he had a great big bloody Warded axe. As it was more men were dying in the collapsed flank because they were panicking and their sergeants and officers couldn't mount an orderly withdrawal.

Arbalests raced along with the Guard, Mages following along behind, with Jans scrambling to get damage control groups into action. Very young Mages, most barely into their teens, were running towards the danger with replacement Ward Posts and other tools. The Journeyman Mage looked frazzled and almost heartbroken to be sending younglings into danger, but in this case younglings were all they had on hand this close to the broken wing. The breach had to be sealed before The Darkness clove any deeper. The Ward posts were thickest on the edges, thinnest where the wings met the center.

Sigsrata roared as he encountered the first Ulanimani, dodging to the side and cutting its legs out from under it. He didn't stop but hammered into the next one, cleaving half of its face away. The axe hummed with power, feeling light in the King's hands. Sigsrata was still angry that the Mage had dared to Ward his axe, but had to admit that the Warding was both stable and effective.

Arbalest bolts snapped out, driving deep, spreading networks of cracks across the Ulanimanis' bodies. The Guard were less effective, having to work in teams to break the beasts' stony hide. This was not working out well for the men.

A guard screamed as he cartwheeled through the air, thrown by an Ulanimani right into the path of another. The second Ulanimani paused to stomp the hapless man into the ground almost daintily. Sigsrata decided that it must be a female.

"Come on, Beastie, my axe is impatient," the King called towards the beast, which appeared to be trying to wipe the smears of the guard off of her hooves.

The Ulanimani looked at Sigsrata, snorted in disdain, and then trotted off in another direction. Yes, Sigsrata decided, the animal was definitely female.

The King shrugged and clove another Ulanimani instead, following up the forward slash with a back swing that tore open another beast from flank to front. Oddly, while some dust spilled out of the wound, no blood flowed. The Ulanimani just seemed to sigh mournfully and then fall over. Sigsrata decided that there was no satisfaction in killing the monsters. Still, it had to be done and he and his men carved out a pocket, allowing the Mages to begin their work.

More reinforcements poured into the area until the Klynsheimers held a wider area, mostly due to the fact that the Ulanimani were less interested in stampeding anymore and milled around, looking to find a way out of the areas that were still Warded.

The great axe glowed sullenly to match Sigsrata's mood. Too many bodies could be glimpsed littering the ground beneath the Ulanimani hooves. Two thousand men had held this wing. At least a thousand were dead.

Sigsrata vented his anger on an Ulanimani that ventured too close. As he did he heard, rather than saw something moving along his right but he was out of position.

"Your Majesty!" a boyish voice screamed.

Sigsrata turned to see a ghostly, blue black hand reaching for him. Bael Wights had snuck among the Ulanimani herd. Sigsrata turned, bringing his axe back around, but too slow as tendrils of fear clawed at his mind and tried to freeze him in place.

Sigsrata was wrong. It hadn't been a boyish voice. A young girl, maybe twelve, holding a thin Ward post like a spear hurled herself at the Wight, the post blazing with light as it connected, hurling the Wight back with a shrieking angry buzz as it clawed at its chest, where Ward light danced.

The girl's eyes were impossibly wide and she panted wildly, fear and amazement filling her face, as she lowered the Ward Post slightly and turned to face the King. Sigsrata didn't know what the apprentice Mage was going to say. Another Wight hit her from the side, well away from the Post, which was already dimming – the girl obviously didn't have the skill to maintain its power on her own.

The girl's mouth was open, which was why Sigsrata could see the Wight's claws pierce the bottom of her mouth, as it casually used its hold to toss the girl over its shoulder. Another Wight made as if to catch the girl, instead ripping her right leg from its socket, which spun her body in another direction where a third Wight ripped off an arm. As the Wights played their terrible game Sigsrata swore that he could hear the girl mewling in agony, unable to scream because of the blood bubbling from the wreck of her mouth.

He saw red and was among the Wights before he even consciously registered that he was moving. Sigsrata's axe lashed out, driving the Wights back. Not killing them, much to his frustration, but forcing the nightmares to give up their game. The Wights circled him now, taunting and chittering, waiting for him to let his guard down. Claws raked out, gouging his armor, but never finding enough purchase. Sigsrata growled in anger, daring any of the Wights to try more.

The King stood over the remnants of the girl who had tried to save him. There wasn't much left but her head and torso. Even so, Sigsrata was not going to let the Wights take even those scraps.

Sigsrata's Guards were trying to reach him but were being driven back time and again by Skrieksgrata in great slashing gouts of blood as the Skrieksgrata's claws rent their armor asunder. Hooting and whistles mingled with cursing, screams and...gurgles as the men fell, bodies ripped open, lungs ruptured.

"Too scared to actually strike me?" Sigsrata said, taunting the Wights.

The Wights cackled and then rushed him from every direction at once. Sigsrata spun like a top, his axe whistling through the air, throwing the Wights back in shrieks of maddened, rune spitting rage as the Wards on Sigsrata's axe ate at their bodies.

The King might have watched fascinated as the Wights drew back, their bodies struggling to reform over the burning Wards. He wasn't that stupid. Sigsrata clove at the Wights, the axe head a blur as it danced in the air. The King wanted to dismember The Darkness much as they had dismembered the girl.

Jans stared around her in wide eyed disbelief. She'd never been this close to death before. Not even when the Grass Titans attacked. Then, Jans had thrown herself into one of Eielson's bolt holes, closed her eyes, and covered her ears.

She couldn't do that here as much as she wanted to. So much blood...it was everywhere. And the screaming. Jans had never known a human being to scream like that. She wanted to fall to the ground and curl up but couldn't. The children needed her.

Jans sobbed when she saw their terrified faces staring at her, asking her to please tell them what to do. The children were dying. She had to do something. Jans grabbed at a replacement Post almost spastically, her eyes still wide and her ears filled with the screams. She charged the post without even thinking about it.

"You!" Jans shouted, gesturing towards a nearby...servant? At least the young man in loose fitting clothes didn't look like a Soldier. Maybe he was a porter of some kind.

"Me?" asked a very feminine voice

"You're a woman? What are you doing here?" Jans asked in surprise.

"You're a woman and you're here," the woman pointed out indignantly.

"Yes, but I'm a Mage," Jans said. "What are you doing here? You're not a Mage and you're not a Soldier."

"Here's a good place to be," the woman said with a shrug. "Better at least than where I was before.

The woman pointed over to the center of the destroyed wing.

"I suppose so," Jans agreed. "Look, take this post. I need you to hold it. We don't have time to ground them all. Angle it away from you, making certain that the butt of the Post is firmly against the ground. That way if anything hits it the counter force will discharge into the ground instead of knocking you backwards."

The woman nodded, controlling whatever fear that she felt and braced herself and the Ward Post. Jans gave her a final look and began repeating her instructions, forming a wall of Posts and flesh, defiant in the face of the Skrieksgrata. Now the real work began, as Jans looked around at a man from the work crews standing their uselessly, panic written across his face as he clutched his tool like a weapon.

"Auger!" she spat at him, moving the man into action.

Sigsrata's breath was coming in bellows and his hair and beard were matted by sweat and stuck to his face. His arms held steady, the axe still slashing at the Wights, though a little slower now. The King's plate armor was gouged, bent, dented, and by some miracle holding. It was almost as if the Wights were afraid to get too close.

Sigsrata couldn't imagine why; he hadn't killed a single one of the nightmares yet. The Wights stilled for a moment, making the King believe that another rush was coming. He tightened his hold on his axe and smiled grimly. Never let them know that you're scared. Sigsrata had said those words to Eielson. The words were as true for the King as they were for the Mage.

A ripple, like a slight breeze flowed over the battlefield. All The Darkness stiffened, shifting their attention to the northeast. The Guunt looked shocked for a moment than the biggest bastard threw back its head and howled.

The Guunt, Skrieksgrata, Ulanimani and Wights fled the field, moving rapidly to the northeast, abandoning the rest of The Darkness, which seemed content to fight on. The pitifully few survivors of Sigsrata's Guard raced forward to take defensive positions around him.

Eielson. That blasted Mage had done something again. Sigsrata knew it and was grateful. The worst of The Darkness had quite the field, giving his men a chance to regroup.

"Prepare the center and right wing to advance. We're taking the fight to The Darkness before they destroy those phalanxes. The reserve units should be moving up by now if any of my subordinates have a brain among them. When the Troopers arrive signal for them to swing wide left and hit The Darkness in the flank," Sigsrata ordered.

Men moved off to relay his commands.

The King was emptying a water skin over his head when he saw Jans move to his side, looking down at the dead girl. The Journeyman Mage had a hand over her mouth and tears were leaking from her eyes.

"What was her name," Sigsrata asked as gently as he was able. His voice was hoarse and he was angry, so he most likely failed at gentle.

"Enie. Enie Rykestruder," Jans said, shaking her head. "She shouldn't be dead. This isn't what Mages do...."

"No!" Sigsrata snapped, unwilling to have the girl's death become lessened.

"This-," he pointed down at the body, "- is exactly what Mages do. Blood and Iron. Ward and Mage. These are our People's defenses. The Twelve would have had you forget this truth and believe that Mages have every right to huddle behind walls. No! Ryskestruder knew her duty. All Honors are hers. Get the Ward Line re-established. We still have plenty of Darkness to fight."

Jans nodded slowly and then gathered up her charges and began strengthening the defenses along the central Line. There would be no salvaging the Left Wing. Sigsrata turned to look out across the plain where two phalanxes of men still struggled to fight their way clear. As soon as he had a few more men at his back he was determined to go join them.

"Push, septa it!" a sergeant yelled from the front rank, pressing into his shield.

Parsons was glad that he was further back in the formation. The Threshers were hammering on the phalanx's shields, their bone and flesh whip like appendages hitting hard enough to break bone.

"Obstacle!"

Parsons sighed. 'Obstacle' was being called out a lot. It meant that the phalanx was walking over a dead Darkness, horse, Trooper or a Soldier fallen in the formation. Parsons cursed as he came across the obstacle – a Soldier – his head smashed in. Looked like his helmet slipped at the wrong moment.

A horn sounded – two long blasts followed by three short ones.

"Tortoise! Arrows incoming!"

The phalanx ground to a halt, the rear ranks turning around and hunkering behind their shields. Parsons and the other men in the center raised shields over their heads, interlocking them and praying.

Three volleys of arrows slammed around the formation, hitting shields, killing Threshers, and wounding men who didn't have their shields positioned properly. Parsons prayed for the arrow volleys to end without him getting struck as 'thunking' sounds peppered the formation. When the horns sounded again he was so thankful.

The horns sounded a third time, issuing further orders. Parsons might have to revise his earlier sense of relief.

"Form square!" yelled the Lieutenant, who, despite a broken arm was managing to hold a shield into position.

The men moved as quickly as exhausted men could, forming a square when all of the men just wanted to make a run for the lines which were tantalizingly close. Drums replaced the horns. The *Klynshipin* rumbled from the drums, a deep bass thrum that escalated rapidly into the thunderous frenzy that had echoed across the most desperate and determined battlefields for centuries. Backs straightened as men felt the energy of the notes thrum through their hearts.

Parsons, whose position in the square was facing back towards the right wing, saw Soldiers marching forth. None of the Soldiers were holding shields – the shields were only good in defensive formations, where swinging the bill was a limited option. The men were moving double time, racing for a hundred feet before returning to a walk for another hundred yards and then repeating the process.

"The King! The King is coming!" someone shouted.

"Forget watching the King!" snapped one of the sergeants. "Watch the grieshtataing Threshers in front of you!"

The Threshers had fallen back during the arrow storm but were now racing forward, lashing out at the Soldiers. Flesh whips curled over the lips of shields, the bone tips striking helmets, shoulders, and faces of men who allowed them too close.

Sickening crunches were more common than screams whenever this happened. Parsons almost wished that the men would scream. Screaming would at least have been normal.

"Drop shields! Attack in triads!"

The advancing units had reached the square. About time. Parsons was glad to drop the shield. The thing was heavy and his arm ached anyway. Of course now they got down to more difficult fighting. Two men to hook the thrasher while the third man stabbed or hacked The Darkness to death. Not easy work.

The King was coming. Parsons could hear the men chanting his name. More than that he could hear the King bellowing a challenge. He didn't bother to look; didn't much feel like dying by being inattentive to the dangers in front of him. The two men who teamed up with him were looking to hook a thrasher already. Parsons would be doing the killing. Lucky him. Apparently he hadn't moved fast enough to get one of the easier jobs.

"Move it, Farmer!" roared his sergeant, pushing him forward. "You've killing to do; no use shirking your duty now."

Parsons sighed and ran forward, his bill raised in a killing strike.

"What are you waiting for, Farmer?" the sergeant yelled. "Don't pose with the blasted thing. Kill it!"

Parsons couldn't stop another sigh as he hammered the creature with a killing stroke.

"You waiting for congratulations, Farmer? Well, here you go; you killed it! Congratulations! Now move your ass and go kill another one!"

Parson's sergeant wasn't a happy man.

Sigsrata strode calmly towards the Threshers, irkanish, garmuts, and pelgs that were all that remained of the Rising. Though their numbers were greatly reduced and the biggest threats had quit the field there were still hundreds of the creatures to deal with. The King looked to be almost ambling across the field, his great axe resting on his shoulder. Sigsrata was far from calm. He was sore, tired and eager to end this fight.

The Darkness was being pincered. The two lines of infantry were converging from either side as the horse archers of the reinforcement contingent drove The Darkness into a tighter and tighter bunch. Infantry archers were volleying into the tightened mass as well, though that would soon have to end as the various forces converged.

Sigsrata had no doubts that The Darkness would be defeated now that the Guunt had quite the field. Lingering uncertainty came from what the total cost of the battle would be. There were many dead Klynsheimer men littering the field already. Horses and dogs too. The wounded were worse, crying, screaming, whimpering or thrashing about.

Sigsrata heard the sergeants calling out a quick pace in preparation for the coming charge almost abstractly. The King was already picking out his targets. Not nearly enough Darkness had bled for his rage.

Sigsrata's side of the pincer hit The Darkness with a deafening crash and a roar of 'Blood and Iron' followed by 'King and Seven'. Sigsrata chose a different battle cry. 'Die you bastards!' roared out of his mouth as his axe smashed into a group of irkanish that were pummeling an unfortunate infantry man to death. The man – boy, really from the looks of his horrified face already locked in a rictus of death – had tripped when the two forces collided.

Irkanish bits flew over the King's shoulder trailing ribbons of blood as he continued to charge forward, ramming the axe head into the stomach of a Thresher that didn't have the time to strike back. The air rushed out of the creature's lungs and it fell backwards. Sigsrata stomped down as he continued to move forward. The Thresher gurgled as its windpipe was crushed.

The King was quite happily killing everything in front of him as panicked bill men and members of his personal guard strove to match his pace. They couldn't, which was why Sigsrata suddenly had a pelg latched onto his left arm.

"Get off you bloody bastard!" the King growled through clenched teeth as he felt his armor slowly being crushed on his left arm. He was grateful that he wore full plate instead of just chain on his arms.

Sigsrata punctuated every curse by slamming the creature into the ground. The pelg showed no indication of letting go. The King couldn't use his axe on the creature without risking cutting his own arm off. Instead he dropped the weapon and pulled out a dagger, fully intending to stab it to death. Several garmuts and irkanish had different ideas and ran at him before Sigsrata had a chance to kill the offending creature.

"Ah, grieshtata," muttered Sigsrata, as he swung the pelg covered arm in front of him like a shield and prepared to charge into the oncoming creatures.

His guards, both regular and those dragged into the duty took one look at what the King intended and threw themselves forward. Bills and hand axes whirled through the air as the men grappled with the enemy, trying to keep the King clear. One man even tackled an irkanish when he lost his weapon. Darkness and Klynsheimer wrestled, rolling around on the ground, each trying to gain the advantage. The irkanish was winning the contest so Sigsrata used the pelg to beat the creature about the head. The pelg didn't like this and tried to bite down harder. The irkanish wasn't amused either and seemed torn over who to attack – the infantryman, Sigsrata or the pelg. Sigsrata decided the matter for the creature, stabbing it repeatedly with his dagger before helping the infantry man regain his feet.

"Help me get this thing off of my arm," Sigsrata growled, handing his dagger to the slightly dazed Klynsheimer who seemed a bit unsteady on his feet.

The infantryman took the dagger and began stabbing the pelg carefully, trying to avoid coming too close to the King's arm. The pelg grumbled as it died, refusing to give up its grip on Sigsrata's arm. The crumbled steel of his vambrace squealed as the pelg's teeth were dragged off of it. The King had to cut the vambrace's straps to get the piece of armor free. It was quite likely that the arm was broken. It was badly bruised at the very least.

Sigsrata looked at his axe mournfully. He was too tired to wield it one handed. With a sigh he snatched up a bill and returned to the melee. The King had enough strength to crush a few more skulls.

"Take care of my axe," the Kind said over his shoulder as he moved forward.

Parsons watched the King laying into a Thresher using a bill. The creature looked as dazed as Parsons felt after the first hit whipped its head to the side. Parsons had no idea what had possessed him to leap at an irkanish bare handed. If the King hadn't rescued him, Parsons was pretty certain that he would have died. The very man Parsons had been trying to protect had saved his life instead.

Parsons wasn't even certain how he had come to be drawn into the unit protecting the King. He vaguely remembered the Lieutenant grabbing him by the shoulder, shouting something, and then pushing him towards where the King battled. Everything was a bit foggy after that; Parsons' head was pounding from where the Irkanish had struck him. Cutting a pelg off of the King's arm hadn't helped.

He stood there, still holding the King's dagger, staring at the battle line that had passed him by. Parsons wanted to sit down. His sergeant noticed him, shouted a string of profanity and Parsons had another bill shoved into his hands before being pushed into the fight. Parsons pointed to the axe and muttered something about the King. The sergeant blinked, shook his head and took the bill back, replacing it with the axe. Parsons almost fell over under the weight. The sergeant sighed and shook his head, pushing Parsons forward again.

Chapter 29

Ilsbruk faced continued attacks all along the Ward Line. He'd spent the better part of a week riding between Way Forts checking on supplies, morale and shifting men to cover the losses. Spriegs led assaults mostly, which were amazingly costly. The Spriegs didn't care how many of their slaves were lost in the attacks. There were plenty of more fodder left crawling around the forest. The problem was that Ilsbruk didn't have plenty of Troopers to replace his dead.

He should be continuing his rounds, but he'd been summoned to the far end of the Ward Line with an urgent message about strange happenings. It was a Rising. How normal was anything that happened during a Rising? But the Way Fort commander was a trusted subordinate, handpicked by Ilsbruk to take over command after the purges following the downfall of the Twelve. The Captain had to trust that the man wouldn't request his presence for nothing.

Ilsbruk rode with a group of twenty – he couldn't spare any more men – and Grieko. Ilsbruk could definitely do without Grieko. The Warder Mage was arrogant, fat and borderline incompetent. He was also the only one available and a Mage had been specifically requested. With the constant attacks, Ilsbruk didn't dare pull any of the more competent Mages off of the Line.

Grieko didn't realize how lucky he was. The Mage hadn't been exposed to too much danger yet. Not like the Warders who'd been with the King at what was being called the 'Battle at the End of the Line' for lack of a better term. No one was happy with the name. The minstrels would come up with something better eventually.

Everyone was less happy with the four thousand, seven hundred and thirty two deaths even though a major incursion had been narrowly avoided.

Ilsbruk's wife was definitely going to be devastated. There were many war dogs among the dead; to Klynsheimer thinking, a Soldier was a Soldier, whether they walk on two legs or four. Betney loved those dogs as much as she did her own children.

Gorgorin was muttering again. The communication had indicated that Ilsbruk would recognize the problem when he saw it. To the sergeant's thinking the message should have been a lot clearer.

Ilsbruk was inclined to agree until his group literally stumbled across the twilight lands. They had been riding in the noon day sun. In fact they were still riding in the noon day sun, but off to their right the forest was definitely in twilight. Warmer too than the brisk chill that hung in the air. Ilsbruk could tell that the area was warmer because a slow and lazy fog was rising where The Road and twilight lands intersected.

"It's that blasted Mage, isn't, Sir?" Gorgorin said, spitting to the side and shaking his head incredulously.

"I assure you, Sergeant, that no Mage is responsible for...whatever this is," Grieko said, inclining his head pompously, which just caused the man's chins to jiggle instead of making him look authoritative. It didn't help matters that the man looked like he was wearing a gaudy tent.

"Well, if it wasn't a Mage," Ilsbruk said, "then you had better determine what did this because if whatever has happened to this area is Darkness wrought we need to know so we can figure out how to counter it."

"I'm not certain this is my area of expertise," Grieko said uncomfortably, shifting in his saddle, which caused no end of irritation to his long suffering horse.

The man would really say anything to avoid manual labor. Ilsbruk gave the Mage one of his smiles. The Mage shifted uncomfortably; the Captain's smiles hadn't improved at all in the months since he'd first tried them.

"Get off your horse and get to work," Gorgorin snapped, dismounting as he spoke, ready to drag the fat Mage off of his mount.

Grieko obviously considered riding away but was wise enough to look at the Troopers who surrounded him. None were looking at Grieko with any friendliness. The man's horse clearly conveyed that it was unwilling to run anywhere with the fat man on its back. The Mage grudgingly dismounted and walked to the edge of the Ward Line and peered over the edge at the forest.

Gorgorin joined him, most likely to ensure that the Mage did something. Ilsbruk and the rest of the men dismounted as well. Several men began looking after the horses while others took up guard positions. Ilsbruk paced impatiently.

"Yup, the Mage did this," Gorgorin said with conviction a few minutes later.

"I had nothing to do with...whatever that is," Grieko said indignantly and waving his hands wildly at the anomaly.

"Not you, you waste of...really gaudy cloth. Seriously, who dresses like that?" Gorgorin asked pointing at Grieko's robes. "Septaed patterning has been giving me a headache all day."

Grieko opened his mouth to defend his fashion choices when Ilsbruk cut him off.

"Sergeant, how do you know that this is Eielson's work?"

"Skill level, Sir," Gorgorin explained. "This here weirdness flows right up to the Ward Line. Seems to mesh with it, creating a seamless joining. Complicated piece of work, that. Haven't met any other Mages capable of doing something like it."

"No Academy Mage created that...that...anomaly!" Grieko insisted, gesturing angrily at the strangely lit forest.

"Yeah, that's what I said," Gorgorin said, looking at Grieko as if the man were a moron. "That 'anomaly' wasn't created by an Academy Mage. It was created by Eielson. The 'Ward of the North'. Ain't nothing Academy about that one."

"But Eielson is an Academy Mage. An Itinerant Mage, I might add," Grieko said indignantly. He did indignant very well or, at least, very persistently. "No matter what fancy titles you men want to give him, it doesn't change the fact that Eielson is an Itinerant. No Itinerant could have changed the way the sun light touches the trees."

"You ever meet Eielson?" Gorgorin asked, his face suddenly blank, which Ilsbruk knew was a sign that the Sergeant was fed up with Grieko.

"No," Grieko admitted, "But I have it on very good authority that -"

"You and your 'authority' don't know nta," Gorgorin barked getting as close to Grieko's face as the man's flab would allow. "You see this Ward Line? Eielson's handy work. All 600 miles of it. Intricate stuff I'm told.

"Eielson also faced down The Darkness at the Battle of the Valley. He burned the grieshtata out of The Darkness before he went down. Terrifying bit of work, let me tell you. Smell bad enough to make you faint. So trust me when I say that, yeah, Eielson could and probably did change that forest.

"But if you actually listened to what I was saying, then you'd realize I agree with you that no Academy Mage could change the forest. Eielson may have gone to The Academy but he's no Academy Mage; not now. I doubt that he ever was."

"Well put, Sergeant," Ilsbruk said, walking over. "But even if Eielson did this – Warding, for lack of a better term, we still need to know what he might have done."

"It's not a Warding," Grieko said stubbornly, crossing his arms. I don't see any Ward Posts or even Wards on the trees."

Gorgorin looked thoughtful for a moment and then pushed the Mage across the Ward Line and into the twilight.

"See anything now?" the Sergeant asked, grinning.

Grieko's eyes widened in blind panic when he realized that he was outside the Ward Line. He shrieked – not like a woman because there was no need to insult women and it was a bit higher pitched than that – and tried to scramble back across the Ward Line. Gorgorin pushed the man back, having the good grace to follow the Mage.

"Kind of pretty," Gorgorin commented, looking around.

"We have to go back!" Grieko practically screamed.

"Can't," Gorgorin said a bit laconically. You couldn't see any Wards from the other side. I figured that you'd have a better vantage from this point. Sooner you find out what's causing this light, the sooner I'll let you back across."

"Sergeant, do you think this is wise?" Ilsbruk asked, unsure. He could care less about the Mage. The Captain didn't want to lose a good sergeant.

"Way I figure it, Sir, Eielson managed to Ward 600 miles by himself. Assuming that he created this...land, I have to think that it's as safe as that Ward Line. That man doesn't do anything by halves."

"And if Eielson didn't create these changes?"

"Then I only have to run faster than tubby," Gorgorin said matter-of-factly.

"Why...I...you...this," Grieko sputtered, looking to see if he could find a way around Gorgorin and get back on The Road.

"This would go faster if you did some investigating," Gorgorin said mildly as he took up a position that ensured that the Mage wasn't going to get past him.

Grieko whimpered, stamped his foot in frustration and then began looking around more thoroughly and with more desperation.

"There's nothing here!" Grieko whined.

"You keep yelling like that and something is sure to come along," Gorgorin observed.

Grieko looked to the heavens, pleaded silently with the Captain and then looked down at the ground in defeat. When he looked at the ground the Mage frowned in puzzlement. He bent down on one knee and began touching the earth.

"The ground is Warded," Grieko said in disbelief, shaking his head. "That shouldn't be possible. The Ward is massive. The amount of power needed... The skill... It's not possible."

"And yet it appears to be," Ilsbruk said with a frown. "The Mage's work indeed. Eielson's been busy."

"I already said that no Mage did this," Grieko said stubbornly.

"Then we'll have to invent a new word to describe him," Ilsbruk said. "In the mean time we need to do some exploring. There are Wardings. Will we be safe enough?"

"I-I don't know. I've never seen something like this. It looks so simple on the surface but there is such complexity underlying the whole construct," Grieko admitted.

Gorgorin and Ilsbruk exchanged a glance.

"Definitely describes Eielson's work," Ilsbruk said.

"Forget the work," Gorgorin said with a shake of his head. "Those words describe the man. Wonderful idiot, unlike this one"

Gorgorin jabbed a thumb in Grieko's direction.

"We'd best get moving and find him." Ilsbruk said with a sigh. "Send a message along the line that we're investigating."

Several hours later and Ilsbruk had to admit that the twilight lands seemed a pleasant place to be. True there had been a bit of occasional worry when Darkness was spotted but once the men realized that The Darkness was avoiding the twilight they relaxed a bit. Not enough to be stupid, but enough to ease a bit of the tension.

That tension came ratcheting back when they neared a Cathedral Oak grove. The land all about was shattered and littered with bones. The Troopers readied weapons and looked around nervously.

"Definitely Eielson," Ilsbruk said, looking around at the destruction.

"The boy does know how to destroy things," Gorgorin said, nodding in pleasant agreement.

"Is that a Guunt?" Grieko asked, scaring everyone until they realized that the Mage was pointing at a massive corpse.

"Nta, it is a Guunt," Gorgorin said, removing his helmet and scratching his head. "How the septa did he kill a Guunt?"

"Lightning," Bob said, coming around from behind one of the support roots.

"Bob," Ilsbruk said, nodding his head in greeting.

"Could you come check out Kawen for me? He was badly wounded. I think he's doing better but I'd like a second opinion," Bob asked wearily, already turning away.

Ilsbruk dismounted and followed Bob. He found Bob leaning over his cousin in a small campsite. There was plenty of fresh water and Bob looked to have foraged a bit. The smell hit Ilsbruk first. He didn't need to look at Kawen, but did so to confirm what he already knew.

"He's dead, Bob," Ilsbruk said softly.

"I know," Bob said sadly. "I haven't had the heart to bury him."

Ilsbruk could see that Kawen had lost his arm. It was hard to tell if infection or any of a dozen other ailments that could beset a man because of such a traumatic injury had killed the Obari.

"Bob, if you've wrapped me in another one of your septa illusions, I'm going to kick your ass," Kawen said, the corpse stirring.

"Kor'nta!" Ilsbruk said, falling backwards

"Oh, you should see your face!" Bob said, laughing hysterically.

The illusion fell away revealing a very much alive, but still badly injured and weak Kawen.

"I swear he does that every time I fall asleep," Kawen muttered.

"What else am I going to do? It's boring watching over you."

"I'm sorry that I had my arm *RIPPED OFF!*" Kawen shouted angrily.

"Well you should be," Bob said benevolently, as if he were accepting a real apology.

"Captain Ilsbruk of the Seven, would you kick my cousin's annoying ass for me?" Kawen requested, glaring at Bob.

"Gladly," Ilsbruk said, regaining his feet and stalking angrily towards Bob.

"Wait now, let's not be hasty. If you injure me I won't be able to show you what Galeb Sonovonol has become," Bob said, backing away hastily.

"What do you mean 'become'?" Ilsbruk asked suspiciously.

"Promise not to take requests from Kawen and I'll show you what you need to see. What you need to understand about Galeb Sonovonol," Bob said solemnly.

Ilsbruk has suspected that Bob was a bit unstable since the Battle of the Valley. Now he was convinced that Bob was completely unhinged.

"What do we need to know about the Mage?" Gorgorin asked, rounding the tree.

"Promise," Bob insisted.

"Alright, Bob, I promise," Ilsbruk said irritably.

Bob smiled and then wove an illusion. It was a life size rendering of Eielson.

"This is how you've known Galeb Sonovonol," Bob said. "This is what he's become."

Another illusion rose up next to the first one. This Eielson was different. He was healthier looking, more muscled, and his skin was darker, ruddier. He stood straight and tall unburdened by injury. Sonovonol was shirtless and bootless, looking untroubled by the cold.

"He has been reborn," Bob said reverently.

"Kawen, what's Bob talking about? Is this true?" Ilsbruk demanded.

Kawen looked over Gorgorin's shoulder. The Sergeant was checking out the Obari's wounds.

"Bob, is this baouc weed you've wrapped the wound in?" Gorgorin asked.

"Yes. It numbs the pain," Bob acknowledged.

"You're using too much. Constant baouc weed use is going to damage the nerves," Gorgorin warned, removing most of the weed.

"Kawen screams if I don't apply a lot," Bob objected.

"I do not," Kawen objected in turn.

"You were screaming your head off!"

"Bob!" Ilsbruk shouted, silencing the two cousins. "Now Kawen, answer my question. Is this what Eielson looks like now?"

The Captain pointed at the second image.

"I don't know," Kawen said, shaking his head. "I was unconscious for most of the day after I...lost my arm. When I woke up Kieri and Galeb Sonovonol were gone."

"Where did they go?" Ilsbruk asked.

"Northeast," Bob answered. "You could see the light flares as Sonovonol extended his Wardings. That and the trees were swaying a lot."

"What's northeast of here?" Ilsbruk asked, thinking.

"Nothing but Darkness," Gorgorin said, shaking his head as he continued to stare at Bob's illusions. "What changes a man so?"

"I killed a Skrieksgrata," Bob said, once again solemn. "That changed me. Galeb Sonovonol killed a Guunt. I imagine that his changes would have to have been that much greater. Though I'll deny that if you ever tell him. His head's big enough as it is."

The implication was disturbing.

"I think that we need a new name to describe what Eielson has changed into," Gorgorin said thoughtfully. "He isn't a Mage anymore. Septaed if I'm sure that he's still human, he's changed that much."

"Changed...," Ilsbruk said, lost in thought for a few moments. "Changed... We need to send word to the King."

Ilsbruk straightened, firmly in command of the situation again.

"Sir?" Gorgorin asked, curious to know his Captain's thinking.

"Eielson's changed," Ilsbruk said. "Who better to explain those changes than a shape shifter?"

"Oh, Sir, you aren't suggesting we get that crazy female to help us?" Gorgorin asked, already wincing at the answer.

"I'm afraid so. We need to know why and how much Eielson has changed. Bob, I need you to send a message for me."

"Wouldn't it be faster to send one of your riders?" Bob asked, looking dubious.

"I need you to send one of your birds, Bob. I need you to craft a sending," Ilsbruk explained impatiently.

"I have no idea what you are talking about," Bob said hastily.

"Bob," Ilsbruk growled, "I don't have time for any platitudes of innocence. Do you seriously think no one, in all of the hundreds of years the Obari and Klynsheimers have co-existed, noticed the Obari's ability to make sendings?"

"It's plausible," Bob said stubbornly.

"Bob, I've seen how far your birds fly," Ilsbruk said bluntly.

"I – hmmm...you've put me in a bit of an awkward spot, Captain of the Seven," Bob admitted. "On one hand you're acknowledging my greatness, which is understandably deserved. On the other hand I obviously have no idea what you are talking about. I mean, one bird looks like another, doesn't it? Perhaps your eye sight is failing?"

It took a half an hour of arguing and some undignified chasing, but, in the end, Bob's sending was winging its way south.

"Galeb?" Kieri asked hesitantly.

"What's the matter?" Galeb asked, staring off into distance as he prepared another Warding.

"I think your ears are a little pointed."

"What?" Galeb asked, turning in alarm.

"Yeah, their definitely a little pointy. Not as pointy as that bitch's ears, but pointy none the less."

"Oh come on!" Galeb said, throwing up his arms. "Haven't I changed enough?"

"I don't know. I've never seen anyone change before," Kieri said with a straight face.

"You're trying to be funny?" Galeb asked, running a finger over his ear absently.

"Well someone has to be. You're far too serious."

"I'm Warding. It's kind of a serious thing to do."

"Yes, but you need to smile more."

"You just told me that my ears are pointy and now you want me to smile about it?"

"I have to laugh or cry, Husband. I'm choosing laughing."

"Easy for you to say," Galeb muttered. "You're not the one who's changing."

"You weren't as worried about these changes before," Kieri pointed out.

"My ears weren't pointy before," Galeb said, scowling.

"Oh, My God, are you vain about your ears?" Kieri asked, clamping a hand over her mouth and giggling.

"It's not funny," Galeb said, sulkily. "Imagine if it were your ears."

"Husband," Kieri said, hugging Galeb tightly, "Don't worry. No matter how much you change, I will love you."

"Thank you," Galeb said, hugging Kieri back.

"Though if you grow a tail, we might have a problem," Kieri said with a laugh.

"Thanks," Galeb said drily, still hugging his wife, his eyes closed.

There was a flash.

"Galeb, are you still Warding?"

"No?"

"Are your eyes closed?"

"No?"

"Stop Warding with your eyes closed!"

Jesia was sulking. She'd been sulking ever since she'd been confined to this stupid tent. Stupid guards wouldn't let her out. It wasn't her fault that the idiot Trooper had died. Jesia had only stabbed him two or three times... Besides the man had forced her to stab him when he'd tried to prevent her from going after her Mage.

Jesia smiled goofily and sighed when she thought about her Mage. But then she remembered that she was stuck in this stupid tent and grimaced. It was so *boring* in the tent.

The tent flap was raised cautiously. Jesia smiled in expectation, hoping that here was some entertainment. Maybe her Mage had come for her? She was giddy at the thought and stood up from the small camp stool she'd been sitting on. Maybe she should strip and lay down seductively for him?

Disappointment was swift in coming. Two men entered holding crossbows cocked and ready, their bolts pointed right at Jesia, who had her hands on the hem of her shirt, but hadn't taken it off yet. The King entered next, making the tent seem that much smaller. An Obari man, nearly as massive as the King came next with a silly looking bird on his shoulder, followed by a Mage woman. Jesia had the feeling that there were many more guards outside the tent. She idly hoped that the bird defecated on the Obari. Jesia seemed to remember that the man was related somehow to that Bitch who thought that she could have Jesia's Mage.

"Have you come to take me to my Mage?" she asked archly, showing these people who was really in charge.

"Perhaps," the King said.

"Why won't you – wait, what? I mean I'm glad that you've finally come to your senses," Jesia said, cutting off her whine in mid-stream before smiling broadly.

She didn't notice how everyone stiffened at the smile which was just a bit deranged. The men with the crossbows tensed slightly, their fingers twitching on the triggers of the crossbows.

"I need you to look at something first," Sigsrata said, gesturing politely to the Obari. "Ebko, if you would please."

The Obari man reached up to his shoulder and tossed the bird into the air. The bird melted into another shape.

"My Mage!" Jesia shrieked in delight that quickly turned to soul wrenching pain. "Wait...He showed his true face! He showed his true face without me!"

Jesia began to sob inconsolably.

The men ignored the outburst. The female Mage moved to comfort Jesia but the King stopped her which was wise. Jesia was grief stricken but also very angry. She would enjoy hurting someone right now.

"Jesia," the King said gruffly. "We need to know what happened to Eielson."

"Don't say his name!" shrieked Jesia before shaking her head savagely. "Oh, what does it matter? He showed his face!"

The King didn't pretend to understand what the woman was going on about.

"Sonovonol," Ebko corrected the King, asserting his daughter's marriage to Galeb. Though whether Ebko was doing so to remind Sigsrata of the treaty between their two people or to remind everyone that Galeb belonged to Kieri was anyone's guess.

"Jesia!" snapped Sigsrata. "What do you know about these changes in Eiel-Sonovonol?"

The King didn't look happy about having to correct himself, but the Obari scouts that Galeb's marriage gained the kingdom were important.

Jesia stilled suddenly as she had a realization. This was another test of her love for her Mage. Yes, it was a test! Jesia was suddenly much happier. She would prove herself worthy! Then there would be sex. Lots of sex. And maybe babies. She wasn't sure yet how many babies. It really depended how much they cried. Jesia hated crying babies. They made her want to smother them...

"Jesia, I asked you a question," Sigsrata said, snapping his fingers and regaining Jesia's attention, which was probably for the best since the woman had been contemplating the best way to kill infants without pissing off one's mate. Jesia hadn't reached a decision yet, though she did feel that experimentation was required.

"I'm not exactly certain, without seeing him in person," Jesia said, turning her attention back to the image and hoping that the King would take her not so subtle hint.

"Tell me what you know from the image and then I'll decide whether or not you need to go see in person," the King said. Sigsrata didn't like the idea of letting the woman have any freedom but he really needed to understand what was happening to Eielson-Sonovonol- whatever his name was now. The King needed to know the repercussions of the man's change. Jesia looked different and there was no denying that she was a very serious threat.

"My Mage," Jesia crooned, feeling that a bit of cooperation was in order to get what she wanted. "Is showing you what he truly is. He's taken off his mask and revealed himself at last."

"What is he then?" Sigsrata demanded.

"The son of a Guunt," Jesia said easily.

"What?" the King exclaimed in surprise.

"What's the matter with you?" Jesia demanded irritably. "Why are you acting shocked? All of you Klynsheimers are sons and daughters of the Guunt. Just like that Obari and his Bitch daughter – yes, I know you are that woman's father and she's a Bitch! – are the sons and daughters of the Bael Wights. Just like my people are the kin of the Shaeloman. This is hardly a secret."

Apparently it was a secret because everyone else in the room was looking shocked. Well, Ebko was looking angry and shocked, but then his daughter had just been insulted. Jesia decided to emphasize her point.

"Bitch," she said, looking straight at Ebko and nodding her head sagely.

"Explain yourself," Sigsrata demanded.

"About the Obari's daughter being a bitch, slut, disease ridden whore who offers favors to any Darkness that happens to wander by or about you being the child of the Guunt?"

Ebko looked ready to explode. Jesia thought about ignoring the man and waiting patiently for the King's answer but decided to gift the man with a little more truth.

"Do not let the truth anger you, Obari Man. I'm sure that your daughter's quite good at sex. Probably had to have a lot of practice to ensnare my Mage. May even have a few brats running around. Probably doesn't even know who the fathers are.

"But don't worry, once my Mage has sex with me, he'll realize what a cheap lay your daughter is and throw her aside. You can take her away to finally hide the shame that she has undoubtedly brought to your Family. Unless you Obari are into

434

wantonness? You do like large families.   I wonder...are you even certain that you're the Bitch's real father? As promiscuous as your daughter obviously must be, I'm sure her mother must have been the same way."

The King had to physically restrain Ebko for a moment before the Obari gave his head a shake to clear it and apologized to the King.

"My apologies, Klynsheim King. I shouldn't have played this woman's game."

"She's certainly...irritating," Sigsrata acknowledged before turning back to Jesia. "Answer my question about the Klynsheim being the children of Guunt. You say one more thing about Kieri Sonovonol and I guarantee you will not be leaving this tent."

Jesia considered the King's warning, decided that the King was being irrational, but then again that *was* the prerogative of royalty, and then answered.

"Well not figuratively children of the Guunt. More in a metaphysical sense. When The Darkness came down from the Tundra in the first Rising they found humanity a bit wanting when it came to prey. The Darkness are all about dominance challenges. Humanity wasn't enough of a challenge so The Darkness 'improved' us," Jesia explained.

"Blood and Iron, as you Klynsheimers like to say, gifted with strength and determination by the Guunt. You had magic before the Rising but the Guunt gave your Wards greater strength.

"Cunning, sneaky and full of false impressions, the Obari gained their illusion powers from the Bael Wights, where my people learned to manipulate form and word from the Shaeloman. It's all in the histories."

Jesia sounded patronizing. To her own ears she sounded benevolent.

"Not in our histories," Jans said, speaking for the first time.

Jesia gave Jans a momentary look of contempt.

"Your histories are woefully inadequate," Jesia said, making another face, her words full of condescension. "I assume that's to be expected. Your old kingdoms died, while my own has endured, though diminished."

"Are these...changes...why your people look so different?" Jans asked, ignoring the insults.

"No, my people are different because we don't pretend to be anything but what we are," Jesia corrected her.

"You realize that you used to dress up as a Shaeloman?" Jans pointed out.

"I don't like you," Jesia said bluntly, unhappy with being contradicted.

"No one is asking you to," Jans said politely. "But I should point out that you're avoiding my question."

"I am avoiding nothing," Jesia said primly. "I just didn't want to answer such a pointless question."

"Why is it a pointless question?" Jans persisted.

"Are all of you Mages stupid?" Jesia asked with what sounded like honest curiosity. "I knew that my Mage was amazing.

I just didn't realize how exceptional he actually was. Somehow it makes me love him more. I didn't think that was possible."

Jesia was hugging herself in glee and dancing around the crowded tent. Everyone else in the tent looked uncomfortable. Well, Jans and the guards looked uncomfortable. Ebko looked angry and Sigsrata held the impassivity of an adult trying not to encourage a particularly troublesome child.

Jesia held onto her moment of joy for a little while before turning her attention back to Jans. The look that she gave the Mage was chilling in both its intensity and seriousness.

"It was a pointless – no, I can't be polite about this seeing as it just might encourage you to further stupidity – it was an exceptionally unintelligent question. Let me know if you need me to use smaller words," Jesia said, pausing as if waiting for Jans to request just that. When Jans just looked at Jesia with an offended expression Jesia continued.

"Yes I have Skin Walked as a Shaeloman. I'm not denying that fact. You seem to imply by doing so that I was hiding who I really am. You couldn't be more wrong. When I Skin Walk I am a Shaeloman. I am not hiding what I am, I'm embracing it."

"That's a bit...disturbing," Jans admitted.

"You get used to it," Jesia said with a shrug. "Though the amount of Walking that we are allowed to do is limited so that we don't become too inclined to Darkness thinking. Hazard of the gift, I suppose."

"I have another question," Sigsrata said, not giving Jesia time to comment on the intelligence of his questioning. "Sonovonol is heading northeast, deeper into The Darkness lands, apparently Warding a path as he goes. Do you have any idea where he is heading?"

Jesia jumped up and down, ecstatic at the news.

"TeraUsuat, of course," Jesia finally answered.

"Your city?" Sigsrata asked, just to make certain.

"Home of the Usatchi, my people," Jesia confirmed. "He goes to save my people! Oh, how the elders are going to be furious! You have to let me go to him!"

Sigsrata didn't answer. He was trying to think about why Eielson would want to help Jesia's people. The Usatchi had brought nothing but misery to Klynsheim... No, it couldn't be, could it? Eielson-Sonovonol hadn't struck the King as that ruthless... Maybe he'd underestimated the man.

"I need to go to him!" Jesia wailed.

"And so you shall," Sigsrata promised. "Along with a suitable enough escort to ensure that Sonovonol returns safely. I have many questions for the man."

Jesia didn't bother paying attention to anything else that was being said. She had her heart's desire. That was all that mattered. She didn't care what these Klynsheimers were muttering about. Useless noise. Six babies. Yes, she would have six babies. That way if she had to kill one or two there would be plenty left to give her Mage a nice loving family.

Chapter 30

Kieri woke to the soft sound of counting. She was still snuggled in Galeb's arms in the bed roll and, while it was difficult to tell time on the Warded path considering it always seemed twilight, Kieri thought that it had to be close to midnight. She suddenly found herself missing being able to see the stars. This time of year the stars shone brilliantly.

Kieri wasn't missing the cold. Galeb had done something that didn't completely erase the chill, but lessened it enough that it was not uncomfortable. They still built a fire every night, which was down to coals at this point, though Kieri didn't feel like stirring to add fuel just yet. Galeb was hot enough on his own and kept their blankets toasty. Rain, however, wasn't something Galeb could do anything about and after their first soggy night the couple chose their sleeping spots very carefully.

"What are you counting?" Kieri asked, whispering into his ear.

"The Guunt," Galeb answered just as softly.

Kieri shuddered, wanting to feel completely safe but knowing better.

"It's alright," Galeb assured her, stroking Kieri's hair as he held her tighter. "They haven't figured out a way to breach the Wards yet."

"'Yet' is not a reassuring word," Kieri complained, worry clear on her face.

"Yes, but it's a pragmatic word," Galeb insisted. "I've found being pragmatic to be much more useful than not."

"You're supposed to tell me that we're completely safe," Kieri insisted.

"Would you believe me?" Galeb asked.

"No," Kieri admitted.

"Then you want me to lie to you?"

"No," Kieri grumbled.

Galeb laughed.

"You know," Kieri said, annoyed, "You never used to be this open or confident."

Galeb looked thoughtful for a moment before disagreeing.

"I've always been open around you. It's just around other people that I learned to be more...circumspect, I guess. Does that make sense?"

"I've never used the word 'circumspect', so no."

"Funny."

Kieri laughed softly.

"I can relax around you, Kieri. I don't have to worry about offending you. I can just be."

Kieri stopped laughing and hugged Galeb tighter. There was a lot of pain hidden under Galeb's words. Kieri decided to change the subject before they both became maudlin.

"What are the Guunts doing?" she asked.

Galeb scrunched up his face, thinking about how best to describe the sensation.

"Kind of poking at the Warding. They know brute force isn't going to work so they are trying to see if I made any mistakes."

"Did you?"

"Seriously, Kieri, who are you talking to?"

"So that's a yes?"

"That's a maybe," Galeb muttered in unfortunate agreement.

"I have to say, once again, that your words aren't very comforting."

"Once again, you don't want me to lie to you."

"Well, you could be a little more circumspect," Kieri said, giving him a look. "I could use a little comforting considering all that I've had to deal with lately."

"I thought that you didn't use that word."

"I'm finding a need to expand my vocabulary since you keep coming up with new ways to disturb me."

"Hmmm. Well, if I made a mistake, which is possible considering that I'm figuring out how to do this as I go along, the Guunts haven't managed to find it."

"What if they do?"

"Let's not borrow trouble. However I have taken some precautions."

"What kinds of precautions?"

"I've finished my personal Wardings. Covered head to toe now."

"That is an improvement, I suppose," Kieri admitted before saying, "Though I will miss the way you looked like you had chicken legs when you were only partially warded."

"Chicken legs? Seriously?"

"Don't worry, Husband, I'm still attracted to you," Kieri said, patting Galeb's cheek.

"Well that's a relief."

"Galeb?"

"We aren't going to sleep at all tonight, are we?"

"You were already awake. In fact it was your counting that woke me up," Kieri said accusingly. "Don't you go blaming this on me."

"I wasn't blaming anyone," Galeb insisted, "just asking for clarification."

Kieri's face scrunched up in irritation as she thought about whether or not his comment was argument worthy. Then she realized that she'd forgotten that she'd been trying to get him to answer a question and decided on a little irritation.

"Stop distracting me," Kieri hissed, punching Galeb in the arm lightly. "I was trying to ask a question."

"Ouch, that hurt!" Galeb grumbled. "What good is finding all of your old aches and pains miraculously gone only to have your wife give you new ones?"

"Don't be a baby," Kieri scolded him. "As I was saying, I was trying to ask a question."

"I can't wait to hear it," Galeb said, keeping his tone even and his face straight.

"Keep it up, Mage, and you're going to end up sleeping alone."

"No," Galeb said confidently.

"Oh, you think that you're so irresistible that I'll come crawling into your blankets no matter what?"

"I wouldn't use those words exactly...."

"Galeb!"

Galeb laughed softly. He was going to make a joke that if Kieri didn't want to share his blankets he was pretty certain that Jesia would, but thought better of it. Not only would saying that anger Kieri, it also disturbed Galeb. He didn't like the imagery in his head.

"What was your question?" Galeb asked, trying to distract himself from the image of Jesia cutting him open as some bizarre form of foreplay.

"Why did you make your Ward seem like we are forever walking in twilight?"

"I like twilight. It's my favorite time of day. The light's gentle and the work is done," Galeb admitted.

Kieri thought about that answer, smiling to have learned something new about her husband. Then she frowned. There had to be more to Galeb's reasoning than liking twilight. Never in all of the years Kieri had known him had Galeb indulged in extravagance.

"And?" she prompted.

"It makes it easier to see The Darkness skulking around the area, especially at night."

Kieri considered letting the matter go but she was still not satisfied with the answer.

"And?"

"I've already explained, Kieri," Galeb said reasonably. Too reasonably.

"Galeb, do you want to sleep tonight?"

"Yes."

"Then answer the question."

"But you might not be able to sleep if I tell you."

"*Now* you're trying to be circumspect?"

"You did say that I needed to do so for your own piece of mind."

Kieri leaned up on an elbow and stared down at her husband.

"Now I'm definitely not going to sleep if you don't tell me."

Kieri's imagination was becoming overworked with the possibilities. Galeb sighed.

"I have a problem with bright sunlight. It hurts my eyes."

"This has something to do with your changes, doesn't it?"

"Undoubtedly. I see best in low light. Full darkness is a bit problematic."

"Why?"

"Because it doesn't look dark. Everything looks tinged in fire."

"That's disconcerting," Kieri said a few moments later after she'd thought about it.

"On the bright side I can always tell when you're feeling amorous."

"Do tell, husband," Kieri said, having not yet decided if she liked this revelation or not.

"Certain parts of your anatomy become a little more...bright? Heated, maybe?"

"You sound unsure, Husband," Kieri said, frowning. She didn't like the implication that she glowed like a torch every time she wanted to have sex.

"I'm just trying to find the best words that won't get me hit."

"Why would I hit you?"

"You have a certain tone that usually promises impending violence."

"First I glow when I'm excited and now I have a tone?" Kieri asked irritably.

Galeb sighed and then pushed the blankets off of himself before standing.

"Where are you going?" Kieri demanded, sitting up. She'd just decided that an argument was in order. "Are you trying to hide something else from me?"

"No, Kieri, I'm just not trying to pick a fight with you," Galeb said as he began to walk away.

"Who said anything about a fight?" Kieri demanded.

"You did."

"I did not! Wait, I suppose I have a tone, don't I? Am I glowing, Galeb? If I am, don't get your hopes up."

"Yes, you have a tone. You're also flailing your arms about. No, you don't look aroused. You look angry, which I think is because what I told you scares you a bit and you've decided to be angry rather than afraid. I'm giving you some space to be angry."

Kieri thought about what Galeb said, didn't like it because he was right, and scowled some more before hugging herself tightly.

"Where are you going?" she asked again in a quieter voice.

"I'm going to stir up a little trouble," Galeb said. "I want to make certain that when we reach Jesia's city we bring a whole lot of Darkness with us. There's no point doing this if we don't draw away the enemy from our peoples."

"Can't it wait until morning?" Kieri asked, suddenly wanting to do nothing more than hold her husband tight and sleep in his arms. Yes, she was afraid of the changes in him but she loved him more than she was afraid. She just needed reassurance and she always felt safe in his arms. Stirring up trouble was the opposite of being reassuring.

"Well, I'm up now. Don't worry, I won't take too long."

"Now I am worried," Kieri muttered, standing as well and following after Galeb.

While her own Wards were quiescent, either because The Darkness weren't that close or because there was no need in the safety of the greater Warding, Galeb's flared to life. He was covered with such an intricacy of Wards from head to toe that it looked almost like he was wearing living golden armor. The Wards were in constant motion, almost appearing to crawl over one another. The appearance was disturbing since only his eyes were visible. His eyes were the worst; they reflected the gold in a very disconcerting fashion.

"You're not leaving the Warding, are you?" Kieri asked worriedly.

"No," Galeb said. "But I want you to cast an illusion that makes it look like I have. That's why I activated my Wards. I want it to look realistic. Do you think that you can replicate my appearance and shroud me in darkness simultaneously?"

Kieri narrowed her eyes.

"I'll take that as a yes."

"Humph! You seem to have this all planned out. How did you know that I was going to follow you?"

Galeb paused and Kieri had the distinct impression that her husband was arching an eyebrow even though she couldn't see it. She decided to scowl and thought about complaining about Galeb making assumptions but decided to hold her tongue. Galeb was right; she was afraid and trying to bury it under anger. Too much anger.

"Whenever you're ready," she said instead, gesturing languidly, as if she were bored instead of angry. "Wait a minute...what happened to your whirlwind?"

The whirlwind or power sump, as Galeb called it, wasn't in its normal position. That and there were two of them. Slightly smaller, more compact than the original, but undoubtedly two whirlwinds.

"I improved them," Galeb said. "The design is more efficient and less prone to stray winds so you won't have to worry about your hair. Everything feeds back into the construct, even the wind, feeding and building at the same time. It's very efficient."

"When did you have time to do all of this?" Kieri said, pointing towards the whirlwinds and Galeb's Wardings. She let the hair comment go.

"You sleep about eight hours a night," Galeb said sheepishly. "I kind of wake up after four."

"You're Warding while you're holding me?" Kieri asked incredulously, letting the four hour comment go. There was too much to focus on at once.

"Theoretically, yes," Galeb confirmed.

"How theoretically?"

"I build it in my mind and don't trigger anything until I'm up and moving."

"Wait, are you triggering these new Wardings when you get up to pee?" Kieri asked suspiciously

"Well..."

"I knew that someone your age didn't have to pee that much at night!"

"Hey, sometimes I do have to pee," Galeb said defensively.

"If you only have to sleep four hours why do you stay with me?"

"Because I like holding you."

Kieri smiled briefly in pleasure. Of course her mind kept the pleasure to a minimum. Questions kept bubbling up to the surface.

"Galeb, what can't you do?" Kieri asked suddenly, worry plainly written on her face as she changed the direction of their conversation.

"Quite a bit, actually," Galeb admitted. "But, I don't know, it's like I have all of these new ideas buzzing around in my head. On the Patrol I was locked in to what I could accomplish. Limited. Now, ever since the Battle of the Valley I've had the freedom to experiment. Every success gives me new ideas. It's amazing."

"What exactly have you failed at?" Kieri demanded.

"Septa it, I knew you would focus in on that," Galeb said lifting his hands and dropping them in irritation.

"Galeb..."

"You remember when we 'found' those conveniently shattered and charred trees that made perfect fire wood?"

"Yes."

"We didn't really 'find' them. I already knew that they were there because something I tried sort of backfired and blew them up."

"What?! When did this happen?"

"You were sort of sleeping and I was experimenting at a distance..."

"How do I sort of sleep?"

"Well, it's more like you were blissfully passed out."

"'Blissfully passed out'? Did you drug me?"

"No! We had sex okay? It was that night you were friskier than usual," Galeb whispered more quietly, giving the distinct impression of blushing.

"Why are you blushing and whispering?" Kieri demanded.

"Because I don't like recounting my sexual escapades in front of The Darkness," Galeb insisted.

Kieri laughed at the absurdity of the statement.

"Don't be such a prude," Kieri said, waving a hand at Galeb. "It's not like The Darkness even understand what we're talking about. Besides, it almost sounds like you are - not very well, mind you – bragging about your prowess. A bit full of yourself. I certainly don't remember passing out 'blissfully'."

"Well, you did," Galeb said smugly. "You had this goofy grin on your face and were drooling a bit."

"I do not drool!"

"Okay."

"I don't!"

Kieri immediately realized that Galeb was trying to distract her and glared at him.

"So you decided to destroy some trees in celebration?" she demanded.

"No. I was trying to – never mind. I don't even know why we're having this discussion."

"Because we barely talked for eight years," Kieri said matter-of-factly. "I'm making up for lost time."

"You ever consider that I might just be the 'strong and silent' type?"

Kieri burst out laughing, holding up her hand to indicate that she needed a minute.

"Really?" Galeb asked indignantly. He hadn't been serious when he said 'strong and silent'. But he didn't think it was that funny. He could be strong and silent if he wanted to be.

Kieri gave a fresh snort of laughter, requiring a few more minutes to calm down.

"Husband, I love you," Kieri said, wiping a tear from her eye and trying to hold in more laughter.

"Glad to be of service," Galeb said, shaking his head and walking to the edge of his Warding. He knew he was being watched. He even knew mostly where the watchers were waiting.

Galeb breathed in deeply, chose his targets and began pulling power from the power sumps. He glanced back at Kieri, noticed her still laughing – she must have been holding in more anxiety than Galeb realized. But then his thoughts changed. A part of him whispered that Kieri might be laughing not because of anxiety but because she doubted his abilities.

He suddenly didn't feel like waiting for Kieri. He knew that he wasn't being rational, but something deep inside of him felt challenged by Kieri's laughter and he felt an equal need to meet that challenge and conquer it. Galeb stepped across the Warding, leaving the twilight and entering full night.

The stars shone magnificently but Galeb wasn't stupid enough to stand there and watch them. There were far too many bodies hidden in the night. His altered sight was quite useful on that regard. A bit disturbing, but useful.

Galeb had decided on small concentrated bursts of heat at the enemy. Enough to burn a decent sized hole, but not wasteful. He struck rapidly, his hands twitching in a dozen directions before he realized that he was being foolish – not only was he indicating where he intended to attack, but the movements were unnecessary. He just had to will the power to flow in the proper direction like any Warding.

Galeb wasn't certain what he killed exactly – he was still trying to figure out how to use his night sight. Unfamiliar shapes were still unfamiliar, possibly even more so when viewed as heat images. A massive shape that Galeb had mistaken for a tree shifted. Galeb almost took a step back across the perimeter of the Ward – he should have already retreated considering what was out here in the night – but he instinctively realized it would be seen as a sign of weakness and that would be a mistake.

Instead, Galeb hammered protective Wards into the ground on either side of him so that other Darkness couldn't attack him while he was focused on the greater threat. The Guunt that he'd mistaken for a tree seemed to accept this move as prudent instead of cowardly. He strode forward, all of twenty five feet tall – small for a Guunt. A very young Guunt perhaps.

The Guunt grinned, opened its mouth as if it was about to give challenge when the Guunt was pushed aside by a sixty foot monstrosity. At least it wasn't the big one, Galeb thought to himself.

The new Guunt roared in challenge, crouched and moved to leap at Galeb, arms extended, mouth agape and massive clawed hands flexing. Galeb pulled from his power sumps and blasted the Guunt before it even had a chance to spring.

Instead of lightning, Galeb went for something more economical, using instead a lance of superheated air that hit the Guunt in the left shoulder at an angle, melting its way deep into the creature's chest cavity. The stone of the Guunt's skin smoked and cracked, the iron instantly liquefying in the affected area.

The Guunt fell on its side in surprise, his mouth frozen in a puzzled look as if the monster was uncertain what had just happened. Galeb looked contemptuously at his fallen opponent. Part of him was swearing in relieved terror that he had killed the creature. A greater part roared in triumph. Galeb shut his mouth when he realized that he was about to try roaring. He would have most likely failed and looked ridiculously undignified, which was why it was good he shut his mouth.

The Mage spun on his heal and strode back across the boundary, unwilling to wait to see what would happen now that he'd killed another Guunt. Galeb was hoping that his Great Warding would prevent anymore Guunt essence from seeping into his body. He really was going to have to come up with a better way of describing the phenomena.

Galeb looked to notice disappointingly that he only had one power sump still active and the remaining one was greatly diminished. So much for not wasting power. Greater disappointment followed. Despite his best intentions Galeb didn't move fast enough. His heel was still on the outside of the Warding when that familiar whooshing sensation hit. Guunt impressions filled his mind with fierce intensity and he stumbled. Thankfully Galeb fell inside of the Warding instead of outside.

The Wards around his body extinguished as molten fire roared through his veins once again. Kieri had the sense of mind to cloak both of them behind an illusion before Galeb fell. Not to hide what was happening to Galeb but because Kieri was furious with how reckless Galeb had just been and didn't feel like having an argument in front of Darkness. Doing so just seemed...unseemly. Which was so ridiculous a thought that it made Kieri even angrier.

Galeb didn't pass out this time. Instead he stood, fists clenched and eyes squeezed shut. It seemed to Kieri that Galeb was fighting the pain, unwilling to be conquered by it, which was the actual truth.

Galeb shuddered slightly, stood straighter and unclenched his hands. His mind was a riot of impressions, which he stilled one at a time, holding them back, like he would Ward The Darkness. Galeb gave his mind time to adjust; he was going to have nasty dreams later.

The Mage wasn't proud that he'd just killed another Guunt. He recognized that he'd been very foolish and was feeling a bit ashamed. The Guuntish part of his nature – as true as that statement was, Galeb was disturbed to have to acknowledge this fact – cautioned against pride. Embrace his strength, yes; feelings of dominance, okay. But no pride, no arrogance. Those emotions were weakness.

"You're taller and more muscled – again," Kieri said through clenched teeth. "That makes this harder."

Kieri jumped up slightly and moved to slap him. Galeb intercepted her hand, holding her by the wrist painfully. He wasn't certain but he may have growled a little.

A flash of fear washed over Kieri's face before Galeb grabbed her up and hugged her tightly. He regretted that he'd scared his wife. He was a bit scared himself by his reaction.

Kieri was stiff in his arms.

"I'm sorry that I did that. I shouldn't have challenged The Darkness like that. I shouldn't have frightened you."

Kieri listened to Galeb's apology and realized that Galeb was in control of himself now. So naturally she kneed him in the groin.

Galeb dropped Kieri as the breath left his body to be replaced by excruciating pain. He might have passed out for moment. He couldn't be certain. He definitely wanted to vomit. He would have thought considering how many changes his body had gone through his genitals wouldn't have still been so vulnerable.

"What the septa were you thinking?!" Kieri screamed at him, kicking him in the side for good measure. "Do you realize how much you scared me?"

Galeb considered grabbing Kieri and hugging her again but he was still rather fond of the fetal position he was laying in. His wife was still kicking him as well, not that the kicks hurt that much with the increased muscle mass. His bones might be denser too. Galeb had a sudden horrifying thought.

"Stop checking your ears!" Kieri shrieked, kicking him harder. "Pay attention! I'm trying to punish you for being so stupid."

Kiesh watched the twilight contemplatively. Omkarl had been quite clever, baiting Kqarush into attacking the Mage. Kqarush was always a bit insecure when it came to his place in the hierarchy. Omkarl battling the Mage and possibly defeating him would have been so unacceptable to Kqarush that the Guunt couldn't even risk Omkarl fighting the man.

The small Guunt bore watching. He was far too intelligent. Kiesh didn't consider killing Omkarl – the Guunt wasn't a threat to Kiesh. Omkarl also had great potential as a Kraalsbriekan. He would be an asset in the seemingly never ending war with the Ptrieshs. The Kraalsbriekan might even regain a bit of their lost range on the tundra under Omkarl's machinations.

Omkarl's quickening, should he live that long, was admittedly quite a distance in the future. Still, Guunt didn't think in days. They thought in decades. This was why they were among the most successful of The Darkness.

The Mage was a puzzlement. His mate was shielding sight of the man, but Kiesh knew that the Mage had strengthened. Kiesh knew exactly what was happening every time the Mage slew a Guunt. The connection went back to the first Rising when the Guunt sought to improve the Klynsheimers. Once that connection between Guunt and Klynsheimer was established it never faded. However it should have been dormant. Kiesh had no idea how the man was drawing the strength of his fallen foes into his body. Kiesh was fairly certain that the man had no idea either. The female certainly didn't based on her shouting. The woman was definitely a bit high strung.

The woman was annoyingly shrill at the moment and Kiesh could hear her complaints quite clearly. The Guunt honestly didn't know why the man put up with the complaints. It must have something to do with needing another being to mate. Probably a weakness. Kiesh almost shuddered at the thought. The idea was rather repugnant.

Maybe Kiesh should capture a Shaeloman and ask it about why the man tolerated the female. Those pests seemed to understand human interaction better than the Guunt. Kiesh sighed. Curiosity was annoying.

He suddenly perked up. Maybe the Mage would put the woman in her place. That might be amusing. He listened for a long time, unsure of what was happening. At least the woman was done screaming. Kiesh scratched an ear absently. The female had quite a voice for such a small body. He hoped the man was putting her in her place.

"Are you done hitting me?" Galeb asked, uncurling from his fetal position.

Kieri was standing nearby, hands on her knees, taking deep breaths. She'd been kicking Galeb steadily for at least ten minutes and was both emotionally and physically exhausted. Still, she managed to glare at him when he asked the question.

"You are never doing something so stupid again," Kieri said fiercely.

Galeb stood, his expression going cold and hard.

"Don't ever give me a command, Kieri," Galeb warned. "I've got quite a bit of Guunt jumbled up in my mind right now and what you just said sounds dangerously like a challenge. Guunt meet challenges with violence."

Kieri straightened, disquieted.

"Are you threatening me, Galeb?" she asked in trepidation.

"No," Galeb assured Kieri, "I just don't want to suffer the embarrassment of you kicking the crap out of me again."

Galeb hoped to diffuse the situation and thankfully it worked. Kieri smiled, hesitantly at first, but eventually grinned broadly.

"Just so you remember what I'm capable of," Kieri said in mock warning. "Seriously, husband, do you realize how much you scared me when you stepped across the Ward and took on another Guunt?"

Kieri looked plaintively at Galeb now, wringing her hands.

"I didn't plan on taking on another Guunt. Honestly I'm surprised that I killed him. He had to be kind of stupid to just stand there and let me blast him."

Kiesh, still listening, had to agree with the Mage's evaluation of Kqarush. The Guunt never would have survived long enough to experience a quickening. The fool always assumed being Guunt meant that there was nothing stronger than his kind below the Tundra. Stupid thinking.

"You can't kill another one," Kieri warned Galeb. "You've changed enough already. I'd hate to see what you would become if you killed more of them."

Kiesh was rather curious himself. Not enough to sacrifice his fellow Guunt to the Mage, but still, he wondered what the end result of absorbing Guunt power would be. Kiesh knew his end point; he would become a Kraalsbriekan. What would a human become?

"You're shivering, Kieri," Galeb said, suddenly noticing the movement.

"I'm not cold," Kieri said hugging herself. "How could I be with the amount of heat you're giving off? I swear that if you were anyone else I'd think you were fever ridden. You're not even sweating.

"I'm just a little stressed, okay? My husband just challenged a Guunt – won that challenge – and and...I'm just trying to handle it all. It's not easy."

"I'm sorry," Galeb said, moving to embrace Kieri.

Kieri held up a hand to stop him. She closed her eyes, took a few breaths and then opened her arms to him. Galeb felt immense relief when he embraced Kieri. He had a very real fear of being rejected.

Kieri burrowed into his embrace, hugging her husband until her arms ached.

"I can't lose you," Kieri whispered. "I just can't."

"I promise that I won't do something like that again," Galeb said, rubbing her back reassuringly.

"No, you'll come up with something even stupider to do. I swear, Galeb you must enjoy scaring me."

"Never. Let's go back to bed. I'll hold you for the rest of the night. No pee breaks."

Kieri snorted before looking up into Galeb's eyes, ignoring the changes that she found there as well. Galeb had always been taller than Kieri, but now his height was becoming annoying. She barely reached his chest.

"I've never been in a real bed," Kieri admitted, wrinkling her nose. "Having one implies having a permanent home."

"Does having a permanent home sound so bad?" Galeb asked softly.

"You tell me. I know that you haven't slept in a bed in at least eight years."

Galeb looked up, thinking.

"I don't know. I haven't stayed in one place in so long that I'm finding it kind of hard to even imagine. I would like to stay in one place for more than a few nights in a row at least."

"You married an Obari woman, Galeb. You married into my Family. That means you go where I and my Family lead," Kieri said, smiling. "The choice isn't really yours."

"Oh, really?" Galeb said, smiling in turn.

"Though you may be able to convince me to give you some say in the matter," Kieri said, waggling her eyebrows.

"I would enjoy that," Galeb said, smiling broadly.

Kiesh definitely needed to find a Shaeloman. He had no idea what the sounds coming from the humans now meant. Maybe they were fighting again? There was some moaning...maybe the Mage was asserting his dominance.

Chapter 31

Killing a Guunt was a good way to attract Darkness, Galeb decided. From the sounds of the fighting going on beyond his Ward the forest seemed to be teeming with beasts. All was going according to his plans, which was good since this would be a first with everything seeming to be working out the way he intended.

As if to sour Galeb's mood and prove him wrong, the sounds of horses and marching men became quite audible. He sighed, rolled off of the blankets – Kieri had complained sometime during the night that it was too hot – and put his shirt on before rummaging for a cloak. Kieri muttered a complaint in her sleep, reaching for him. Considering her state of undress Galeb felt it was prudent to wake her. Kieri looked around blearily, demanded to know why Galeb was suddenly putting on a cloak, and then scrambled to get dressed when she realized that they were about to have company.

"Septa it!" Kieri swore. "I was looking forward to more comforting."

"Well, if you want to put on a show," Galeb offered, "I'll comfort you as much as you want. When did we start calling it comforting?"

"Behave," Kieri said with a smirk as she pulled on her boots. "Stall them until I fix my hair."

"Why are you so worried about your hair?"

"Because I want to look presentable, not like I just woke up after a night of being ravished by my husband."

"I don't know," Galeb said, hesitantly. "I'm kind of proud of ravishing you. I might want to brag. Maybe you should keep your hair the way it is. Wait, I thought that we were calling it 'comforting'?"

"There'll be no bragging," Kieri hissed, though she gave Galeb a quick smile. "Unless you want to take that cloak off?"

"Do you really think it prudent to step in front of a group of armed Klynsheimer infantry and Troopers looking like I do without some sort of warning first."

"You're being ridiculous. You don't look that different, aside from being a bit taller and stronger. Okay, your skin has a definite reddish tinge to it, but you don't look that different."

"What about my ears?"

"Will you stop obsessing about your ears? They aren't that noticeable."

"You noticed."

"I have keen powers of observation and fondle them on a regular basis."

Galeb grinned and then paused as if in thought.

"Do we have time for a quickie?"

"No! Now go stall them."

Galeb sighed. He'd only been half serious but still felt some disappointment. It had been nearly a week since he'd killed the second Guunt and his progress had been steady. Between Warding all day and Kieri's affections at night it was a good thing that he didn't require much sleep. Well, Kieri had been complaining that he wasn't letting her sleep enough at night but

Galeb was unrepentant. Mostly. No, he didn't feel a bit of remorse.

Familiar faces greeted Galeb as he walked around a few trees and approached the Klynsheimer contingent. Captain Ilsbruk rode at the head of a column of Troopers, maybe a hundreds strong. Trailing behind was twice that many infantry. Riding uncomfortably behind the Captain was Jans and some woman who looked familiar but Galeb couldn't place her. Galeb couldn't be certain but he had the distinct impression that Bob was about somewhere.

"Greetings, Galeb Sonovonol," Ilsbruk greeted him, raising a hand.

Galeb hesitated before returning the greeting, not out of disrespect, but because he was momentarily overcome with old behaviors from his long years on The Road. Galeb ruthlessly squashed these feelings, standing straighter even though a small voice warned him against calling attention to himself. Being noticed was dangerous, the voice warned. Galeb told the voice to shut up. He may have even growled at it.

"You don't have to wear that cloak," Ilsbruk said, smiling, which had the usual result of making him look constipated, angry and confused all at once. "We are well aware of how you've changed. Bob showed us. The men have been prepared."

Galeb quirked an eyebrow at that explanation.

"How's Kawen?" he asked, annoyed that his voice, unlike the rest of him was still as damaged as ever. Galeb couldn't figure that one out. Kieri insisted that it must be a mental hang up.

"Alive and well enough the last time I saw him. He was taken back south of the Line by Family members. He will need some time to heal," Ilsbruk explained. "Where's your wife, if I might ask? Her family was asking after her well-being even though Bob insisted quite colorfully that you would kill anything that dared try to harm her."

In a fit of humor, Galeb decided to acquiesce to the Captain's request and take off his cloak. Besides, Kieri had insisted that he stall the Klynsheimers until she was presentable. Ilsbruk sucked in a breath at the sight.

"I don't think that Bob was being colorful at all," Gorgorin said, riding up beside Ilsbruk. "Boy's gotten septa big."

"His size is the least of the changes," Jans said, peering at Galeb.

"Begging your pardon, Ma'am," Gorgorin said with a shake of his head. "You didn't see the Mage before. Nothing but gristle and scars. Trust me, his size is a big change. Of course there's his eyes and skin tone. Not to mention the ears."

"I told Kieri that they were noticeable!" Galeb hissed in annoyance. He was going to have to grow out his hair.

"She's well, I trust?" Ilsbruk asked.

"Yes," Galeb said, resisting the impulse to cover his ears. "I imagine Bob's bothering her right now."

"Your blankets smell like sweat and sex," Bob complained as he sat down next to Kieri who was running a comb hurriedly through her hair. "You do as well."

"I'm married, Bob. I have sex. Galeb's body temperature is quite high now. It's like sleeping next to a camp fire. I sweat."

"No excuse for not washing," Bob replied, looking around as if everything around him was fascinating.

"We just woke up, Bob," Kieri said defensively.

"Always with the excuses," Bob said mournfully, shaking his head. "Galeb Sonovonol has changed some more."

"He killed another Guunt."

"He should stop doing that."

"I already told him that."

"Is he not listening? Is that why you're trying to distract him with sex?"

"Stop asking about my sex life, Bob. How's Kawen doing?"

"He's crabby. He was complaining the whole time when Ebko came to take him back to the Family."

"Kawen lost an arm, Bob. He's entitled to some complaining."

"Hey, I killed a Skrieksgrata. You don't hear me bragging about it all of the time."

Kieri stopped brushing her hair and looked straight into Bob's eyes.

"Bob, that's how you start most conversations. And Kawen's not bragging about losing his arm."

"How do you know? Were you there when Ebko came?"

Kieri sighed. She did feel bad about leaving Kawen, but Galeb needed her more.

"No, Bob, I wasn't."

"I was and trust me, he was bragging."

"Do you have any more complaints about me, Kawen or the rest of the Family?" Kieri asked as she finished her hair.

"Not really. I'm just trying to distract you from the fact that Ilsbruk brought Jesia with him."

"My Mage!"

Galeb groaned when he heard those words and the scuffling that was ensuing as Jesia was trying to force her way past her guards and reach Galeb.

"Why did you bring her?" Galeb demanded, glaring at Ilsbruk.

"The King wanted an expert on weird nta to evaluate your current condition," Gorgorin explained helpfully.

"You know she's insane, right?"

"Yup," Gorgorin said with a sniff. "Your problem, not mine."

Apparently Jesia won the struggle with her guards because she skidded to a halt in front of Galeb and looked at him with adoring eyes.

"I knew that you'd be magnificent when you took off your mask," Jesia said softly, licking her lips and raising her hand as if to stroke Galeb's arm.

Galeb never had a chance to stop Jesia because suddenly Kieri was standing between the two of them, glaring at Jesia, with a dagger drawn.

"Stay away from my husband," Kieri warned.

"You're just a place holder," Jesia said dismissively. "Now that I'm here feel free to wander away and get eaten by something."

Kieri glared harder. Jesia smirked, the expression freezing on her face as her nose twitched.

"You smell like sex," Jesia said, her eyebrows plunging as she scowled. "You better not have been having sex with my Mage!"

Bob wandered up, looking amused.

"Oh, wait, were you just having sex with your cousin? That's okay then."

Bob no longer looked amused.

"Jesia, you are supposed to stay to your guards," Ilsbruk said, pinching the bridge of his nose in frustration.

"It's not my fault that they can't keep up," Jesia grumbled, testing Kieri to see if she could find a way around her rival.

"You better not have killed them," Ilsbruk warned.

"I promised you that I wouldn't kill them," Jesia said pouting. Mostly because she couldn't find a way past Kieri. "I want to have sex with my Mage. Get out of the way."

Kieri narrowed her eyes, gripping the dagger tighter.

"She's being difficult," Jesia complained, pointing at Kieri.

"I can't imagine why," Gorgorin said, shaking his head.

"If you didn't kill them, where are they?" Ilsbruk demanded.

"Somewhere back there," said Jesia pointing vaguely behind her. "One of them was having trouble with his arm. The other was having foot issues."

"Jesia!"

"I promised not to kill them. I didn't say anything about hurting them," Jesia said petulantly.

"Septa it I told those idiots not to underestimate you," Ilsbruk growled.

"Maybe if you killed one of them the rest would follow your orders better," Jesia suggested before stepping back from Kieri to ponder the problem.

"Tell her to move," Jesia finally said, looking at Galeb and smiling.

"Galeb, you better not even consider telling me to move," Kieri said angrily.

"Why would I tell you to move?" Galeb asked, confused. "Why would I want to even encourage her?"

"Because you love me, of course," Jesia said smugly.

"I do not," Galeb protested.

"He's just trying to spare your feelings," Jesia said to Kieri confidently.

"I am not – why am I even arguing with you?" Galeb said, shaking his head.

"Because I'm irresistible. Don't worry though, I'm not going to resist you," Jesia said to Galeb, batting her eyelashes.

"So, to what do we owe this pleasure?" Galeb asked Ilsbruk, looking at the Captain sourly, folding his arms and trying to ignore Jesia.

"Have you looked at yourself lately, Mage?" Gorgorin said with a harsh laugh. "You might call yourself a curiosity at this point. The King wants to know more about what's going on with you."

"It's the ears, isn't it?" Galeb muttered turning and walking away. "Investigate all that you want but it will have to be while we walk. I have Warding to do."

"Well, he's as friendly as ever," Gorgorin said, looking at Ilsbruk.

"I know. He's perfect," Jesia said, grinning dreamily.

"Are you ready to explain what you're doing here, Sharni?" Parsons asked, walking up to his sister who was stretching stiffly after hours in the saddle.

Parsons had found himself assigned to the expeditionary force sent after the Warder Mage. He was part of a newly formed company made up of the survivors of units from the left fighting wing. Neither of his brothers were in the new company. Both had been wounded in the fighting. Parsons wasn't certain how badly – he'd been mustered into the new unit and sent off before he could find out anything.

"I'm Journeyman Warder Mage Sepsrigga's assistant," Sharni said, scowling at her brother. "I'm here because it's my job."

"No need to be testy, Sharni," Parsons said, shaking his head.

"I'm tired, I'm sore from riding and now I have my brother treating me like I'm a child. How would you react?

"No one's treating you like a child. I just wanted to know why you're here. I'm concerned, especially since you didn't tell anyone that you were heading off into the wilderness.

"As for being sore, I walked the whole way. You should try it; you wouldn't be complaining about riding."

"I'm old enough to make my own decisions. Journeyman Sepsrigga offered me a position. I took the offer. It's not like any of us had many options," Sharni said sourly.

"No, but following a Mage into the wilderness isn't exactly the safest choice," Parsons said. He wished that he had never advocated becoming settlers. Sharni was right; none of them had many options anymore.

"No, but then it's your job to keep me safe. If you haven't noticed the King sent several hundreds of Soldiers and Troopers along with Sepsrigga."

"Not to protect you," Parsons said disagreeing. "I think that we're along to guard that strange woman."

"How dangerous can she be?" Sharni said, grimacing as she stretched her back.

"She just wounded the two men assigned to guard her. The Captain is angry about it. The rest of us are worried about what happened. You should be worried."

"I have nothing to do with her," Sharni assured her brother.

"You do. The woman's obsessed with the Ward we've come chasing. Your mistress is investigating the Ward. You will come into contact with one another. I'm just asking you to be careful."

"The Obari woman pulled a knife on her already. I don't think that I'm the one that needs to be careful," Sharni said with a weak grin.

"No, it means that you have to be even more careful."

Sharni shook her head, still irritated by her brother's hovering.

"Do you think it's him?" Sharni asked. Maybe here was safer ground and her brother would stop badgering her.

"The Mage from The Road? I don't know. I had heard that he'd been killed in the Battle of the Valley. If it is him, he's changed an awful lot since we last saw him."

"I want it to be him."

"You want the Mage to be alive."

"Of course. He got hurt saving us from ourselves and then disappeared. He deserves to be alive."

"A lot of people deserve to be alive," Parsons disagreed, flashing back to the fighting where so many men in his original unit had fallen.   "It doesn't make it so."

"I can still hope," Sharni said, scowling at her brother.

"Sharni!" called Sepsrigga. "We're moving on. Grab my small pack and a canteen. We'll be walking."

"I have to go," Sharni said, moving to gather up the items.

Parsons watched his sister walk away still worried.

Jans had grown increasingly annoyed over the last day and a half now that their expedition had caught up with the Ward. While it was true that she and Eielson – Sonovonol, she had to remember that; the wife was mad enough as it was without further provocation – had never been close at The Academy, they hadn't been enemies. The point of which being that the man should just answer her questions and stop being so close mouthed.

Case in point. Jans had just asked him another question about his transformation – she had a list of about four hundred questions that she was working methodically through – and low and behold Galeb had to stop again and needed silence. Admittedly watching the man Ward was fascinating. The scale was breathtaking, the Wards themselves simple and dizzyingly complex all at once. Then there were the power sumps. Three lazily spinning whirlwinds that seemed tethered to Eiel-Sonovonol's will.

Jans didn't know a single Mage who could create such things. The more she hung around Sonovonol- there, she'd done it – the more Jans realized how utterly alien the man's thinking was as opposed to Academy doctrine. The Trade Road had forged something Jans didn't understand and she desperately wanted to. She needed to know if the man was unique or if his achievements could be replicated.

Admittedly not for altruistic reasons. Obel was gleaning a lot of notoriety over his small changes to Galeb's innovations when it came to defensive Wardings in subprime conditions. No one yet believed that Obel had created these new techniques himself. However, it was only a matter of time before people did believe Obel's version of the truth. He was fast becoming a power in the new Academy – only differentiated from the old Academy in that no one yet held leadership since the King was still directly commanding the Warders. Obel was primed to become part of the new leadership and Jans needed her own boost to find a position to rival his own.

Galeb Eiel – septa it – Sonovonol – why couldn't the man have the decency to marry Klynsheim – was Jans chance to gain notoriety of her own. So far the man was not cooperating.   Still, she was learning from observation.

"Two," Jans said, holding her hand out.

Sharni, her assistant, reached into the satchel and pulled out the second notebook. Jans kept separate notebooks depending on the line of questioning. Notebook one was for examining Sonovonol's transformation. Notebook two was for examining his Wardings, which were as vastly different from the Warding techniques the man had used on The Road as those techniques were from traditional Academy methodology.

Jans appreciated the woman's efficiency and lack of commentary. Sharni knew her place quite well, understanding her role as a servant impeccably. Jans was also pleased that the woman didn't frighten easily. The Good Lord knew that Sonovonol attracted his share of trouble. The racket that The Darkness raised every time they tested his Wardings made sleep all but impossible despite the Ward's assurance that you 'got used to it' and everyone should be more worried when it was silent. Silence indicated that The Darkness was up to something.

Jans quickly began writing down observations as the Warding built, flowing around them and outward in a sudden rush. She could see the results – Jans could hear the results as The Darkness infested woods erupted in hate filled sounds as the new Warding took hold – but she couldn't see the formation of the Wards themselves. There were too many twists and turns as familiar Wardings combined in combinations that Jans could theoretically comprehend but saw no way to build herself. Not without a full kit of tools, a medium to carve on and days – okay weeks- to lay the ground work. Being able to power such Wards was another consideration that Jans didn't even want to think about.

She'd asked Sonovonol – yes! She was going to continue to get his name right – to explain his methodologies in detail. All Jans had asked for was a deconstruction of techniques. The man's reply every time was to 'observe before questioning'.

Jans was beginning to suspect that the man couldn't explain what he did – that or he refused, which would be just petty. Well, he had given daily demonstrations, even tried to show her how to fashion his light Wards. Once again Jans could grasp the concepts but the actual execution slipped through her fingers. Eiel-Sonovonol! Septa it! – had politely explained that Jans needed to shift her mindset and once again suggested watching instead of questioning.

Even so, Jans suspected that there was some fundamental point that she was missing. It didn't help matters that Eiel- son of a bitch! – Sonovonol was excessively distrustful of Jans and anyone associated with The Academy. While Jans couldn't blame...Sonovonol...for this attitude she really wished that he would just suck it up and get over past wrongs. He needed to be more cooperative and was just being stubborn for the sake of being stubborn.

Jans finished up the description of the latest Warding and decided on a different approach. She handed the notebook back to Sharni and walked over to the Wife. Yes, just call her the Wife and there is no fear of mixing up her family name. Not that Jans should care; the woman was an Obari, and one couldn't be held accountable for any lapses when dealing with barbarians. Still, appearances were important.

Now was a good time to approach the Wife; her annoying cousin was currently absent. There was something fundamentally wrong with Bob – idiotic name – and it didn't help that he was constantly propositioning her. There was also the incident when she was washing last night. Jans could have sworn she heard the man giggling even though there seemed to be no one around. This was after...Sonovonol – good... suggesting watching the creation of Obari illusions so that Jans could grasp what the Ward was talking about when he mentioned mindsets. The Wife had flatly refused to be of help, not that the Ward had suggested she should do so. Bob had offered to help; he followed up the offer by suggesting that Obari illusions were best watched naked.

Jans pushed away the uncomfortable thought and smiled, turning on her full, friendly, almost matronly air that she'd been cultivating with the younger Mages over the past year or so. The Wife, who was never far from...Sonovonol...or a weapon since Jesia was about, glanced over at Jans and frowned. Suspicious woman.

"Good morning, Mrs. Eiel-Sonovonol," Jans said, stumbling.

"Sonovonol," Kieri snapped. "Surely someone as educated as you, Mage Sepsrigga, can manage a proper form of address. We Obari do not hold with the honorifics either. Kieri Sonovonol will do."

Jans almost frowned at being corrected by the foreign woman. Almost. Instead she decided to ignore the insult.

"You must forgive me," Jans said, maintaining her smile, "Our cultures are so different that it can be difficult to remember every custom."

"Galeb doesn't seem to have a problem. Maybe it's just you."

Ouch. The woman wasn't even trying to be polite. Probably Jesia's fault. That one seemed to bring out the worst in everyone. Somehow the Ward seemed to sense Jans' thoughts – which was a disturbing possibility with how strange the man now appeared. The cloak he insisted on wearing wasn't helping. Especially since Bob kept putting that hideous illusion on it.

"Kieri has a very low opinion of The Academy and all associated with it," Galeb explained, flexing his shoulders.

"If you're hot take the cloak off," Kieri said, putting her hands on her hips and shaking her head in exasperation.

"I'm tired of getting stared at," Galeb muttered.

"You've seen what Bob keeps doing to the cloak. You're getting stared at with or without it."

Jans was confused. The air was chill, almost cold. Another few weeks and it would be exclusively cold from what some of the Troopers had told her. Constant rains as well. Eielson shouldn't be hot. She held out her hand and Sharni gave her the appropriate notebook immediately and Jans made a quick notation. Eielson's wife – hah! Take that, you barbarian! – narrowed her eyes at the sight of the notebook disapprovingly.

"Sonovonol," Kieri said, as if she'd heard the silent use of Galeb's former name.

Jans frowned in disquiet at the thought but decided to continue with her new approach.

"It is quite understandable that your wife has concerns about The Academy after your unforgiveable treatment. I assure you that I am not a Twelve loyalist. I firmly associate myself with the King.

"I have a name," Kieri said, "And you know that I am standing right here."

"Always use an Obari's name," Galeb advised. "It is considered impolite not to do so. First and surname always."

"You don't do that," Jans pointed out.

"I'm Family. You're an outsider," Galeb said with a shrug, as if the reasoning was obvious.

"I don't need you telling Mage Sepsrigga how to address me," Kieri snapped at her husband before Jans could say anything else.

"Hey, be angry at her, not me," Galeb protested, as he finally decided to take off the cloak.

As soon as he did there was some excited chattering among the corps of Mages analyzing the boundaries of the Warding. These Mages were research types that seldom saw much field experience mostly because, while they understood theory exceptionally well, they lacked the power or finesse for field Warding. The corps had been following behind the main expedition taking their time analyzing the effects of Sonovonol's Wardings and The Darkness' reaction. Another hundreds of infantry escorted the men and women, having the unenviable duty of keeping the researchers from getting themselves killed.

"That's why I wear the cloak," Galeb muttered, eyeing the excited researchers who were pointing and jabbering at one another. A few more excited fellows had to be grabbed by the arm by their escort and quickly moved away from the edge of the Warding before the researchers crossed the boundary.

"They are annoying," Kieri admitted, having apparently forgotten her earlier anger. "But also funny. Bob keeps entertaining them with wilder and wilder descriptions of your exploits."

The couple shared a laugh.

Jans considered laughing with them but contented herself with a small smile, feeling it unwise to interrupt the moment.

"My apologies again for not knowing your customs better," Jans said, in an attempt to restart the conversation. She needed the prickly Obari on her side to help her make the Ward more cooperative. "I have seldom left the capital and in consequence my knowledge of the North Lands is a bit limited."

Kieri quirked an eyebrow. Jans was a bit disconcerted. The Obari seemed to have the ability to raise an eyebrow half way to her hairline. It was somewhat intimidating in a weird way.

"Galeb went to the same school that you did, Mage Sepsrigga. He had no problems adapting to our ways," Kieri pointed out again.

Galeb distinctly remembered more than one lecture on the differences between reading information in a book and putting that information into practice. There had been an extensive learning curve when it came to adapting to Obari customs. Wisely he kept his mouth closed.

"Well, Galeb Sonovonol seems to be an exceptional man," Jans said with a smile of triumph as she managed the correct form of address.

The woman didn't seem appeased, her eyes narrowing in thought at the compliment Jans had just given her husband. Lord, Jans hoped that the woman was not being jealous. Jans had no designs on Sonovonol other than as a means to increase her standing in the Mage ranks. He was too different to be attractive to her; especially those ears... It was best to keep the conversation moving. Maybe catch the woman off guard. Yes, that would do nicely.

"I'm certain that Galeb Sonovonol's mother has had difficulty following your customs," Jans said sweetly. "I hope that you will allow me the same latitude as I learn."

Galeb stiffened. Kieri's eyes widened and then narrowed dangerously, one hand going to her hip and the other pointing right in her husband's face.

"You told me that your mother was dead!"

Jans tried not to smile over the victory that seemed to be unfolding quite nicely in front of her.

"I never said that my mother was dead," Galeb argued back. "You assumed that she was dead."

"Because you would never talk about her!"

Eielson-Sonovonol definitely had a pained expression on his face.

"You never talk about her?" Jans asked, affecting surprise. Well, emphasizing her surprise, certainly. "Your mother was asking after you the last time I was in the capital. I was quite angry with you when she told me that you hadn't been in contact with her in years. I see now that my anger was justified."

"I wrote," Galeb said defensively. "She never wrote back so I gave up writing to her. How is this any of your concern? We're not friends; we were never close in The Academy. You certainly went out of your way to shun 'poor Galeb with his silly notions' while we were in school."

"Our schooling was ages ago. We all had our focuses; just because my interests were in a different direction didn't mean that I shunned you. Obel did, yes, but I never participated in anything to make you an outsider. You isolated yourself quite nicely all on your own.

"But that's not important. Ignoring your mother is the issue. You said that your mother never tried to get in contact with you once we graduated. Did you ever try to find out why?" Jans asked.

"Most likely the doings of that septaed Academy," Kieri growled, still glaring at her husband and not giving him the opportunity to answer. "You need to fix this."

Jans knew enough to understand how important family was to Obari. She had gained the ally she needed.

"Most likely," Jans agreed sympathetically. "Especially in light of everything that was discovered during the King's purge.

"Oh my goodness! There was an announcement of your death in the capital right after the Battle of the Valley. Your mother must think you're dead."

"Galeb, you are going to write to your mother immediately," Kieri insisted. "I'm certain that Mage Sepsrigga can arrange it so that the letter actually reaches your mother."

Kieri looked over at Jans a little more warmly. Not much, but Jans could work with it.

"After we have finished this task," Kieri continued, "We are going to find your mother. She is Family."

"Yes," Galeb said, still uncomfortable over the mentioning of his mother and looking alternately guilty and irritated. He was also shutting down, closing off his emotions, which earned him another poke and warning look from his wife.

Jans wasn't really surprised by Galeb's reaction. Like most Mages, Galeb had been raised in The Academy from a very early age. From what Jans understood Galeb's acceptance to The

Academy had been a relief to his mother, a widow, since she had one less financial burden to worry about. Any relationship was more than likely strained even before Galeb had been assigned to The Road. And once on The Road, the Ward's world had narrowed considerably and dangerously.

Things seemed to be changing. From what Jans could tell, the Ward had changed more than physically, becoming more open.   At least that was what Captain Ilsbruk and the Sergeant seemed to indicate, though Jans saw no sign of this openness. Apparently the wife had a great deal to do with this transformation and was determined to allow no regression. The Ward for his part seemed to have gone from withdrawn to cantankerous.

Not that Jans really cared either way now that she had created some common cause with the Wife. Jans had to work on developing that connection. Maybe then she could get the Ward to start giving her more detailed information about his methods. As it was Jans already had enough material for the introductory treatise but she needed something of more substance before she could begin designing the centerpiece of her masterwork.

Besides, she had promised Mrs. Eielson – the mother, not the foreign wife – to inquire after her son. True, it had taken much longer than she had originally anticipated, but Jans should be able to spin the eventual reunion in her favor. The capital would buzz with the news of how she brought the renowned hero of the realm and his poor mother back together. It had nothing to do with the letter that Jans had had to write to Enie Rykestruder's family after the King insisted that she had a duty to her subordinates to inform their loved ones of their passing. Well, not too much to do with that task. Jans grimaced just thinking about her death. Poor girl. Rykestruder should have been working with the researchers – weak in power but filled with determination. She'd been a good spy for Jans as well.

Speaking of poor – which both mother and son undoubtedly were since Jans had heard nothing about the King rectifying the Ward's economic status – Jans might also be able to arrange some financial compensation for Galeb's mother. Times had to be tough for the woman given the strain the Rising had put on the nation's economy. The military was monopolizing supplies so finding spirits for Mrs. Eielson's paltry tap room had to be prohibitively expensive as well. Even the price of rot gut had risen exponentially.

There was a lot of opportunity if Jans could just take advantage of it. Getting the Ward to cooperate was the key to everything.

"Mrs. Eielson – his mother," Jans said quickly lest the Wife take offense, "is really a very nice woman. She owns a small tap room in the capital. Mrs. Eielson has run it herself ever since Galeb Sonovonol's father died."

Kieri was glaring almost apocalyptically at her husband now.

"Why is it that Mage Sepsrigga has told me more about your family in the last few minutes than you have ever told me?" she demanded.

"You never asked?" Galeb said, instantly regretting the words as soon as Kieri heard them since she began poking him in the ribs to punctuate her words.

"Never asked? You should have volunteered the information without me asking."

"Ouch! Will you stop poking me?!"

Kieri poked harder.

"I never even knew my father!" he said almost desperately. "He died when I was three."

"Then you knew him."

"Who remembers being three?"

Jans did, mostly because her mother had the foresight to hire a chronicler of what Marsin Sepsrigga already knew would be a life full of her daughter's outstanding achievements.

The argument continued for several moments, attracting a bit of a crowd which caused Sonovonol to become increasingly withdrawn. Kieri at this point was insisting that Jans tell her everything that she knew about the Ward's mother. Jans was happy to oblige. Then all septa broke loose with two simple words.

"My Mage!"

Jesia was running over with a dozen guards in hot pursuit. The Obari woman suddenly lost all interest in the Ward's family and took up position in front of her husband who was actually walking away as fast as a man could without running. It was almost a relief when the Bael Wights attacked the Warding.

Soldiers were shouting, officers and sergeants issuing orders and researchers were trying to find the optimal place from which to study the attack without appearing to be trying to hide behind the Soldiers. Galeb Sonovonol looked at the scene with a shake of his head and a self-conscious touching of one ear.

A sigh was the only warning that Jans received before the air filled with a rain of light that pierced the surrounding forest at precise intervals that totally ignored the attacking Wights. Sharni was doing her best not to show her fear, which was difficult since fear seemed to thrum through the air. The woman handed Jans the appropriate notebook and waited patiently, though slightly hunched behind her mistress.

Jesia, crazy as ever had stopped running towards the Ward and was watching him adoringly, doing a jig as she crooned.

"What are you doing? Jans asked, confused as to why Sonovonol was ignoring the Wights themselves.

"The Wights aren't really there," Galeb said, a slight sound of strain in his voice. "What you see are solid state illusions. Capable of hurting you, yes, but not the source. The source is hiding further out. You just have to find the range and burn them. The light you see are concentrated bursts of heat. Call it a 'burning rain' if you want. It's really an experimentation. I'm not certain that it will work, but I keep trying variations to maximize efficiency."

Jans was stunned. This was more information than the Ward had shared since her arrival. No, that wasn't true; it was simply the most understandable information that the Ward had shared since Jans' arrival. Of course the man wasn't explaining how he formed this Warding or how it operated independent of a firm medium or at such a distance. Yes Jans could see the Ward combinations crawling all over Sonovonol's arms and chest – apparently he could fully Ward his body, which seemed recklessly stupid. Just because Jans could see the Wards didn't mean that she understood their creation. Not that she wanted too; once again, warding your own body seemed recklessly stupid.

Then the man had to go and make matters worse.

"I've included an explanation of this in an addendum to my treatise "Unlocking the Knowledge of Our Ancestors: A Field Guide on Darkness and Wards," Galeb explained.

"I drew the illustrations," Kieri said proudly.

"You submitted a treatise?" Jans asked carefully. The title indicated that the man wouldn't even take credit for his ideas. He was annoyingly humble. Or more likely the Ward wanted to deflect some of the attention off of himself and make fewer enemies by claiming his techniques were only rediscoveries.

"Yes," Galeb said, matter-of-factly. "The King insisted that I do so while I was recovering. I revised my earlier treatise that got rejected so it didn't really take that long."

"The King pretty much figured that Galeb Sonovonol attracts trouble and it was better to have his knowledge preserved in case that trouble became too much to handle," Bob said, wandering over and giving Jans a flirtatious wink. "I'm surprised that you didn't know; there were scribes coming in and out of his tent for days."

"I thought they were just taking testimony," Jans admitted.

"No," Bob said with a snort. "Captain Ilsbruk took care of that even before we met up with the King. From what I cared to understand, the King is having copies of the treatise put in every major Warder Institution and Chapter House."

Well, on the bright side, Obel was in for a bit of a shock. No, Jans had to be positive. She'd read Sonovonol's earlier work; it hadn't been exactly stimulating reading. The man's reputation as unconventional would work against him as well.

There was an angry shriek and the Wights began to wink out of existence.

"The only problem is I don't know if I'm actually doing more than temporarily inconveniencing the creatures," Galeb said thoughtfully before shrugging. He was walking away before Jans could ask any more questions.

Kiesh watched the Wights failure with a hint of satisfaction. The human was Guunt touched; his dominance over the grubs was to be as expected as it was necessary. Kiesh knew where the human Mage was heading and such behavior needed to be encouraged. The man believed that he was drawing The Darkness after him. He never stopped to consider that he, himself, was being herded.

Kiesh watched the exchange between the three females – was it four? Kiesh couldn't be certain whether or not to count the female that kept handing objects to the female Mage. He shook his head in irritation before deciding on three.

He'd captured a Shaeloman and forced the creature to watch the interactions between the Mage and his females. The Shaeloman had tried to explain the interactions but Kiel suspected that not even the Shaeloman could fully understand the dynamics between the humans. One was mated to the Mage. One wanted to be mated to the Mage. A third could go either way. How was Kiesh supposed to make sense out of all of that?

Kiesh pondered the issue for a while – he wanted to understand his enemy's weaknesses - which meant that he idly scratched something with a claw while lost in thought. The sounds the claw made were soothing. Well, the sounds were soothing once the Shaeloman stopped whimpering and finally died, which admittedly wouldn't have taken so long if Kiesh had realized what exactly it was he was scratching.

Kiesh finally reached a decision. The humans were insane. He was happy with that realization until he realized that maybe he shouldn't try to understand the humans and simply think like a Guunt. The Mage was Guunt touched after all. Perhaps the Mage was building his own pack of Guunt. That made more sense. Or did it?

Kiesh didn't like the Mage; the man tangled up his thoughts and made his head hurt.

Chapter 32

Galeb woke up, with the realization he was holding a naked body. He was thankfully still dressed, but the person that he was holding was definitely naked. Oh, and not Kieri. Galeb cracked an eye and saw Jesia trying to yank his pants off while holding him tightly.

"Gargh!" Galeb said as he jolted awake from what was definitely a nightmare.

"Smgpmph," Kieri muttered softly from the stranglehold she had on his chest. "...really a nice girl...Mrs. Eielson..."

Galeb looked down at his wife and quirked an eyebrow. He really didn't want to know what kind of dream Kieri was having. Especially since it reminded him that he had to reconnect with his mother. Corinne Eielson had been a loving woman, he seemed to remember. The sad truth was that he hadn't been that close to his mother in nearly two decades. The Academy had its ways of promoting separation.

He was in some ways not looking forward to that reunion. It was bound to be awkward and Galeb wasn't very good at that sort of thing.

"Ah! You're finally awake!" Bob said looking down at Galeb. Bob was sitting on a root of the tree that Galeb and Kieri had camped beneath for the little bit of privacy it afforded.

"...don't think that's an appropriate question to ask about your son...," Kieri mumbled, blushing bright red.

"What is she dreaming about?" Bob asked curiously.

"None of your business, Bob," Galeb said. "Don't you dare wake her up to ask her either."

"Wouldn't think of it," Bob said, continuing to keep his voice down.

"What do you want, Bob?"

"I have some questions," Bob announced with a smile. "Well, not really my questions. More like Mage Sepsrigga's questions, which I promised to ask."

"Why are you asking questions for Jans?"

"She promised we'd spend some time together if I asked the questions," Bob said with a shrug. "I figured that it was a fair trade."

"She's just using you, Bob," Galeb warned.

"Of course she is," Bob agreed. "Doesn't mean that I can't use her back."

Galeb closed his eyes to think about it for a few moments.

"I suppose it can't hurt," Galeb finally relented.

"Good!" Bob whispered eagerly. "First question: Why is the Warded Road that you're creating so winding?"

"Because it reflects Obari sensibilities, not Klynsheim," Galeb admitted. "I would have thought you'd know that, Bob."

"Why else?"

"There is no other reason."

"Oh? I didn't think the answer was that obvious."

"But I don't want to wear an apron...," Kieri mumbled.

"Are you certain that I can't wake her up and ask her what she's dreaming about?" Bob asked as he and Galeb glanced back down at Kieri.

"No."

"Okay. Why's it always twilight on the Path?"

"I've used Wards to bend the way the light enters the path during the day. The Wards of the Path illuminate it at night. I've already answered that question for both Jans and the researchers."

"How do you bend the light?"

Galeb explained how he'd gotten the idea from watching Obari illusions and went on to describe the process that he'd worked out to accomplish the effect.

"I...don't really understand anything that you just said," Bob admitted.

"Neither did Jans or the researchers," Galeb admitted as well. "It's kind of a mesh of Obari and Klynsheim ideas. You have to be able to think in both ways simultaneously."

"...haven't really discussed children...no, I don't want a chicken," Kieri whispered, moving her hands as if she was pushing away something before shifting against Galeb and nestling even closer.

"I really want to wake her up," Bob whined.

"No," Galeb insisted. "Don't you have any other questions?"

"Well, this one's more of a repeat of the last one since you didn't really answer it completely. Why's it always twilight? Not how you've accomplished the effect, but more why use the effect in the first place."

"Aesthetic reasons," Galeb answered.

"Really?" Bob asked, arching an eyebrow.

"What? I like twilight."

"That's an awful lot of power to be throwing around simply for aesthetic reasons," Bob pointed out.

"It also makes it easier to both see the boundaries of the Warding and find the Path without using Ward Posts," Galeb pointed out.

"Nothing to do with your freaky eyes?" Bob asked.

"There's nothing wrong with my eyes," Galeb protested even though he felt oddly relieved that Bob wasn't pointing out his ears.

"If you say so," Bob said with a shrug. "One more question: when are we sneaking away to get a look at this city?" Bob asked.

"You are not sneaking off!" Kieri insisted, suddenly sitting up.

"Now she wakes up," Bob muttered and then said more loudly, "Having pleasant dreams, were we?"

"My dreams are none of your business, Bob," Kieri insisted, looking at her cousin suspiciously.

"I've heard that the mess cooks are preparing chicken," Bob offered conversationally.

Kieri looked momentarily panicked before glaring at Bob suspiciously.

"Bob was just leaving," Galeb insisted, snaking an arm around Kieri and holding her tight in case Bob got any ideas to cause more trouble.

"You aren't sneaking off," Kieri insisted, snuggling under Galeb's arm.

Ever since the nights had gotten cold enough to feel it on the path, due to the season and the fact that the Path was heading further north, Kieri took great advantage of her husband's higher than normal body heat. Galeb didn't mind too much, though occasionally his arm would fall asleep when Kieri held him in one position for too long.

"I'm not going to sneak off," Galeb insisted again. "I am – unfortunately – going to have to talk to Jesia."

He could feel Kieri frown against him. That his wife wasn't throwing a fit at the moment was progress he supposed. Galeb was a bit suspicious of how well Kieri was taking that pronouncement.

"Not alone, you're not," she warned him.

"Not alone," Galeb agreed. "But I will talk to her. I need to understand more about this city of hers."

"TeraUsuat," Kieri said.

"Yes," Galeb agreed. "I need to know more information about the walls of the city."

"You have a plan to deal with these people?" she asked, her voice already softening as she fell back asleep.

"I've got an idea," Galeb admitted.

Kieri was already asleep. Bob looked gravely at Galeb and then walked away without another word. Bob didn't like it when Galeb had ideas. He'd had to kill a Skrieksgrata the last time Galeb Sonovonol had ideas.

Galeb had to admit that his interview with Jesia went surprisingly well, aside from or perhaps because of Jesia's determination to ignore Kieri's presence. Jesia chatted pleasantly, answered every one of his questions promptly, and attempted to flirt, which was admittedly painful to watch. All that mattered was that he had the information he needed.

He sought out Ilsbruk afterwards, who sat outside his tent at a camp desk looking over reports. The Captain looked at ease, probably glad of the respite from fighting. Ilsbruk didn't look up when Galeb approached, simply starting a conversation as he shuffled papers.

"I'm still getting complaints about your insistence on limiting the amount of trees that can be cut down for firewood," Ilsbruk said. "It's getting colder and we need a lot of fuel to support the size of our expedition."

"This isn't a Klynsheim road," Galeb explained, again. "Obari standards will be maintained."

"This isn't Obari territory and you are Klynsheim – a member of The Academy of Mages," Ilsbruk argued, leaning over to poke at a small heating brazier that he'd stolen from the cook's supplies.

"I'm not changing my mind," Galeb insisted.

"I liked you better when you were more withdrawn," Ilsbruk said, glancing up.

What Ilsbruk didn't realize was that it was taking a considerable amount of self-control for Galeb not to fall back into that pattern. Kieri had insisted and Galeb had to agree that he couldn't afford to show weakness, not if he was going to keep the Path the way that he wanted it. That and avoid being taken advantage of at the same time. The fact that the memories of two Guunts were swirling about his brain urging him to smash down the Captain for challenging his decision helped strengthen Galeb's resolve.

"We all change," Galeb said, forcing his hands still.

"We need more firewood," Ilsbruk insisted.

"Take it from anywhere but the places I've designated," Galeb insisted back.

"Your designated locations require us to expend twice the amount of effort."

"Most of the Soldiers don't have much to do," Galeb pointed out.

"They'll be busy enough when needed."

"Until then they can stay in shape gathering fire wood from everywhere but the designated locations."

"You've grown more backbone, Ward," Ilsbruk said, putting his papers down and leaning back to look up at Galeb.

"Everyone changes," Galeb insisted again.

"No they don't, which is often a pity."

"Not everyone is married to Kieri Sonovonol."

"Yes, I imagine that would toughen you up," Ilsbruk said with a slight grin. "My own wife is said to have mellowed me a bit."

"They give us what we need," Galeb agreed. "I am not budging on the firewood issue."

"You know that I could simply ignore your mandates and take the wood from wherever I wish instead of leaving copses of wood throughout this Path you've forged."

"I've built the King a secondary defensive line," Galeb pointed out. "I doubt the King would risk losing such a defense over a few trees."

"See, now that's a threat, Ward Sonovonol," Ilsbruk said, leaning back on his stool and looking coldly into Galeb's eyes. "You forget yourself and you forget the reality of your situation. Ward or no, you answer to the King. Your continued fulfillment of your role ensures the continued protection of your Family and associated Obari within Klynsheimer lands. You do not make threats."

For a moment Galeb felt a bit of the old fear roil in his gut. The voice in his head was shrieking that he should back down. Don't be noticed. Avoid conflict. Focus on the duty until the people walk away.

Another part of himself roared in rage, silencing the voice, wanting to rend the source of such cowardice. The rage won out, oddly smoothing his thoughts, strengthening his resolve. If any of this inner turmoil showed in his face, Ilsbruk chose not to comment. The Captain did notice that Galeb's eyes were redder than they should have been, almost with a feral gleam in them. Ilsbruk kept his own expression neutral as he processed this information.

"I am not making threats, Captain Ilsbruk, towards my King or my country. I am stating a fact. Those copses will remain untouched. Consider them Way points, integral to the Path. But don't forget that this Path is not a Klynsheim Road, looking to serve dual purposes as both defense and transport way. This route is just a means to an end. I highly doubt anyone will want to make the journey north once I have finished my task," Galeb said, standing straighter, not menacingly, but powerful none the less.

"What is your task?" Ilsbruk asked. "Let us get to the point that has brought me here. What will you do once you reach TeraUsuat?"

"What I do or not do at TeraUsuat isn't why you're here, Captain. You're here to determine what I have become," Galeb said with a shake of his head. "But as to what I'll do at TeraUsuat I will give The Darkness what they want. I will give them the city."

"Are you Darkness then?" Ilsbruk demanded sourly. "Are you going to murder people now?

"No, I'm not Darkness," Galeb said, with just the slightest note of uncertainty in his voice. "Nor will I murder anyone. I said that I would give The Darkness the city. I didn't say anything about the people inside of it.

"The Path heads south as much as it heads north. The people will have a choice. The Usatchi can stay and die or they can flee, submitting themselves to the King's authority."

"Klynsheimer, Obari and Usatchi. You've brought quite a collection of people to the King," Ilsbruk spat. "Did you ever stop to consider the strain the influx of population is putting on our resources? No, you wouldn't, would you? At heart you are still an Itinerant Warder Mage walking his Patrol."

Ilsbruk stood, leaning on the camp desk and glaring at Galeb.

"That's the problem with you, Galeb Sonovonol. You're a Power beyond anything our People have seen since perhaps the First Rising. All that ability and yet you still think small.

"Let me explain in terms you can understand, Ward or whatever you have become. Perhaps that's a problem as well. We need a new word to describe you. Maybe then you can break old expectations.

"Regardless of titles you need to hear this. You are not the cripple, self-absorbed Warder that I met on The Road. You are not the loner too afraid to be around his own people. You are more than that and you have to start thinking that way. Everything you do effects not just the people around you but everyone in the Kingdom."

"I Ward," Galeb protested, uncomfortable with what Ilsbruk insisted he do. He'd never thought past the need to Ward before. Even Galeb could admit that it was a sad existence, but familiar at least.

He also thought that Ilsbruk was being unfair. Galeb was well aware of the problems of population. Whether or not the Klynsheim wanted to admit it, the constant influx of settlers into Obari lands had put a strain on resources in the north. Before the Rising, the Klynsheim and Obari had been a generation away from war. The Obari would have lost that war but the settlements of the North would have burned first.

Ilsbruk was wrong. Galeb did understand the problems of adding two distinct peoples to Klynsheim lands. Well, he understood some of the problems at least. Galeb just didn't know what else to do. There also was the grim reality that no matter how many Darkness Galeb drew north the Rising was not over. The Darkness would consume TeraUsuat and then head south again. Many more were going to die before all of this was over. Galeb was only buying his People some time.

Ilsbruk didn't give Galeb a chance to defend himself.

"You stride big," Ilsbruk hissed, slamming a fist into the table. "You're like a great big boulder that falls off a cliff into a small pond. You don't see any problem while the water is thrown everywhere and the creatures within it struggle to survive the aftermath of your arrival.

"Yes, I am here to see what you have become. More than that I'm here to see if you can co-exist with your own people without causing greater destruction."

"And what if I can't?" Galeb said in challenge, suddenly forgetting the arguments that he could make in his own defense. The influence of the Guunt was very evident in his posture and words. He'd worry about that later.

"Well, you see that's a very interesting question," Ilsbruk said, leaning back and crossing his arms. "The plain truth is that you don't have a choice. That's another reason why I'm here. I'm your nursemaid. It's my job to ensure that you start behaving according to the King's expectations.

"And before you argue with me, Galeb Sonovonol, and I admit it's a good sign that you are arguing considering how you used to behave, remember that you're not immortal. You can be killed. So can your wife and her entire Family."

Galeb clenched his fists and made to step forward. Ilsbruk held up a hand to stop him.

"This is politics boy. The nation matters a whole septa of a lot more than you do. Nothing personal. You will abide," Ilsbruk said softly, with a hint of sudden sympathy. "Nothing much has to change at the heart of it. You can still Ward and protect what's important to you. But you will do so with more direction and more forethought. No more harrowing off on your own initiative without careful planning.

"Look on the bright side, Sonovonol. Your wife will probably thank you for staying out of trouble."

Galeb was angry.

"We are servants of the realm," Ilsbruk reminded Galeb. "We are the shield of our People. In your case the shield of your Peoples.

"King and Seven. Central Command and Academy. We all have our place. You lost yours for a time. I'm here to make certain you find it again. When you do, it'd be best not forget so we can avoid future problems."

"As you say, Captain Ilsbruk," Galeb agreed, "Just as you should remember that I married into an Obari Family. Obari are never alone."

"I've killed a Skrieksgrata," Bob said conversationally as he stepped out of Ilsbruk's tent, leaning on his short spear. "Never killed a Klynsheimer. Don't imagine it would be that hard comparatively.

"Fact is you spoke some truths, Captain Ilsbruk of the Seven. Do some good for Galeb Sonovonol to listen. Problem is that you threatened the Family. Shouldn't do that. It makes people a bit prickly. I suppose I could let it go this time seeing as Galeb Sonovonol doesn't seem to want to cause any unnecessary trouble.

"He and I have a bit of disagreement when it comes to you Klynsheimers. Me, I think that we could dispose of a body very easily. Just have to chuck it over the Ward boundary and all that Darkness will swallow up the evidence in an eye blink.

"Galeb Sonovonol doesn't agree. He seems to think that Kieri Sonovonol would look unkindly upon such an action. Admittedly she probably would. Not much of a sense of humor in that woman."

Ilsbruk stood stiffly, watching both men carefully. He knew that he could take the Ward in a fight. The man might be strong, had some fighting skills, but had trained to fight Darkness. Ilsbruk had a broader skill set. The man wasn't even carrying his quarter staff any more, though the Ward still had his fighting knife belted to his waist.

Bob was an unknown. The man was unstable and looked far too comfortable with that spear.

"Not the real problem with what you've done anyway," Bob continued. "Best not to threaten Kieri Sonovonol. She's the only thing that holds Galeb Sonovonol restrained. You think that he's bad now; you don't want to imagine what he would do if she were harmed."

Ilsbruk watched the Ward's face when Bob mentioned harm befalling the man's wife. No, Ilsbruk agreed, he didn't want to imagine what the Ward would do. There had been nothing remotely human or remorseful upon the man's face. Only a promise of the world burning.

"But these are hypotheticals," Bob said affably. "No need to worry about anything as long as we all get along. Especially considering how many Obari are now living around your own family, Captain."

"Of course," Ilsbruk agreed sourly, sitting down. He didn't like threats to his family any more than the Sonovonols had enjoyed the threats to their Family. He decided to ignore Bob and focused back on the Ward.

"You came to me for a reason besides arguing," Ilsbruk said.

"Yes," Galeb agreed, suddenly remembering why he'd sought the Captain out. "I have two requests."

"Yes?" Ilsbruk asked, noticing that Bob had disappeared and so had his small heating brazier. He cursed silently.

"We are getting closer to the city. We need to formulate a plan for how to deal with the Usatchi. I have some ideas," Galeb said.

"It's good to see you thinking ahead. What's your other request?"

Galeb suddenly looked a bit uncomfortable.

"I need to send a letter to my mother letting her know that I'm still alive. Since the King hasn't seen fit to reverse my death declaration I wasn't certain how to go about that."

Ilsbruk was almost surprised. He hadn't given any thought to Sonovonol's Klynsheim relatives. Given the Ward's last eight – almost nine- years, Ilsbruk had assumed that neither had Galeb.

"There's no need to reverse the declaration. Word's already spread through the medical trains carrying wounded south that you're alive," Ilsbruk explained. "Since that won't be a problem, I don't see why you need my help with sending the letter."

"I want to make certain that the letter actually arrives," Galeb said.

"The Twelve are dead, Sonovonol. I've told you that enough times. No one is going to interfere with a letter you send," Ilsbruk assured him.

"I have your word?"

"As much as you trust it, I give my word that the letter will reach your mother."

"Thank you."

"Bring the letter to me when you finish it."

Galeb reached into a pouch and took out a many folded piece of paper and handed it to Ilsbruk. Ilsbruk took the letter and then looked at his pile of paper work.

"Come back in an hour and we'll discuss our approach to TeraUsuat."

Galeb nodded and walked away.

When the Ward was gone Ilsbruk unfolded the letter. He would ensure its delivery. He would also read it to assess Sonovonol's state of mind.

A few minutes later Ilsbruk refolded the letter and looked thoughtfully at the paper. That was nearly the most awkward letter that the Captain had ever read. It was only topped by the letter that Kieri Sonovonol had given him to deliver to the Ward's mother nearly an hour before. The two were well matched it seemed. Bob's letter had been funny at least. Though why Bob felt the need to write a letter to Corinne Eielson was anyone's guess.

Chapter 34

Life in the capital was anything but pleasant in the poorer quarters of the city during normal times. With a Rising there were food restrictions, shortages, drafts and rioting. The drafts took care of much of the rioting as the hot-headed youth were mustered into the defense of the Kingdom. Little could be done about the food shortages until the southern lords finished sorting the harvest by the triad – military, civilian and lord's share.

Koring entered the cramped but well-kept tap room of his Aunt Corinne, which was crammed between a chandler's shop and a general merchandise store that specialized in thrice owned items. Rumor had it that there had once been an alley between the two stores and Aunt Corinne had built her tap room without anyone's by your leave in the open space.

Koring had started checking on her daily ever since the announcement of his cousin's death. Those first few weeks had been difficult with his aunt alternatingly listless and crying. Koring had felt sympathy, though in reality he wondered just how much feeling Aunt Corinne had for her son. Neither one of them had visited much during Galeb's Academy days due to both written and economical restrictions. It had been eight years since his Aunt had even received a letter from his cousin. Still, Corinne had been devastated; Koring could only assume that his Aunt had held out hope of reconciling with her son.

His Aunt had been overjoyed when word had filtered through the city that not only was Galeb Eielson alive but he was fighting The Darkness in the North Country as part of the King's battle strategy against the Rising. Koring's reaction had been more restrained. As a King's Speaker he had greater access to casualty reports than the average civilian. One of his regrettable duties now was delivering death notifications to families.

Four thousand or more lost in the King's battle. Another two thousand or so wounded. Nearly a thousand dead along the Ward Line. Twice that wounded and by all accounts the Rising had barely begun. Galeb might be alive now; there was no guarantee that the man would survive much longer.

There were also the disturbing reports circulating about his cousin. Some said that he was fast becoming a Dread Power to rival The Darkness. While Koring discounted such extreme talk there were enough rumors of strangeness to be disconcerting.

Today Aunt Corinne was sitting at one of the tiny tables crammed inside of her establishment. Short, too thin, and old were the best ways to describe Corinne; life had neither been kind or forgiving. Still, Koring's Aunt had a sense of pride about herself normally. Everything that Corinne Eielson had, she'd earned.

At the moment Aunt Corinne was staring down at three letters looking very confused. From the condition of the letters they had travelled a very long distance. There were more than a few stains marring the paper.

"Are you alright, Aunt Corinne?" Koring asked, easing his bulk into the seat across from her.

"The entire city's on half rations and you still look fat, Nephew," Corinne pointed out.

"Everyone looks fat next to you, Aunt Corinne," Koring responded politely.

Even with restrictions Koring knew how to get extra supplies. Not that Corinne of all people should be complaining. Those contacts were one of the few reasons why Corinne was still able to serve alcohol to her customers. Not the best grade alcohol, but then again Corinne had only ever served tolerable alcohol.

His Aunt clucked at Koring disapprovingly and then returned to looking at the letters perplexedly.

"Who are the letters from?" Koring asked, seeing that the letters were the reason why his Aunt seemed out of sorts.

"This one," Corinne said, pointing to the first letter, "Is from my son. Decades of education at The Academy and he still writes poorly. It took me an age to piece together the meaning of his words. Apparently he's written a treatise and yet he can't put coherent sentences together when writing his own mother. He apologizes for not writing sooner. Apparently the Twelve had prevented his correspondences. That's something, I guess."

She sighed, shaking her head slightly in exasperation.

"The boy never did know how to express himself. He was always too quite. Now this one," Corinne said, pointing to the second letter, "is apparently from my daughter – in - law. I didn't even know that he got married. She's foreign. Obari, it says. Very polite. Very nervous. I don't know how I feel about this."

There was a look of consternation and annoyance on his Aunt's face.

"Could have had the decency to meet his mother before marrying him," Corinne muttered. "Bad enough that my boy didn't bring her to meet me. Woman should know better.   Foreign too...can you imagine what kind of strange customs the woman must be used to? I've heard that those Obari are savages. I hope that she hasn't corrupted him."

Koring thought back to the rumors and thought it likely that if anyone was demonstrating strange behavior it was his cousin Galeb, not his foreign wife.

"Still, I shouldn't complain too much," Corinne said, shaking her head, "I have the chance for grandchildren now. Be good to see young ones running around. Even if they will be half savage. I suppose that they can be taught manners. At least I hope so."

Koring's Aunt looked wistful for a moment before shaking her head and looking at the final letter with total bewilderment.

"This last one here is from some man named 'Bob' – you ever hear of such a name? Claims to be my daughter – in - law Kieri's – that's my boy's wife's name – cousin."

"What does this Bob want?" Koring asked.

"Aside from drawing pictures of birds all over his letter? He starts by telling me that he killed a Skrieksgrata and apparently it's Galeb's fault. Strange man. Bob also wanted to assure me that my son isn't as frightening as he looks. Apparently he's at least twice as frightening. I have no idea how that's reassuring or what it means."

Koring had an uncomfortable idea of what this Bob meant.

"Bob finishes his letter by offering a bit of advice. Apparently I should offer Kieri chicken when I meet her.   Must be some sort of Obari custom."

Corinne looked up at her nephew as if he could offer some advice on how to deal with the letters.

"What has Galeb gotten himself into?" Corinne asked.

Koring reached down and looked at the letters. Once he was done skimming through them he straightened up and leaned back. The chair protested the movement but Koring ignored the sound. All chairs seemed to protest being sat on by him.

"Well, Aunt, there is a lot to ponder on, I will give you that," Koring agreed.

"I can't help but feel that my boy is finding trouble just like his father. Must be an Eielson trait," Corinne grumbled.

"Apparently his surname's now 'Sonovonol'," Koring said helpfully. He'd always enjoyed learning new information, which was why he made such a good Speaker.

"Foreign nonsense," his aunt said dismissively. "There's also the problem of the fourth letter."

"There's a fourth letter?" Koring asked, looking back down at the papers.

"This one," Corinne said, flipping over the letter from her son. On the back was a quick message.

Koring looked closer and his eyes widened when he noticed that the message was written by Ilsbruk of the Seven. The Captain was offering his Aunt an escort north to see her son.

"What are you going to do?" Koring asked.

"I'll probably wait a week and then go," Corinne admitted. "I can't afford to buy any more spirits, so once my supplies run out my customers will run out as well."

Koring thought about offering his Aunt support but things were becoming tight even for him. Without the income from her tap room there was no way for his Aunt to support herself. It would probably be best to accept Captain Ilsbruk's invitation. Corinne wouldn't have to worry about starvation for a time at least.

"I'm an old woman," Corinne said, leaning back in her chair. "It's time my son showed some responsibility and helped support me."

Koring's eyes widened slightly. His Aunt had always been one for self-sufficiency.

"Don't look at me like that," Corinne snapped. "I've earned a rest."

"I'm not arguing," Koring insisted.

"Besides, my son obviously needs a firm hand if he's taking up with a foreign woman."

"Aunt Corinne, Galeb's in his late twenties. He's an acclaimed Ward with Battle Honors," Koring protested.

"Nephew, my son's hanging around with someone who calls himself '*Bob*'," Corinne pointed out. "Not to mentioning taking up with a foreign woman. Oh my God! Do you think that he actually married her or is he just – what is it you young people call it? Co-existing?"

"Co-habitation, Aunt Corinne. That's rare and only indulged by South Land intellectuals who are out of favor with the Church," Koring pointed out.

"He better not be co-habitating," Corinne said fiercely. "No boy of mine is going to ruin a woman's reputation, foreign or not.

Oh my God! I hope that he actually had proper marriage rites. What if they just went through some barbarian custom?"

"The Obari believe in God, Aunt Corinne."

"Do they have proper priests?"

"I...don't know."

It was best not to lie to Aunt Corinne.

"You know anything about Obari marriage rites?"

"No."

Koring was quite glad that he didn't know anything about Obari marriage rites. Particularly since Koring had never heard of an Obari priest. He couldn't deny that the Obari lacked priests but he couldn't confirm it either.

Corinne looked contemplative.

"Well, I suppose that you'll find out," she finally said.

"Wait – what?"

"You didn't think that I was going to the North Lands without a relative escorting me, did you? I'm old Koring. Show some consideration."

"You're not that old. Besides I have a job, Aunt Corinne. I can't leave."

"You'll be on detached duty. I've already arranged it."

"What! You had no right!"

"I suppose not. That's why I asked your mother to take care of the particulars. Your Senior Speaker was most understanding. He also liked the idea of getting some more King's Speakers into the North Lands. Something about not letting the Military Speakers have too much control over information."

Koring couldn't think of any excuse besides whining that he didn't want to go to the North Lands. There was danger there and short rations. Especially short rations.

"But I don't want to go on a diet," Koring complained.

"This is not all about you, Nephew," Corinne snapped. "This is about my son and his savage of a wife. And possibly Bob. I have a feeling a man that strange is going to be underfoot. Besides, Koring, you could stand to lose some weight."

Koring slouched sullenly into his chair. The chair complained. Koring ignored the chair's complaint. The chair collapsed. Corinne explained politely that he now owed her several coins for the chair.   Koring lay on the floor scowling and mourning the fact that he was too old for a tantrum.

"Look on the bright side, Nephew. Maybe we can find you a foreigner to marry."

Chapter 35

Sigsrata sat on what he referred to as his 'travel throne'. It was just a large chest that offered more support than a camp stool. He was enjoying a nice lunch and reading correspondence while his clerk wrote a letter to the Queen. Sigsrata's wife insisted on regular missives. The King was obliging by directing his clerk to write regularly for him. Sigsrata had come to find the letter writing rather relaxing since he was no longer the one doing it.

The sounds of thousands of men working filled the air, the only thing marring an otherwise perfect day. The Ward Line was being extended slowly but surely towards the mountains. Obel was directing the efforts and relishing his chance at command. Thankfully the men serving under the Mage resented his presence so Sigsrata wasn't too worried about the Journeyman expanding his influence.

The King was reading an expeditionary dispatch. Ilsbruk's reports were regular and concise, which the King appreciated. Sigsrata had to agree with the Captain's analysis that Sonovonol needed a new rank. The man was too strange to fit normal ranks and too powerful to fall under conventional authority. This created a problem because Sonovonol was a man of duty and habit. Without a clearly delineated position, the man was floundering a bit. Give him the familiar and the Mage would become more biddable. Truthfully the man would still be walking his Patrol on The Road if Ilsbruk hadn't dragged him away.

The problem was coming up with a rank. Something without too much authority. Sonovonol was not a leader. But something with enough authority that others couldn't seek to use the man for their own gains. Which reminded the King about another nagging problem. He was going to have to place a heavy guard around Sonovonol at all times given the man's remarkable abilities. There would be many within both the Warder Mages and the Nobility who would like to see such a powerful asset removed from the King's grasp.

Maybe 'King's Mage'? Was the man even a Mage anymore? Not to mention how The Academy would react to having a man independent of their authority and working directly for the King. Not that the man trusted The Academy or that Sigsrata particularly cared. Admittedly Sigsrata was enjoying the deaths of the Twelve. Life was much more satisfying without the constant nagging and machinations of old men who should've known better.

No. The title had to be more nationalistic. Not something associated with either the King or The Academy. Something grand that transcended petty arguments over authority and firmly tied Sonovonol to his duties.

The title also had to consider Sonovonol's character. They referred to him as a Ward but that title didn't fit well. Wards built defenses. Sonovonol had gone on the offensive and kicked The Darkness in the teeth on multiple occasions. No, something more aggressive...'Spear of Klynsheim'? Not particularly imaginative, but it did have a nice martial ring to it.

But there were the man's Obari connections to consider. Sigsrata enjoyed the scouting abilities of the Obari and didn't want to lose their service. Not to mention avoiding a war. The Klynsheim settlements in the North Lands had been leading in that direction as the Obari felt more pressured. 'Spear of the North', perhaps. No, too regional. The Southern lords might take offense.

Just keep it simple; 'The Spear' or 'Spear'. Yes, the King liked the sound of that; it would do. Especially when paired with a title for Kieri Sonovonol.

By titling the Obari woman he tied her people tighter under his authority and gave the woman some ground of her own to stand on when it came to dealing with obstinate people. Call her 'The Shield'. Yes, that would do well. 'The Spear and the Shield'. The writers would enjoy romanticizing the pair.

Elder Klisisil of TeraUsuat, a stork of a man in overlarge robes, frowned as he glanced out the window of his opulent receiving room. The view was of a carefully manicured garden and a massive, almost absurdly thick wall. The wall was about more than defense. The wall prevented any of the elders from having to view the outside world and The Darkness that threatened their existence. Here in the heart of the city the elders maintained their illusions of past glories without any real concern about danger.

It was growing harder to maintain those illusions with the sky brightening at all hours. The light was growing closer. None of the scouts had an answer as to what the light might be, which was why Telmut, Master of Scouts, was kneeling in the center of the room, staring at the floor.

"How can you possibly have no idea what is causing that light?" Klisisil demanded. "We have branded over two dozen of your scouts in recent days. Their Walks should have garnered us some information."

Klisisil cursed the fact that it was his turn to deal with matters outside the city center. The other elders were pleasantly indulging in a garden party despite the lateness of the season. He'd heard that someone had found a cask of Tslisil dating back two hundred years. The Elder's mouth watered at the thought of the pungent drink.

"The Darkness swarms around the light. The giant Guunt commands the beasts and he watches any new arrivals suspiciously. I've lost half the scouts," Telmut explained. The Master of Scouts was a squat man, hairy and wild looking from years of Walking as one form of Darkness or another.

"Are you certain that Abrms and his lot aren't interfering? Their discontent has spread like a rot. We'd be better off killing him instead of just denying him the brand," Klisisil complained.

Telmut wanted to sigh in agitation but kept himself still and his gaze lowered. The elders had no concept of the difficulties his scouts faced. Septa, the elders were lost to reality on most days. Telmut was considering aligning himself with Abrms' faction; he'd grown sick of petty demands.

But then there was the magic. Telmut, like all scouts, craved the brands that allowed them to Walk. The elders controlled the brands, keeping them locked away behind intricate defenses. Telmut couldn't fathom not being able to Walk but dreamed of being able to walk forever.

"Abrms hasn't Walked since you decreed him confined to the outer wall," Telmut objected respectfully.

"If The Darkness are swarming so thick, why haven't they been diverted south as is customary?" Klisisil complained, seeming to ignore Telmut's earlier explanation. The Elder swore that he could smell the Tslisil on the breeze.

Telmut wanted to curse. He really did. The elders had no concept of the sacrifices that the young made in this mausoleum of a city.

"The Darkness swarm the light, Elder. There is no turning them. The Giant Guunt holds sway and none dare challenge him," Telmut repeated.

"Then kill the Guunt. We have enough skins to swarm him under," Klisisil argued as if he had found the perfect solution.

Telmut was exceedingly doubtful on that matter. There were some Skrieksgrata skins, a thrasher, and an assortment of more minor Darkness. Jesia Ulbrms had disappeared with their prized Shaeloman pelt. Telmut had reported the odd woman dead to satisfy any Elder curiosity on the matter but in reality Telmut had no idea what had happened to her.

There was no information coming into the city and there would likely be none for the foreseeable future. There was certainly a Rising in action and that Rising seemed to be moving in unprecedented numbers towards TeraUsuat. Well, unprecedented for the last several hundred years at least. Something massive had collapsed all of the other outer walls, so Telmut assumed that there had to have been large Risings against the city before.

"We do not have the numbers," he admitted to the Elder.

"Why not?" snapped the Elder.

Telmut felt that it was like dealing with petulant children some days. Elder Armisa was worse, but at least she was senile.

"Because of Elder mandate, attrition and sheer lack of population," Telmut said honestly, which wasn't always the best practice when dealing with the elders.

"Our walls are manned by the strongest warriors in all the human lands!" Klisisil insisted almost hysterically. "Upon the stone is a forest of spears ready to smash The Darkness!"

The Usatchi military hadn't been a forest of spears since the First Rising. They hadn't even been a woodland of spears in the last hundred years. They had barely one man for every thirty feet of wall when Telmut had been born. Now they averaged one man or woman for every five hundred feet. If it wasn't for the scouts the outer wall would have been overrun decades ago despite the sheer size and thickness of the defenses. As it was the wall was deeply pitted and covered with the dried blood of Darkness.

The Elder seemed to calm down as he gazed out the window.

"How long before the light reaches the city?

"Estimates put it at least a few weeks away."

The light had started as a pin prick on the horizon. It had steadily swollen day by day.

"I want our warriors prepared to repulse the attack when it gets here," Klisisil commanded. "See that the defenses are ready."

This was not Telmut's job. The Master of Arms oversaw the Wall's defense. Telmut didn't bother to correct the Elder. The elders treated all of the young as if they were interchangeable. He would simply pass the order on to the appropriate person.

Afterwards he had to talk to Abrms. Telmut had a feeling that he would not want to remain once the light arrived.

Chapter 36

The Walls of TeraUsuat were just over the horizon. The expeditionary force was drawn and tired, cold and often miserable. Galeb slept comfortably enough though on most nights a canvas shelter was required to keep out the rain. Kieri had no objections other than the squelching mud that seemed to constantly be miring the expedition's progress.

They were nearly a month behind Galeb's original projections. Jesia complained bitterly and loudly on a daily basis that it was unfair that Kieri got to sleep warmly next to Galeb and she didn't. Bob countered Jesia's arguments by offering to keep any unrelated woman in the expeditionary force warm by sleeping with them. Ilsbruk was still trying to get the brazier Bob had stolen back.

The expedition was currently halted and had been halted for several days. Ilsbruk was finalizing plans for the approach to the city. The Darkness was growing impatient but seemed unwilling to challenge the Great Warding as the research Mages were calling it, except for occasional forays that seemed more out of boredom than true malice.

Galeb was building power. Six of the power sumps whirled along the edges of the Great Warding. Six was his limit; Ilsbruk was still angry at the spectacular failure experienced when Galeb had tried for seven. Thankfully the blast had been directed outward. Galeb couldn't be certain but he thought even the Guunt were shocked by the power of the explosion. Kieri hadn't been shocked; she'd been pissed. Jesia had offered to comfort Galeb after his failure, which had only made Kieri angrier.

Bob hadn't helped matters by loudly volunteering to comfort any frightened women.

Galeb was left intensifying the sumps he had, compacting them further, which increased the airspeed and pressure, doubling the energy produced by the winds.

Everyone stayed well clear of the power sumps. Not just because of the failure of the seventh, though no few people had a few gray hairs because of the incident. No, everyone avoided the power sumps because it was cold and wet enough without having rain pelted at you at high velocity.

When Galeb wasn't building power he was being lectured. Ilsbruk was hammering home Galeb's role in the plans to confront the city. The Captain was fairly confident that if he didn't constantly remind Galeb about restraint, team work and a myriad of other things Galeb would mess up.

Galeb knew that Ilsbruk had a point. He was just tired of hearing that point repeated to him as if he were a child. In a fit of temper, after Bob made the mistake of mocking his interactions with the Captain, Galeb Warded Bob.

It wasn't a full Warding. Instead Galeb created a blood red rope of Wards snaking loosely around Bob's body. The effect was eerie, with the Wards moving sinuously around Bob, a turgid flow that began where it ended.

Bob was terrified at first. Then he realized the amount of attention he was getting from the research Mages as well as Jans. Bob began strutting after that, insisting that he would only answer the questions of females. Preferably scantily dressed ones. Kieri hit him for that comment.

Bob protested the indignity of her treatment, pointing to his Wards as a sign of his elevated status. Kieri glared at Galeb. Not being stupid, Galeb triggered Kieri's Wards. Bob's Wards were a serpent, dark and dangerous. Kieri's had the cold brutality of a winter storm raging out of the tundra. Bob wisely backed down, agreeing that the women could be fully dressed when they talked to him. Kieri hit him again for good measure.

Approaching TeraUsuat was like approaching the decaying ruins of a civilization that had once thought too highly of itself. Which was a perfect way to describe Usatchi sensibilities.

The shattered remnants of the Usatchi were immortalized by fallen wall after fallen wall of startling magnitude. None of the expeditionary force could help but be impressed by the stubborn tenacity that had erected those walls. None could help but be humbled by the brute force that had shattered those defenses. Everyone was solemn, even Bob – at least for a few moments.

Abrms growled in frustration as he watched the approaching people bathed in that impossible twilight. Jesia was supposed to have smuggled the Mage to the city, allowing Abrms and his supporters to slip away. Instead the Mage was announcing himself in impossible glory.

The Warding, for that was what the light must be, stopped just short of the Outer Wall near one of the hidden sally ports. The wind picked up as six whirl winds could be seen moving sedately along the Warding, crackling with power. People moved along the length of the Warding which seemed to be a Pathway a hundred yards wide.

While most of the people held back, a group strode forward. The Mage was easy to pick out because he seemed a mighty figure, looking faintly Usatchi and so unlike his brethren. Two dozen Soldiers marched on either side of him, an honor guard.

"Southerners," spat Bormuth, one of the three elders chosen to come to the Wall and oversee the visitors. Bormuth was similar to every one of the elders, stick thin, awkward and delusional. Bormuth distinguished himself from the others only by having quite horrible bad breath.

"They had an Old One," commented Sirareichie, tugging on one of her thick white locks. "I didn't think the Southerners had any of those left; I thought we'd had them killed off years ago."

More like centuries ago.

"What does it matter?" Klisisil snapped, displeased at once again having to deal with outside matters. "Tell them to go away before we unleash the might of the Usatchi upon them."

Abrms kept his mouth shut and face blank when Telmut glared at him. Mentally Abrms snarled. 'Might of the Usatchi'? The elders were wearing robes that, while once magnificent, were worn and tattered, showing many signs of repeated mending. This section of Wall bristled with spears, true, but only because the Master of Arms had to strip defenders away from the rest of the Wall.

Abrms wasn't certain that doing so was a good idea. Sure the Usatchi made an impressive display but the sheer amount of Darkness roaming around the edges of the Warding was daunting.

"Ask him what he wants," demanded Sirareichie, "I want to go back to my chamber."

Gebilin, Master of Arms, a well-muscled warrior just one year shy of being eligible to move into the Inner Wall, snapped a precise salute and walked to the edge of the Wall between two huge ballista.

"What do you want?" Gebilin demanded in turn, yelling down at the Southerners. He wasn't the brightest of men.

"I meant for you to ask in a more dignified manner," Sirareichie snapped, stamping a foot in anger.

"Oh-uh," Gebilin stuttered before leaning back over the edge of the Wall. "Why have you come to TeraUsuat, City of Cities, home of the mighty Usatchi?"

"I suppose that's better," Sirareichie grumbled.

"I, Galeb Sonovonol, Spear of the Southern Lands, have come to take the Usatchi out of these ruins and back to the safety of Klynsheim and Obari lands," the Mage answered, his voice booming despite sounding quiet and gravelly.

There had been much arguing between Galeb and Ilsbruk over using the new title. Galeb had found the term 'Spear' a bit ridiculous. Bob had thought the title lacked something and suggested 'Spear of Death'. Ilsbruk had told Bob to shut up and Galeb that the title was non-negotiable. It was Galeb's new rank and the Mage better get used to it. To emphasize the point, Ilsbruk had smiled. Galeb had grumbled and given up the argument at the time.

Now, in a fit of rebellion Galeb had elaborated on the basic speech that he'd been told to memorize. He'd added the bit about 'Klynsheim and Obari lands'. Ilsbruk was most likely going to be angry. Galeb thought the addition emphasized the point that he represented both Klynsheim and Obari interests.

"Fancy title," muttered Bormuth enviously.

"How dare he criticize mighty TeraUsuat, City of Walls," muttered Klisisil.

"He's a big one," Sirareichie commented. "Kill him."

One of the ballista fired into the group of Southerners, the iron tipped three foot bolt slamming through the chest of the Mage and embedding deep into the ground.

"As I mentioned," the Mage said, looking at the Usatchi with pity, "I am the Spear of Klynsheim and Obari. The Obari part is what you should pay attention to. After having spent some time in the company of one of your women I'm not stupid enough to approach your walls directly when an illusion will do."

Telmut glanced over at Abrms in condemnation. Abrms gritted his teeth. Both men knew who the Southerner was talking about.

"You have one day to lay down your arms and prepare to evacuate south," the Mage warned.

"We do not obey you," Bormuth bellowed, his scrawny frame shaking with rage. "We are Usatchi! We command!"

"You are murderers who have brought death and destruction to my Peoples for centuries. We will no longer allow this city to stand so that it can create further devastation."

"We are Usatchi, you filthy barbarian!" howled Bormuth.

"I told Ilsbruk that you wouldn't understand. This was a waste of time. I should have gone with the demonstration first and then laid out the demands," the Mage said, his image closing his eyes.

The Warding suddenly branched in two directions, racing along the outside of the Wall, not touching and leaving a wide space around where the Usatchi were gathered. The Mage seemed to breathe in deeply and hunch his shoulders forward. The two branches of the Warding slammed into the outer Wall, which, as Jesia had promised, was stained with the blood of Darkness. Whenever the Usatchi killed a Darkness they smeared the blood of their defeated enemy upon the stones as a warning. Through this practice the Usatchi had given Galeb the instrument of their own destruction.

The stones of the Wall groaned as the Warding sought to repel The Darkness essence that had soaked within it. The groaning intensified as the whirlwinds seemed to lessen. Soon sharp cracks could be heard as stone began to crumble under the weight of the Warding.

The light drew back. Bormuth opened his mouth to taunt the Mage for his failure but froze with his mouth unfortunately open. Guunts raced forward towards the damaged walls, each one trying to be the first to reach the fractured stone. The biggest Guunt collided with the wall sending shockwaves in the stone and throwing many people off their feet.

The walls groaned in halfhearted protest before languidly collapsing around the Guunt who continued to hammer away at more and more sections. The Usatchi soon found themselves standing on a ragged island in the middle of the destruction as a thick cloud of dust engulfed them.

With the Wall down, the Warding flew forward, curling around the remaining portion of the Wall and racing towards the inner Wall. Darkness poured over the broken Wall, hunting among the exposed city section for any Usatchi unfortunate enough to be caught within the broken defenses. There weren't many, but their screams could be heard quite clearly.

"You have one day," the Mage warned and then the illusion faded.

Kiesh roared with the rest as The Darkness celebrated the destruction of another hated Wall. The prey was unfortunately few and far between but they were already attacking the next Wall and the Guunt were optimistic. Especially since the collapsed outer wall made for effective projectiles to throw at the remaining barrier.

Galeb sat down on the ground with a sigh, ignoring Ilsbruk's glare at the wanton destruction of the Wall. Jesia was gratefully silent, mouth agape as she watched The Darkness pour into the outer city. Kieri looked down at Galeb with concern. He knew he looked exhausted; he was probably twice as exhausted as he looked.

"I'm going to sleep now," Galeb said, yawning. He was out before his head fully touched the ground.

The elders were refusing to leave, so caught in their delusions that they thought they could withstand the attack of a man who was willing to help The Darkness collapse the very walls around them. Of course none realized the truth; Galeb couldn't help to collapse the inner wall. There was no Darkness essence upon those stones for him to work with.

The elders ordered the scouts to attack, bringing out the brands to empower the all of the remaining Skin Walkers. Telmut acquiesced to the elder's demands, having smuggled in a single skin to the branding chamber, normally an offense punishable by death. The elders were horrified when Abrms, in his Skrieksgrata skin, tore them to pieces. Abrms, for his part, roared his pleasure as he slaughtered the elders, painting the walls with their blood.

Telmut angrily ordered Abrms to stop, but Abrms refused to give up the skin, instead tearing out of the room with a hooting whistle to go join The Darkness rampaging in the ruins of the outer city. Telmut watched the Skin Walker go with more than some trepidation.

After the death of the elders the bulk of the population agreed to evacuate. The constant 'CRACK' of stones slamming into the inner wall also convinced many to agree. Those people who wanted to remain were going to be left to die.

It would take three days to evacuate, which the Southerners graciously gave them. The families hurried to get ready to leave, trying to decide what was best to take on the upcoming journey. The Southerners offered no guidance, waiting silently.

The Skrieksgrata rambled through the street smashing buildings with arbitrary glee. He was happy with the freedom of the movements, only regretting when his claws sunk to their full length in the stone or wood and could go no deeper. Still, it was only a minor regret and barely hampered his fun.

"Septa, Brother," Jesia said, slipping out of a doorway to confront him. Jesia's long Walks as a Shaeloman had given her the grace and skills to avoid being seen if she didn't want to be. This was how she constantly slipped away from her guards.

Everyone in the encampment had been so busy arranging the evacuation that it had been even easier than usual. All Jesia had needed to do was throw a bit of a fit, insult the Obari whore – the whore better not have given her Mage any diseases – and everyone thought she was sulking in her tent. Have a history of stabbing a few people out of boredom and no one was eager to entice Jesia out of the tent. More than likely because the Klynsheimers were happy Jesia was staying out of the way.

The Skrieksgrata's eyes flared in an angry glee and a paw swiped out at head level. Jesia skipped to the side easily, waving a finger at her brother in admonishment.

"Behave," she said in a sing song voice. "I'm only here to help you."

The Skrieksgrata looked as skeptical as its face allowed.

"Well, I'm here to help myself, but by helping me, you help you. Think about it Abrms; that brand on your back is only going to stay empowered for nine, ten months before it is exhausted. What are you going to do then?

"If you think that the elders were stingy, wait until you meet the Klynsheimer King. He will confiscate the brands and do you really think he will give us access to them? Our people have brought death and misery down upon the Southerners for centuries. The King will lock the brands away, if he doesn't outright destroy them."

The Skrieksgrata glared and slammed his fists into the cobblestone street, shaking the nearby houses with the intensity of his growing rage.

"Oh, you think that you can resist? Don't be foolish, Brother. The Southerners are demanding we lay down our weapons when we leave the city. How can we fight them then?

"No, we must strike when the Southerners least expect it. We take the Mage and he will grant you your wish, Brother. You've seen his Warding; it stretches hundreds of miles back to the Great Northern Road. He is a Power that can infuse the brand with so much strength that you can Walk for decades without fear of the brand fading. Think of it, Abrms; decades of Walking, embracing your inner Darkness.

"Not only that, but with the Mage we can negotiate with the Southerners from a position of strength. We will not be beholden to their whims. The Usatchi will make the demands and the Southerner will dance to our tune as has always been the way of things."

The Skrieksgrata stared at Jesia intently. He'd stopped paying attention after his sister mentioned the possibility of Walking for years without having to receive another brand. Jesia saw the greed on the Skrieksgrata's face and smiled.

"Here's what I need you to do..."

Galeb had extended the Warding to a gate of the inner wall, which The Darkness continued to assault, making great strides in weakening the defensive work. The Warding was the only thing that had saved the gate from destruction. The evacuation was meant to be orderly but between a small breach in the wall and the frenzy of The Darkness upon seeing the Usatchi fleeing the city, the families came in a panicked flood.

Ilsbruk was trying his best to bring the panic under control and the infantry was stretched to its limit keeping people moving and away from the edge of the Warding. Even the research Mages were drafted into helping with the exodus. Jans took charge of this group, asserting her lead position.

The Master of Arms had been easy to convince to assert the Usatchi position. As much as everyone had hated the elders and the city, they had, as a people, an overwhelming sense of their own importance. No one, not even if they were helping, could be allowed to dictate terms to the Usatchi.

One hundred and fifty warriors had agreed the Southerners needed to be put in their place after speaking to Abrms. The Usatchi warriors waited and then took advantage of the panic, moving in small groups through the civilians until they were in position to strike. The first group of Klynsheimer infantry found themselves overwhelmed, the lucky ones quickly stabbed. The unlucky ones were knocked clear of the Warding and swarmed over by The Darkness. The Guunt approached the growing melee of panicked civilians and struggling Soldiers and sat to watch in idle curiosity.

Civilians were being knocked clear of the Ward, falling with blood curdling screams as they were torn apart or were used to amuse The Darkness. The Guunts only occasionally smashed a Usatchi into a blood soaked smear. They seemed more intent on the dominance battle playing out. To the Guunt this was the first human activity that seemed to make sense. Kiesh, in particular, was relieved to see that these tiny creatures were finally showing some appropriate behavior. The Giant Guunt licked absently at his one hand, smeared with human blood and grimaced at the taste.

Ilsbruk was cursing so loudly and vilely that even Gorgorin paused in admiration. He was trying to help the septaed Usatchi and they were intent on killing his men and each other. The insanity of these people shouldn't have been surprising considering his time with Jesia. Still their lack of any survival sense was unbelievable.

The Captain had managed to pull the remnants of his infantry back and formed a defensive line. The surviving research Mages were running away as fast as they could – which meant that every hundred yards or so the wide eyed men and women had to pause to catch their breath. Jans and her assistant were already well ahead of the rest.

Usatchi civilians were being held back, Ilsbruk not daring to let any through the line lest warriors try to take advantage of any gaps. The Usatchi warriors were hiding among the increasingly tightly packed mass of people and were firing arrows from the safety of the crowded and panicked civilians, hoping to whittle away at his forces without fear of reprisal and it was working.

Troopers were hanging back, ready to charge upon command. Ilsbruk could end this quickly if he wanted to kill a great many of the civilians but there were too many women and children in the heaving mass of people. Ilsbruk also didn't want to turn the civilians against him. At the moment they weren't a threat. Kill some of them and they might join the warriors. He was hoping for a more peaceful solution. He just had to wait on the rider who'd been sent back to the main camp a mile from the walls.

Unfortunately Ilsbruk might not be able to wait much longer. That small breach in the wall had widened and Darkness were pouring through, attacking the Usatchi who couldn't push their way into the Ward's protection because of the stalled mass before them.

"Line, Battle withdrawal twenty feet!" Ilsbruk ordered.

The surviving infantry officers repeated the command and the infantry began a slow retreat, facing the crowd, weapons leveled.

Parsons had thought that the Battle at the End of the Line had been horrible but this...this was worse. Watching panicked civilians being pushed out of the Ward, hearing the horrifying, burbling screams of people being rent apart. It was all too much.

At least the terrible fight inside of the crowd was over. The gut wrenching moments in which Usatchi warriors stalked among the people, leaping out to cut down Parson's fellow Soldiers had been filled with brief bursts of stark terror and terrible anger. The command to fall back and form a line had almost made Parsons want to sob with relief.

Now they were retreating again to give the civilians more room. The Darkness was inside the inner wall and anyone not inside the safety of the Ward was dying. The Usatchi warriors didn't seem to care; they were still intent on slaughtering the Klynsheimers.

Parsons hated these people with a passion that burned his throat with its acid touch.

"We're getting more of our people killed," Eadsadch, one of the Master of Arms most loyal fighters complained even as he launched another arrow at the retreating line of infantry.

"It can't be avoided," snapped the Master of Arms, worried himself. "We have to give Jesia and the advance group time to grab the Mage."

"How will we know when she has him?"

"Calekish will sound a horn," the Master of Arms explained, taking his own aim at the Southerners. Calekish was a trustworthy warrior. He wouldn't make them wait any longer than necessary.

Chapter 37

Jesia sauntered through the encampment with a short spear slung over her shoulder. She mused that the Southerners and Usatchi had much in common. Both peoples only saw what they wanted to and blinded themselves to the rest. The Klynsheimer Captain should have been prepared for an attack; the Usatchi were meant to command, not follow the rules of others. Jesia's people didn't respond well when lesser races forgot their place.

It had been far too easy for a group of ten warriors to slip through the early fighting and make their way to the Southerner's camp. The Klynsheimers had been focused forward, never looking to their rear. It was a lapse for which, even now, the encampment was paying the price.

The support staff were in the process of dying as Jesia's people ran riot searching out their quarry. Soon Jesia would finally have her Mage. After she killed the Bitch. And thoroughly washed him; the man had been slumming for far too long. He was bound to be a bit unclean. Jesia sighed, shaking her head at what women were forced to forgive their men.

Jesia admittedly got distracted with thoughts of what she would do with her Mage. She'd forgotten about Bob. She remembered him when the twilight descended into a smothering blackness and Calekish shrieked as a spear took him under the arm pit. Bob's battle cry of 'I killed a Skrieksgrata' was unmistakable.

Bob was not the source of the choking night that was so black and thick it seemed to squirm its way into every pore of the body and then gnaw its way to the marrow. It would have been better if this had been one of Bob's illusions. It was something far worse.

Galeb altered the light under Kieri's guidance, as she explained how her Family had blinded Ilsbruk's men on The Road during their attempt to rescue him. That act was his last rational one.

Galeb was not angry. He vibrated with a rage that Kiesh would greatly appreciate. His blood roared in his ears and his skin burned at the touch. Galeb had given the Usatchi a chance. They repaid him with the blood of his countrymen. He would smash the Usatchi until only a bloody paste remained to drip from his hands.

Hmmm...Kieri might not like that; Galeb decided to use a weapon instead. A bill wasn't that much different than a staff and he had no intention of using it properly anyway. He stalked through the dark, muscles tense and ready, his eyes glowing with a feral gleam, his personal Wards stilled. At that moment, Galeb was as much of a Darkness as the creatures that prowled outside of his Great Ward. He was worse though because there were no Wards to stop him.

The two Usatchi warriors saw a pair of red glowing eyes approaching through the unnatural night. They heard a whistling sound accompanying the eyes. They felt the blade of the bill impact with a sickening crunch that sent their bodies tumbling in several different directions at once, blood splattering canvas and ground. Neither man had time to scream. The eyes didn't pause nor did the weapon as it struck again, rending flesh from bone. A smile, gleaming white, joined the eyes.

Jesia frowned; there was a lot of screaming and it sounded suspiciously like her countrymen. It also seemed to be raining again. Only this rain was hot and sticky. Strange. Jesia didn't ponder the curiosity for very long. Her frown turned into a wide grin as she saw a strip of moonlight walking towards her.

Kieri stopped, allowing the illusion to spread, bathing the immediate area in a gentle white glow. Her sword was held ready and she waited impassively.

Jesia's grin became a bit manic, stretching her face painfully. The Bitch was considerate enough to come to her; no sense in making the Obari wait. She launched herself forward, jabbing with her spear with Shaeloman quickness. Kieri's blade lashed out, knocking the spear aside and countering with slash of her own.

The blade tip whistled just past Jesia's nose as the Usatchi woman leaned back. She knocked the blade aside as another slash was aimed at her middle and parried a thrust aimed at her head. Jesia couldn't keep the grin off of her face. She was having so much fun!

Kieri was scowling, not taking any pleasure from the fight. She wanted this ended and Jesia dead. Kieri launched another series of fast blows fully intending to do just that; Jesia danced around her, responding with a series of quick jabs that were a feint.

Kieri barely had time to dodge to the side as the butt of the spear slammed at her head. She stumbled backwards. Jesia took advantage, jabbing and slashing at her in a frenzy of moves. Kieri couldn't block them all and felt a sting on her left side and arm as the spear edge sliced through leather and left shallow cuts before Jesia slid to the side, giving Kieri some breathing room.

Kieri scowled more. The crazy woman better not be toying with her.

The two women circled each other, weapons clashing and blood dripping from minor cuts. The bridge of Jesia's nose was split open and a jagged cut stretched across one hand. Kieri had two more shallow wounds on her right arm and left shoulder.

Jesia slashed at Kieri's midsection, slammed the butt of the spear at her head, and then kicked out at Kieri's right knee, connecting painfully. As Kieri stumbled Jesia followed through with an elbow to the head.

Kieri was staggering, falling to the ground and just managing to role away as Jesia stabbed downwards. She couldn't get to her feet, continuing to scramble away as Jesia pursued. Jesia was laughing hysterically - probably the only thing keeping Kieri alive.

Jesia's laughter cut off in mid syllable, turning into a puzzled mewl. Kieri scrambled to her feet, her eyesight a little blurry, blade held ready. She needn't have bothered. The Usatchi woman was kneeling on the ground, held in place by Bob's spear. The weapon had entered her back at an angle and the blade protruded a foot beyond her stomach.

Kieri looked up at Bob, slowly bringing her eyes into focus, mouth agape.

"What?" Bob asked, looking concerned. "Were we supposed to be fighting fair? No one told me we were fighting fair."

Kieri didn't answer. She limped her way over to Jesia, grabbed the woman's hair, pulled her head back and slit her throat.

"Oh, we're not fighting fair. Good. Because if we were you're not going to like what Galeb's been up to," Bob said with a sigh of relief.

Bob supported Kieri, who was still a bit unsteady, her knee throbbing as they walked through the encampment looking for Galeb. They found plenty of evidence of his passing. Blood was splashed everywhere and body parts littered the area, the Usatchi warriors violently dismembered. At one point Galeb must have broken the bill he was using because the bodies became more crushed than dismembered, bones sickeningly shattered, piercing the skin and skulls caved in with brains seeping through the cracks.

The Obari found Galeb standing in a small clearing near one of the cook wagons. He'd slammed an Usatchi's head through the side of the wagon and then torn the woman out long ways, reducing the wooden side to kindling. It was best not to dwell on what the woman's head looked like.

Kieri didn't think that Galeb knew that she and Bob were there until he spoke.

"Are there any more left alive, Bob?"

"No," Bob assured him. "I killed two and three quarters. Kieri killed one quarter. You seem to have killed eight though it's hard to confirm. There's a lot of body parts that need matching up."

"Good," Galeb said, swallowing deeply.

The sounds of a rider moving haltingly through the night could be heard. Galeb idly restored the twilight.

Kieri could see that he was blood soaked, gore caking his arms in a thick paste up to his elbows.

"Jesia?" Galeb asked.

"My three quarter. Kieri's one quarter."

"I'm glad I didn't have to kill her," Galeb said absently, rubbing a hand on one encrusted arm. "She might have thanked me while I did it."

"She was strange," Bob agreed.

"Galeb, are you alright?" Kieri asked as she let go of Bob and limped over to her husband.

"Not particularly," he admitted. "I enjoyed killing them. I don't know how to feel about that."

Kieri grabbed his hand, careful not to wince at the feeling of slick blood and other unidentifiable substances.

"It's okay," she reassured him. "They needed killing."

"Yes," Galeb said, looking at her with a puzzled expression. "It was...fun."

Kieri kept her expression neutral and just held his hand. She didn't want him to see her worry.

"It's over now," she told him carefully. "There's no more need for killing."

"I know," Galeb said, shaking his head viciously as if to clear his thoughts. "I know."

He hugged her fiercely until Kieri began beating him about the back and demanding that he let her go. She didn't know what felt worse – the squelching sound of the blood as their bodies connected or the pain from her various injuries.

Galeb let her go, finally realizing that she was hurt. He looked panicked for a moment until Kieri assured him that she was going to be okay. Galeb ordered Bob to get water and then began checking over Kieri's wounds. She pushed him away, pointing out that as filthy as he was it was better that he didn't touch any of her cuts.

The rider, one of Ilsbruk's Troopers, found them. The horse stomped nervously, its eyes rolling as it saw Galeb. The Trooper looked pale as a ghost and trembled a bit when he looked at Galeb himself. Haltingly he delivered Ilsbruk's message. Galeb sighed and allowed Bob to push him aside. The Obari began looking over his cousin.

"I have to stop this," Galeb said, once he explained Ilsbruk's message to Kieri.

"I know. Finish this, Husband, so we can leave this cursed place."

"I am the Spear and the Usatchi have transgressed," Galeb said, nodding, as his mouth quirked into a sardonic smile. He turned away and closed his eyes concentrating. He never noticed how Bob stilled, looked intently at him, and then launched a flock of birds, swirling carrion crows, instead of bobwhites, that called raucously as they winged north.

Parsons steadied himself as the line ground to a halt once again. They had fallen back nearly a half a mile and the Usatchi were still pressing close.

At least the arrows had finally stopped. He supposed the sudden darkness that had fallen over the Warding had something to do with that. It was so dark he could barely see the man standing next to him.

Usatchi were wailing, cursing and making every noise that a terrified people were capable of uttering. The Darkness then lifted as suddenly as it had come, twilight returning in less than an eye blink. Parsons braced himself waiting for the return of the arrows but he needn't have bothered.

A murder of crows, heralds of death, swirled into the space between the Usatchi and the Klynsheimers. A spiral of feathers tightened dizzyingly before exploding outward, dripping a viscous black ichor. The ichor pooled and swelled upward turning the color of viscera before solidifying into a shape.

The Spear stepped forward, a fiend out of Darkness wrought nightmare. The Mage looked to have bathed in blood, the kind of unspeakable filth only found deep in the innards of the human body caking his arms. His gaze was terrible. Then he grinned and the Usatchi recoiled.

"I am the Spear," the specter spoke, his voice the rattle of bone, "and the Usatchi have transgressed."

The Usatchi recoiled again, and truth be told so did the Klynsheimers.

"Bob's outdone himself," Parsons heard Captain Ilsbruk say.

"Not even Bob has this good of an imagination," Sergeant Gorgorin argued with a slow shake of his head. "I have no doubt that this is one of Bob's sendings. But grieshtata me if that ain't an actual rendering of Sonovonol."

"Dispatch a squad back to the encampment. Find out what the septa happened there," Ilsbruk snapped.

Gorgorin saluted and wheeled his horse away.

The Guunt chose that moment to voice their approval of the image. Gargantuan hands slammed the earth in accompaniment of their cries.

The Ward shifted. Gradually at first and then it split, dividing the Usatchi into smaller and smaller squares. The Usatchi clumped together tighter and tighter as The Darkness flowed into the gaps upon a wave of claw, fang, fur and talon.

As the groups got smaller, both through the division of the Ward and through misfortune that ended with screams, it was easier and easier to see the Usatchi warriors hiding among the civilians.

The infantry fell back out of bow range and waited. The Usatchi watched, trapped, for over an hour before Sonovonol arrived on the scene. He no longer resembled Bob's sending, which had faded with his appearance. The blood had dried and was even now flaking off of him. If anything he looked more terrifying. He stopped out of bow range as well.

The Mage carried a large sack with him and reached inside of it once he stopped. His hand reappeared holding a head which he flung towards the trapped Usatchi. He did this eleven times, finishing with Jesia's head. A Skrieksgrata caught Jesia's head and crushed it in its jaws, shaking savagely before running off with its prize.

Once finished Galeb stood staring at the Usatchi, letting them squirm for another half an hour before speaking.

"We Klynsheimers and Obari came here bringing hope to an undeserving people. A selfish people who returned our kindness with the murder of our own. We should not be surprised; the

Usatchi have had no problem murdering Klynsheimer and Obari for centuries with impunity."

Galeb paused, shaking his head.

"You will no longer go unpunished."

The square with the largest concentration of Usatchi warriors collapsed letting The Darkness in. Death was brutal and swift for most. A few of the stronger warriors became playthings.

"I will spare some of you," Galeb said, paralyzing fear sweeping across the Usatchi with every pass of his gaze. "I will give you a path, a narrow path back to the rest of the Warding. Only civilians will cross this path. Any warriors attempting to cross over will immediately result in the forfeit of the life of every Usatchi in that square."

A group of warriors tested Galeb's resolve. More Usatchi died. Finally after hours, the last of the civilians crossed into the main Ward, sobbing hysterically as they were led away. Only warriors were left, staring angrily or fearfully at Galeb. He counted nearly a hundred of them. If he considered pitying them the thought did not cross his face. Instead he looked over at the Guunt, looked at Kiesh, and said:

"They are yours."

Kiesh nodded his understanding and the final squares dissolved. The Darkness fought one another to reach them.

Chapter 38

Ilsbruk walked over to Sonovonol making sure that the man saw him as he approached.

"You've looked better, Galeb Sonovonol," Ilsbruk commented.

"I feel remarkably good," Galeb admitted, watching The Darkness thoughtfully.

Ilsbruk was worried that the man was watching the dying warriors but was relieved to see that Sonovonol was instead watching the largest Guunt who was lording over the slaughter with surprising dignity.

"What are you thinking, Sonovonol?" Ilsbruk asked.

"How many warriors do you think the Usatchi have left?"

"Probably several hundred that abided by the original terms. They are unarmed but still dangerous."

"We need time to sort the warriors out. We need time free from so much fear so we can plan and prepare better defenses," Galeb said, gesturing towards the Darkness.

"What are you going to do, Sonovonol?" Ilsbruk asked again worriedly, edging forward as if he could stop the man from any foolishness.

"Buying us time."

He thrust his hands out, Wards flaring as they struck the largest Guunt.

Kiesh roared in surprise. He hadn't thought that the human Mage would be so daring. Pain flowed through him before becoming something...else. He paused in mid rage pondering what was happening. He was experiencing the quickening.

Kiesh was momentarily insulted that the Mage thought that he had the right to initiate quickening. Then, being practical, he decided to embrace the transformation, knowing that he was being spared a hundred years of waiting.

Galeb was careful with the amount of power being unleashed. He could kill the Guunt...maybe...he was a big beast after all.... But killing wasn't his purpose – besides he didn't want any more Guuntness flowing into his body. He really had to come up with a more dignified way to describe the experience.

It was better this way; Galeb was enjoying the killing too much. He could barely muster up any heartache over the civilians he'd killed along with the warriors when he let The Darkness take them. He needed to step back before he lost himself.

The giant Guunt reared up and slammed his fists into the ground meaningfully. Galeb understood and quenched the Wardings. The Guunt was glowing softly, lines of red gold fire appearing and disappearing on its stony hide with every breath.

The creature nodded to him and then spun around running north, uncaring of what trees it smashed out of its way.

"What did you do?" asked Ilsbruk, his voice hoarse with disbelief.

"I created a power vacuum," Galeb explained. "The Guunt will war among themselves to establish the new dominant. The rest of The Darkness will flee the Guunt's violence. I've bought us some time."

"Is that all you've done?"

"It's all I intended."

"That's always been your problem, Sonovonol. You've never recognized the difference between the two," Ilsbruk said, shaking his head. "We need to organize the refugees. Get gone from this place. "You need to bathe. I can smell you."

"I would like to head southeast and link up this Warding with the Great Trade Road," Galeb said wistfully. "I think it would be good to get away from people for a while."

"No," Ilsbruk said simply.

"I didn't think I would be allowed," Galeb said with regret. "Keep everyone you can away from me."

It took hours to sort out the refugee train. There were several thousand extremely traumatized Usatchi trying to solidify their position of superiority over the Klynsheimers. Ilsbruk was not above using Sonovonol as a threat. In the end the survivors were divided into groups of two hundred. Each group was spaced a half a mile apart. The gap was rigidly maintained with the promise that anyone violating the marching order would be relegated to the rear of the column. Sonovonol was at the rear of the column; the Usatchi were willing to fight one another not to be at the rear along with him. Especially since Sonovonol seemed to be brooding most of the time and glaring the rest.

A full day went by before the march south began. Ilsbruk, with Sonovonol's help, took time to raid the Usatchi's libraries, carting south as many books as possible in the wagons. When the wagons ran out of room, Usatchi were delegated to carry two books each. There was no need to threaten reprisal should the books be damaged or disappear. One look towards the Mage and everyone was more than eager to comply.

It was a cold and miserable march, rains constant and little shelter or fire wood to be had. The copses of trees that Galeb had decreed untouchable remained so. The Klynsheimers were all too eager to enforce that extra discipline even if they, themselves had complained about the very same thing on The Road north.

Galeb allowed the gap between himself and the refugee groups to increase steadily. Mostly through his desire to avoid people, partly through Kieri's insistence that he be scrubbed clean. She would not let him do it himself. Kieri worked over every inch of him until she had convinced herself that not a bit of the madness that had claimed her husband remained.

His clothing she burned. There was no salvaging it. Not while maintaining any piece of mind anyway.

Not that the replacement clothing was much better, but dead men's clothing had to do even though it was ill fitting.

Obari hunters joined up with the refugee column during the third week bringing much needed game. The weak were already dying by this point.

At the half way point a relief column of twelve hundred infantry arrived, filling out the ranks and reminding the Usatchi of their status. None protested other than the occasional defiant glare. The Usatchi survivors were still a proud people; they just weren't stupid.

The King was waiting at Union. 'Union' was the official name given to where the Great Warding joined the Ward Line. It was also being used to unofficially describe the fact that Sigsrata now considered himself the overlord of the Klynsheim, Obari and Usatchi peoples.

The Obari ignored the King's assumption. They huddled deep in Ilsbruk's domain, a large land grant that had lesser woods than the Barshom Forest but plentiful streams and game. The woods nestled up to the Eastern mountains, giving the Obari the opportunity to slip away if they so desired. None dreamt of returning to the Northlands. The Rising might last a generation or more.

The Usatchi schemed among themselves, taking note of relationships between the powerful, already plotting their assimilation into this new culture and their eventual return to power. It might take a hundred years or more but the Usatchi were convinced their blood would be among the most powerful. Their exotic looks were already garnering attention among the nobility.

Sigsrata watched the Usatchi trudge pass him impatiently. Frankly he didn't want to waste food on these people but he would. Jesia had shown that the Usatchi had knowledge that his own people lacked. There was too much unknown about The Darkness to waste the resource.

Come spring the Usatchi would become farmers, resettled in the sparsely populated valleys of the Southwest, known as the Deeping Dells. The original homelands of the Klynsheim, long abandoned in favor of the more fertile plains. He could contain them there, limit their influence; Sigsrata knew that these people were already scheming and was taking steps to ban intermarriage. Given the Usatchi's history of bringing death to Klynsheim the King didn't think getting the Justicers to agree would be that difficult.

Sigsrata was also considering a fostering program to get the young away from their manipulative parents. There too, was the matter of the brands that were already on their way south to be locked away until he could find the best uses for the shape shifters. The brands' surrender had been a condition of the allowing the Usatchi sanctuary. However, Sigsrata wasn't foolish enough to think that all of the brands had been surrendered. He was already devising ways to ferret out the remaining tools.

He needed to be careful; Sigsrata had to ensure that he didn't turn Usatchi arrogance into hatred. He also had to make certain that the Usatchi didn't turn the valleys into a stronghold.

The King was impatient to see his Spear. He wanted the man to inspect the new Ward Line to the Western Mountains. An easy duty meant to allow Sonovonol to rest, recuperate, and avoid trouble as much as possible.

Sigsrata needed to see how far gone Sonovonol was; Ilsbruk's reports of the man's ruthlessness in handling the Usatchi were disturbing and uncharacteristic of the man. He needed to talk to his Shield as well; Kieri Sonovonol was the key to the Spear. She would want him kept safe and would not mince words about Galeb Sonovonol's overall condition. Sigsrata found the woman as refreshingly honest as he found her annoying.

Besides, Sigsrata had a surprise for the Spear and Shield and it was going to be funny. The King was determined on this point.

The Sonovonols kept Sigsrata waiting three days. Three days that bled much of the humor from the King's surprise. Especially since Galeb Sonovonol scared the crap out of the King when he arrived. Sigsrata was sitting on his travel throne pretending to read over some documents so his assistant wouldn't force him to read one of his wife's incipient letters. He was sipping on a mug of tea – his wife wouldn't let him guzzle as was proper for a man – when Sonovonol and his wife were suddenly standing in front of him. Bob, of course, was leaning over his shoulder.

"You're holding the paper upside down, you know," Bob commented.

Sigsrata spewed his tea, choking in startlement.

"See, I told you it was going to be funny," Bob said, grinning.

Kieri Sonovonol smiled slightly, enjoying the irreverence to a government authority as only an Obari could. The corners of Galeb Sonovonol's face twitched slightly. It was a discomfiting sight; almost as if the man had been taking smiling lessons from Ilsbruk.

Who just so happened to walk up as the King spit his tea.

Sigsrata wiped at his mouth, scowling, and looked at the three new arrivals. They were all travel worn, in need of cleaning and rest. Perfect.

"Now that you've had your amusement, we have business," Sigsrata said standing and trying to regain some dignity. "Follow me."

The Sonovonols exchanged a look. Kieri shrugged and the group fell in behind the King.

There was quite the encampment at Union, a new Way Fort under construction and research Mages writing whole dissertations on the methodology used to link the two Wardings. Sigsrata had it on good authority that most of the dissertations were garbage. Of course it was competing researchers who assured Sigsrata of this fact; not that he cared. If he asked, Sonovonol could probably explain the Union in an incomprehensible manner that would have even the researchers scratching their heads before informing the man that he didn't know what he was talking about. Warders could be annoyingly obtuse.

Third row of tents to the left. Yes. Sigsrata had the route memorized, knowing that Sonovonol wouldn't be able to see until it was too late. There she was, predictable as ever, sitting in front of her tent enjoying a cup of tea on one of the few non-rainy days of the season. Her nephew was about somewhere annoying the military speakers.

Sigsrata stepped to the side at the last moment just as the woman looked up. Sonovonol and her eyes locked.

"Momma?" Sonovonol asked in a very much undignified manner, the words seemed torn from his mouth as his eyes widened.

Sigsrata was already chortling. This was turning out as well as he'd hoped. Ilsbruk tried smiling. Everyone winced.

"Son?" Corinne Eielson stood up slowly taking in a man whom she barely recognized.

Sigsrata had had the decency to make her aware of the physical changes. The woman had taken the changes in stride, asking pointedly if her son's foreign wife was responsible. The King had assured her that the changes were all her son's doing. Mrs. Eielson was unconvinced.

Despite seeing her son for the first time in eight years, Corinne still took the time to curtsey to the King before glaring up at her son who stood like a lamp post and looking as intelligent as one.

"Eep!" said Kieri Sonovonol, ducking behind her husband, eyes wide and mouth gaping. This was not the way she wanted to meet her mother-in-law. Illusion was already rising up around her, hiding the dirt and raggedness of her dress. Galeb was on his own. Kieri was in full dither behind her husband.

Corinne Eielson took immediate charge, looking around Galeb at Kieri. The older woman shook her head, walked around the side of her tent and came back holding a chicken.

Bob began grinning wildly. Kieri Sonovonol looked ready to faint, blushing beat red, her eyes wide in panic.

"A gift for you," Corinne said, holding the chicken out impatiently until Kieri took the bird, which looked as bored as the

Obari woman looked terrified. If Sigsrata wasn't mistaken, the poor woman was shaking. The King was awfully glad he'd procured the chicken at Mrs. Eielson's request.

Bob was outright choking on his laughter. Corinne looked at Bob, shook her head disapprovingly and poked the man in the stomach.

"Hey!" Bob sputtered. "She stabbed me!"

Bob pointed accusingly at the Mage's mother, outrage clear on his face.

"Stop being a baby and behave," Corinne admonished Bob.

"You stabbed me!" Bob complained louder. "Do you know who I am?"

"Bob," Corinne said, deadpan.

"No, I'm – wait, yes, yes I am! I'm glad to know my fame proceeds me," Bob said, flashing between confused, surprised and preening. He stood taller and took a strutting step. "Since you clearly know who I am, I would have expected more respect and less poking."

"You're still acting like a child," Corinne pointed out.

"I am not!" Bob huffed. "You are aware that I've killed a Skrieksgrata? I'd like to see a child do that!"

Corinne poked him again.

"OUCH! Stop doing that, Woman!" Bob protested, dancing away.

"Behave," Corinne warned Bob.

"Septa woman has Skrieksgrata claws for fingers," Bob muttered, rubbing his stomach.

Corinne gave Bob one last warning glare before turning her attention back to her son.

"You married this woman?" Corinne asked, nodding towards Kieri, who was still staring at the chicken as if the bird was going to try to eat her and trying not to hyperventilate.

"Yes, Momma," Galeb said, wincing. Why couldn't he just call her 'mother'? It probably had something to do with the fact that the last time he'd spent any significant amount of time around his mother was when he was five.

"You had the rites? A priest performed the ceremony?"

"I believe the Sonovonols married according to Obari tradition," Sigsrata said helpfully.

Corinne Eielson had researched Obari tradition. Sigsrata had been quite helpful in that regard.

Faster than the King would have given Mrs. Eielson credit for she had reached up and grabbed her son by the ear, twisting. She pulled him down and glared into his face.

"I raised you better!" she hissed, shaking his head and threatening to tear off his ear. She then turned to look at Kieri. "Nice to meet you, dear. You probably don't understand how my son's turned you into a loose woman. Don't worry; we're going to fix that."

Corinne then turned, not letting go of her son's ear and began to drag one of the most powerful men in the kingdom through the encampment. Kieri gaped after her mother-in-law alternating between shock at the sight of Galeb being dragged off and anger at being called a 'loose woman'. The chicken was forgotten and scampered away.

"Ouch! Let go! Where are we going?" Galeb demanded.

'Manners!" snapped his mother.

"This is fun!" Bob said with a big grin, bouncing excitedly.

Corinne stopped and shot Bob another warning glare. Bob danced backwards hastily, covering his stomach defensively.

"You are getting married properly. Shame on you for living in sin with this woman! Didn't you think about her reputation at all?" Corinne snapped.

"But we're married," Kieri protested, finally speaking up.

"Not properly," Corinne insisted. "It's not your fault, dear, my son should have known better. I can only blame that Academy. I raised him to have better manners which The Academy has seen fit to erase."

Galeb was wise enough to not point out that he'd spent the first few years of his life in a tap room. His impressionable mind had learned a few things, manners not really being among them.

"There's nothing wrong with Obari traditions," Kieri snapped, growing angrier. She was glaring at Galeb as if this was all his fault.

"Of course not, dear," Corinne said, still dragging her son towards the priest's tent. The size of the encampment justified having a priest in residence. Even if it didn't, Sigsrata would have had one brought here just for this occasion.

Corinne didn't let go of her son's ear until the marriage rites were ended even though the priest kept insisting how irregular it was to have the groom's mother twisting her son's ear during the entire ceremony. It didn't help matters that Kieri kept poking him in the side angrily. Or that the chicken had made a reappearance at some point and Bob was now holding it and Kieri kept scampering away every time Bob brought the Chicken too close.

"Now," Corinne said, turning to Kieri, once the ceremony was finished and she let go of Galeb's ear, "let's have some tea and get to know one another."

Corinne linked arms with Kieri who was alternatingly glaring at Galeb and looking panicked. Galeb could tell that Kieri was walking carefully to maintain the illusion around her.

"I suggest you find some clothes that fit and take a bath," Galeb's mother said to him as she walked off. "I must apologize for my son again, my dear. You'd think that he'd at least know to bathe. You don't have that problem, do you? Is it an Obari thing?"

"Tell her about Jesia," Bob offered Galeb helpfully, "It might distract your mother long enough for Kieri to escape."

"Shut up, Bob," Galeb growled, rubbing his ear.

"Manners!" snapped Corinne, dragging Kieri to a stop and turning to glare at her son. "That Academy has spoiled you, allowing you to behave quite badly. I suggest you think long and hard about your behavior and find a way to fix it. I would also think that it would be best not to let any of your children attend that institution when the time comes."

Galeb was affronted. Actually affronted. Not about the comment about letting children attend The Academy – he wasn't going to even before Kieri had told him flat out it wasn't going to happen – but about the comment of The Academy doing anything for him, good or bad. He opened his mouth to argue but Bob elbowed him in the stomach.

"Do you want to get poked?" Bob hissed.

Corinne arched an eyebrow at Bob. Bob visibly paled.

"Or talk about your ears," Bob suggested, feeling a keen need to change the topic. "Everybody notices your ears."

Galeb had opened his mouth to yell at Bob but snapped his mouth shut, fingering his ears self-consciously.

Epilogue

The Watcher stood in the entrance to the cave, his senses open. There. He felt it again – a warmth on the breeze, unwelcome and alien in his glacial home.

A Guunt had quickened a century before estimations. A minor inconvenience considering the Kraalsbriekans never had the numbers to truly threaten the glacier. But the precedent was disturbing. The estimations were never wrong. This was not a natural quickening; it couldn't be. The Guunts had found a way to hasten their maturity.

This was unacceptable; the glacier must not be allowed to be threatened on its slow march. The Watcher tasted the breeze again, noticing nuances. Whatever had quickened the Guunt was far south. Beyond the tundra and the taiga. Beyond the Great Forest in the Southern lands.

Hmmm.... Strange creatures dwelt there. Physically weak and Darkness touched but with powerful magics that let them resist The Darkness. It did not matter. The Ptrieshs were not Darkness...no such magics would touch them.

The Watcher turned and began to pound a staccato rhythm on the ice. A return pattern let him know the message had been received. An Arc would be sent south along the Eastern Mountains to find this new source of power for the Kraalsbriekans. The Arc would deal with this threat the only way the Ptrieshs knew how – they would kill everything in the South lands to ensure a one hundred percent chance of the successful elimination of their target.

54991304R00333

Made in the USA
Middletown, DE
07 December 2017